Libby stared at her [obscured]
Tomorrow Ned w[obscured]
it—chip it and stri[obscured]
to be excited, but [obscured]

Her child hadn't gone straight home from [obscured],
Libby knew because she'd phoned home at 4:00 pm and
Reva hadn't answered. Libby hadn't bothered to leave a
message on the answering machine. What would she say?
"Reva, you're breaking my heart!" But she'd asked Reva
about it, and Reva had said she'd taken a nap and she must
have slept right through the phone's ringing.

Reva was a teenager. The sensory nerves in her body
were wired to vibrate wildly at the sound of a ringing
telephone. No way could an eighth-grade girl sleep
through that sound.

Damn. Libby didn't even know what Reva was doing. She
was a terrible mother, that much was certain.

She stared glumly at her fireplace and pondered the likelihood that her choices of late represented one huge mistake
after another. The hugest had been signing all those papers
at the bank to buy this apartment. Buying it meant that not
only would she never be able to retire, but she'd have to be
reincarnated so she could finish paying off the mortgage
and her ex's loan in her next lifetime. She would never
be able to come home at three o'clock to keep an eye on
Reva, and Reva would run wild through New York City.

And Ned…another huge mistake. She didn't even know
what was going on between them. She couldn't kiss him
ever again, because lousy mothers up to their eyeballs in
debt weren't entitled to such pleasures.

If she tried to explain, he wouldn't understand. He didn't
seem to possess the gene for guilt. Not only wasn't he
Jewish, but he was from Vermont. Did they even know
what guilt was in Vermont?

JUDITH ARNOLD
~ THE ~
FIXER UPPER

MIRA

First published in Great Britain 2006.
MIRA Books, Eton House, 18-24 Paradise Road,
Richmond, Surrey, TW9 1SR

© Barbara Keiler 2005

ISBN 0 7783 2193 2

58-0306

Printed and bound in Spain
by Litografia Rosés S.A., Barcelona

To Cathy, Kathy, Mary-Lou and Terry.
There's a reason this book is dedicated to you, but
it's long-winded and convoluted, so I'll spare you.
Just know that I treasure our friendship and
I'm glad you're all in my life.

ACKNOWLEDGEMENTS

As always, I am immeasurably grateful to my agent, Charles Schlessiger, and my editor, Beverly Sotolov, for their insights and their unflagging support. I am also grateful to Lawrence Watt-Evans for his wisdom and his skill at Web surfing, and to everyone at MIRA® Books.

One

On the first Friday of October, Libby Kimmelman arrived at her office to find two bouquets of flowers in glass vases, a gold-foil box of Godiva chocolates, a CD and at least a hundred file folders on her desk. "Oy," she groaned. "It's starting."

Tara bounced into the office behind her. Tara was so bouncy Libby sometimes wondered whether she wore shoes with springs embedded in the soles. Maybe it was easy to be bouncy when you were twenty-three and naturally blond and you could afford to work as a glorified secretary at subsistence wages because your parents were willing to subsidize you.

Libby was thirty-five and naturally bland. Her job paid a respectable salary, but if someone offered to subsidize her, she'd say yes in an instant.

"I printed out all the online applications that came in this week," Tara said, gesturing toward the piles. "That's what's in the folders. I've labeled them and sorted them into kindergarten applicants and transfers." The kindergarten pile was significantly higher than the transfer pile. Not surprising—most parents trying to get their children into the Hudson School wanted to get them in right at the start, so the youngsters could benefit from the full Hudson experience.

And why shouldn't they want that? The Hudson experience was terrific. Compared with the city's public schools, it was exponentially better than terrific. Small classes, devoted teachers, funding for laboratories and studios, foreign language instruction starting in first grade… A child couldn't get a better education in New York City. Libby knew this not only because she was director of admissions for the lower school but also because Reva had been enjoying the full Hudson experience since even before kindergarten, when Libby had enrolled her in the Hudson preschool created for the children of employees.

Libby understood why parents pushed to get their kids into the school. She didn't have to like their pushiness, though. She was starting her second year as director of admissions, and already the thought of all those pushy parents sending her flowers and chocolate and God knew what else was enough to give her hives.

Dropping her briefcase onto her chair, she plucked the envelope poking out of the larger bouquet from its plastic clip, lifted the flap and pulled out the card, which she read aloud so Tara could enjoy it with her: "'To Ms. Libby Kimmelman, Director of Admissions, Hudson School—Please accept these flowers as a token of our respect and admiration for the very difficult task you perform. Sincerely, Roger Haverford, Jr., Evelyn Haverford and little Roger Haverford III.'"

"Ick," Tara said. "You're not going to accept anyone named little Roger Haverford III, are you?"

"I'm going to be objective," Libby said. That was her mantra: *I'm going to be objective.* With thousands of parents jockeying to get their precious darlings into the school, Libby had no choice but to be as objective as possible.

She wondered if little Roger Haverford III had his heart set on attending Hudson. Doubtful. More likely, the kid had his heart set on a bag of M&M's and a SpongeBob SquarePants DVD. Over the years, Libby had interviewed a lot of four- and five-year-olds, and none of them had mentioned that attending the Hudson School was their abiding goal. The parents might be obsessed, but the kids had their priorities in order.

She reached for the card from the other bouquet and slid it from its envelope. "'Lib Kimmelman: Hope you love flowers as much as we love the Hudson School. The Springelhoffen Family.'"

"Eeuw," Tara said.

"Take the flowers and put them somewhere I can't see them," Libby requested. "One bouquet out by the reception area, and the other in the teachers' lounge. And take the chocolates, too."

"You're not going to eat the candy?" Tara gazed longingly at the gold Godiva box.

"I can't," Libby said. "It would be unethical. It would also be fattening. My tush doesn't need chocolate."

Tara lifted the box. "It's a one-pound ballotin. Do you know what Godiva charges for this?"

"I'm guessing a lot. Was there a card with the chocolates?"

"Here." Tara handed her the gift card, which had been wedged under the gift-wrap ribbon.

Libby opened it. "'Dear Dr. Kimmelman…' Hey, they've given me a doctorate!" she boasted. The rest of the note was typical: Shane Fourtney's parents thought these chocolates might sustain her as she tackled the arduous task of choosing the next kindergarten class at Hudson. "We hope you like truffles!" the note concluded cheerily.

"Take the candy to the lounge with the flowers," she urged Tara. "You can open it there and pig out if you want. Just don't tell me about it."

Tara grinned and bounced out of Libby's office, juggling both bouquets and the candy.

Libby moved her briefcase to the floor and sank into her chair. What the hell was a *ballotin*, anyway? What kind of word was that? Flemish? Why couldn't the folks at Godiva just call it a box?

Staring at the piles of folders on her desk, she sighed. Last year, her first behind this majestic walnut desk in the stately, paneled office of the director of admissions, she'd been overwhelmed by the flood of gifts. Bribes, really. As Anthony Caruthers, who'd warmed this chair for thirty years and trained Libby as his replacement before retiring to a thatch-roof cottage in Tahiti to paint and study Plato, had told Libby many times, "The only gifts a director of admissions should ever accept are those that dwell within the soul of a deserving child."

Someone ought to stitch that into a sampler, Libby thought glumly as she stared at the piles heaped atop her leather-trimmed blotter. Perhaps Anthony could do needlepoint if the painting-and-Plato didn't work out. Libby, unfortunately, had no time to master needlepoint. She had hundreds of applications to plow through—and the season was just beginning.

She lifted the CD that lay on top of the taller pile. A label had been tucked inside the jewel case: "Samantha McNally Performs Her Favorite Songs" was printed in block letters; below them was a slightly blurry photo of a beaming young girl with an oversize red ribbon in her hair. Opening the case,

Libby scanned the label on the CD, which listed the songs Samantha McNally performed on the disk: "My Bonnie Lies Over the Ocean," a medley of "Twinkle, Twinkle Little Star," "Baa Baa Black Sheep" and "The Alphabet Song," and "Un bel dì, vedremo" from *Madama Butterfly*.

Libby shuddered.

She shifted one pile of folders to the left so she'd have an unobstructed view of her desk calendar. Her ex-mother-in-law had given her a Palm Pilot for her birthday last year— "So you can keep track of all your dates," Gilda had said, a bizarre comment from the mother of a man who'd walked out on Libby ten years ago—but Libby preferred her archaic day-by-day paper calendar, which she didn't first have to turn on if she wanted to find out what was on her schedule. Nothing, she noted as she gazed at the blank page. Not a single date.

Libby didn't date much. Her ex-mother-in-law knew that. But a decade after the divorce, Gilda kept showering Libby with gifts and taking an inordinate interest in Libby's non-existent social life. She was obviously still trying to compensate for her son's idiotic decision to leave Libby for a skinny fashion editor who sounded as if she had cotton balls stuffed into her sinuses when she talked.

Don't think about it, Libby ordered herself. *Don't think about Harry and his fancy-schmancy wife and their hoity-toity apartment…and the fact that you and Reva are teetering on the verge of homelessness.*

She gazed at the towering pile of kindergarten applicants, and weariness seeped through her, even though she hadn't yet glanced at a single file. Instead, she reached for the top folder from the shorter pile. Flipping it open, she skimmed the first page of the application form, which mainly provided basic information—name, address, birth date, parents' names and places of employment. On the second page Libby read that Amanda Starrett's family would be moving from Massachusetts to New York in January and would like to transfer her to Hudson. According to the essay her mother had written in answer to the question "Please describe your child," Amanda, all of nine years old, had already proved herself astonishingly gifted at soccer, and her painting style merited comparisons with Jackson Pollack's.

Not to gloat, but Reva was painting like Jackson Pollack when she was two. Libby snorted and set aside the folder.

The next applicant was Vijay Bannerjee, whose parents had both recently joined the faculty of Rockefeller University. They predicted that young Vijay would be an Intel Science Competition finalist by the time he was fifteen. Surely the Hudson School should be eager to experience his brilliance before he moved on to fame and glory and a likely Nobel Prize.

Libby sighed. Weren't there any *normal* children applying to Hudson? Children who painted like no one famous and whose scientific prowess extended to building model solar systems out of Ping-Pong balls, fish wire and pipe cleaners? Parents were so afraid to admit that their children were just children. If they got to know Hudson students, they'd realize that most were not destined to win Nobel Prizes or create paintings that hung in the Museum of Modern Art, or to sing Puccini at the Met. They were just kids, lucky enough to get a good, solid education before they entered the world. The school hoped most of them would contribute something worthwhile to society—but for God's sake, they didn't have to be geniuses.

Her wonderfully nongenius daughter poked her head around the open doorway. "Hey, Mom?"

Warmth billowed inside Libby whenever she saw Reva, the same warmth she'd felt the first time she'd held her damp, whimpering newborn in her arms. Reva was thirteen now, in her final year of Hudson's middle-school program, and the only time she was damp and whimpering these days was when she got caught in a downpour. Today was sunny, though, and her hair hung in a glossy brown fall down her back, each strand as straight as a plumb line. Her face had lost its baby fat in the past year; suddenly, she had cheek-bones. She'd started tweezing her eyebrows, and their spare shape gave her a startled look. Her shirt covered the waist-band of her jeans. Thank God for the Hudson dress code, which banned exposed navels.

"What's up?" Libby asked.

"Kim and I have to go to Central Park after school today, okay?"

"Why?"

"We have to collect leaves for this project."

"How late will you be?"

"Five?"

Libby shook her head. "It's getting dark earlier. I don't want you in the park once the sun starts setting."

"It doesn't get dark before five."

"It gets *darker*," Libby declared.

"We need to get a lot of leaves. It'll take awhile. I don't know if we can get it done by five."

How long did it take to collect leaves? "What's the project?" Libby asked.

Reva rolled her eyes and sighed dramatically. "God, Mom. It's a science project on deciduous trees. Deciduous are the kind of trees that lose their leaves. Okay?"

Libby knew what *deciduous* meant. That Reva did, too, implied that her science class must be spending time on the subject. "Okay," she said, opting not to comment on Reva's exasperated tone. "But I want you home by four-thirty."

"I don't know if we can get it done by then," Reva protested.

"Try," Libby suggested. "And don't go north of 79th Street."

With another profound sigh, Reva pivoted on her sneak-ered heel and stormed out of the office.

Whatever warmth Libby had felt at Reva's arrival was gone now. Sometimes Reva was the sweetest, most lovable girl in the universe, and sometimes she most definitely was not. Libby wished Reva would give some warning about which daughter she intended to be at any given moment—the sweet, lovable one or the exasperated eye-rolling one. Maybe she could send Libby a hand signal—thumb up or thumb down. Maybe she could wear a T-shirt that read I Love You, Mom on one side and The Bitch Is Back on the other.

Libby glanced at her desk calendar again. Only five more years before Reva left for college. Only seven before she was officially no longer a teenager. God willing, they'd both survive until then.

Shaking her head, she reached for the next folder on the pile. She flipped past the first page and zeroed in on the essay the parents of Eric Donovan had written about why the Hudson School should be thrilled by the opportunity to educate their son.

"My name is Eric Donovan," the essay began, and Libby sat back in her chair and stopped skimming. Rarely did a child write his own essay. For this application, she'd take her time.

"My name is Eric Donovan, and I'm ten years old. Me and my dad just moved to New York from Vermont, and I like the city a lot. The only problem is, I'm in this public school a few blocks away and it's really crowded. My class is too big, thirty-four kids, and it's always so noisy it's hard for me to concentrate. I used to do really good in my school in Vermont, pretty much all As except for stuff like penmanship (you can't tell how bad my handwriting is because I'm writing this on my computer) and music. I don't have such a great voice, but I know all the words to 'Ninety-nine Bottles Of Beer' (ha-ha.) Anyway, I'm smart and I work hard and I think I'd do much better in a school with smaller classes and less shoving and shouting in the halls. I asked my dad if I could go to private school and he said sure, as long as I can get financhal aid. (I'm not sure I spelled that right.) He's I guess what you'd call a fixer upper, he fixes old houses, only now we're in New York and it's mostly apartment buildings instead.

"Anyway, I really like the way the Hudson School looks on the Web site, and I like that it was named after an explorer. We studied Henry Hudson in my third-grade class in Vermont last year, and I wrote a really excellent term paper, which I would be happy to show you if you'd like to see it. So it just seems like I should go to the Hudson School. If I can get some financhal aid. And if I get accepted, which you never know."

Libby read Eric Donovan's essay twice more. Nothing in his application implied that he could sing Puccini or paint like Pollack. Her first promising applicant, she thought with a smile as she closed his folder and placed it on top of the pile.

"See, the thing is," Eric was saying, "Mrs. Karpinsky smells like oatmeal."

Ned shook the water from his hands, reached for a paper towel and tried to remember what oatmeal smelled like. Right now, his nostrils were locked on to the smell of the onion powder he'd shaken all over the pan of chicken pieces and chunks of potato. Onion powder and garlic powder were the extent of his culinary creativity, along with an occasional dash of salt.

Fortunately, Eric ate just about everything, including oatmeal. Why the fact that his babysitter smelled like oatmeal was a problem, Ned couldn't guess. "Maybe you should sprinkle some brown sugar on her," he joked as he lifted the pan from the tiny rectangle of counter that separated the sink from the stove, and slid it into the oven. He still found it amazing that he could cook an entire meal, featuring all the major food groups, in this kitchen without having to take more than three steps in any one direction. The stove, the oven, the sink and the fridge were all within easy reach, no matter where he stood in the room.

Back in Vermont, the kitchen of their house had been sixteen by twenty feet, big enough that he could get an aerobic workout fixing dinner as he jogged from sink to stove to table. The kitchen in this cozy Upper West Side apartment was too small to contain a table. Or a refrigerator with side-by-side doors and an external water dispenser. Or a double-basin sink. Or a window.

Deborah would have hated this kitchen. But Ned liked it well enough, if only because it wasn't in Vermont.

"So," he said, swinging the oven door shut and turning to face Eric, who had planted himself in the doorway between the kitchen and the dining nook. "What are you really trying to tell me about Mrs. Karpinsky? You don't like her?"

Eric shrugged his bony shoulders. "I don't like the way she smells," he said.

At some point in the not-too-distant future, Eric would be a teenager and Ned would no longer be able to decipher his cryptic grunts and snorts. But he was still on the safe side of adolescence, and Ned could read him reasonably well. Eric had a wonderfully open face, parts of which were currently hidden behind a mop of wheat-colored hair that cried out for a trim. Despite its shagginess, however, Ned could see the glint of mischief in Eric's blue eyes, the slight skew of his mouth, the way his chin shifted as he gnawed on the inside of his cheek. Ned could also see that the jeans Eric had on, bought just a month ago, were looking a little short at the ankles. He mentally added trips to the barber and Filene's Basement to the weekend schedule.

"Oatmeal smells good," he pointed out when no explanation of Eric's problems with Mrs. Karpinsky was forthcoming. "What's really bothering you about her?"

Eric tucked one foot behind the other and kicked his toe against his heel. "Okay, it's just that I don't need a babysitter. I could come home from school and—"

"No." Ned cut him off quietly but firmly. Maybe he was overprotective, but damn, this was New York City, and he wasn't going to let his son become a latchkey statistic, stuck alone in an apartment with all the locks bolted until Ned got home from work. Maybe in another couple of years, but not now. Eric was too young.

"Okay, so I thought, like, if there was someplace I could go after school. You know, like a program or something."

"I researched after-school programs. All the programs in this neighborhood had waiting lists a mile long."

"Well, see…" Eric reversed feet and kicked his other heel. "The Hudson School has an after-school program for kids. I read about it on the Web. After class you can stay as late as five o'clock and do all kinds of things, like art or go to the gym and shoot hoops or play indoor soccer, or you can do homework or extra-credit stuff. They've got a computer lab, too. I could learn Java. Or even Linux."

"If you went to the Hudson School," Ned reminded him, leaning left a few inches so he could reach into the refrigerator for lettuce and tomatoes. "Which you don't."

"I applied, though, so if I got in—"

"You what?" Ned twisted around so fast a tomato went

flying from his hand. Fortunately, it landed in the sink instead of smashing on the floor.

"I applied to the Hudson School."

One thing Ned admired about his son was that he never retreated. If he did something, he owned up to it, not in a tiny, apologetic voice but at full volume and with his chin raised. Ned had always taught him that if you were going to do something, you might as well be proud of it—and if you weren't going to be proud of it, you were better off not doing it.

Evidently, Eric was proud of having applied to the Hudson School. He'd mentioned the place to Ned once, about a week ago, casually remarking that it was only a few blocks away and that he could probably get a good education there. Ned had pointed out that private schools in Manhattan generally carried tuition fees resembling the gross national product of certain third-world nations. Eric had raised the idea of scholarships and Ned had said scholarships were great, and then the conversation had shifted to whether Eric was obligated to root for the Yankees now that he lived in New York.

They weren't poor. Ned had gotten a good price for their house in Woodstock and his business—enough money to enable him to buy a four-room walk-up in a brownstone on West 73rd off Riverside Drive. The place had needed some work, but Ned was an expert at renovations. He'd refinished the hardwood floors, constructed a wall between the living room and the L-shaped extension that was supposed to be a dining area, and converted the newly created room into a den with built-ins and a window seat from which a half inch of the Hudson River was visible, and he'd built a loft bed for Eric so he'd have more floor space in his bedroom. Not a major overhaul, but Ned had turned the place from a dowdy flat into a bright, livable home.

So other than the monthly fees and taxes, housing was paid for, and his income covered expenses and the occasional luxury. But private-school tuition? Ned would have to win the lottery, and he'd rather spend his disposable income on visits to the Hayden Planetarium or skiing trips with Eric than on tickets for Mega-Millions.

Eric must have read Ned's mind. "I asked for financial aid," he said. "I think I misspelled *financial*, though. I probably should have looked it up." He stopped kicking his heel. "So they probably won't accept me, anyway."

"Because you misspelled *financial?*" Ned took a deep breath. At times like these, he really resented Deborah for having gone and died on him. Call him sexist, but women knew how to get through these conversations better than men did. They knew how to zero in on a kid's insecurities and doubts, how to cut through the crap and figure out what was really going on. Ned could cook chicken, he could handle clothes shopping and haircuts, he could bandage a scrape and make funny British voices while reading *Harry Potter* aloud—and he could do things Deborah would never have done, like camping with Eric or teaching him how to throw a curve. But these discussions in which Ned sensed he and Eric were talking about something they weren't actually talking about…

He busied himself rinsing the salad ingredients while he scrambled for the right thing to say. Eric had applied to a private school. Without telling Ned. Because he didn't want a babysitter, especially one who smelled like oatmeal. *Add it up, Donovan,* he ordered himself. *Do the math. Figure it out.*

"Was there an application fee?" he asked.

"Um, yeah."

He considerately didn't turn to face Eric. That "um" warned him that Eric was squirming, and no kid liked to squirm in front of a witness. "And you paid for this application fee how?"

"Well, I applied online," Eric explained. "They have this online form, so I just filled it out and sent it in."

"And paid for it how?"

"With your Visa."

"I see." Ned washed the hell out of the lettuce and waited for Eric to say what he knew he had to say.

"I'm sorry. I shoulda asked."

"Yeah."

"It was only forty dollars."

"*Only* forty dollars?" Forty dollars wasn't too awful, but if Eric was feeling guilty, Ned would just as soon ratchet up his guilt to an uncomfortable level.

"I got the account number from a bill. You keep them in that drawer, you know which one? In the desk."

"Of course I know which drawer I keep the bills in." Ned didn't want to snap at Eric, but damn. If the kid could give Ned's credit card number to some posh private school via the Web, he could just as easily give it to an online vendor. He could buy hundreds of CDs—he'd recently discovered hip-hop, much to Ned's dismay—or silly T-shirts or pasta makers or—Jesus!—*porn.* He was only ten years old, but his voice was beginning to sink from soprano to alto, and the hair on his spindly legs, while still pale, was beginning to thicken. With Ned's credit card, Eric could rack up hundreds of dollars on the Internet visiting sites that showed breast-enlarged women having sex with farm animals.

That was why Eric needed Mrs. Karpinsky babysitting him. She might be sixty-seven, but she knew a thing or two about the Internet. She'd taken a course at the local branch library, she'd told Ned when he hired her. "I got a set of Victorian napkin rings to die for on eBay, sterling silver, the real McCoy," she'd boasted. "If I told you how much I paid for them, you'd want to kill yourself." She tended toward morbid imagery, but at least she was computer-savvy.

Ned tore the lettuce onto two plates. He tried to reduce the violence of his motions, but when you were pissed, it was better to rip into a head of lettuce than the head of your son. By the time his temper had cooled off, he'd heaped each plate with enough lettuce to feed a visiting army, but at least he could trust himself not to throttle Eric. "You are never, ever to use my credit card without asking me," he said in a tight voice. "Now put these plates on the table."

"You forgot the tomato," Eric pointed out, his expression not nearly as contrite as Ned would have liked.

"Fine." Ned slapped the plates onto the counter and hacked the shit out of the tomato. He divided the mangled chunks between the two plates and handed them to Eric.

He waited until the chicken was done and he and Eric were seated, facing each other in the dining nook he'd created at one end of the living room, before revisiting the subject. The credit card use was one thing. The Hudson School was another. "Look, Eric," he said. "We agreed on the move to New York. You said you wanted to live here."

"I do," Eric said.

"And now you're hitting me with this school thing."

"I don't like my school," Eric said bluntly. "It's too noisy."

"Like you're the quietest kid in the world."

"If *I* think it's too noisy, you can imagine," Eric said.

Damn him for coming up with such a smart response. "I can't afford the Hudson School. Do you know what private schools cost?"

"That's why I asked for financial aid."

Hell. The school's cost wasn't the worst of it. Eric had already figured out how to get around that obstacle: type in Ned's Visa account number and click on Send.

The problem, the issue that bit into Ned's gut with greater force than he could ever bite into his chicken, was that Eric was apparently unhappy. With school, with Mrs. Karpinsky, with everything. With this new life, which Ned had been so certain was just what they both needed. "You want to go back to Vermont?" he asked, bracing himself so he wouldn't cringe if his son said yes.

"Nah," Eric said, to Ned's enormous relief. "New York's cool."

"So it's just school that's bugging you?"

"The school is okay. I mean, I could survive. I told you about Gilbert, right? This kid in my class. He's like always pushing kids and stuff. He calls me Monty because I'm from Vermont. I mean, that's really stupid."

"Definitely stupid," Ned agreed.

"Anyway, this other kid, Leo, he and Gilbert got in trouble today because they were using all the rubber cement to make a ball, and Ms. Martinez said they were wasting it, and they kept doing it, so she made them leave the room. And Gilbert kept shoving Leo the whole time. I don't know why Leo didn't shove him back. I would have."

"So…" Ned scrambled to get the conversation back to where he wanted it. "So there are obnoxious kids in your class—"

"And not enough rubber cement."

"So that's why you want to go to the Hudson School?"

"And the after-school stuff they have there. And…" Eric jabbed the tines of his fork into a chunk of potato, then pulled them out, then jabbed again, as if he believed the potato might still be alive. "It's just, the kids all look so happy when they leave the Hudson School. I see them sometimes when I'm walking home with Mrs. Karpinsky. The ones who don't do the after-school program are leaving right when we walk past. The school's in this row of brownstones

on I think it's 78th Street, between West End and Broadway.
And they look, I don't know, like they really had a good time
while they were there."

If anyone was experiencing a guilt glut now, it was Ned.
His son wanted to have a good time in school. What kind of
father was he if he wouldn't move heaven and earth to send
Eric to a school where he could be happy?

He was the kind of father who didn't have twenty-five
thousand dollars a year to spare for tuition.

"Okay," he said, letting out a long breath. "You submitted this application. You asked for financial aid. I guess
we'll just have to wait and see what happens, right?"

Eric's face brightened. Ned hadn't said, *No, you can
never go to the Hudson School.* He hadn't said, *You will do
chores of my choosing at three bucks an hour until you've
repaid me the forty dollars you charged on my Visa card.*
All he'd said was, *We'll see.* The two most wishy-washy
words a father could ever utter. And Eric's smile was wide
enough to split his face.

Two

If Reva didn't love Kim, she would hate her. Kim was just so totally *perfect.* She had that whole Japanese-American tough-but-dainty thing going for her. Her hair was so black the highlights were blue, and it was naturally straight, not like Reva's, which she had to press the waves out of with her straightening iron. Kim was petite and wore size-two jeans, *size freaking two,* and she was incredibly smart, and she played the piano really well, even though she said she hated it and wanted to quit. Her older brother, who played the violin, was a freshman at Juilliard and her older sister, who attended the Hudson upper school, took cello lessons at Juilliard, and Kim's parents were already saying they expected Kim to take piano lessons at Juilliard once she started ninth grade. Kim insisted that would never happen because she hated hated hated the piano, but she never said so to her parents. She just complained to Reva.

The thing was, Kim was really a great person, so Reva had to forgive her for being perfect. Also, Reva had a few things on Kim. For instance, she could invent the best excuses to spend Friday afternoon at Central Park, checking out Darryl J. Kim never came up with good excuses for anything. It was always up to Reva to devise their cover stories. Kim said this was because Reva had a much better imagination, and Reva didn't argue. She liked having at least one thing better than Kim, and an imagination was a pretty cool thing to have.

Collecting leaves for a school project. Kim considered Reva some kind of genius for thinking that story up.

"We've got to remember to bring home some leaves, though," Reva reminded her as they jogged into the park at the West 77th Street entrance. She figured they could collect leaves on the way to the Band Shell, which was where Darryl J would probably be. That was where he was last weekend, when she and Kim had seen him and fallen in love.

Reva wondered what the "J" stood for. She wondered where he would go once it started getting really cold. She wondered whether he had a girlfriend. At thirteen, she was too young for him, but maybe he'd wait for her. Like, he could date other girls now, as long as he was willing to dump them all when Reva turned fifteen. Okay, sixteen.

Kim picked up a maple leaf that was lying on a bench. "How's this?"

"It's torn. This is supposed to be for a school project, remember?"

Tossing the leaf to the ground, Kim shrugged. "What kind of project? My parents will ask. You know them."

"Botany," Reva said. Eighth-grade science was mostly about the scientific method and lab technique and how to keep a proper notebook. It was pretty boring except for when they actually *did* something. Like, they were currently studying the properties of magnets. Writing out the labs in a notebook was about as exciting as getting a tooth drilled, especially all those details about what the metal nail weighed and how far it was from the magnet when it reacted to the magnet's attraction. But actually doing stuff with the magnets was fun. If Reva decided to become a scientist when she grew up—not likely, but stranger things had been known to happen—she would have an assistant do all the measurements and write everything in her lab notebook for her.

Magnetism was physics. Leaves were botany, which was biology, which meant she and Kim were doing absolutely nothing like it in their science class. The last time Reva had to collect leaves for school, it was for an art project in second grade, when the class made autumn place mats by sealing colored leaves between rectangular layers of transparent contact paper. Reva's place mats had come out ugly, but her mother had used them every day until Thanksgiving. She was that kind of mom.

"Ashleigh Goldstein is so weird," Kim said, picking up a couple of aspen leaves and handing one to Reva. "Wasn't that weird, what she did in gym today?"

"You mean, refusing to play field hockey because it's too militaristic?"

"What's militaristic about field hockey?" Kim asked as Reva scooped a couple of oak leaves off the path. "You just run back and forth with a stick."

"I thought Ashleigh's protest was cool," Reva argued. "I mean, yeah, she's weird, the way she wears that ankh necklace and the black nail polish and everything. It's like, she can't decide if she's Goth or hippie."

"I bet she just didn't feel like playing hockey so she made that up, about it being militaristic," Kim said. "That's just so her."

"She wants fewer team sports and more stuff like modern dance and yoga. I think it's because she sucks at sports."

"I heard Ashleigh tell Monica Ditmer in the bathroom
yesterday that her mother had breast reduction surgery."

"Really?" Reva could not imagine why anyone would
want to reduce the size of her breasts. At the moment, she
measured 32A. Her dream in life was to make it to B. Her
real dream was to have cleavage, but she was pretty sure you
had to be at least a C for that, and she didn't dare to hope
for too much. Her mother wasn't that chesty, and she'd said
these things tended to be hereditary, so Reva was probably
doomed. The idea of having boobs so big you wanted to
shrink them was just too bizarre.

Darryl J undoubtedly liked big boobs. All guys did. If
they didn't, a dozen magazines, a zillion Web sites and thousands of plastic surgeons would go out of business.

"What if he's not there?" Kim asked. She was always
worrying about stuff not going the way it was supposed to.

Reva didn't worry too much. Things usually seemed to
work out, one way or another. "If he's not there, we'll go
home with a bunch of leaves," she said. "And then we'll go
back to the park tomorrow. You know he'll be there on the
weekend. That's where the money is—the weekends."

"I wonder how much he makes," Kim said, kicking a few
brown leaves on the paved walk. Her sneakers had little
rhinestones glued on the toes in star shapes, and when the
sun caught them they sparkled. Reva had considered getting
sneakers like that, but her feet weren't the sparkly type.
They were too large, for one thing. She already wore the
same size shoe as her mother—not that her mother owned
any shoes Reva would ever want to borrow. For work she
wore low-heeled pumps, and at home she wore flats with
wide toes, like the shape of your actual feet. They were
ugly, but she said they were comfortable, and someday Reva

would understand that comfortable was more important than stylish when it came to shoes. Reva hoped that day wouldn't arrive too soon.

Her mind drifted back to Darryl J—specifically, Kim's comment about how much he made. Reva had heard that some street performers actually earned enough to live on just from the coins and bills people tossed into their instrument cases. She'd also heard that serious musicians had to audition for spots in the subway stations. The real money must be there, she figured.

"Hey, maybe you and your sister and brother can set up a trio on the sidewalk and make some bucks," she teased. "You could play… I don't know. Who writes music for piano, violin and cello?"

"Mendelssohn," Kim said glumly. "Well, lots of people, but we're all learning a Mendelssohn trio now. My parents want us to perform at a holiday party they're hosting this December." She wrinkled her nose in disgust.

"Leave your brother's violin case open at the party," Reva suggested. "Maybe the guests'll throw some money into it."

Kim laughed. That was another thing Reva could do—say things that made people laugh. Most of the time, she didn't think what she was saying was all that funny, but if people laughed, that had to be a good thing. About the only person Reva couldn't make laugh was her stepmother, Bony. Her real name was Bonnie, but she was so skinny Bony fit her better. One thing Bony would never need was breast-reduction surgery. She always picked at her food and gave Reva warning looks when she took seconds. Okay, so Reva didn't wear size-two jeans like Kim. She wore size four and sometimes six, depending on the style. Like, she should put Weight Watchers on her speed dial.

"The thing is," she said, "Darryl J is going to be rich

someday. He's going to be discovered, and then he'll get a huge contract and do concerts and sell lots of CDs. Tracy Chapman used to sing on street corners in Boston, or somewhere around there, and then she got discovered and she wound up famous."

"Who's Tracy Chapman?" Kim asked.

Of course Kim wouldn't know. Her parents listened only to classical music, Mendelssohn and that stuff. Reva had nothing against classical music, and Ms. Froiken, who taught music at Hudson, told interesting stories about how Haydn wrote the "Surprise Symphony" to wake up people in the audience who nodded off during concerts, and how Stravinsky's ballet "The Rite of Spring" caused a riot the first time it was performed. She made classical music fun.

But other music was fun, too—not just the stuff Reva listened to but also the stuff her mother listened to. Old rock. Some of it was pretty good. Her mother had a Tracy Chapman CD that was full of wistful, plainspoken songs that Reva could just imagine someone singing while strumming an acoustic guitar on a street corner in some city and hoping people would throw money into the open guitar case at her feet.

Tracy Chapman wasn't poor anymore. And someday Darryl J, because he was so talented and so incredibly gorgeous, wouldn't be poor, either. He'd be riding to concert arenas in a limousine. And Reva would be riding with him, because he'd be in love with her.

The mall at the heart of Central Park wasn't as crowded as on the weekends, but since the afternoon was mild and sunny, people were out. Maybe they'd left work early—folks liked to do that on Fridays. Maybe some of them were unemployed and had nothing better to do than hang out and search for someone to play chess with, or feed the pigeons stale bread, or just stroll along the paths that meandered through the park. Maybe some were so rich they didn't have to work. And the younger people, the punky boys on skateboards and the girls like Kim and Reva, had probably just been let out of school. Maybe they'd told their mothers they had to collect leaves, too.

A mime stood at one end of the Band Shell, doing that whole icky-jerky-movement thing. Why did mimes paint their faces white? And the silly black hat with the flower sticking out of the hatband, and the striped shirt—what was that all about? No one was interested in this mime, anyway; people walked right past him. Poor guy, trapped inside an invisible box and no one cared enough to watch him break out.

She and Kim hurried past, following the twangy sound of a guitar. There was Darryl J, surrounded by a small cluster of people. The mime must be jealous, Reva thought, but that was his problem.

She and Kim joined the crowd gathered around Darryl J. They didn't move directly to the front—that would be too obvious—but found a spot that offered a good view of him. He was as handsome as ever, his hair in neat, even braids, his skin smooth and the color of caramel, his guitar and mike plugged into a small amp. He wasn't too tall—Reva liked that about him—and he had dark eyes that glowed like mood-ring stones, and a smile that could turn solid rock to lava. His jeans were baggy, but they weren't torn, and the crotch didn't droop to his knees. On top he wore a kind of woven hippie-ish shirt.

He couldn't be much older than eighteen, she estimated. And in January she'd be fourteen. A few years from now, they'd be perfect for each other.

He was singing something fast and catchy, the words spilling from him in a cascade of rhymes that almost sounded like rap, only he was singing instead of just chanting them. "'When I see you, I wanna be you, so I could know you inside out, and I could show you what I'm about,'" he crooned.

Reva sighed and clutched Kim's arm. Kim was beaming. She probably loved him as much as Reva did, but she was too well behaved and obedient to follow through. She'd never ride in a limo with him, because her parents would shit a brick if she did, and for all her fussing and complaining about stuff, she never liked to upset her parents.

Reva didn't care. True love was more important than her mother.

His guitar case, open at his feet with his little white Darryl J sign propped up inside it, contained a fair amount of coins and paper money. Reva wished she had enough money that she could toss some into his case, but she got only five dollars a week allowance—probably the smallest allowance of anybody in the entire eighth grade at Hudson—and if she gave Darryl J some money, that would mean no ice cream cones or lattes after school with her friends, and nothing to set aside for a movie outing or mascara, which she really desperately needed because her eyelashes were pale at the tips. Her mother said she was too young for mascara, which meant Reva had to buy her own and sneak it on when her mom wasn't looking.

If she got together with Darryl J, she wouldn't have to worry about budgeting her puny allowance to pay for mascara. Not that he was rich now, but he would be. She had faith. He was that talented. He'd fill arenas. No—more intimate settings, cooler places. Downtown clubs, and then maybe Roseland. Not Madison Square Garden, where the performers were just tiny dots on the stage and the only place you could actually make out their faces was on the JumboTrons.

Of course, she wouldn't be seated out there in the vast

darkness of the upper tiers, staring at the monitor. She'd be backstage in the wings, where Darryl J could see her. He'd glance her way between numbers and send her a secret smile that said, "I'm pretending to sing these songs for all those people out there, but I'm really singing them for you."

That was how she felt today, standing with maybe twenty other appreciative listeners as he sang, "'If I could be you, then I could free you. One and one are one, flunk the math and feel the sun.'"

Reva felt the sun, burning deep inside her. *One and one are one,* she thought, allowing herself a grin at how Mr. Rodriguez would react if she ran that equation by him in math class. He wouldn't understand. He was married and paunchy and he was always making stupid puns: "Where do rectangular trees come from? Square roots," and "I will now sing an imaginary number," and he'd pretend to sing, mouthing the words but not making a sound.

Darryl J made golden sounds, sounds that planted the sun right inside Reva's heart. One of these days, when she was just a little older…

Reva totally believed that anything was possible.

Vivienne had come to talk Libby into attending Saturday-morning services with her, but Libby had instead talked Vivienne into skipping services and having a cup of coffee. Libby wasn't exactly the most observant Jew in the world. She hadn't been in a synagogue since Reva's bat mitzvah last January—and that had been organized and overseen by Harry, who for some reason had felt that ushering Reva through this ritual was his paternal duty. Also, he'd gotten to host a fancy reception afterward, to which he'd invited assorted clients and colleagues, thus turning Reva's coming-of-age observance into a useful networking opportunity.

"I'm not trying to convert you," Vivienne said, settling

into her chair at the minuscule table Libby had managed to wedge into one corner of her kitchen. She and Reva ate a fair number of their meals there, which enabled Libby to boast that she had an eat-in kitchen.

How much longer she would have an eat-in kitchen was anybody's guess, of course.

Vivienne crossed one leg over the other. She wore tailored wool slacks and a multicolored tunic that hurt Libby's eyes. No one should have to look at that many colors at eight o'clock on a Saturday morning. The slacks were boring, at least, a dark blue as restful on the eyes as the top was painful. That was Vivienne in a nutshell—a combination of traditional and zany, boring and wild, restful and painful. Libby deeply hoped that Vivienne would be restful and not painful this morning.

"You want a bagel or something?" Libby asked. She was still in her robe, a faded green wraparound beginning to fray at the collar.

"A bagel?"

"I bought them fresh at Bloom's yesterday on my way home from work."

"In that case..." Vivienne fingered her hair. It was a garish red, cut spiky and short. Ever since Vivienne had gotten married, she'd been experimenting with different hairstyles. Libby wondered what Leonard thought about that. Maybe he liked it. Maybe each time she changed her hair, he felt as if he was sleeping with a new woman. "I was planning to eat at the kiddush," she said, "but if we aren't going to synagogue, sure, I'll take a bagel." She leaned back in her chair, which bumped into a counter. "What's this, dead leaves?" she asked when her hand accidentally brushed against the plastic bag of foliage.

"Reva collected them for a school project," Libby said as she sliced a second bagel.

"Is she still asleep?" Vivienne glanced toward the doorway. Maybe she expected Sleeping Beauty herself to materialize there. "You spoil her, Libby."

"She's allowed to sleep late on a Saturday morning."

"When you could instead be bringing her to shul. Actually, no." Vivienne contradicted herself, waving a manicured hand through the air, pretending to erase the thought from an invisible chalkboard in front of her. "You don't want to bring her with you right now. There are some new members of the congregation. Single men. A nice Jewish man, Libby—you could do worse."

"I married a nice Jewish man," Libby reminded her as she arranged the bagels in the oven to warm.

"That wasn't a nice Jewish man," Vivienne argued. "That was my brother."

For some reason, Libby had received custody of Harry's family along with Reva and the apartment in the divorce. Gilda and Irwin and their daughter, Vivienne, all believed Harry had been a first-class schmuck to leave Libby. At the time, Libby had agreed wholeheartedly with them. But when she thought about the kind of man he'd become—the kind of man he'd probably been all along, although she hadn't had the luxury of noticing that at the time because she'd been pregnant and eager to tie the knot—she realized she was better off without him. He seemed much happier with Bonnie, who was so unlike Libby she knew he couldn't have possibly remained happy with her.

"I just think you ought to be a little more socially active, Libby. You're, what, thirty-five years old? Time is gaining on you. You wait too long, no man is going to be interested."

"What apocalyptic women's magazine did you read that in?" Libby joked as she filled two mugs with coffee and carried them to the table.

"Have you got any Splenda?" Vivienne asked, nudging the sugar bowl away. "I'm trying to lose five pounds."

Vivienne was always trying to lose five pounds, which was why Libby always kept packets of artificial sweetener on hand. She pulled a few from a cabinet shelf and set them on the table next to Vivienne's elbow.

"So these gentlemen, these new members of the congregation… All I'm saying, Libby, is you could do worse."

"I'm not looking for a boyfriend," Libby said. "If one comes along, fine, but I've got too much else on my plate right now. You want any orange juice?"

"If you're pouring…" Vivienne accepted a glass of juice with a shrug. "What do you have on your plate that you don't have time for a love life? And don't tell me Reva. If she can adjust to her father getting remarried, she could adjust to you going out on a date every now and then."

"I do go out on dates every now and then," Libby said, silently acknowledging that her dates were more *then* than *now.* "And Reva doesn't dictate my life." Yeah, right. Reva was the first thing Libby thought about when she woke up every morning and the last thing she thought about before drifting off to sleep every night. Reva was the light burning in her soul—and the headache burning in her skull. Who had time for dates with all that burning?

Still, she shouldn't be so quick to dismiss the opportunity Vivienne had laid before her. "Tell me," she said casually as she slid the bagels out of the oven and onto a plate. "Are any of these nice Jewish men at your synagogue rich? If they are, I could be interested." She laughed to indicate she was joking.

Vivienne didn't join her laughter. "You need money? That hoo-ha school isn't paying you enough?"

"The pay is fine." Libby settled into the chair beside Vivienne and smeared some cream cheese onto her bagel. "It's not the school."

Vivienne examined the tub of cream cheese. "This isn't the low-fat kind, is it? Well, what the hell. You only live once." She scooped a large dollop of cream cheese out of the tub and slathered it onto her bagel. "So, what is it? Reva's running up big bills at Bergdorf's?"

"It's the apartment," Libby told her. She hadn't mentioned the problem to anyone yet, and even though Vivienne was aggressively opinionated, she was a true and loyal friend, a better sister-in-law than her brother had ever been a husband. Libby trusted her, and she needed to unburden herself. "Remember when the building went co-op, maybe eight years ago?"

"Way behind the curve," Vivienne recalled. "Everyone else was going co-op in the '80s, but this building hung on until much later. You never bought, did you."

"I couldn't afford it. We were divorced and Harry let me keep the lease. I could manage the rent, but buying, even at the insider's price, was out of the question."

"But anyone who didn't want to buy at the time got to keep their leases, right? You were grandfathered in."

"Well…" Libby sighed. "Grampa died."

Bagel poised in midair, Vivienne gaped at her. "He died?"

"The company that owned all the apartments that didn't go co-op overextended itself. They have properties all over the city, and the market isn't as strong as it was a few years ago, and they had to raise cash. So they sold their ownership of the units in this building to another company, which claims we either have to buy or move out."

"Don't they have to honor the terms of your lease?"

"My lease comes up for renewal next January, and they're not going to renew it. I've got to figure out a way to buy this place, or else Reva and I will have to move."

"You'll never find a place like this for what you're paying," Vivienne said, words Libby certainly didn't need to hear. She knew she was paying a remarkably low rent for her six-room pre-war, with its nine-foot ceilings, its tall, sun-lit windows and its fireplace. She could afford a rent increase. She could even afford the monthly costs of a mortgage. But she didn't have the funds for a down payment, even at the cut-rate insider's price the new company had quoted.

"And you need how much?" Vivienne asked her.

Libby winced. "A quarter million, minimum."

"Oy vey." Vivienne dropped her bagel and pressed a hand to her chest, as if to contain the convulsions of her heart. "Where are you going to come up with money like that?"

"You know any rich single guys?" Libby said, then grinned so Vivienne would understand she was kidding. Vivienne tended to take things literally. If Libby wasn't careful, Vivienne would start interrogating the new bachelor members of her synagogue about their net worth.

Vivienne's heart must have calmed down, because she lowered her hand to her mug and sipped her coffee. "I know a rich married guy," she said.

"Thanks, but I'm not *that* desperate."

"Harry," Vivienne said.

"Harry?" Libby's ex-husband?

"He's rich. He pulls down a huge income working at that law firm—a position that you, let us not forget, supported him through law school to obtain. Plus Reva is his one and only child, and he has a moral obligation not to allow her to become homeless."

"She wouldn't be homeless," Libby protested. "We could move someplace less expensive."

"Where? Jersey?" Vivienne wrinkled her nose.

"I'm not asking Harry for money." Asking her ex-husband for money would be an admission of failure—and Libby wasn't the one who'd failed. The real-estate company that owned her apartment failed. But Harry wouldn't see it that way. He'd give her a hard time. After all, he'd wanted the apartment as much as she had when they'd decided to get a divorce. Back then, the odds of its going co-op were minimal, and the lease had locked them into a remarkably affordable rent, but after a bit of back and forth, Harry had acquiesced.

As divorces went, hers wasn't bad. She and Harry could speak civilly to each other. Harry generally deferred to her when it came to Reva, and he'd let Libby have primary custody, although she felt that was largely because his wife was too busy being glamorous to fuss with a stepdaughter. Whenever Reva returned from a visit with her father, she regaled Libby with stories about how utterly inept Bonnie was as a stepmother.

"I think you should ask him," Vivienne said. "He's such a schmuck. He owes you, Libby."

"He's your brother," Libby reminded her.

"Yeah, and I've been exposed to his schmuckiness my whole life. Get the money from him."

Libby pursed her lips and shook her head. Harry Kimmelman might be her last resort, but she hoped she'd find a few other resorts first. Anything to avoid having to go to him, hat in hand, and plead with him for—God!—a quarter of a million dollars.

"What, you're too proud to ask?" Vivienne pressed. "You'd rather wind up homeless than hit him up for money?"

"It's not just asking for money, Viv. It's asking for a small fortune."

"He's got a big fortune. He can afford it."

"Can he?" Harry didn't discuss his finances with Libby. But he was a partner at his firm, and Bonnie had to earn a decent salary as a fashion editor for one of the major glossies, and they were dinks—double income, no kids.

Libby had never been grasping and greedy during their divorce, however, and Harry had been generous in the settlement. In addition to giving her the apartment, he'd agreed to provide liberal child support and cover many of Reva's other expenses. The private school was free, of course, because Libby worked there, so he was spared the staggering cost of Hudson's tuition, but he paid for pretty much everything else Reva needed.

Maybe Libby could have Reva ask him for the money…. No, she wasn't going to put her daughter in the middle of this. She didn't even want Reva to know there was a chance they might have to move, at least not unless a move became unavoidable.

"Would you like me to ask him for you?" Vivienne offered.

"No. If I have to go to him, I'll do it myself."

"My parents might be able to help you out," Vivienne said. "Not that they've got a lot of spare cash lying around, but they'd do anything for you. I'd contribute, but Leonard and I are still newlyweds. We're still trying to figure out how to handle a joint checking account."

"I hate this, Viv. I hate having to beg people for money."

"To finance an apartment like this in Manhattan, you've got to beg," Vivienne said before taking a decisive bite out of her bagel. "Get used to it. You want to keep your house? You beg."

If anyone else had spoken to her that way, so officious and blunt, Libby would have erupted in anger. But when Vivienne issued her opinions in her slightly nasal New York accent, with bits of cream cheese edging her teeth like the grouting between the tiles in her bathroom, Libby could only laugh. She didn't have much to laugh about—a weekend that would be spent listening to a CD of a five-year-old girl singing Puccini, fretting about her apartment situation and bickering with Reva over nonsense—but laughing beat any of the alternatives she could come up with.

Laugh today, beg tomorrow, she thought. Or beg Monday. She could visit a bank. She could inquire about borrowing against her retirement account at Hudson. Maybe she could find a kindhearted loan shark down in Times Square.

Anything would be better than having to ask Harry for money.

Three

What Ned knew about private schools he could fit on the point of a penny nail. What he *felt* about private schools could cover a two-by-four, but those feelings were based mostly on Hollywood movies featuring arrogant preppies in crested blue blazers and gray pants and speaking with snooty British accents. He'd become acquainted with a few prep-school alums in college, and they hadn't been anything like the Hollywood stereotype. They'd been presumptuous, though, astonished that not all teenagers received a new car for graduation and allowances large enough to cover spring-break jaunts to the Bahamas.

All right, so he was a little biased. If private school was Eric's dream, Ned would bulldoze whatever obstacles stood in the way of that dream.

He stood on the corner of West End Avenue and 78th, watching youngsters—none of them wearing uniforms—

stream down the sidewalk and sort themselves into the three adjacent brownstones that all appeared to be part of the Hudson School. He wasn't sure which building he should enter, but the brownstone on the left seemed to be attracting most of the smaller children. That must be the lower school, the one Eric had applied to.

That Eric had sent in the application without even telling Ned still shook him. The kid had asked some questions about private school a couple of weeks ago, but Ned hadn't realized he was actually thinking of applying. That he'd gone ahead and done it—helping himself to Ned's Visa card—had left Ned uneasy and awash in guilt. Had moving to Manhattan been a mistake? Ned asked himself again. Had he destroyed his son's educational opportunities?

He and Eric had made the decision together to move to Manhattan, he reminded himself. They'd agreed that they had to leave Vermont, and he'd sent feelers out to various friends who might be able to find him work. His old classmate at college, Mitch Moskowitz, ran a rehab-and-renovation business in New York, and he'd come through with a job offer. When Ned had run the idea past Eric, Eric had freaked out. "New York! That's so cool! Let's go!"

Ned had planned the move carefully. He'd done research. The apartment he'd found for them was right near a primary school with a solid reputation, and it fell within the district of a high-scoring middle school. By the time Eric was ready for high school, Ned had assumed he'd either get into one of the elite public high schools—Eric was, after all, a flipping genius—or they'd rethink their plans and maybe leave the city.

He'd met Eric's fourth-grade teacher at the local elementary school, and she'd impressed him as a tough, smart woman. Ned had believed that things would work out. And they would, he assured himself, even if Eric didn't get into the Hudson School. But if Eric wanted the Hudson School, Ned would do what he could to get him in.

He waited for a few stragglers to race up the steps ahead of him, then climbed the front stairs and entered the building on the left. The vaulted entry smelled like lemon, leather and money. The walls were paneled with dark wainscoting, and a turned mahogany staircase ascended out of sight. A few framed bulletin boards held fliers and announcements, and an easel in the curve of the stairway displayed a placard with the date printed on it in bright block letters. High-pitched voices echoed from above, tumbling down the stairs.

An open door to his left led into an office. He glanced at his watch. Eight-fifty. He'd phoned Mitch to say he'd be arriving at the Colwyn job a half hour late, but he hoped this wouldn't take that long.

Smoothing the collar of his shirt beneath his denim jacket, he wondered whether he should have worn a tie. Maybe he ought to have splashed on a little cologne, too, instead of his usual no-name aftershave. Did he even own any cologne? He recalled buying a bottle when he'd decided it was time to start dating again, but given how messy that whole period had been, he'd left the bottle behind when he and Eric had packed up their belongings and moved.

Drawing in a steadying breath, he strode through the doorway and smiled at the woman behind the counter. She stood at a long worktable, inserting papers into an electric stapler that bit down on them in a crisp, quick tempo. Glancing up, she smiled hesitantly. She appeared middle-aged, her brown hair streaked with silver and her eyes obscured by large-framed glasses that gave her face a buglike appearance. "May I help you?" she asked.

"I need to see whoever's in charge of admissions," he said, moving a step to his left so the huge bouquet of flowers balanced in a vase on the counter wouldn't block his view of her.

Her smile chilled. "I'm not sure if Ms. Kimmelman is available for unscheduled meetings with parents," she told him.

"Well, if you're not sure, perhaps you could find out." She didn't seem convinced, so he added, "My name is Ned Donovan. I'm here for my son, Eric," as if that would make a difference.

Refusing to shift her gaze from him, the woman pursed her lips and crossed to a desk. She lifted a phone, pushed a button and listened for a moment before speaking. "Tara? There's a gentleman here who wants to see Libby. He says he's here for his son—" she eyed Ned quizzically "—Eric Donovan." She paused, then said, "I have no idea." Another pause, and, "All right." She lowered the phone and told him, "Ms. Kimmelman's assistant said she'd check."

Ned nodded and tried to guess what the assistant was checking. He didn't have a police record. Nor did he have a legacy of family members who had attended the school, or a well-connected associate who would vouch for his son, or a history of making huge donations to the endowment fund.

Feeling the woman's gaze on him, he turned to study the cubbyhole mailboxes fastened to one wall. Most of the boxes had papers or envelopes in them. A table beneath them held another bouquet of flowers. Such an abundance of flowers—had someone died?

A quiet buzz jolted him. He turned back to the counter to see the woman lift her phone. "Oh. Well, all right, then," she said, then hung up and gave him a suspicious glare. "Ms. Kimmelman is willing to meet with you," she said, her tone conveying that such a willingness was a rare thing. "Tara will be here in a minute."

Exactly one minute passed before a young blond woman entered the office through the glass door. Clad in a short skirt, a cotton sweater and enough costume jewelry to lead a Mardi Gras parade, she exuded more perkiness than he could handle on only one cup of coffee. "Hi, I'm Tara," she said, then beckoned for him to follow her.

They headed down a hall. "Libby usually doesn't meet parents without appointments," she informed him. "I don't know why she agreed to meet with you, but I'll warn you, things are really hectic right now. So don't take it personally if she can give you only a couple of minutes. You can schedule an appointment with her for some future date, if you'd like."

Libby Kimmelman. He repeated the name silently a few times until it was permanently imprinted on his brain.

"Today," Tara told him, "she got five bouquets. It's a good thing you didn't bring flowers. She'd hold it against you."

Flowers had never even crossed his mind. Was he supposed to accompany an application to a prestigious private school with a gift? Or would a flat-out cash bribe be just as effective? How big a bribe?

Tara swept through another door, passed an empty anteroom with a huge bouquet perched on a table just inside, and led him down a narrow hall to the end. She rapped on the door marked Director of Admissions, then inched it open. "Libby? Eric Donovan's father is here."

A woman's voice drifted out. "Send him in."

Tara pushed the door wider and stepped aside, gesturing Ned ahead of her. He entered the office and hesitated. His gaze took in more walls of walnut paneling, an elegantly patterned rug that looked authentically Middle Eastern and old, and a grand, varnished walnut desk.

The woman seated behind the desk was surprisingly

young—mid-thirties, tops—and her dark shoulder-length hair was held off her face with a barrette. Her suit jacket hung across the back of her chair and the sleeves of her blouse were rolled up. Her brown eyes took up half her face, and a knife-sharp nose sliced straight down between them. Her desk was cluttered with towering piles of folders and a vase stuffed with flowers. She seemed exhausted, and it was barely 9:00 a.m.

"Ms. Kimmelman?" He approached the desk, right hand outstretched. "I'm Ned Donovan."

Despite the fatigue shadowing her eyes, her smile struck him as genuine. She rose from her chair and shook his hand. "Libby Kimmelman. It's a pleasure to meet you."

A pleasure? Did she even know who he was? Or was she just relieved that he hadn't brought her flowers?

He liked the feel of her hand, cool and smooth, her nails short and shiny. He liked the curve of her smile, too, even though he sensed tension in it. She waved toward an armchair facing her across the desk, then busied herself shoving piles of folders around until he could see her without tilting his head.

"I wasn't aware that flowers were part of the deal," he said, motioning toward the vase.

"Flowers, chocolates, fruit baskets and a hamper filled with bubble bath, natural sponges and loofahs. That's today's haul. Tara, could you take the chocolates with you when you go?"

"Sure." The perky blonde bounded into the office and lifted a box of chocolates from a corner of the desk. Cradling the box in her arm, she started toward the door. "If you don't want the bubble bath, I could use it."

"I was thinking I'd send it to a nursing home, along with some of the flowers."

"If no nursing home wants it, send it my way." Tara

closed the door, leaving Ned and the director of admissions alone in the stately office.

Something was clearly going on that Ned didn't get. Flowers. Chocolates. Loofahs, whatever the hell they were.

He refused to be intimidated. He'd come to the Hudson School on a mission, his favorite, most important mission: Eric. Getting him into this school and finding the funding to pay for it. If loofahs were part of the deal, so be it.

He straightened in his chair and his gaze collided with Ms. Kimmelman's. For a brief, weird moment, he forgot his mission. She had amazing eyes.

He should have worn cologne.

Shit, Donovan—get it together, he ordered himself. The right time would come to meet women, socialize, have a sex life and all that kind of thing—but the right time wasn't now. And this lioness guarding the majestic gates of the Hudson School wasn't a woman he ought to be thinking about in the context of his sex life.

"What can I do for you, Mr. Donovan?" she asked pleasantly.

Let my son into your school. He cleared his throat and shifted in the chair, which was surprisingly comfortable, upholstered in burgundy leather that had grown smooth and hard with age. For some perverse reason, the chair irked him. Maybe because it was so classy. Like Libby Kimmelman, with her gold-button earrings and her tasteful apparel. Like the Hudson School itself. Ned wasn't used to feeling outclassed, but this office was classy, no question about it.

He cleared his throat again. "My son applied to the Hudson School. He sent in the application before I even saw it."

"Are there parts of it you'd like to amend?" she asked, rummaging through one of the piles on her desk.

"He saved to disk what he sent you, and it looked okay to me, as far as it went." Ned wished he had a pencil or something to hold. He wasn't sure what to do with his hands. They sat inert on his knees, his fingers hot and itching to move. "He didn't... Look." Ned took another deep breath and went for broke. "He really wants to attend this school, and if that's what he wants, that's what I want for him. He'd do well here. He's a terrific kid. And I just—I don't know the ins and outs of this thing. I've never had any dealings with private schools before. I didn't know about the flowers and chocolates and the...whatever they are. The loofahs."

Her smile was reassuring. "Flowers and all the other gifts do applicants no good at all. I get rid of them. The Hudson School doesn't accept students based on the presents their parents send me."

Okay, then. "So, how do kids get in?"

"I have a committee. We review the applications. We interview the children, and sometimes their parents. Then we sit around a table and discuss each applicant. We try to figure out who will contribute the most to the school and who will benefit the most from it. It's not an exact science, Mr. Donovan, but we work hard and we usually wind up with an excellent group of children. Now, your son, Eric—" she rummaged through the pile again and pulled out a folder "—is applying as a transfer student. I don't know how many openings we'll have in his grade for next year. We usually have a few."

"A *few?*" Anger and skepticism flared inside Ned, but he tamped it back down. "How many kids apply for those few openings?"

"It varies. We accept applications through the end of October, and the number of openings—"

"In other words, my son's got as much chance of getting into this school as a cow has of swimming to France."

She smiled again, all dark eyes and white teeth. "Can cows swim?"

Ned wished he could share her grin, but he was too annoyed. A *few* openings? Hell.

"There are always openings for transfers, Mr. Donovan," she assured him, "and nowhere near as many applications as we get for the kindergarten class. Your son has as good a chance of getting in as anyone else. A better chance, probably. A much better chance than a cow swimming to France."

"And why would that be?" he asked.

"He wrote his own application, for one thing." She tapped the folder without opening it. "I've received hundreds of applications this fall, and Eric's was the only one that gave me a genuine feeling for who he was. All the others were written by anxious parents. Your son had the guts to write his own application. That's worth a few points in my book."

"He's got more than guts," Ned said. "He's smart and funny." *And he's got his heart set on this damn school.*

"According to his application, he can't sing very well."

Ned was surprised that she could say that without refreshing her memory by skimming Eric's application. "Is singing required for the Hudson School?" he asked cautiously.

"Only if Eric goes out for the chorus. Tell me some more about him, Mr. Donovan."

What should he say? He could tell her Eric was the most wonderful boy in the universe, but he somehow doubted she would view his opinion as objective.

"In his application," she said, helping him out, "he mentioned that he used to live in Vermont."

Ned nodded. "We moved this past summer. He loves the city, but he's not crazy about his public school. He told me…." Ned sighed. Eric's words twisted like a key inside him, releasing worry. "He told me he sees students leaving Hudson at the end of school and they all look so happy. That's what he wants—to leave school feeling happy. He also likes the

after-school programs you offer. He's not crazy about his babysitter."

"He's what, ten?"

"You've got a good memory." He glanced at the un-
opened folder.

"Ten's a difficult age when it comes to babysitters. My
daughter's thirteen, so I have an idea what you're going
through. Ten-year-olds feel they're old enough to *be* babysitters and way too old to *have* babysitters." She flipped the
folder open, then shut, too quickly to have actually read anything. "He said you're a fixer upper." Her voice rose, turning the statement into a question. "I was a little confused by
that. Isn't a fixer upper a house that's falling apart?"

"I'm in construction," he explained. "Vermont is full of
fixer uppers. Lots of New Yorkers go to Vermont and buy
old barns and shacks, and they hired me to turn them into
fancy weekend places. So I fixed up the fixer uppers. I guess
that makes me a fixer upper."

"Or maybe a fixer upper fixer upper," she said with a grin.

Like a fool, he grinned back. "Down here, I'm doing
apartment renovations. Same idea, except there are no drive-
ways or front yards."

She stared expectantly at him. What else should he say?
What would win Eric a desk and chair in this school?

Since the topic of his work had come up, he figured now
was as good a time as any to raise a related subject. "I saw
nothing on your Web site about how much the Hudson
School costs."

"We haven't set the tuition schedule for next year yet,"
she explained.

"Well, whatever you set it to, I think it's going to be out
of my price range. What's the deal with financial aid? Or
am I screwing my kid's chances of getting in by asking?"

"No," she said gently. "You're not screwing your kid's

chances. We do offer financial aid. You'll have to fill out an application." She opened a drawer in her massive desk and pulled out some papers and a dark blue folder with a silhouette of the Hudson School's three buildings embossed on the front in gold. "I suggest you fill this out yourself, rather than having Eric do it."

"Right."

"I'm afraid it's nosy," she said, "but we need to know your entire household's financial situation. If Eric's mother—"

"Eric's mother is dead," Ned said matter-of-factly. Deborah hadn't earned much when she was alive, and she'd quit her job when Eric was born.

One thing Ned and Eric had never had to miss was her income. Everything else, yes—her little-girl voice, her blueberry pancakes, her uncanny skill at the board game Clue. Her silvery-blond hair, her wire-rimmed glasses, her inability to carry a tune—a flaw Eric had unfortunately inherited from her. Her lack of joke-telling skills—thank God Eric hadn't inherited *that* weakness. He was a lot funnier than his mother ever was. Deborah had been nothing if not earnest.

"I'm sorry," Ms. Kimmelman said. She fished a pen from between two stacks of folders, opened the folder in front of her and jotted something down.

Ned bristled. "Do you give an edge to kids whose mothers are dead?" Much as he wanted Eric to get into the Hudson School, he'd be damned if he'd let this lady accept his son out of pity.

She glanced up, her eyes flashing and her smile gone. "No. But we do like to have as much information as possible about our applicants. I'd say this would be a pretty important part of Eric's life."

Ned couldn't argue about that.

"If there are other important parts of his life you think we ought to be aware of, I'd appreciate your telling me."

Ned rummaged through his mind. It was overloaded with irrelevancies—the fancy rug at his feet, the faint scent of the flowers on her desk. Her eyes, as dark and intense as espresso.

Shoving that thought aside, he considered what was most important about Eric. His insistence on freeing every salamander he'd ever caught within five minutes of catching it. His natural grace on skis. His love of books—not just *Harry Potter* but *Horatio Hornblower* and the *Hitchhiker's Guide* and his Bart Simpson books. His enjoyment of historical research. His budding interest in hip-hop. His skill with computers. Would any of this make a difference in Eric's application?

Ned didn't even know how to talk about the most important thing of all: Eric's spirit, his refusal to allow his mother's death to destroy him, the way he'd looked at his father one day, more than a year ago, and said, "Crying isn't going to bring her back, and I'm tired of being sad. Is it okay to stop crying? We can miss her and still be happy."

If Ned said to Libby Kimmelman, "Accept my son because he understands the importance of happiness," would she let him into the Hudson School?

"He's an incredible kid" was all he could say. "If you don't take him, you're crazy."

"There are times I question my sanity, Mr. Donovan," she said, then laughed. "Please make sure you get these financial aid forms back to my office as soon as possible. Let me give you my card…." She pulled one from her desk drawer and paper-clipped it to the folder before she handed it to him. "The fax number is on there, if you want to fax the forms. And my phone number, if you have any questions."

He nodded in thanks as he accepted the folder, shook her

hand one more time and wished Eric had asked him for something he could guarantee, like a new bicycle, or Red Hat software for his computer, or tickets to a Rangers game. Admission to the Hudson School was a crap shoot, and Ned had never played with these dice before. He couldn't begin to guess the odds.

But damn it, he wanted his kid to win.

Four

Well, that was interesting.

No it wasn't. *Interesting* was Eric Donovan's application, the fact that he'd written it himself and sent it in without informing his father. The upper school received more applications written by the prospective students themselves, but since the majority of Libby's applicants were five years old, an application submitted directly by the student, without any adult input—which had obviously been the case with Eric's application—was…*interesting.*

But Eric's father was a whole other thing. *Interesting* barely scratched the surface. The broad shoulders, the callused hands and defiantly working-class apparel, the tousled hair too dark to be blond and too light to be brown, the smile constantly warring with the obvious tension in his jaw, those sleepy blue eyes…

Libby bet she wouldn't find too many guys like him wandering around Vivienne's synagogue.

Of course, Ned Donovan was the father of an applicant, and she'd met him only because, like most parents of Hudson applicants, he was pushy. But his parental pushiness wasn't the usual type. He hadn't wasted Libby's time extolling his son's superlative qualities. He hadn't mentioned Eric's IQ, his grasp of quantum physics, his theories about the stone sculptures on Easter Island or his fluency in French. Nor, thank God, had he brought Libby candy or flowers. Or loofahs.

Even so, he'd had his own subtle pushiness. The guy had charisma, and he'd used it. When he'd been sitting across the desk from her, staring at her with those bedroom eyes, she'd had to fight to keep herself from getting sucked in.

She heard a rap on the door, and then Tara cracked it open, peered inside and pushed it wider. "What a stud," she whispered as she bounced into the room.

Okay, so Libby hadn't been the only one susceptible to Ned Donovan's charisma. "He's an applicant's father," she said primly.

"I wish all our students had fathers like that." Tara's eyes twinkled with mischief. "We could raise funds by publishing a pinup calendar. 'Hunky Dads of the Hudson School.' If they all looked like that guy, we'd sell enough to provide scholarships to the entire student body."

Libby laughed, even though imagining Ned Donovan as a pinup boy, in a strong stance, with his shirt unbuttoned to reveal a well-muscled chest and his heavy-lidded eyes gazing seductively at the camera, was unsettling. "It would certainly be the hit at the Holiday Fair," she said, setting Eric's folder aside and wishing she could set Eric's father aside as easily. "When I start doing the interviews, I'll make a note of any candidates for Mr. February or Mr. November. Who's on for today?" She nudged a few more folders around, clearing the clutter away from her desk calendar. The only dates written on the page were with prospective students.

Tara pulled a pad from the hip pocket of her miniskirt and flipped a page. "In ten minutes you've got Astrid Morgensen. At eleven you've got twins—Daisy and Violet Fleur. At one-thirty you've got Will Billicki, although—" she squinted at her notes "—if he's still napping, his mother says they may arrive late, because he can be a wee bit testy if she wakes him up before he's ready to get up."

"A wee bit?"

"Her exact words."

"I'm sure. And twins, too. Oy." Libby sighed. Two five-year-olds were more than double the work of one, and she couldn't interview them separately, because the earth would stop spinning if Hudson accepted one twin and not the other. Twins were a set; the school would accept both or none. Libby might as well interview them together.

"Now, I know you're going to be objective," Tara remarked before Libby could recite her mantra. "All I'm saying is, if the kid has a gorgeous father, it could be relevant to his application. A Hudson Hunks calendar could do wonders for the annual fund-raising drive." With that, she waltzed out of Libby's office.

If the Hudson School published such a calendar, Libby would certainly buy a copy. Ogling students' fathers would be a pleasant way to pass the time when her ex-sister-in-law wasn't trying to set her up with members of her congregation. Unfortunately, most of those students' fathers were married to students' mothers, so ogling would be the beginning and the end of it.

Ned Donovan wasn't married, though.

And his son wasn't a student at the Hudson School. Yet. And might never be, depending on his interview and the number of openings for his grade and a host of other considerations. And if he did wind up at Hudson, his father would be a student's father, which would put him off-limits. And he was already off-limits, anyway.

Besides, he wasn't rich. If she was going to set her sights on an unattached man, she might as well find someone who could help her hang on to her apartment.

She restacked her folders and centered Astrid Morgensen's on her blotter. Opening it, she read what Astrid's mother, Hilga Eydendahl-Morgensen had to say about her spectacular daughter. Not yet five, Astrid was an expert on Nordic history. "She believes she is a descendent of Erik the Red," her mother wrote in the essay, "and who are we to say she's wrong?"

The mantra rose to Libby's lips: *I'm going to be objective.* If Astrid Morgensen wanted to believe she was Erik the Red's however-many-times-great-granddaughter, so be it. The Hudson School could always use a Viking maiden in its kindergarten class.

Macie Colwyn was an artist, although what her art was Ned had no idea. Her husband, whom he'd never met, did something that involved sitting at a desk and earning oceans of money, and with that money Macie had purchased a two-thousand-square-foot loft in a neighborhood just north of the West Village, which Mitch had told him was the Meatpacking District. Not a particularly charming name, and it didn't strike Ned as a charming neighborhood, either, but Mitch had assured him it was going to be the next TriBeCa.

After living for two months in the city, Ned almost understood what that meant. Manhattan was an island of neighborhoods, each with its own special personality. People who bought lofts in the Meatpacking District would be looking for a different sort of renovation than people who bought penthouses on the Upper East Side or town houses in Murray Hill or flophouses in the Bowery. The only important thing such clients had in common was access to more money than Midas. A person couldn't buy a residence worth the sort of rehab work Greater Manhattan Design Associates did unless that person was filthy rich.

Thanks to her husband, Macie Colwyn was filthy rich. She looked as if she'd undergone a bit of rehab work herself. Her bosom was disproportionately large, given her otherwise petite physique, her lips were permanently puckered and her eyebrows never moved. What she wasn't spending on this loft she was apparently passing along to some lucky plastic surgeon.

"She wants a new wall," Mitch muttered to Ned as he entered the loft.

He acknowledged his good luck in having stopped by Libby Kimmelman's office before arriving at the site. If he hadn't detoured to the Hudson School before work, he would have arrived at the Colwyn loft on time, which meant Mitch might not have been there. Although Mitch had landed the commission, drawn up the preliminary designs and signed all the contracts, he'd been letting Ned oversee the actual project. It was big and complex, but Ned had an architecture degree and plenty of experience. The job itself was nothing he couldn't handle.

He wasn't sure he could handle Macie Colwyn, however. "What do you mean, she wants a new wall?" he muttered back as he closed the door behind him and removed his denim jacket. The loft spread out around him, its old linoleum flooring torn up to expose the discolored plywood underneath, its enormous windows admitting glaring rivers of morning sunlight into the open space, wires and surge protectors, tools and worktables scattered around and three crew members working their retractable tape measures as they marked off areas into what would eventually become rooms. One of the worktables had a roll of papers spread out across it, Mitch's blueprints for the project. Macie stared at the plans, her arms folded over her pumped-up bosom and her eyes narrowed, as if she wasn't sure how to interpret what she was looking at.

Mitch ran a hand through his hair, which was already standing in dark tufts, as if he'd been tearing at it. "She says the living room in the original spec is too big and she wants to divide it into a front parlor and a back parlor. I explained that if she does that, the front parlor isn't going to have a window in it. She's trying to figure out how to put one in."

"Put a window in?" Ned's gaze circled the loft. "Opening onto what? The back half of the living room?"

"Talk to her. She won't listen to me."

Ned let out a breath. The hardest part of home renovation work was dealing with insane clients who believed their riches could buy anything, even a wall with a window that opened onto nothing.

He had already dealt with one woman today—a woman who'd hinted that she might be crazy, but seemed remarkably sane to him. He couldn't imagine Libby Kimmelman demanding an exterior window on an interior wall. He also couldn't imagine her injecting her lips full of whatever it was that made Macie Colwyn's lips look as if someone had whacked her hard on the mouth. And Libby Kimmelman clearly hadn't injected her forehead with Botox, given the worry lines that creased it.

What had she been worried about? he wondered. Breaking the news to Ned that his boy wouldn't be able to attend Hudson, or just the challenge of dealing with unwanted bouquets of flowers?

Mitch raked his fingers through his hair again, a gesture

that forced Ned's thoughts back to the challenge at hand. Ned had to try to fix things. It was his job.

Tossing his jacket into a corner on the dusty subfloor, he strode over to the table where Macie stood before the un-scrolled floor plan, studying it as if it were a biblical arti-fact, written in Aramaic so she couldn't read it. "Mitch says you've got an idea about breaking the living room into two rooms," he said.

She peered up at him. Her eyes were ringed with smudgy black liner and her hair, cut in layers that reminded him a little of an artichoke, had a purple undertone. She smelled like some kind of herb. Given his lack of culinary exper-tise, he couldn't identify it, but it reminded him of Thai food. "I understand that redoing the design will add to the ex-pense," she said. "That's not a problem."

"No, it's not," Ned agreed. Every damn change she de-manded, from wall moldings to light fixtures to backsplash tiles in the kitchen, would add to the expense, and Mitch would happily bill her for it. "The problem is, if you put a wall up in the middle of the living room—" he pointed to that section of the blueprint "—you'll wind up with a room without a window. Not only will it be gloomy, but you might have building code problems." He wasn't sure about the Manhattan building codes, but mentioning them might be enough to scare her away from her idiotic notion about the new wall.

"Who would we have to pay to make those problems go away?" she asked.

He had no idea. He hadn't been working in New York long enough to know the ins and outs of local corruption. "I'm not sure all building inspectors are on the take," he fudged. "You offer payment to the one honest guy and you'll wind up…" He concluded with a shrug, letting the threat re-main unspoken. "But there are other ways to break up the living room," he continued, before she could grill him on the sentencing guidelines for bribing public officials. "For instance, we could put in a broad arch here." He indicated the midpoint of the living room on the floor plan. "Something wide enough to let natural light flow throughout the entire room, but it would still break the room up for you. Another possibility would be columns."

"Columns?"

"You know. Like pillars."

"Ooh, columns!" Her face lit up. "Like the Parthenon. Could we get Corinthian columns?"

"Whatever style you want. I'd have to check with Mitch on suppliers, but I'm sure we could get Corinthian columns, if that's what you'd like. A pillar on each side would suggest a division of the room, but you'd still have the flow."

"I love Corinthian," Macie gushed. "All those leaves and scrolls around the top. It makes such a statement, don't you think?"

A statement about the pretentiousness of the home owner, perhaps, but Ned kept his mouth shut. If Macie was enthusiastic about the idea, he'd push it for all it was worth.

"Would we have to have just one on each side? Maybe we could install four of them, spaced evenly across the room."

Jesus, that would look dumb. Ned smiled. "We can explore different placements once we've got the room framed. The columns wouldn't be weight bearing, so we could put them wherever you want them."

"Columns." Macie sighed happily and gave herself a little hug. "I feel like Athena just thinking about it."

If he and Mitch didn't have to add a stupid wall in the middle of her living room, she could be Athena, Hera and Aphrodite rolled into one. "Great," he said. "Let's get to work."

* * *

"Can I sit here?" Ashleigh Goldstein asked as she approached Reva's table. One table over had empty seats, too, but the girls sitting there were Larissa LeMoyne and her friends, a group of stuck-up divas who probably IMed each other every morning before school because they always were dressed alike, in Marc Jacobs stuff from Barney's. If Larissa was wearing a black miniskirt and tights, they'd all be wearing black miniskirts and tights. If she was wearing hoop earrings, they all wore hoop earrings. It was really gross.

Ashleigh Goldstein belonged at that table like Darth Vader belonged at a Sweet Sixteen party. Reva waved at the empty chair next to her and said, "Help yourself."

Kim appeared less than pleased, but Reva didn't mind Ashleigh's company. She considered Ashleigh cool in a perverse way. Today, Ashleigh was dressed like a bag lady, in layers of faded denim and linen. Her hair was dyed black, but it looked sooty instead of sleek like Kim's, and around her neck she wore her ankh on a velvet cord and a *chai* on a gold chain. She had big boobs, too. That thing about breast size being hereditary must be true.

"I hate gym," Ashleigh announced, as if that had any possible relevance to anything in the world. Gym had come and gone hours ago, and during that period Ashleigh had continued her antiwar protest against field hockey. "I think you guys should sit out with me."

"I like hockey," Kim told her.

"You don't strike me as the violent type," Ashleigh commented, tilting her head to study Kim. Then she shrugged and unrolled her insulated lunch bag. She pulled out a box of lemonade and some sort of icky vegetarian sandwich with sprouts and other green stuff leaking out of the whole-wheat roll.

Reva could not imagine being a vegetarian. It sounded like a noble gesture, a great sacrifice—but not being able to eat a burger? Chicken fingers? Shrimp scampi? She'd rather die. Her lunch today was turkey breast on rye bread. She felt sorry for Ashleigh for being unable to enjoy such a culinary treat.

Kim wasn't a vegetarian, but she always brought weird lunches to school. Even though both her parents had grown up in the United States, they were into their Japanese heritage and liked to send Kim to school with little Rubbermaid tubs full of miso soup and strips of teriyaki beef that Kim would have to reheat in the microwave by the soda vending machine.

"Field hockey is not violent," Kim argued. "If anything, sports is a way to get out the violence inside us. Like, you're pissed at your mother so you whack the ball with your stick, and then you're not so pissed anymore."

"That's my point exactly," Ashleigh said. "We're using hockey to sublimate our violence, rather than trying not to be violent in the first place."

"Ooh, *sublimate*," Reva said, wiggling her eyebrows. "Ash used a ten-dollar word."

Both Ashleigh and Kim laughed, which was what Reva had hoped they'd do. She hated when her friends bickered.

Kim scooped a spoonful of soup out of one of her plastic containers and sipped it. "Do you think Ms. Froiken is going to start auditioning soloists today for the fall concert?"

"I heard we're doing excerpts from *Tommy*," Ashleigh said.

"That's what I heard, too," Kim confirmed.

"*Tommy* is so seventies," Ashleigh said, crinkling her nose. "It's like, my parents listened to that stuff."

"It's good music," Reva argued. "A lot of old rock is good. And besides, did you ever see pictures of Roger Daltrey when he was young?"

"Who's Roger Daltrey?" Kim asked.

"The guy who sang *Tommy* in the seventies. He'd go on-stage without his shirt, and he had this incredible chest. And no tattoos, either." Reva couldn't stand the tattoos all the rock stars seemed to have nowadays. It had become such a cliché, and they looked kind of dirty, like when she got ink smudges on her fingers. Whenever she saw a tattoo on a musical artist, she always wanted to tell him to take a shower.

She hoped Darryl J didn't have any tattoos.

"Are you going to try out for a solo?" Kim asked.

"Who, me?" Ashleigh wrinkled her nose again. "I'm lucky Ms. Froiken hasn't kicked me out of chorus. She always stares straight at me when she says, 'Someone's flat in the second soprano section.'"

Ashleigh Goldstein was definitely not flat, but Reva refrained from making any boob jokes. If her mother had had that breast reduction surgery, it might be a sensitive subject with Ashleigh, too.

"Actually, I meant Reva," Kim said, turning to her. "Are you going to try out?"

Reva snorted. "I don't know. Ms. Froiken never gives me solos." It was true; Reva thought she had a decent voice, and she tried out for solos every year. Last year, when they'd performed a medley of songs from the *Lion King,* she got to make a little introductory speech about the circle of life before the chorus started to sing, but that was talking, not a real solo.

"You should try out," Kim urged her. "You've got such a great voice."

Kim was just saying that because she was a good friend—but one reason she was a good friend was that she said such things. "You should try out, too," Reva told her.

Kim shook her head. "Ms. Froiken always says my voice

doesn't carry. Anyway, she's probably going to ask me to do the piano accompaniment."

"Maybe she'll ask me to turn the pages for you," Ashleigh remarked. "That would be one way to get me from ruining the second sopranos."

"You don't ruin the second sopranos," Kim said, which Reva thought was really sweet, given that Kim wasn't crazy about Ashleigh. "I'm a second soprano, and I've never heard you sing flat. I think Ms. Froiken is staring at Kirsten Hough when she says that." Kim jerked her head toward Larissa's table. Kirsten sat at Larissa's left, wearing a sheer white blouse with a pink camisole under it, just like Larissa. "Anyway, you should go for it, Reva. You've got a great voice."

"Yeah." Reva took a swig of her milk and shrugged. "Like, maybe someday I'll wind up on a street corner, singing for spare change."

"Or singing backup for another street singer," Kim murmured, then winked.

Oh, God, how cool would that be? Singing backup for Darryl J... Not that he needed a backup singer. Not that his songs needed any embellishment from anyone at all whatsoever. But if Reva was his backup singer, she'd get to travel with him and appear with him on the stage of the Knitting Factory or the Mercury Lounge, and she'd step up to the mike with him on the parts of his songs where she was supposed to sing, and they'd both lean in toward the mike together with their lips so close they were practically kissing.

"Okay, you guys." Ashleigh used her thumb to nudge a stray sprout into her mouth. Black nail polish, Reva decided, was almost as bad as tattoos. It made a person's fingers seem dirty. "What are you talking about?"

"What do you mean, what are we talking about?" Kim asked innocently.

"You're talking about some actual street singer, right?"

Reva and Kim exchanged a glance. Ashleigh was more perceptive than they'd realized. Should they tell her about Darryl J?

He wasn't their private property, after all. The more fans he had, the quicker his rise to the top would be. He deserved to have lots of people seeking out his music. He was so talented. And Ashleigh wasn't like the divas, who'd sneer at anyone who listened to a performer who wasn't already famous. Ashleigh was open to new things.

"There's this guy who sings in Central Park," Reva said.

"He's *really* cute," Kim added.

"And talented. His name is Darryl J."

"We've heard him sing lots of times," Kim boasted.

"Darryl Jay? Like the bird, *j-a-y?*" Ashleigh asked.

"No. Just the letter *J*," Reva told her.

"What does it stand for?"

"We don't know," Reva said, savoring the mystery of it.

"And he's good?" Ashleigh asked.

"Not only that, but he's really cute," Kim declared.

"What kind of music does he play?"

"Melodic rock," Kim explained.

"But slightly hip-hop," Reva added.

"Only, it's melodic."

"A little like Ben Harper, only better," Reva said. "And he plays the guitar."

"And he's very cute," Kim said.

"Yeah, I got that part, about him being cute." Ashleigh grinned. "So, like, what? You guys just stumbled over him one day or something?"

"Something like that, yeah. And now we're his most devoted fans," Reva boasted. Telling Ashleigh about him was fine, because no matter how much she might love Darryl J— if she ever bothered to find him and listen to him—and no matter how many friends she told about him, and how fast his rise to stardom occurred, Reva and Kim had priority over everyone else. They'd discovered him. They'd gotten there first.

"So…where would I find him in the park?"

"He's been playing at the Band Shell," Reva said. "We'll be going on Saturday, if you want to join us."

Ashleigh got kind of aloof. "I don't know. I might have plans," she hedged, which probably meant she wasn't sure she wanted to traipse through Central Park with Kim and Reva on a Saturday. Reva had no idea where Ashleigh hung out on her weekends. Somewhere grungy and Goth, she supposed.

"Well, let us know," Kim said, shrugging as if it was nothing to her one way or the other. Which was pretty much how Reva felt about the whole thing, too. If she and Kim could build Darryl J's fan base, that would be great. And if they couldn't, they wouldn't have to share him with anyone. He'd be all theirs.

Either way, Darryl J belonged to them, and Saturday afternoon they'd get to bask in his beautiful music and his magical smile.

Five

"I'm home," Libby called out as she swung open the door. Her briefcase was crammed with folders and her head still resounded with nerve-grating echoes of Will Billicki's whine.

Apparently, Will would have happily napped all afternoon if his mother hadn't brought him to the Hudson School for his interview. "A wee bit" scarcely scratched the surface of how cranky he'd been, and Libby had urged his mother to reschedule. But she'd insisted he would be fine. "Just give him a few minutes," she'd pleaded.

Libby had given him a painful half hour. She often coined nicknames for the children she interviewed, in order to jog her memory once the committee met to decide which applicants would be accepted into Hudson. In her mind, Will Billicki became "Shrill Will."

I'm going to be objective, Libby had chanted to herself

as she'd soldiered through her thirty minutes of hell with the boy. One Shrill Will had been twice as much work as two Fleurs, whom Libby had barely been able to tell apart and who had talked to each other and ignored her completely throughout their interview. As for the Viking girl, she'd actually had some interesting things to say about longboats.

Too bad Libby had given away all the chocolates she'd received in the past week. Her headache might respond to a couple of Godivas—or, better yet, a glass of wine. If a prospective Hudson parent sent her a bottle of merlot, the kid would definitely have an edge in the admissions process.

Seconds after Libby closed and locked the apartment door, Reva appeared in the doorway to the living room, pressing the handset from the cordless kitchen phone to her ear. *It's Grandma,* she mouthed, before saying into the phone, "Uh-huh. Uh-huh. Yeah, math's okay. In science we're doing magnetism—oh, and leaves. Listen, Grandma, Mom just got home. I'll put her on. Bye." She thrust the phone at her mother.

Libby set her briefcase on the mail table in the foyer. Ridding herself of it made her realize how heavy the damn thing was, crammed with applications she had to review before tomorrow. "Hi, Gilda," she said into the phone. She knew the caller was her mother-in-law. Her mother phoned rarely, and when she did Reva called her "Dee-Dee" because she insisted she was too young to be called anything that hinted of grandparenthood. Her name was Delia, and "Dee-Dee" sounded youthful.

"Libby!" Gilda exclaimed, as if astonished to hear her voice. "Did you know they've got fresh swordfish steaks on sale at Gristede's? Only $6.99 a pound. I picked up a couple for Irwin and me. You should stock up. They say swordfish has that fat in it, the one that makes your good cholesterol go up."

"I think that's salmon, not swordfish," Libby murmured, switching the phone from hand to hand as she wiggled out of her blazer. "Salmon's the one with the omega-3 fatty acids in it."

"Well, swordfish is good for something. I should have picked some up for you."

"Thanks, but my fridge is full."

"Reva should eat more fish. It's brain food, did you know that? It makes you smart."

"Reva's already smart," Libby said, thinking about Reva's frequent smart-ass attitude.

"Vivienne says she sleeps all day."

"Only on the weekends. She's a teenager. Teenagers need a lot of sleep." Libby strolled toward the kitchen, tossing her blazer over the back of a dining-room chair on her way. Gilda could talk all she wanted about fish, but Libby had to deal with real food.

"So, Vivienne said she stopped by to see you on Saturday," Gilda commented. Libby braced herself, expecting her ex-mother-in-law to pester her about her refusal to socialize with the eligible men Vivienne had lined up for her at the synagogue. Gilda surprised her by saying, "Vivienne said you're having financial problems."

Libby wasn't sure how to respond. She bought time by yanking open the fridge and pulling out the package of ground beef she'd left in there to defrost that morning. It was still half-frozen, but it would thaw quickly enough when she browned it before mixing it into the tomato sauce for her pasta. "I'm okay," she finally said, exercising discretion. Reva wasn't within earshot, but she could appear at any moment. Libby didn't want her to hear about the housing catastrophe that loomed before them.

"According to Vivienne, you aren't okay at all. Libby, *bubbela,* what's a family for if you won't turn to them in times of trouble? Tell me what we can do. Irwin and I can help."

"No, Gilda." Wedging the phone between her ear and her shoulder, she unwrapped the meat, plopped it into a skillet and turned on the heat. Then she used the edge of a spatula to hack the frozen red core into smaller pieces. "It's sweet of you to offer, but no."

"I'm not sweet. Ask Irwin. He calls me his little *chrain*. You know what that is?"

"Horseradish," Libby said. She had to eat the stuff every spring at Gilda's Passover seder, and it always made her nose run.

"What a guy." Gilda's sigh sounded oddly affectionate. Her voice lost its gentle undertone when she continued. "Vivienne says if you don't raise a lot of money, you might lose your apartment. She says it's going co-op."

Vivienne talks too much, Libby thought, although she supposed she herself talked too much. She shouldn't have told Vivienne about her financial crisis with the apartment— or else she should have told Vivienne not to share the news with her mother. Gilda might have the personality of a horse-radish, but she had a cream-puff heart, and of course once she heard Libby was in trouble, she would want to intervene. Even if Libby wasn't in trouble, she'd want to intervene.

"So what kind of money are we talking about?" Gilda pressed.

"A lot. But really, Gilda, you and Irwin shouldn't be worrying about this."

"If we could help—"

"You can't. I mean it." She wedged the phone between her ear and shoulder again, this time so she could fill a pot with water for the pasta. "Irwin's retiring in, what, five years? You should be saving money for that. You can't count on Social Security."

"We're saving, we're saving. We have a nice fund, Libby. Don't worry about us. We could spare a little."

"A little won't help," Libby explained.

Gilda said nothing for a minute, then, "If it's that much, you should ask Harry. Giving you money is the least he could do, the way he walked out on you and Reva for that new wife of his."

"He does give me money," Libby said. She hated defending her ex-husband, but she wasn't going to lie about him. "He sends me a check every month."

"For Reva. What does he ever do for you?"

He leaves me alone, Libby answered silently, grateful for the fact that he did. "We both work," she said, forcing patience into her tone. "We both earn incomes. We both agreed there was no need for alimony."

"But he left you. A good woman, the mother of his child, and he left you for that stuck-up lady. You should've taken him to the cleaners, Libby, I always said."

"He's your son," Libby reminded her.

"I should've raised him better...."

"Gilda. Stop it." She stirred the browning meat vigorously. It sizzled and spat, just the way her temper would sizzle and spit if she loosened her grip on herself. After being trapped in the interview room with Shrill Will, she didn't care to spend her evening listening to Shrill Gilda wallow in guilt over her son's stupidity. Nor did Libby want to think about her housing situation. She *had* to think about it, but she didn't want to. Thinking about it fried her, just like the meat in the pan.

She couldn't give in to anger, though. Being a single parent meant staying in control, projecting confidence and serenity and not indulging in temper tantrums, even when they were called for and there was no therapeutic chocolate or wine within reach.

"Go to him, Libby," Gilda urged her. "Tell him to be a mensch. He owes you, *bubby.*"

"That's the problem. He *doesn't* owe me."

"He left you."

And good riddance, Libby thought. "A long time ago," she said. "Everything was settled ten years ago. I can't throw our divorce in his face and ask for more money. "

"But it's okay to let him throw his own daughter out in the street?"

Libby reminded herself that she really did love the woman on the other end of the line. "I appreciate your concern, Gilda, but I'll figure out how to deal with this situation on my own, okay? It's not Harry's problem. It's not your problem. Give me a chance to work on it."

"I should take a hint, right? Fine. You're upset and you wish I'd shut up—even though it's my fault. I botched things when raising Harry, and now he's a schmuck. Take it out on me. I deserve it for raising such a schmuck."

"You didn't raise a schmuck, Gilda," Libby assured her, wincing at the sheer falsehood of that statement. "Just stop worrying, okay? Things will work out somehow."

"They always do," Gilda said, apparently trying to sound comforting, although her words lacked conviction. "But remember, he's there, and it's his daughter."

"Okay. I'll think about it," Libby assured her. "I've got to go. The meat is burning." She said goodbye and disconnected the call.

"So what's going to work out somehow?" Reva asked from the doorway.

Great. She'd caught the end of the conversation. What else had she heard? "You know Grandma," Libby said casually, pulling a box of linguini from a shelf and shaking out enough for their dinner. "She gets worried about nonsense."

"What kind of nonsense?"

"Stuff about when Grandpa retires," Libby said, pleased that that wasn't a lie.

It wasn't the truth, either, and Reva was too smart to let her get away with fudging. "If you don't want to tell me, why don't you just say so?" she asked petulantly, her mouth curving in a self-righteous scowl.

Libby didn't want to tell her—but she couldn't say so. Who knew how Reva would react to the news that they might lose their home? Nowadays, asking her to straighten up her room could trigger outrage and door slamming. Informing her that she soon might not have a room to straighten up… Libby didn't even want to imagine the hysteria that would ensue.

Still, lying wasn't a great strategy, either. "It's just that this apartment is going co-op," Libby said, praying that Reva wouldn't understand the ramifications of her statement.

"Yeah, so?"

"So, I have to do a little recalculating."

"Going co-op…" Reva entered the kitchen, sidestepped her mother and flopped onto one of the chairs at the tiny corner table. "Like, what exactly does that mean?"

"It means that our apartment will no longer be for rent, so if we're going to stay here we have to buy it. Well, not outright buy it, but buy shares in the building proportionate to our unit. It's kind of confusing."

"I'm not an idiot," Reva said. "Buying shares in the building is like buying the apartment, right?"

Libby sighed. "Right."

"How much do we have to pay?"

Libby sighed again. "Too much."

Reva shrugged. "Get the money from Dad."

"Reva." Was Libby the only person in the world who hated the idea of hitting up her ex-husband for large quantities of cash?

"He's got plenty," Reva pointed out. "You know what he charges his clients? Hundreds of dollars an hour. I figured it out once, and he's hauling in like over half a million dollars a year. And he doesn't spend it all on food, because Bony never eats. She's so skinny it's disgusting."

Reva's mention of food drew Libby's attention back to the stove. The water was boiling, and she added some dry linguini to it, then nudged the sticks of pasta down into the pot as the water softened them.

"You should buy fresh pasta," Reva remarked. "Kim says it tastes better."

Fresh pasta costs more, too. If Libby had any hope of financing her apartment purchase without begging Harry for assistance—as everyone in the whole damn world seemed to think she should—she was going to have to start watching her pennies. No fresh pasta. Chuck steak, not sirloin. Store-brand ice cream instead of Ben & Jerry's. Maybe she ought to race over to Gristede's and stock up while the swordfish steak was on sale.

"Dry pasta tastes fine," she said, then clamped her mouth shut before her frustration spilled out. Shrill Will's whines had subsided to a background din in her skull, a grating accompaniment to the messy condition of her life. She did *not* want to go to Harry. She did *not* want to lose her apartment. She did *not* want the water to boil over the top of the pot, but it was doing just that, hissing as it spattered against the stove's glowing red coils. She turned down the heat and stirred the pasta until the water sank back below the rim, then dealt with the meat, which was brown and dry, nearly burned.

She was an utter, abject failure. She couldn't budget, she couldn't cook and she couldn't maintain her objectivity when she interviewed brats.

"So Kim and Ash and I are going to the park this Saturday," Reva was saying, evidently no longer interested in discussing financial crises with her mother.

Frankly, Libby was no longer interested in the subject,

either. She wished it would just go away. "Who's Ash?" she asked as she pulled a jar of tomato sauce from a shelf in the door of the refrigerator.

"Ashleigh Goldstein."

"That girl with the black nail polish?"

"You don't like black nail polish?"

"I didn't say that," Libby replied, eager to avoid an argument with Reva. One of the advantages of working at the Hudson School was that she was familiar with most of the kids and their manicures. Ashleigh Goldstein's father was a Park Avenue orthodontist, and Ashleigh seemed determined to present herself as anything but the daughter of a Park Avenue orthodontist.

"What's going on in the park on Saturday?" she asked. "You don't have to collect more leaves, do you?"

"There's always something going on in the park on Saturday," Reva said.

"I meant, something specific. One of those toy boat regattas, or a kite-flying contest?"

Reva rolled her eyes. "Yeah, like Kim and me and Ash would want to watch a bunch of assholes fly kites or play with their little toy boats."

"You used to love those regattas," Libby reminded her. "Everybody lined up along the edge of the pond with their remote controls, steering their boats around the buoys, and people cheering.…"

Reva made a retching sound. "No, we don't want to watch the boats," she said. "We just want to hang out."

"I guess it's all right, if you don't have too much homework."

Reva opened her mouth as if to comment on her homework, then changed the subject altogether. "They had tryouts for the fall concert solos today. Ashleigh was really good. She says her voice is flat, but it's not."

"Did you try out?"

"Yeah. I sucked."

"Ask Muriel Froiken if you can try out again."

"Mom." She rolled her eyes again. "What, you think she'll give me a solo because my mom works at the school? Forget that. I'm not going to ask for favors."

Libby refused to apologize for being on the Hudson staff. "Why don't you set the table," she suggested, struggling to filter her annoyance out of her voice.

Looking gravely put-upon, Reva pushed herself to her feet and crossed to the silverware drawer. Libby considered telling her to set the dining-room table, instead. Every now and then they ate dinner at the big table, and they even lit a centerpiece candle sometimes, which made the meal seem terribly grand. Maybe eating in there and not at the cramped table tucked into the corner of the kitchen would cheer them both up.

But the big table might emphasize how alone Libby felt right now. No Harry to bail her out financially. No other adult to vent to, to dump all the tension of her long, wearying day on. No one to assure her that she could afford to splurge on fresh pasta every now and then, that she wouldn't lose her home, that her daughter would never paint her nails black like Ashleigh Goldstein's. No one to say to her, "I can't promise everything's going to work out, but I can sympathize."

Her mind filled, involuntarily, with a picture of Ned Donovan. He was probably rattling around his apartment with his son right now, fixing dinner just like Libby. He would have removed his jacket and his thick-soled work boots; he might be wearing form-fitting jeans and a snug T-shirt—and thank you, God, for giving men physiques that looked so good in jeans and T-shirts. His hair would be mussed because, living alone with his son, he had no one to comb it for. No one to shave off his five o'clock shadow for. Just him and his son and a plate of—why not?—spaghetti and meat sauce.

What was she thinking? A guy like him would undoubtedly have a girlfriend, someone young and attractive and solvent, someone without an obnoxious teenage daughter and a looming housing disaster. His girlfriend would be puttering around the kitchen with him right now, all the while assuring him that his son would get into Hudson or some equally esteemed private school. She would listen as he described his day, his hard work fixing things up. She'd ask him how things went at the Hudson School that morning, and he'd say, "Tell me, honey, what the hell is a loofah?"

Other adults had adults. Libby did, too—although a ridiculous number of them were her ex-husband's relatives. Vivienne was right; she needed some men in her life to turn to, to sleep with, simply to lean on. If they wanted to help her buy her apartment, that would be fine, too. But right now, just having a man to talk to would be nice.

"So, you like those jeans?" Ned asked Eric.

"They're okay."

Given what Ned had spent on them, Eric ought to demonstrate a little more enthusiasm. But then, the kid was ten years old, and boys that age would rather die than pretend they cared about clothes.

One thing Ned missed about Vermont was normal prices. In Manhattan, even the discount stores charged obscene amounts for kids' dungarees, plus a staggering sales tax. And Eric was going to outgrow the jeans Ned had just bought him before he came close to wearing them out.

Still, Manhattan had its compensations, Ned conceded as he and Eric strolled down Broadway. Manhattan had life, sidewalks teeming with people chattering, nudging one another, holding hands. Couples. Healthy adult couples whose body language shouted that they had sex on their minds.

Not that Ned had sex on his mind. He was out shopping with his son, for God's sake. Sex was the furthest thing from his mind.

Yet the young couple with their arms looped around each other's shoulders and their hips colliding with every step dragged the subject just a little closer to Ned's mind. The couple disappeared through the door of a seedy-looking bar. They hadn't looked seedy themselves; maybe the bar was nicer than it appeared from the street.

Now that Ned was living hundreds of miles from Woodstock, Vermont, he might just have the opportunity to usher a woman into a bar. Or out of a bar and somewhere more private, more intimate, somewhere conducive to the sort of activity that should have been the furthest thing from his mind but wasn't.

He'd usher the woman into a nicer establishment, of course, and he'd take his time to learn if she was someone he'd really want to share that particular activity with. He wasn't desperate. He'd gone without for quite a while, and he could go without for a little longer. He could be picky. He could wait for a woman who wasn't too young or too old, a woman who was smart and involved in an interesting career…a woman with thick brown hair and eyes as big as silver dollars, only dark and luminous.

Someone like Libby Kimmelman, for instance.

Well, no. He didn't want to waste his time with a snooty prep school admissions director.

Libby Kimmelman hadn't seemed particularly snooty, though. She'd been remarkably accessible, and she'd had a warm smile, and when she'd said the word *loofah* it had sounded inexplicably erotic. He wondered what it would be like to make *loofah* to a woman like her.

Before he could congratulate himself on his clever pun, Eric said, "You think maybe I could get some new T-shirts, too? Everybody wears them real baggy here."

T-shirts. His son. Right. "If we can find some that aren't too expensive, sure," he said, resolving to put sex and Libby Kimmelman and loofahs where they belonged—in that region a man could convince himself was the furthest thing from his mind even when it was located at the very center of his consciousness.

Six

Finally. Saturday. This had to have been the longest week in Reva's life.

Every night after dinner for the past week, her mother had emptied her briefcase onto the dining-room table and read applications, a task that turned her into a total bitch. Reva supposed that having to read hundreds of essays about five-year-olds who could speak three languages and design rocket ships might get old pretty fast, but still.

Adding to her mother's crabbiness was the whole money thing. She refused to consider getting money from Reva's father. Not only did she refuse, but she actually got into a worse mood whenever Reva raised the subject.

And last night, when Reva had done her mother the favor of changing the subject, and asked if she could get a second hole pierced in each ear, her mother had gone ballistic. It wasn't like Reva was asking to get her nipple pierced, or her belly button, or even an eyebrow. Just an extra hole so she could wear two earrings per ear. Lots of girls had more than one hole. But when her mother got like this, she was so unreasonable.

Aunt Vivienne had stopped by Thursday evening. She'd said she couldn't stay for supper, but after chugging down the wine Reva's mother had poured for her, she'd wound up calling her husband and saying she'd be home later, and she'd shared their dinner of broiled swordfish steaks, which had tasted pretty dry and bland to Reva, even though her mother and Aunt Vivienne had insisted they were delicious.

Aunt Vivienne, too, believed Reva's mother should ask Reva's father for money. Over dinner she'd remarked that guys were jerks so you might as well get what you could out of them. Reva had considered that an odd thing for a newlywed to say. Aunt Vivienne had gotten married only a year ago, and Reva had to admit that her husband, Leonard, definitely lived on the asshole side of the street, but Aunt Vivienne had married him of her own free will, so how bad could he actually be? Anyway, the bottom line was that Aunt Vivienne agreed with Reva that her mother ought to hit up old Harry for the money she needed. And her mother had said absolutely no way.

Pride could be pretty stupid—to say nothing of costly.

But Reva wasn't going to think about her mother or her father or the apartment today. The sky was sunny, the air was mild and she had eight dollars and change in her purse—enough to buy a hot pretzel and an ice cream or one of those souvlaki subs they sold from pushcarts around the park. Kim probably had even more money with her. She got ten bucks a week allowance, and her parents bought her most of what she needed. Reva didn't know how much Ashleigh got, but she probably spent it all on cosmetics—the black hair dye, the nail polish, the pale powder and dark eyeliner she liked to wear. Makeup cost real money if you bought the quality brands.

Reva met up with Kim and Ashleigh at the park entrance by Strawberry Fields. Kim was dressed like a normal person, in blue jeans and a cotton sweater. Reva was dressed normally, too, in black jeans and long-sleeved T. Ashleigh wore an ankle-length paisley skirt and a black shirt with a studded leather belt cinching her waist, ankle-high black boots with big buckles on them, her ankh and her *chai* on chains around her neck, peacock feathers dangling from her ears and small gold hoops poking through them—she had two holes per ear, and it obviously hadn't turned her into a monster—and gobs of black liner edging her eyelids.

"So, where's this fabulous musician?" she asked. Her voice held a challenge, as if she suspected that Reva and Kim had been exaggerating when they'd told her how cool Darryl J was.

Reva caught Kim's eye. Kim clearly wasn't thrilled about including Ashleigh on this outing. Maybe Reva had made a mistake by inviting her to join them. But Darryl J needed a bigger audience, and who better than his most loyal, devoted fans—Reva and Kim—to bring that audience to him? Today Ashleigh, next week Monica Ditmer and Katie Staver, and maybe the week after that Reva could entice Katie's brother Matt and those guys he hung out with, Micah Schlutt and Luke Rodelle. The record companies probably wouldn't take Darryl J seriously if he didn't have some guy fans.

In any case, she wasn't going to let Ashleigh's presence or Kim's scowl ruin the day she'd been waiting for all week long. "This fabulous musician," she said calmly, "is probably performing near the Band Shell." She strode past the Imagine mosaic imbedded in the ground—her mother always got teary-eyed when she saw the mosaic, but it didn't do much for Reva, even though it usually had some candle or withered flower lying on it in memory of that Beatle who got killed—and on to the road that looped around the lower park. It was closed to automobiles today, but the traffic was still pretty dense. Bikers, skaters, skateboarders and joggers all sped past, moving in the same direction. Jogging was supposed to improve your health, but it seemed to Reva that jogging amid all those bikers and skaters could cost a person his life. Just crossing the roadway, she felt she was risking major bodily harm.

Ashleigh and Kim kept up with her, though, and they made it to the other side of the road without injury. The sky above the Sheep Meadow was filled with kites, and Reva remembered her mother's corny question about whether Reva wanted to go to the park to see the kites. Flying a kite seemed like about the most boring activity a person could do voluntarily. Sitting through Mr. Calaturo's European history class was probably a little more boring, but a class was mandatory. People had a choice about flying a kite, and there were dozens of folks at the park today who'd freely chosen to stand on the sprawling expanse of grass, clutching a reel of string and craning their necks to observe their kites. Like this was so exciting, a big colorful thing held up in the sky by a breeze.

"So, when do you think Froiken is going to announce the *Tommy* soloists?" Ashleigh asked as they worked their way along the path that bordered the Sheep Meadow.

"A couple of weeks," Kim said with a certain authority. Since she would be playing the piano accompaniment, it figured she would have the inside scoop on Ms. Froiken's schedule.

"The later, the better," Reva grumbled. "As long as I don't know who the soloists are, I can pretend I've got a chance."

"I thought you sounded fantastic at your audition," Ashleigh argued. "You definitely have a chance."

Reva eyed Kim, who nodded. "You sounded really good," she confirmed.

Reva trusted Kim's judgment more than Ashleigh's, but she wasn't convinced. "I had a tickle in my throat when I was singing. I kept feeling like I was going to cough or something."

"You didn't sound that way," Kim assured her. "You sounded great."

"You sounded fantastic," Ashleigh insisted.

"I don't have that good a voice," Reva said, wishing she could believe her friends. They were only trying to make her feel better, and she appreciated their effort. "Now, Darryl J...*that's* a good voice."

Ashleigh raised her eyebrows, doing her best to look skeptical. It was hard to look skeptical when you were wearing an ankle-length paisley skirt.

By the time they reached the eastern edge of the Sheep Meadow, music from the performers at the mall was already drifting toward them—too much music and too much crowd noise for Reva to detect Darryl J's guitar and voice, but she was sure he'd be set up in his usual spot near the Band Shell. It was such a balmy day, and the park was so mobbed with people enjoying the weather he couldn't afford not to be there. On a day like today, a street musician could probably clean up.

She and Kim accelerated their pace as they neared the mall. Ashleigh managed to keep up, which was good because the walkway was really crowded, and if they lost her they might never find her again, no matter how much she stood out with her pale face and those shit-kicker boots.

"There he is," Kim said, slipping past Reva and dodging a guy on a unicycle juggling stuffed teddy bears. It was easy for Kim to move through the throng, because she was so tiny. Reva managed to follow in her wake, glancing over her shoulder every now and then to make sure Ashleigh was still with them. And then she heard one of those broad, rich guitar chords that she associated with Darryl J's music, and her face broke into a smile, almost literally, as if her skin were cracking open to let her happiness escape.

How could this one musician have such a strong effect on her? She didn't know and she didn't care. All that mattered was that she'd survived a long week and now, at last, she would receive her reward: standing in Darryl J's presence and listening to him sing.

She wove through the crowd surrounding him—a much larger crowd than last week's, maybe because it was a Saturday, maybe because it was so warm and sunny. He wore a denim shirt, a leather vest and jeans today, and his sleeves were rolled up to his elbows. No tattoos visible. She sighed in relief.

God, he was so good! His voice was like this spiced cider she'd drunk at Grandma's house last winter—smooth and tangy, cool on the tongue but warm going down, a warmth she felt moving through her, in her throat, in her chest, in her gut and in her blood, which carried it throughout her body. It made her want to sway.

Next to her, Kim stood transfixed. Behind her, Ashleigh whispered, "Ooh, he's cute."

Cute didn't begin to describe him. He was beyond awesome. He was magical. He was going to wait for Reva to get a few years older, and then he was going to fall madly in love with her.

He started singing a slower song, in a minor key. "'I close my eyes because it's all been such a loss, and the cost, baby, the cost is the price of my soul,'" he crooned. Reva wasn't sure what he meant by "the price of my soul," but it was such a sad lyric, and the chords were so melancholy, the riffs so bluesy, she wanted to break free of the crowd and give him a hug. She wondered who had broken his heart so badly—surely he couldn't have made up this song out of thin air. It had to have been wrung from some mournful experience he'd suffered.

She would never break his heart. Never.

The song ended and he smiled. As the crowd burst into applause, Reva forced herself to acknowledge that maybe he *had* just made the song up. Maybe he'd been sitting around, writing a bunch of happy songs, and he suddenly said, "Man, I ought to write something sad, just to show how wide my range is," and he'd knocked off this song about the price of his soul.

People broke free of the crowd and stepped forward to drop money into his open guitar case. Reva thought about the eight dollars she had in her purse and the pain Darryl J had revealed in his song. He deserved to be paid for his music. If he didn't make enough money he might just quit the whole music thing and get a job in a bank or at McDonald's. She couldn't bear that happening.

Gathering her courage, she pushed forward, unzipped her purse and pulled out a dollar. Dropping it into his guitar case brought her closer to him than she'd ever been before. He was even handsomer up close—no acne scars flawed his tawny skin and his teeth were a brilliant white. "Hey," he said as she straightened.

She glanced around to see who he was talking to, then realized he was smiling right at her. At *her.*

"Hey," she managed to croak out. If she thought she'd sounded bad at the *Tommy* audition, she sounded about a thousand times worse now, like an asthmatic frog.

"I've seen you before," he said.

Omigod. He'd *seen* her. He'd *noticed* her.

She was glad she'd already dropped the dollar bill into his guitar case. Her hands were suddenly so slick with perspiration the money might have disintegrated in her palm.

She had to say something. He was still smiling at her. "I love listening to you," she said, hoping she wasn't blushing or oozing sweat in her armpits. She didn't have any zits, did she? Was her hair sleek and shiny? Did she look fat to him? She really wasn't fat, regardless of what Bony said, but next to Kim she resembled a porker.

Fortunately, she wasn't next to Kim. Kim was standing with Ashleigh in the crowd, watching her.

"Well, thank you," he said.

So polite! No tattoos and polite—but African-American and cornrowed and earning money by playing music in the park, so it wasn't as if he was exactly safe. Plus his being years and years older than her, of course.

But his smile seemed safe, almost. Safe and sexy both. She felt more of that cider warmth slide down from her face into her chest and through her whole body.

She had to say something. She couldn't waste this moment. It might be the only time she ever talked to him. "I should thank you," she said, sounding much calmer than she felt. "Because your music is really cool. I think you should be making records. You're that good. My name is Reva." Shit! She'd been doing so well, and suddenly she was blurting out *My name is Reva,* as if she were brain damaged or something.

"Well, hey, Reva," he said affably. "I'm gonna play another song now." In other words, bug off.

He was too polite to say *Bug off,* of course. He had to be polite because she'd stuck a dollar bill in his guitar case. But now he knew her name. And maybe he wasn't just being polite. Maybe he was actually pleased to have met her. Maybe, just maybe, he'd go home tonight, to wherever his home was—she wanted to imagine him in some tiny, artsy flat on the Lower East Side or an interesting old brownstone in Harlem—and fall asleep remembering the girl who thought he should be making records, who had that much faith in him.

She smiled, hoping her expression didn't seem forced, and strolled back to where her friends were standing. "Omigod!" Kim squealed softly.

"He's really cute," Ashleigh declared once again.

"Do you think he likes you?" Kim asked.

"Shh." Reva clung desperately to her poise. She didn't want them to know how rattled she was, how wet her hands were, how fluttery her heart felt, beating like a ticking time bomb in her throat. "He's playing a song."

Darryl J swept the crowd with his gaze and then zeroed in on her. "This one's for my new friend, Reva," he said, then let loose with a rowdy flurry of guitar chords.

He was singing this song for her! Just the way she'd dreamed, just the way she'd fantasized. He was singing to her…and she could scarcely even listen to the song because she had to concentrate all her energies on remaining upright when she was *this* close to fainting dead away.

The girls stormed the apartment in a tumble of chatter, laughter and stomping feet. They shouted a chorus of "Hi's" at Libby on their way to the kitchen, where they armed themselves with a two-liter bottle of Diet Pepsi and a bag of cheddar-cheese popcorn, and then they vanished into Reva's bedroom. Hearing Reva's door slam shut, Libby shook her head and grinned.

She would rather die than have to relive her thirteenth year. Her memories of that year were ghastly. She'd been gangly and mismatched, her nose suddenly too big for her face, her chin too small, her figure devoid of curves and her knees and elbows as rough as sandpaper. And as much as she would have liked to ignore her appearance altogether, her mother had constantly harped on it: "Don't eat that, it'll give you pimples!" "Don't wear that skirt, it makes you look chubby." "I wish you'd let me do something with your hair, Libby." Her mother had undoubtedly meant well, but every comment had informed Libby that she was a disaster.

Her mother had been beautiful, and still was. Her father appreciated his wife's beauty more than any of her other traits, which was probably a good thing, given that Libby's mother had been a dreadful cook, an even worse housekeeper, a dilettante who always swore she'd get a job but never did, and a sometime volunteer who complained about the hard work she was doing without compensation. "I'm answering phones for this outfit all day. The least they could do is pay me," she'd grouse, even if the outfit was a soup kitchen or an organization raising money for research on dyslexia.

"Better yet, they should make you their spokeswoman," her father would say. "A beautiful woman like you, all you'd have to do is smile and the donations would pour in."

Libby had promised herself then that she'd never harp on her own daughter's appearance—assuming she ever had a daughter. Once Reva had been born, Libby held on to that promise. In truth, she believed Reva was the most beautiful girl in the world, but she never said so. If she did, she would undoubtedly embarrass Reva. To be thirteen was to be overly conscious of every minor flaw, every misplaced freckle and torn cuticle. If Reva asked, "Does this shirt match these pants?" or "Is my hair straight in back?" Libby would answer honestly, but other than that she kept her mouth shut about her daughter's appearance.

Through the closed bedroom door Libby heard muffled giggling and shrieks. She turned her attention back to the application open in front of her. Phoebe Evans was apparently quite the four-year-old, already capable of writing the entire alphabet backward, a talent Libby supposed would come in handy if she ever became a subversive inventor like Leonardo da Vinci and wanted to write her notebooks in code. Her parents pointed out on the application that they'd managed to secure a place for her in her extremely prestigious preschool two months before she was born. "We believe in planning ahead, and so does Phoebe," her parents wrote.

Libby set aside Phoebe's application and opened the next folder. Madison Harkinian was a spectacular gymnast, according to her father, with hopes of competing in the 2016 Summer Olympics. This sounded familiar to Libby…and then she saw the Post-it fastened to the inside of the folder, with her preliminary notes on Madison's application jotted onto it. She'd already reviewed this application. Her piles must have gotten mixed up.

She leaned back in the dining room chair and groaned. Not even two weeks into the process, and all the applications were sounding alike to her. She'd read at least four essays about youngsters who hoped to compete in the 2016 Summer Olympics, and a few more who expected to compete in the 2018 Winter Olympics. Shoving Madison's folder away, she reached for the next one in the pile and prayed that the child had no Olympics aspirations.

She opened the folder and immediately noticed a Post-it with her handwriting on it: "Fin Aid App." This was Eric Donovan's application. She'd jotted the reminder to make sure his father filed the form. Flipping through the folder, she found a copy of Eric's financial-aid application, several faxed sheets. Tara must have filed them.

Libby pulled out the financial-aid application and studied it. Ned Donovan was neither rich nor poor. He lived in New York and worked for a firm called Greater Manhattan Design Associates, where he got paid what would be considered a comfortably middle-class income in any other community but what in Manhattan was a just-getting-by income. He'd bought his apartment for a typically obscene amount of money. He had a savings account but no investments. He and his son were clearly not caviar class.

But he owned his apartment outright. Libby would be thrilled just to have a mortgage. To qualify for one, however, she needed a down payment.

She'd already visited the Human Resources Department at Hudson to discuss the possibility of borrowing against her pension; they'd advised her not to do it. She'd also visited her bank, where a loan officer told her he'd be happy to discuss mortgages with her once she had a sufficient down payment. Vivienne didn't seem to be coming through with any rich single guys from her synagogue.

Libby wondered if Ned knew how lucky he was. He might not be able to afford the Hudson School's annual tuition—hell, she couldn't afford it, either, and if Reva hadn't been eligible for a free ride at the school, she'd be stuck, like Eric, in an overcrowded public school. Or else Libby would have left the city, moved to a more affordable suburb and enrolled her daughter in the local school district. Nowadays, though, the suburbs were almost as expensive as the city. Imagine having to bankrupt herself to buy a tract house somewhere, miles from everything, with sky-high property taxes. And she'd have to buy a car, and Reva wouldn't have Central Park to hang out in with her friends, or a student subscription to Mostly Mozart.

Life was too damn expensive.

Sighing, Libby shut Eric Donovan's folder and tossed it onto the dining-room table. Then she pushed herself out of her chair and trudged to the kitchen. Her ex-husband's phone number was programmed into the cordless phone's memory to make Reva's life easier—she phoned Harry far more often than Libby did—but Libby had assigned him number nine on the memory list. No way did he deserve one of the first few numbers.

She pressed the memory button and nine and listened to the phone ring on the other end. Maybe she'd get lucky and no one would be home. That would give her a few more days to prepare herself mentally for the difficult task of begging him for assistance. Not that she had a lot of time to spare. She needed to come up with the money or move by January.

"Hello?" Bonnie spoke into the phone. She had an odd accent, nasal Brooklyn burnished with polished notes of Westchester, kind of like Dijon mustard on a greasy hot dog.

"Bonnie? It's Libby," she said. "Is Harry there?"

"If you'd called ten minutes later, he wouldn't be," Bonnie told her. "He has a squash date with Gerald Wexler." Bonnie liked to engage in friendly small talk with Libby. She probably considered it terribly civilized that a former wife and a current wife could shoot the breeze rather than each other.

Libby tried to recall who Gerald Wexler was, then decided she didn't care. "Can I talk to him?" she asked, a part of her wishing she'd waited ten minutes before phoning, and another part of her lecturing herself to be mature and sensible and get this god-awful conversation over with.

"Let me see if I can grab him before he bolts," Bonnie said. "You know how he can be."

Actually, Libby didn't know how he could be. The only time he'd ever bolted during their marriage was when he'd bolted from the marriage itself.

She heard a click as Bonnie put her on hold—why the woman couldn't just put down the phone and holler for Harry was a mystery—and then, after a few seconds, another click. "What's up?" Harry said. Unlike Bonnie, he didn't seem to feel any compulsion to be civilized.

Libby steeled herself for her mission. To call him and complain about his failure to pick Reva up on time or his letting her watch R-rated movies when she visited him was one thing; to ask him for financial help was quite another. "I need to talk to you," she began, then realized she couldn't possibly talk to him about her apartment if he was on the verge of bolting.

"About what?"

If he were any more brusque, Libby would get windburn from his words, right through the phone. "It's important, and I can't go into it when you're on your way out."

"Is it about Reva? Is she okay?"

She'd give him half a point for remembering that they had a child together. "Reva is fine," she assured him. "But what I have to discuss with you affects her. When can we talk?"

"You're the one who's asking for this talk," he said. "When do you want to talk?"

"I want to talk now," she told him, striving mightily to keep her tone calm and even. "We can't talk now because you've got a squash game."

"How long a talk are you anticipating? Can we do it when I get Reva tomorrow?" Reva usually saw her father Sundays, a routine they'd developed a few years ago, when he'd taken charge of her Hebrew-school classes in preparation for her bat mitzvah, and the classes had met on Sundays. Now they just spent the day together. Reva had dinner with him and Bonnie and then she returned home to sleep, since she had school the next morning.

"All right—but I'd rather not discuss this in front of her. Or Bonnie, for that matter."

"It's a big secret?" His voice held a touch of mockery. "Oh, boy. I love secrets. Fine. We'll talk tomorrow. I've got to go."

"Go. We'll talk tomorrow." Libby hung up before she

could say anything else, like *Fuck you, shithead.* No one could bring out the bad language in her like Harry.

She dreaded having to ask him for money face-to-face, but maybe it would be harder for him to say no when he understood that Reva's home and her stability were at stake. He did care about her, and although fatherhood clearly didn't come naturally to him, he put some effort into it.

Libby carried the phone back to its base in the kitchen and felt her shoulders slump. What had she accomplished with that call? She'd laid some groundwork. She'd bought herself twenty-four hours to figure out how to persuade Harry to help her out. She'd made herself nauseous.

She returned to the dining-room table and saw Eric Donovan's folder lying open in front of her chair. If only there were a scholarship fund for people like her, who were desperate to hang on to their overpriced apartments. She'd fill out an application just as Ned Donovan had, and fax it to someone, and hope that a bouncy assistant stuck it into the correct file, and then—because she was a good person and a hard worker and she deserved to keep her apartment— she'd receive a letter saying she'd been approved for aid. And she and Reva would live happily ever after, right here in this place that had been their home for thirteen years.

She heard a surge of trilling laughter from behind Reva's closed door. For her, Libby thought. Harry had damn well better come through for his daughter.

Seven

"You want me to what?" Harry bellowed.

"Shh!" Libby batted the air with her hand, signaling him to lower his voice. Reva had vanished into her bedroom as soon as she and Harry had arrived at the apartment, but even through her closed door she would hear every word of this difficult discussion if he insisted on shouting. For that matter, the Shapiros downstairs and the Gordons upstairs would probably hear every word. When Harry got worked up, his voice had the resonance of a foghorn.

It wasn't as if Reva needed to be protected from the idea that her mother would ask her father for money, given that she herself had suggested it. But Libby would prefer not to have her daughter witness an argument. She and Harry had done a decent job of divorcing without rancor, and when they disagreed, they did so as calmly as possible for Reva's sake.

Libby really hoped this talk would be calm. Harry's reaction didn't bode well.

"Sit," she said, gesturing toward the faded sofa in the living room—a sofa that had entered the apartment when Harry still called the place home. "I'll make some coffee."

"I don't want coffee," he retorted in a tone maybe one or two decibels lower than before. "I just ate a very nice dinner with Reva and Bonnie."

As if someone who'd eaten a very nice dinner couldn't possibly follow it with a cup of coffee. Libby wondered where the very nice dinner had been—somewhere near his downtown apartment, she assumed, since he'd told her he had dropped Bonnie off at home before driving Reva to the Upper West Side to engage in this conversation Libby had requested.

"Well, sit anyway," she said, steering him to the sofa. The coffee table—a scuffed but solid oak piece that also dated back to Harry's marriage to Libby—was strewn with sections of the Sunday *Times,* and Libby made a halfhearted attempt to straighten them into a pile before settling into one of the wingback chairs.

Even glowering at her from the other side of the coffee table, Harry was a handsome man, lean and buffed, his dark hair brushed straight back from his polished face. When she'd started dating him at Columbia, her friends had nicknamed him "Ken" because he looked a little like a Ken doll. Unlike Ken dolls, however, he was anatomically correct, which was how she'd wound up pregnant just weeks before graduation.

He'd done the right thing. He'd offered to accompany her to a clinic if she wanted an abortion, and when she'd told him she didn't—a decision that had surprised her as much as him, although as soon as she'd reached it she'd been certain she'd made the right choice—he had agreed to marry her. He'd been finishing his first year at Columbia Law School, and a dean he'd gotten chummy with had somehow finagled them into this apartment. The wedding had been simple, Libby in a loose-fitting white dress, Harry in a beautifully tailored suit that had cost more than her dress, a ceremony at his parents' synagogue followed by an elegant dinner hosted by her parents at the Faculty House on campus. Everyone had told her the food was terrific, but she'd been suffering from morning sickness, which in her case had been morning, noon and night sickness until well into her fifth month. Her only memory of the wedding dinner was that it had returned on her as soon as they'd arrived home.

The rooms of this apartment had been empty when they were newlyweds, the windows uncurtained, the fireplace dusty, the naked hardwood floors echoing Libby's and Harry's footsteps. Gilda and Irwin had scrounged some cast-off furniture for them, and after a few months, once Libby had landed a job as an administrative assistant in the admissions department of the lower school at Hudson, she had replaced the inflatable mattress she and Harry had been sleeping on with a real bed and purchased the living-room sofa at a discount outlet in the Bronx. She'd set up the crib Gilda had located for her—Gilda's neighbor's niece's colleague at work had been willing to sell the thing for fifty bucks when her youngest child graduated to a junior bed—just days before Reva arrived.

Libby had nursed her daughter through countless sleepless nights in this apartment. She'd scraped strained peas off the walls, mopped fingerpaints off the moldings and rescued LEGO blocks from the hearth of the never-used fireplace. She'd splurged on a few multicolored rugs to warm the hardwood floors and muffle her footsteps. She'd observed pigeons roosting on the sill outside the kitchen window. She'd read *Green Eggs and Ham* a thousand times to Reva, seated side by side with her on the couch where Harry now sat, and then she'd watched Reva prance around the room shouting, "That Sam-I-Am! That Sam-I-Am!"

She was *not* going to give up this apartment. Not without a fight—or a grovel, if that was what it took.

"Harry," she said, "I hate asking you for money, but I'm in a bind. Either I buy this apartment or we move. Moving would mean a long schlep for Reva to get to school. It would mean longer trips for you to visit her. A quarter of a million dollars—" she raced through the figure, hoping he wouldn't think too hard about it "—isn't that much when you consider how essential it is for her to stay in the only home she's ever known."

Libby held her breath, fearing he might propose something ridiculous, like taking primary custody of Reva and having her move into his SoHo loft so she wouldn't have such a long schlep. But from SoHo to the Upper West Side wasn't exactly a short schlep, and anyway, Bonnie would never want to be a full-time mother. Besides, Harry didn't want to be a full-time father. That was one reason he and his second wife were such a good match. The only other reason, as far as Libby could tell, was that they both liked money a lot.

Not that Libby was in any position to criticize. Right now, money was one of her favorite things, too—or it would be if she had any.

Harry sighed and rubbed his Adam's apple, as if swallowing had become a challenge for him. Swallowing Libby's plea for assistance obviously had. "I know you don't want to leave this apartment, Libby. *I* didn't want to leave, but I had to."

Under other, less desperate circumstances, Libby would have pointed out that he'd had to leave the apartment only because he'd chosen to leave their marriage. He'd had his law degree and his megabucks job as an associate at a fat-cat Wall Street firm, and he'd yearned for a glamorous life, not one that included a decidedly down-to-earth wife and a three-year-old daughter with dried ketchup on her shirt and pink Play-Doh in her hair.

"But the amount of money you're asking for—I mean, Libby! It's outrageous!" he declared, barely managing to keep from shouting. Libby could see his exertion. Some people had difficulty projecting their voices. Harry had difficulty not projecting his.

"What's outrageous about it?" Libby asked. "The only outrageous thing about this is the cost of real estate in Manhattan."

"Why the hell can't you cover the down payment?"

"I can cover part of it," she said defensively.

"All you need is a quarter-million dollars. Christ." He closed his eyes, as if the situation presented a gruesome spectacle he couldn't bear to view. "What did you do with all your money?"

"All what money? My salary at the Hudson School doesn't compare with what you corporate lawyers earn. I pay the rent, I pay for food, I pay for supplemental life insurance, I pay for Reva's subscription to Mostly Mozart, and every now and then I buy new stockings. My old ones get runs in them." She felt herself scowling and tried hard to relax her face. If she came across as too angry, he'd have an excuse to say no. "It's a miracle I've saved as much money as I have," she argued, thinking wistfully of how she'd earmarked that money for a special vacation trip with Reva someday, and Reva's college, and even a wedding at the Faculty House at Columbia if that was what Reva wished. Now all her savings would have to go toward the down payment on the apartment. Libby could only hope Harry would pay for Reva's college and her wedding. She highly doubted that he'd offer to pay for a special vacation trip.

"Is the apartment actually worth that much? Have you had it appraised?"

"It's worth more than they're asking," she told him. "They're offering me an insider's price. Other apartments in this row—" she gestured up and down to indicate the identical apartments above and below hers "—have gone for much more in the past few years."

"In other words, buying this place would be an investment."

"Yes!" She felt triumphant, delighted that Harry could regard the purchase as a positive thing. Her triumph faded fast, though. If he provided the down payment, would the apartment become *his* investment? Would he think he owned it? Even if she paid the mortgage?

Oh, shit. Would they have to draw up a formal agreement, with the title in both their names? Would she have to hire a lawyer to negotiate terms with Harry? Lawyers cost too much money. Some—like the one currently sitting on her sofa—got paid several hundred dollars an hour.

She slumped against the chair's slack upholstery. Like the sofa, the two armchairs in the living room dated back to her newlywed days. Harry had taken a few items with him when he'd left: a brass coat tree that used to stand in the entry, the Wedgwood-china serving for four that had been a gift from his dour aunt Ethel—it was the same pattern as her own china, and Libby had always suspected Aunt Ethel had simply given them some extra settings that she didn't need—and a fussy pair of lamps with overly ornate pseudo-Ming Dynasty bases that Gilda had donated to Libby and Harry after buying herself new bedroom lamps. But most of the furniture had been too shabby to match Harry's upwardly mobile self-image, so he'd left it behind. The apartment's furnishings were ten years shabbier now, but familiar and comfortable. Libby couldn't imagine redecorating, even if she could afford to. The chairs were indented to cup her tush; the sofa cushions cradled her shoulders perfectly. The upholstery colors—at one time teal and dun, but now a sort of murky bluish-green and brownish-green that reminded her of the ocean—worked with the rugs and the curtains.

Sitting in her beloved old chair, she eyed Harry cautiously. For a casual Sunday dinner with his daughter, he'd dressed awfully formally, in a crisp shirt, a blazer, tailored trousers and loafers so thoroughly polished they gleamed like chrome on a hot rod. Even when he'd been a struggling law school student, he'd dressed with precision. Libby suspected that when he played squash with Gerald Wexler, he wore starched white shorts and a polo shirt with a pocket-embroidered logo so exclusive no one knew who the designer was.

"If I supplied the down payment," he said slowly, his dark eyes narrowing on her, "and mind you, I said *if,* I'd expect to be paid back."

"Of course," she assured him, proving she could be eminently reasonable as long as he wasn't going to claim ownership of the apartment.

"And how would you pay me back?"

"We could work out a payment schedule once I paid off the mortgage."

"In other words, I'd have to wait thirty years for you to reimburse me."

"I was figuring on a fifteen-year mortgage," she said, even though she hadn't given it much thought. She'd be thrilled to qualify for any mortgage at all.

"We could all be dead in fifteen years," he pointed out.

That was a cheery notion. Maybe as a lawyer, he found it useful to consider worst-case scenarios. In fifteen years, a high-tech war might vaporize the planet, and then this building would be gone, and Harry's precious investment would be worthless. In fifteen years, Martians might take over Manhattan and choose this West End Avenue address as their headquarters. In fifteen years, Reva might be married and Libby might be insane, muttering gibberish in a cozy padded cell somewhere. In which case, Harry could sell the damn apartment and get his down payment back.

"Why don't we operate on the assumption that that won't happen," she said sweetly.

"Well." He surveyed the living room, his gaze lingering for a moment on the painting hanging on the wall next to the fireplace, a trite but inspiring rendering of the Brooklyn Bridge in the fog. Libby had bought it a few years ago from a sidewalk artist who was clearly not destined to have his own show at the Museum of Modern Art anytime soon, but she loved it. Harry registered his disapproval of the painting with a grimace. "A quarter of a million dollars, Libby. It ain't chopped liver."

"It certainly ain't." She'd agree with anything he said, including bad grammar, if he would come through for her.

"I have to think about this."

Think fast, she wanted to demand. She didn't have much time. In less than three months, the new owners would expect her to buy or move. "Of course," she said, determined to be nice. "Of course you have to think about it."

"Given the investment value of the place," he added, his gaze sweeping the room once more and his upper lip twitching slightly as he glimpsed the Brooklyn Bridge painting, "you really ought to do more to maintain it."

"If I owned the place, I'd do more," she said, although it had never occurred to her to do anything with the apartment, other than vacuum it whenever the dust bunnies threatened to crawl out from under the sofa and raid the refrigerator. What would she do to it? Paint the walls? Install a marble vanity in the bathroom? Hell, if she bought the place, she would hardly be able to afford toilet paper, let alone new vanities.

"I'll get back to you." He pushed himself to stand, as lean and slim as he'd been when she'd first met him. As arrogant, too. As snooty and superficial and Ken-doll plastic.

But he hadn't said no. He'd said he would think about it. He could be as arrogant and snooty as he wanted to be; if he said yes, she would consider him the most wonderful Ken doll in the world.

She walked him to the door, ever the gracious hostess, and gave him her most winning smile. He didn't return it. Smiling had never been one of his talents. She tried to recall moments in their lives when she'd seen him smile with genuine pleasure. At their wedding? No, but then, she herself hadn't smiled that day, given her profound nausea. When Reva was born? He might have cracked a glimmer of a smile that day, but mostly she remembered him sitting beside her in her hospital room in the maternity ward and outlining the financial pressures this new baby placed upon them. "All right, we can name her Reva," he'd said, as if this was a huge concession for him when he'd been the one to suggest the name, which had belonged to his late paternal grandmother. "Now, how soon will you be able to return to work?"

He might have smiled the day their divorce was finalized. Libby vaguely recalled his mouth curving when she'd told him he could take the lamps, Ethel's ugly china and the coat tree in the foyer.

So he didn't smile on a regular basis. She could smile enough for both of them. And if he came through with the down payment, she'd be smiling enough for the entire population of New York.

As soon as he left, Reva emerged from her bedroom, smiling enough for Libby. "That went pretty well, huh, Mom?"

"You were eavesdropping?"

"Daddy yells," Reva said with a shrug. She bounded past Libby, into the kitchen, and pulled a box of chocolate-chip cookies from a cabinet shelf. They were a low-fat brand, which meant they tasted like dried spackle, but the chocolate chips still resonated. "He always talks like he's addressing the Supreme Court, you know? And he's not even a…what's the word? It sounds like an alligator."

"A litigator," Libby said helpfully.

"Yeah, that's it. I mean, it's like, he doesn't exactly argue cases in some courtroom like the guy on *Law & Order* and make big moral speeches or something. All he does is sit in his office, reading the fine print."

"Maybe he likes to orate to us because he doesn't get a chance to orate professionally," Libby suggested. Insulting Harry in front of Reva wasn't exactly kosher, but the kid had her father so perfectly pegged nothing Libby could say would alter Reva's opinion of him. "Why are you eating cookies? Didn't you just have dinner?"

Reva glanced at the cookie in her hand, as if she'd forgotten it was there. Shrugging again, she popped it into her mouth. "Bonnie wouldn't let me order dessert. She wouldn't hear of it. Her words. 'I wouldn't *hear* of it,'" Reva said in an affectedly nasal voice.

Libby laughed. "You're a very bad girl," she said, reaching for the box and helping herself to a cookie. "You shouldn't mimic Bonnie like that."

Reva ignored her. "So, we get to keep the apartment, right?"

"You heard your father. He said he has to think about it."

"That means yes," Reva said with blithe certainty. She grabbed another cookie from the box and set it on the counter. "I've gotta call Kim about *The Waste Land.* Bony told me T. S. Eliot was an anti-Semite. That sucks." She chomped down on her cookie and waltzed out of the kitchen.

Libby watched her, envying her energy, her optimism and her ability to consume cookies without fretting over calories like her stepmother. Or her mother, who tucked in the box's lid and replaced the cookies on their cabinet shelf. Someday Reva would be thirty-five, and she'd have to worry about cookies and mortgages and even, possibly, God forbid, an ex-husband. But now she was thirteen and all she had to worry about was a dead poet.

Lucky girl.

Eight

"She's hot for you," Mitch murmured.

One reason he'd put Ned in charge of the Colwyn project was so he could focus his energies on preparing bids for other jobs. This was why he'd been so glad to take Ned on, he'd explained; he knew Ned had the expertise to manage jobs, freeing Mitch to pursue new projects. In time, Ned would start writing specs and bids, too. But specs and bids for New York City renovations were different from specs and bids for tottering old farmhouses nestled among the rolling green hills of Vermont, so until Ned became more familiar with the local regulations and the costs of doing business in the city, Mitch wanted him on site, overseeing the actual labor.

That was fine with Ned. Unlike a lot of his architecture classmates in college, he had always enjoyed getting his hands dirty. He was the son of a cop and a housewife, and growing up, he'd shared his bedroom with two brothers. Desks and drafting tables were no more his natural element than ritzy private schools were.

But although Mitch had installed Ned as the manager of the Colwyn job, he still came around to monitor its progress. Today, in fact, Ned had asked him to take over at three so he could leave early. By three-thirty, Mrs. Karpinsky would have delivered Eric to Libby Kimmelman's office at the Hudson School for his interview. Ned had to be there in time to walk his son home.

He'd spent the day trying not to obsess about the interview. Eric wasn't the least bit anxious about it. He believed being granted admission to the Hudson School would represent the fulfillment of his destiny. Nice to be so sure of yourself, Ned thought—not that he'd ever been overwhelmed by self-doubt, but he had a passing acquaintance with reality, and he knew damn well that sometimes things didn't work out the way they were supposed to.

Eric could handle the director of admissions. He wouldn't notice her big dark eyes and that intriguing hesitancy in her smile. He'd think nothing of her rippling brown hair, and if he shook her hand he wouldn't be aware of how soft her skin was, and how firm her grip. Yeah, Eric would probably do just fine in his thirty-minute face-off with her.

The scent of coffee dragged Ned's attention back to the brightly lit loft in the Meatpacking District. Most of the walls had been framed, and the place resembled a rustic jail, lots of vertical two-by-fours dividing the loft into room-size cages. Macie Colwyn had swept in just minutes after Mitch arrived, and she'd brought with her a cardboard tray filled with cups of coffee from a café she swore was so exquisite, Starbucks ought to change its name to Earthbucks. Ned wasn't sure what that meant, but then, he was no coffee con-

noisseur. As long as it was strong, black and heavily caf-
feinated, he had no complaints.

The three carpenters on the crew had helped themselves
to cups of coffee and were hard at work shaping the door-
ways and positioning the electric boxes for the sockets and
light switches. Ned had joined Mitch by the card table to
drink his coffee while reviewing everything that had been accomplished so far. He'd left the lid on the cup—pine-scented
sawdust floated in the air, and he didn't want it floating in
his coffee—and drinking through the square opening lent the
gourmet brew a plastic taste. If it was better than Starbucks,
he couldn't tell.

"Who's hot for me?" he asked Mitch.

"Macie Colwyn. Look at the way she's watching you. No,
don't look," Mitch murmured, peering past Ned. The woman
must be somewhere behind him. When she'd made her
grand entrance with the coffee ten minutes ago, she'd resembled an ostrich, her long, thin legs wobbly thanks to her
spike-heeled boots, and her tufted purple-tinged hair reminding Ned of gaudy feathers. "She wants you," Mitch insisted.

Ned kept his gaze steady on his friend's face. Mitch was
the antithesis of Macie Colwyn, a complete absence of
whimsy. His dark hair was unremarkably short and he
dressed, like Ned, in faded jeans, sturdy shirts and steel-toed
boots, even on days when he spent most of his time in the
office. When he and Ned had been classmates at Penn, he'd
worn his hair down past his shoulders and refused to sport
jeans that didn't have at least a few holes in them. But age
and the responsibility of running a business could compel
a man to groom himself.

"I can practically see her breathing from here," Mitch
warned. "We're talking heavy breathing, Ned. Panting."

"Maybe she's got asthma," Ned suggested, keeping his

voice as subdued as Mitch's. Then he added, because it needed to be said, "She's married." Under the din of one crew member's hammer, another's power drill and a third's boom box, which played syncopated salsa through pathetically tinny speakers, Macie was unlikely to hear them.

"Have you met her husband? He's a gargoyle," Mitch said.

"Yeah, but he's a billionaire gargoyle. When you're that rich, your looks don't matter."

"So she's married," Mitch argued. "She's still lusting. I bet she got turned on by your suggestion of the columns last week. Columns are phallic."

She had indeed been excited by Ned's column idea for her living room. Every day when he showed up at the loft, she asked when the columns would be arriving. Every day he explained to her that they would be among the final pieces installed. They were merely decorative, which meant they got added after all the structural work was done.

"If she's lusting," he deadpanned, "it's only because I'm so irresistible. I don't need columns for sex appeal."

"Not construction columns, anyway. Just stay alert for her," Mitch said, barely moving his lips. "She's a Greek goddess. She wants a temple, and you're just the guy to give her one."

Ned grinned. His anatomical column had no interest in her whatsoever, and he hoped she would find another temple to worship in. He took a final slurp of coffee before lifting his jacket from one of the chairs and putting it on. "I've gotta go, Mitch," he said. "Keep your fingers crossed that Eric does okay at this interview."

"He'll do great," Mitch predicted. "And if it doesn't work out, you can always move to the 'burbs. Some of them have terrific school systems." Mitch lived in a pricey town up in Westchester—the smallest house in town, he always joked, but Ned had seen it and it was pretty big for a small house—and his kids were allegedly getting a superlative education thanks to that town's public schools, for which Mitch paid almost as much in taxes as a private school's tuition would run. Ned wasn't knocking Mitch's choice, but in his mind suburbs were for intact families, husband-and-wife pairings, two drivers to make use of the two-car garage. Besides, he and Eric really liked the city. They liked the noise and the bustle and their cozy little apartment. Eric's public school was the only gripe.

Ned wondered if Macie Colwyn was watching him as he strode around a wall of vertical two-by-fours to the door and out. The only reason he cared was that if she wanted him, other women might want him, too. One reason he'd moved to New York, after all, was to meet women—smart, attractive women who didn't hire plastic surgeons to remodel their faces and bodies with the same ease they hired people like him to remodel their real estate.

A gray gloom hovered over the city as he exited the building onto West 12th Street. Sometimes, Ned had discovered, the city seemed gloomy even on a sunny day because the buildings were so tall they blocked out half the sky and most of the sun. But the buildings in the Meatpacking District weren't that tall, and the gray was definitely caused by heavy clouds that must have rolled in while he'd been working. He lifted the collar of his denim jacket around his neck and jogged to the nearest subway station.

The train was relatively empty—a big change from his usual ride home at the end of the day, when half the city seemed to be crammed into a single subway car with him. Settling onto one of the molded plastic seats, he recalled life in Woodstock, Vermont, where folks would joke that rush hour meant four cows crossing the road from one pasture to another at the same time.

The subway's tremors and sways were easier to take sitting down. Ned stretched his legs out in front of him, closed his eyes and tried to picture Eric walking into Libby Kimmelman's elegant paneled office. Would he be impressed? Probably not. He knew a few things about quality construction, thanks to his dad, but he was too young to care about the trappings of power. And Ms. Kimmelman was young and pretty. She wouldn't scare him. He'd probably tell her all about his research on Henry Hudson, his interest in learning Linux computer programming, his preference for contoured skis and the difference between cold fronts and occluded fronts.

Ned hoped these were areas of interest that the Hudson School valued in a kid. If they weren't, Ms. Kimmelman could stuff Eric's application up her snobby nose with a sterling-silver spoon.

Actually, her nose wasn't that little, he recalled. It was a prominent nose. An interesting nose.

That was what he'd come to New York for: not just women who wanted him, but women with interesting noses. The thought made him laugh, which eased his tension a little.

He got off the train at West 79th and climbed the stairs to the street. A drizzle had begun, and he darted among the raindrops down the block and around the corner to the Hudson School's trio of brownstones. He raced up the stairs of the one on the left and ducked inside.

He remembered the woman behind the counter in the front office—same drab, gray-streaked hair, same oversize eyeglasses—but a whole new battalion of flowers decorated the place. One bouquet consisted entirely of yellow roses, one featured an array of autumn-hued chrysanthemums, one comprised a cluster of exotic blooms he couldn't identify and one was a tortured arrangement of bent branches, dried flowers and minimalist leaves. He wondered if they'd all accompanied applications—and if he should have ignored Libby Kimmelman and her assistant and sent some flowers to ensure that Eric's application would be viewed favorably. Maybe he should have sent a loofah—or better yet, hand-delivered one.

"May I help you?" the woman in the eyeglasses asked.

"I'm Ned Donovan. My son is having an interview with Libby Kimmelman," he said, moving toward the corridor he'd gone down the last time he'd been here.

She stopped him with a sharp reprimand. "You can't go wandering around the building unescorted. Please wait."

He might have responded that he had no interest in wandering around the building, except that wouldn't be true. He would love to roam the halls of the grand old building and peek into classrooms. He'd scope out the facilities to see what kind of library, gym, art studio and science lab twenty-plus grand a year in tuition would pay for. Eric had told him the students emerging from the Hudson School always looked happy, and Ned would like to observe some of those happy students.

But he supposed he wouldn't want his kid attending a school where strange men wandered around the building unescorted, so he gathered his patience and stood where he was while Eyeglasses summoned someone over the phone. The chipper blond girl. He recognized her the moment she appeared at the end of the corridor, jangling costume jewelry and wearing a short skirt that showed off her youthful legs. What had her name been? Tina? Tessa? Something pert.

"Libby is interviewing your son right now," she told him as she accompanied him down the corridor to the admissions office.

"How is the interview going?" he asked.

She shrugged. "He hasn't raced out of the office in tears, if that means anything."

Ned found her words less than reassuring. Trying not to frown, he followed her into the waiting area. Mrs. Karpinsky sat in one of the chairs, a bulky tote bag emblazoned with the logo for Channel Thirteen, the city's public TV station, propped on the floor between her legs, and a Game Boy clasped in her hands. She worked the buttons deftly despite the arthritic bumps that swelled from the joints of her thumbs, and the toy emitted metallic beeping sounds.

"Hello, Mrs. Karpinsky," he said in greeting. Even though he was her employer, he always called her Mrs. Karpinsky because she looked like someone's grandmother—which, in fact, she was. In deference to her age, he wouldn't feel comfortable calling her Fannie.

She glanced up and smiled, her gray hair mussed and her eyes overly bright from focusing on the game's tiny screen. "So, you finally decided to get here?"

He checked his watch. "I got here when I said I would."

"You're wet." She gestured toward his drizzle-damp hair. "Fortunately, I had the good sense to bring an umbrella. Two umbrellas. One is mine. The other one I found in your closet. I brought it so you and Eric can get home without catching pneumonia." She poked around in her tote and pulled out a compact umbrella. When Ned leaned toward her to take it, he caught a whiff of a familiar scent.

Oatmeal.

"I don't suppose you need me anymore," she announced, turning off her game and tucking it inside her tote. "I expect to get paid for the entire afternoon, of course."

"Of course." Her bluntness amused him.

"And remind Eric to do his homework. He hasn't even glanced at it yet. I'm out of here." Mrs. Karpinsky enunciated the slang phrase too clearly, as if she wasn't speaking her native tongue.

"Thanks for bringing Eric," Ned said. He remained standing until she'd gathered her tote and sauntered out of the room, her crepe-soled shoes squeaking against the polished floor.

The blond girl skipped off and Ned settled into one of the seats. A few magazines lay on the end table by his elbow, but they were the same sort of child-oriented magazines Eric's pediatrician in Vermont had always left out for the parents to thumb through, and those magazines invariably troubled Ned. Reading them made him far too aware of how inept he was as a parent. Articles answered questions he would never have thought to ask: "Will forcing my child to use the potty cause him to become neurotic?" "Can you publish a few recipes for legumes that my children will enjoy?" "What are some effective reading-readiness exercises?"

Reading-readiness exercises? Were they like sit-ups and push-ups? Ned and Deborah had read to Eric until one day, when Eric was about five, he'd started reading the books to them. Was that an exercise or simply sharing a book with a kid? Was Ned a deficient dad for not knowing the difference?

The top magazine on the pile at his elbow blared headlines that reinforced his decision to avoid such publications: Holiday Etiquette for Tots. The Truth Behind Weekend Soccer Headaches. Everything You Should Know about Palate Expanders.

He shifted the umbrella from hand to hand, unbuttoned his jacket and stared at the wall across from him, which featured a framed watercolor of children frolicking across a pastel-green field under a sunny blue sky—an idyllic scene as far removed from Manhattan's Upper West Side as the

planet Pluto. He glanced at his watch: two minutes had
passed since Mrs. Karpinsky's departure. He stared at a
bowl of cellophane-wrapped hard candies and wondered
whether they'd been sent by an applicant as a bribe or were
supplied by the school. Maybe Libby Kimmelman liked to
pump the interviewees full of sugar to see just how rowdy
they might get.

A girl peered into the waiting area, then stepped inside.
Ned estimated her to be in her early teens. Her hair hung
straight and dark past her shoulders, and she wore a snug-
fitting, long-sleeved T-shirt and bell-bottom jeans. He issued
a silent prayer of thanks that he'd never owned a pair of bell-
bottoms. The last time they were popular, back in the seventies, he'd been too young for them, and now he was too
old.

She seemed a little breathless, her cheeks flushed and her
dark eyes glowing. When she moved her head her hair
shifted, revealing dangly gold earrings. She carried a backpack slung over one shoulder and a nylon windbreaker in
her hand. "Are you the only one here?" she asked him.

He had to think about his answer. Obviously, he was the
only person in the waiting area, but other people were
around somewhere, picking his boy apart. "My son is being
interviewed right now," he said. "And there was a reception-
ist—" he figured that title came close to describing the
blonde "—but I don't know where she went."

"That's Tara," the girl said. She struggled against a smile,
as if she didn't want him to see how happy she was. He
didn't need her smile to sense her mood, however. Joy
seemed to radiate from her eyes and vibrate in her limbs.
"Who's interviewing your son?"

"Libby Kimmelman," he said, then paused. Should he be
telling her this? Who was she? A Hudson student, he assumed, but still...

"Oh. Okay, great." She flopped onto a chair across the waiting area from him, tossed her backpack and jacket onto an adjacent chair and swung her legs, too antsy to sit still.

After watching her for a moment, he lowered his eyes so she wouldn't think he was staring at her. He checked his watch, then glanced up to notice her checking her watch.

Tara returned. "Hey, Reva!" she greeted the girl.

"Hi." Once again, a smile threatened to explode across the girl's face.

"Waiting for your mom?" Tara asked.

She nodded. "He said she's interviewing his son," she whispered.

The blonde smiled at Ned, then turned back to Reva. "Does your mom know you're waiting for her?"

So this girl was Libby Kimmelman's daughter. Ned recalled her mentioning a daughter when he'd met her, and here she was. This shouldn't intrigue him, but it did. He immediately started analyzing the girl's features. The eyes were her mother's, large and dark, like those of a character in a Disney cartoon. The nose was not so much her mother's. The cheeks and chin, yes. Libby Kimmelman's hair was wavier than the girl's.

Reva Kimmelman had a spectacular smile, even when she was trying to wrestle it into submission. He wondered if a full-fledged smile from the mother would light up the world the way the daughter's did.

"You seem psyched about something," Tara commented.

"I am," Reva said, "but I've gotta tell my mom first."

She turned her dark eyes to Ned. Did she resent him because his son was taking up her mother's time? Well, she'd just have to cool her heels. He figured the longer Eric's interview went, the better. He hoped Tara wouldn't buzz Libby and mention that her daughter was bubbling over in the waiting room; he didn't want Libby to rush Eric out the door so she could see Reva.

"So how's school going for you?" Tara asked Reva.

"Great. Really good," Reva said, her leg swinging faster.

"Getting excited about moving on to the upper school next year?"

"I guess." Reva shrugged and examined a lock of her hair, picking through it with her fingers. "How do you get your nails to grow in, Tara? Mine always come in uneven, and then they break."

"Maybe you need more calcium in your diet," the blonde said. "Or gelatin."

"My friend Kim has to keep hers short because she plays the piano," Reva said. "If she grows them too long, they tap on the keys and then her piano teacher gets pissed off. My other friend, Ashleigh, paints her nails black. They aren't long, but they're kind of disgusting. Do you think fake nails look real?"

"It depends. If they're high quality and you shape and polish them, they can look pretty good."

"Yours are real, though, right?"

"Yeah." Tara scrutinized her hands and, apparently, liked what she saw.

Ned stifled a groan. One definition of hell might be finding yourself trapped with two females discussing their manicures.

The magazines at his elbow tempted him. Surely reading about palate expanders had to be more exciting than eavesdropping on the nails discussion. He lifted the top magazine, flipped through it and discovered it filled with photos of cheerful mothers playing with their children, concerned mothers measuring cough syrup into teaspoons for their children and an occasional mother-and-father pair flanking a child. No single fathers in this magazine.

At last, he heard a door open down the hall, and then voices—Eric's and Libby Kimmelman's. "So the thing about Linux," Eric was saying, "is that it's free. This guy who invented it believes software should be free. I really want to learn how to use Linux, but when I try to read about it on the Web, most of the stuff's written in German."

"That could be a problem," Libby Kimmelman said. "Maybe you need to learn German."

"Do they teach that here?"

"Not until sixth grade, I'm afraid," she said. "Everyone gets some basic Spanish and French in the lower grades. Over in the upper school, they teach Latin."

"That's cool," Eric said. "Nobody talks Latin, so it's kind of like a secret language."

They turned the corner into the waiting area, and Eric raced over to Ned just as Reva leaped from her chair and hurled herself at her mother. Before Ned could say hello, Reva let out a shriek. "Mom, guess what? I got a solo! Ms. Froiken gave me a solo!" She flung her arms around her mother and jumped up and down. "I get to sing 'See me, feel me, touch me, heal me'!"

Ned caught Libby Kimmelman's eye as he rose from his chair. Her daughter was clinging to her and leaping up and down, shaking her so wildly she could barely remain on her feet. She burst into laughter.

Ned laughed, too, because she looked pretty funny, her daughter bobbing like that, jerking her shoulders and babbling about a choral concert. Libby's hair was tousled, her blazer pushed askew and her eyes as bright and full as her daughter's. "Calm down, sweetie, and tell me everything," she said.

Reva released her and danced in a little circle around the waiting area. "I tried out, remember? And at rehearsal today she announced the soloists. And I got a solo!" She pirouetted, giving her foot a graceful thrust into the air. "We're doing *Tommy,* and I get to sing 'See me, feel me, touch me, heal me.' I can't believe she gave me a solo!"

"She didn't give it to you," Libby said. "You earned it." Ned thought that sounded like the kind of statement the magazine in his hand would advise a parent to make.

He glanced down at Eric, who wore a smirky smile, apparently finding Reva's exuberance hilarious. Or maybe the smile reflected Eric's assessment of how his interview went. Jesus, the kid was only ten. What did he know about interviews? He probably thought it was a huge success because he'd had a good time talking to Ms. Kimmelman. Ned had had a good time talking to her, too. Or it *would* have been a good time if he hadn't been so damn conscious of the stakes.

Eric was carrying his warm-up jacket, and Ned tugged on it. "What do you say we hit the road," he suggested quietly, not wishing to interrupt the Kimmelman celebration just a few feet away. "I see Mrs. Karpinsky made sure you were prepared for the weather." The jacket was waterproof, with a hood. Ned wished he had his own warm-up jacket instead of the denim. At least he had an umbrella, thanks to Mrs. Karpinsky.

Eric donned the jacket and started toward the door, shouting, "G'bye, Ms. Kimmelman!" over his shoulder as if they were buddies likely to see each other again in a day or two.

Ned cringed at Eric's informality, but the kid's shout caught her attention. She extricated herself from her daughter's crazed embrace and called across the room, "Goodbye, Eric. It was a pleasure meeting you."

"It was a pleasure meeting you, too," Eric said. From him the words emerged a little stilted, but he sounded earnest. He surprised Ned by adding, "So, I'll e-mail you my Henry Hudson research paper, okay?"

"Okay," she said, then lifted her gaze to Ned and gave him a smile that lit a fire in his gut.

Whoa. Why would she be smiling at him? She wouldn't, except as a courtesy. The fact that he liked being the recipient of her smile a little too much was his problem, not hers. He nodded toward her, mumbled a quick thank-you and followed Eric out the door. Eric was already halfway down the hall and Ned had to jog to catch up to him.

At the building's entry, Ned pulled Eric to a halt. Rain was now streaming down. "We're going to need this sucker," he said, studying the umbrella. He couldn't recall the last time he'd used it. It had been Deborah's. Umbrellas were a girl thing.

He was confident enough in his own manhood to use an umbrella, though—especially in a downpour. If only he could figure out how to open it. He pushed the button in the handle, but nothing happened.

"You have to take the outside part off first," Eric pointed out.

Oh. Right. Ned pulled at the sleeve that enclosed the umbrella. It didn't slide off easily; the ribs pressed against it. Probably because he'd pushed the handle button. The umbrella had opened inside the sleeve.

He tried to squeeze the ribs shut. He tried to peel off the sleeve. He tried to keep from cursing. Maybe umbrellas were a girl thing because guys were too stupid to figure them out.

Eventually, the sleeve slid off and the umbrella burst open. As soon as it did, he heard a shout from down the hall: "No!" Turning, he saw the Kimmelmans, mother and daughter, hurrying toward him. The daughter had donned her windbreaker; her backpack was slung over one shoulder. The mother carried a leather briefcase. Her shout seemed to have been directed at him.

"Something wrong?" he asked.

She raced toward him, although her speed was limited by her slim-fitting skirt and her stack-heeled shoes. "You shouldn't open an umbrella indoors," she explained. "It's bad luck."

Ned laughed. Then he stopped laughing, because she looked so serious. "Bad luck?"

"Don't walk under a ladder. Don't let a black cat cross your path. Don't open an umbrella indoors. Didn't your mother teach you anything?" She smiled slightly, but he was pretty sure she believed what she was saying.

"That's superstition," he argued.

Her expression was oddly defiant. "Who cares? You're still not supposed to open an umbrella indoors."

"Well, I guess we'll just take this thing outside, then," Ned said, leaning against the door to open it. Eric scooted out, and Ned continued to hold the door for the Kimmelmans. They eyed the rain, the water-slick stairs leading down to the sidewalk and, finally, each other.

It dawned on Ned that they didn't have an umbrella— which seemed like a lot worse luck than anything that might befall him because he'd opened his indoors.

His gaze traveled from the rain to Libby Kimmelman in her neatly tailored suit. "Where are you heading?" he asked.

"Home. West End Avenue at 75th. We'll be fine," she assured him, although her eyes narrowed as she stared out at the rain.

"That's on our way," he told her, extending the umbrella toward her. "Here you go."

"Oh, no, I couldn't—"

"I don't need an umbrella," Reva said, darting between her mother and Ned and joining Eric outside on the rain-spattered steps. "'I'm free!'" she sang in a sweet soprano. She stood with her arms outstretched, her face turned up to catch the rain, and sang, more loudly, "'I'm fre-e-ee!'" Ned recognized it as an excerpt from *Tommy*.

"What she is is wet," her mother muttered.

"Come on." Ned crossed the threshold, the umbrella arched over his head and Libby's. "Let the kids get wet. It won't kill them." Before she could object, he angled the umbrella toward the stairs, beckoning her to join him.

She could have remained behind and let the rain soak her, but she was obviously too smart for that. With a shy smile, she fell into step beside him.

Nine

It wasn't his fault that he had to stand so close to her; if they didn't huddle together under the umbrella, they'd get wet. So he cozied up to her, the umbrella's handle between them, and headed down the street.

The kids wanted no part of the umbrella, which didn't surprise him. Up in Vermont, Eric had acted impervious to the weather. He would have worn shorts year-round if Ned had let him, and on a few occasions he'd tried to leave for school without a jacket in the dead of winter. "I've got a sweatshirt on," he'd complain when Ned hauled him back inside and ordered him to put on his parka.

Today was fairly warm, at least, so while his son and Libby Kimmelman's daughter might get wet, they wouldn't get chilled. Eric probably wouldn't even get that wet, since Mrs. Karpinsky had had the foresight to make him bring an appropriate jacket. Reva's windbreaker offered her a little protection—not much, but her behavior implied that she didn't care. She loped ahead of Libby and Ned, zigzagging between the buildings and the curb and belting out excerpts from *Tommy.* "'Tommy, can you hear me?'" she sang at top volume. If Tommy was anywhere within the five boroughs or northern Jersey, Ned thought, he could hear her.

"She's been trying out for solos for the past few years, but she never got one," Libby explained. She seemed almost as excited as her daughter, her smile filling the half of her face that wasn't taken up by her eyes. "I know how badly she wanted a solo, and this is her last year in the lower school. I'm so thrilled for her."

Reva was obviously even more thrilled. Teenagers often acted blasé about things that really ought to turn them on. *Blasé* didn't apply to Libby's daughter, however. She jogged to and fro, arms outstretched, backpack bobbing against her shoulder as she sang. Eric appeared bewildered by her behavior, but he was still at the age when boys believed girls were congenitally insane. Reva's zany exuberance probably strengthened that conviction. He gave her a wide berth so she wouldn't stampede him in her romps around the sidewalk, but he watched her like an entomologist observing a new species of insect.

"Won't she ruin her voice, trying to sing louder than all the street noise?" Ned asked Libby. If he could hear her over the din of auto and bus traffic, she had to be singing pretty loudly.

"What noise?" Libby laughed. "Your Vermont roots are showing. This is quiet for New York."

If this—the honking horns, the rumbling engines, the whoosh of tires spinning through puddles and the drumming of rain on the taut umbrella—was Libby Kimmelman's idea of quiet, he'd hate to think what her idea of loud was. Maybe, if Eric got into the Hudson School and they decided to remain in Manhattan instead of moving to a suburb, Ned would get used to the noise, too.

And he wasn't sure he and Eric would stay in Manhattan if he couldn't get Eric into a better school than the one he was currently attending.

How did the kid's interview go? Did Libby even remember it? Ever since she'd emerged from her office, she'd been one hundred percent focused on her own child. Ned didn't blame her, but what about Eric? He struggled to figure out a discreet way of asking Libby about the time—nearly an hour—she'd spent with his son.

She glanced at him and, evidently, saw the unvoiced question in his expression. "You're curious about Eric's interview," she guessed.

"Yeah," he confessed. "Can you tell me anything?"

She studied his face for a moment, then turned forward as they approached a corner. "It went fine."

Now, that was an informative answer, he thought sarcastically.

"I really—I'm sorry, but it would be unethical for me to go into detail with you, Mr. Donovan."

"Ned," he corrected.

"Ned." A smile flickered across her lips. "Eric is a smart, funny boy. Poised and self-confident. I would never have suspected that he was new to the city, or that he…well, he's faced some challenges most kids his age never have to know."

Ned's pity meter sent out a preliminary warning signal, but before he could say anything about Deborah, Libby continued. "I'm still not sure how many openings we'll have in next year's fifth-grade class, or how many applicants we'll have for those openings. But for what it's worth, Eric's right in the thick of it."

Still not what Ned hoped to hear. He wanted her to say

she'd been blown away by Eric, downright flabbergasted by his brilliance and charm, willing to kick someone out of the Hudson School to make room for him, if necessary.

"Right in the thick of it" wasn't bad, though.

"He and I discussed Egyptology," she added. "I gather you took him to the Egypt exhibit at the Met recently."

"A couple of months ago," Ned told her. "He liked walking through the pyramid."

"He liked more than that. He told me he's been reading up on the Internet about hieroglyphics. He seems fascinated with codes and languages."

"Either that, or he's fascinated with the Internet." That she continued to talk about Eric while her daughter danced around a puddle and let her voice soar over West End Avenue struck Ned as a good sign. He waited for Libby to tell him more—did a fascination with codes and languages give a Hudson School applicant an edge?—but she fell silent when her shoulder bumped his and she stumbled on an uneven slab of sidewalk.

He reflexively cupped her elbow with his hand to steady her. The rain lifted a tangy scent from her hair, which glistened with drops of moisture. As soon as she'd regained her footing he let go of her and reminded himself that he shouldn't be thinking about the way her hair smelled, or the delicate feel of her elbow. She was the woman who could decide his son's fate, and she was a mother, and she probably had a loving husband hurrying home through the rain right now, eager to arrive at her apartment at the same time she and their daughter did.

"That's our building," she said, pointing to a large limestone structure. He didn't spot any fatherly men racing toward it and waving at them, but he did notice the building: classic prewar, the pale stone edifice lined with broad windows set into ornate brickwork in the facade. A large permanent awning trimmed in wrought iron extended above the leaded-glass double doors.

Reva darted ahead and stood in the shelter of the awning. Eric arrived beneath the overhang two steps behind her, leaving as much space between them as he could.

"Can we have champagne, Mom?" Reva asked once Libby and Ned joined them.

"Of course," Libby said.

Champagne? Reva was just a kid. Ned wasn't a stickler for rules, but he couldn't imagine giving Eric champagne. That might be because Ned didn't think much of the stuff himself. If he wanted something bubbly and alcoholic, beer worked better.

Libby must have once again guessed his thoughts, because she chuckled. "Ginger ale in champagne flutes," she explained. "It's the way we celebrate big events. Want to join us in a toast?" As soon as the invitation was out, she appeared startled. Her cheeks darkened slightly, although that could have just been an illusion caused by the awning's shadow. "It was so nice of you to walk us home, sharing your umbrella and all," she added, justifying her hospitality.

If he was smart, he'd say no. He remembered all the reasons he wasn't supposed to think about Libby Kimmelman as anyone other than a school administrator who could change his son's life—and the likely existence of a husband was the most important reason. She wasn't wearing a wedding band, he noticed as he glimpsed her left hand, but nowadays that didn't mean much.

Yet this building, this magnificent old prewar with its rococo facade… Damn, but he'd love to see what her apartment looked like. "Sure," he said. "How about it, Eric? You want some ginger ale in a champagne flute?"

"What's a champagne flute?" Eric asked.

"A fancy glass."

Eric considered for about a second. "I like ginger ale," he informed Libby.

She smiled tentatively, as if she wasn't quite thrilled about the way things were turning out. If Ned changed his mind and declined the invitation, would Eric fare better in his application?

The hell with it. He wanted to get inside this building. And she was right—it had been mighty nice of him to walk her home.

They entered the building together, Ned carefully folding his umbrella shut to avoid offending her superstitions. A bored doorman in a navy blue topcoat and hat smiled and nodded mechanically at Libby, gave Ned a questioning stare and then went back to the magazine he was flipping through. "Let me just check my mail," she asked, ducking into a room off the lobby. Ned watched her fumble with her key for a minute before she finally inserted it in the narrow door and pulled it open. Several envelopes spilled to the floor. He considered entering the mail room to help her gather the letters, but thought she might read too much into his chivalry. So he remained where he was and let her scoop them up. She stuffed them into a side pocket of her briefcase, straightened and shoved her hair back. It seemed to have doubled in volume during her walk home. The rain had made it thick with waves and curls, and droplets glistened as if someone had spread a net of diamonds over it.

They moved as a group to the elevators, pressed the button and piled into the car. The lobby hadn't been too unusual—a floor of black and white marble tiles in a checkerboard pattern, black marble accents on the walls, bronze sconces that produced a little less light than he deemed safe in an apartment lobby. But the elevator was something else. It was paneled, the wood polished to a high sheen and trimmed with bright brass fittings. The buttons on the control panel appeared fairly new—no numbers worn off—but they were dark tortoise shell, a classy touch.

"The apartment's probably a mess," Libby apologized as they rode up. "Things are usually chaotic in the morning when we're rushing around, and—"

"Don't worry about it. I'm sure our place is worse."

"Mrs. Karpinsky makes me pick up all my stuff," Eric complained.

"Good woman. She's worth every penny I pay her." Even if she smelled like oatmeal, Ned added silently.

The elevator bumped to a halt and they emerged. The air had a familiar, pleasant scent. Clean laundry, Ned identified it. A few years ago, he wouldn't have recognized that dryer-sheet fragrance, but he'd learned a lot about laundry since Deborah had died.

Libby didn't fumble her keys this time. She opened an apartment door and stepped inside. Ned held Eric back to let Reva in first—he'd have to work with the boy on his manners. Reva waltzed through the entry, singing once more. "'See me…fe-e-eel me…'"

Ned paused in the entry. It was spectacular.

Chaotic, maybe—if one had a low tolerance for chaos. A closet door hung open, revealing a jumble of coats, jackets, hangers and enough scarves to warm every neck in Alaska. A sloppy pile of fliers occupied a small mail table, and Libby hastily set her briefcase atop them, effectively hiding them. A single pink shower sandal lay on the floor of the hallway.

But what a floor! Herringbone parquet in various oak stains, bordered with a dark oak trim. The finish was dull and scuffed, but the craftsmanship blew Ned away.

So did the square footage. The foyer alone was as large as his kitchen, and the living room that opened off it had a fireplace.

Without asking for permission, he strode into the living room. If the hearth, which held nothing but a thin layer of dust, was any indication, no one had burned a fire here in years. But the fireplace was a thing of beauty, flanked by ridged moldings and topped by an ornate mantel, which, like the moldings, was slathered in off-white enamel paint. He rapped his knuckles on the shelf and heard wood under the paint—and something else under the wood. Marble, he'd bet.

"This is incredible," he said.

Eric laughed. "I told you my dad was a fixer upper," he reminded Libby. "Wherever he goes, he has to check stuff out and figure out how to fix it up."

A drop of water hit the toe of Ned's work boot, and he carried the dripping umbrella back into the foyer. Seeing no obvious storage place, he propped it in a corner as Libby shoved the closet door shut. Opposite the living-room door, another doorway opened onto the dining room, and through it he saw a long trestle table covered with papers and files. The furniture in the living room and dining room was old and shabby. The apartment was old and shabby, too, but God, what potential.

"Is the fireplace operational?" he asked.

Libby smiled awkwardly. "I have no idea."

"You don't know?"

"I've never used it. Eric, can I take your coat?" She extended her arm to Eric, who obediently unzipped his jacket and handed it to her. She hooked the hood over the cut-glass doorknob of the closet.

"How can you have a fireplace and not use it?"

"I've never built a fire," she admitted. "The house I grew up in didn't have a fireplace, and I never joined the Girl Scouts."

"The one time we tried to roast marshmallows, we had

to do it over a burner on the stove," Reva muttered, shaking her head.

"That was a disaster," Libby added with a laugh. "The marshmallows dripped all over the coils. What a mess!"

Ned turned back to study the fireplace from a distance. "You ought to strip the paint off the mantel and moldings and find out what's underneath. A fireplace like that is a treasure."

"Oh, sure." She laughed again, but stopped when he didn't join her. He hadn't said anything funny, certainly not about her fireplace.

"These floors are terrific, too," he added. "If you polished them and slapped on a fresh layer of polyurethane, the place could pass for a ballroom." He fell silent when he realized she was staring at him. What kind of asshole was he, to come into this woman's home, go nuts over the construction and then advise her to renovate the place?

"If I could afford a fixer upper, I'd refinish those floors and unbury the fireplace treasure," she said, startling him even more. How could she live in an apartment this spacious, with its high ceilings and crown moldings, and *not* be able to afford a renovation? The place had to be worth a fortune. If she could afford to live here, surely she could afford whatever she wanted.

Or maybe not. What did he know? He should just shut up, chug some ginger ale and take off before he put his foot in it again.

"Reva…" she addressed her daughter. "Why don't you give your father a call while I get the champagne."

Reva scowled. "If I call him, he'll be out of his office and I'll just wind up leaving a message that he'll never get."

"Then call him at home and leave a message there. He'll want to hear about the solo, and the date of the concert. It's such exciting news."

While Reva yanked her windbreaker over her head, Ned processed what Libby had just said. *Call him at home.* She wasn't married to Reva's father. "If I leave a message there," Reva said, "Bony'll get it and make a big deal out of it."

"It *is* a big deal."

"She'll say I should lose weight so I don't sound fat while I sing."

"If she does, I'll punch her in the nose," Libby promised. "I bet she'll say you need a new outfit for the concert, and she'll bring you to some fancy boutique and spend a lot of money on you."

Reva considered her mother's words and grinned. "I'll call," she said, yanking off one wet sneaker and then the other, and padding down the hall, hopping over the stranded shower sandal rather than stopping to pick it up.

Call him at home. Ned shouldn't be thinking what he was thinking…but Libby had such gorgeous eyes and a vulnerable smile, and he'd liked the feel of her shoulder bumping his under the umbrella, the graceful curve of her arm as he'd helped her regain her balance…and he *really* shouldn't be thinking what he was thinking. Totally inappropriate. She was the flipping Hudson School director of admissions.

She sauntered through the dining room and, although she hadn't invited him to accompany her, he followed, registering the dining-room's chair rails and beveled windowsill, all of it coated in gloppy white paint. He unbuttoned his jacket, which wasn't leaking water like Eric's because he'd stayed relatively dry under the umbrella. Libby wasn't too wet, either. In the kitchen, she kicked off her shoes and lost an inch and a half in height. Her skirt fell to her knees, but what he could see of her legs he liked. She shrugged out of the blazer of her suit and tossed it onto a chair, and he liked what he could see of her back, too, the slope of her shoulders under her white blouse, the wild waves of her hair.

More than inappropriate, he scolded himself. Demented. For all he knew, Libby could have a husband making his way home right now. Just because she wasn't married to Reva's father didn't mean she wasn't married. And even if she wasn't…damn it, she held Eric's educational fate in her hands. Ned could find other women to admire, women with pretty eyes and crazy hair and great legs. Women who couldn't wield any power over his son.

There was always Macie Colwyn, after all. Her hair would qualify as crazy. Merely thinking about it made him wince.

Hovering in the kitchen doorway, he watched Libby pull several inexpensive-looking champagne flutes from a cabinet shelf and arrange them on a metal tray. The kitchen was small, but it was larger than his—big enough to fit a tiny table into one corner—and it had a window. It also had more than its share of clutter: a box of Grape-Nuts cereal on the table, a pile of dirty dishes in the sink, an empty gallon-size milk jug on the Formica counter. With stone counters, the kitchen would look so much better. And with the paint removed from the cabinets. Someone who lived here must have really had a thing for ugly white enamel. The stuff was slathered over practically every surface.

But whatever lurked under all that paint might be magnificent. "This apartment is really something," he said.

"Thanks." She removed a bottle of ginger ale from a shelf in her refrigerator.

He tried to focus on the kitchen, but his attention refused to shift from her. He shouldn't have asked her about how Eric's interview had gone, but he'd asked anyway. And he realized—because he wasn't good at playing games or stifling his curiosity—that he was going to ask her something else he shouldn't. "It's none of my business, but…"

She twisted off the cap, and the bottle of soda hissed. As

she filled the glasses, she said, "For all I know, the fireplace *does* work. One of my neighbors told me a long time ago that the flues had been sealed off as a safety precaution. But maybe he was pulling my leg."

She was giving Ned an opportunity to back off, but he was too foolish to grab that opportunity. "I meant, about Reva's father. It's none of my business, but are you divorced?"

She lowered the bottle and stared at him. He wished he were as skilled at guessing her thoughts as she was at guessing his, because for the life of him he had no idea what was going through her mind. She wasn't smiling, but she didn't seem angry or affronted. Nor did she seem entirely comfortable. Uneasy, possibly pissed. Maybe even panicked, but he wouldn't bet on it.

"Yes," she answered. "I'm divorced."

"And there's someone named Bony?"

"Bonnie," she corrected him. "Reva's stepmother. Reva calls her Bony."

Okay. Libby hadn't slapped him, hadn't told him to take a hike, so he pushed a little more. "Does Reva have a stepfather?"

Libby gave the question far more consideration than it deserved. Either she was married or she wasn't. Was there some gray area he wasn't aware of?

"No," she finally said. "No stepfather." As if she wanted to cut him off before he could venture any further, she turned from him, lifted the tray and started toward the door, leaving him no choice but to move out of her way. "Where's the superstar?" she shouted as she carried the ginger ale through the dining room. "It's time for a toast! And then the Donovans have to leave."

Well, there was an answer for him. *The Donovans have to leave.* What he'd seen shimmering in her big brown eyes must have been panic after all.

Maybe he ought to develop his mind-reading ability before he attempted to put the moves on a woman. Libby was
clearly a mind-reading master. She'd read what was on his
mind just now—and read, as well, that he was mind-illiter-
ate, so she'd helpfully spelled out her sentiments: *The
Donovans have to leave.*

He might be dense, but he could take a hint. Gorgeous
woman, gorgeous fireplace, and neither would get stripped by
him. At one time, he'd known what he was doing around
women, but his skills must have atrophied. Marriage could do
that to a guy. He'd have to polish his moves—and practice on
a woman who didn't work at the Hudson School, for God's
sake.

In the meantime, he'd choke down a little ginger ale,
grab Eric and his umbrella and get the hell out of there.

Ten

Reva felt giddy and light-headed, as if she'd actually been drinking champagne instead of ginger ale. Too much singing, probably. She'd hyperventilated or something. Too much dancing, as well. Her hair was still damp from bopping around in the rain, and it was going to get all weird—not as awful as her mother's, but she'd have to wash and straighten it tonight if she wanted to show her face in school tomorrow.

And she definitely wanted to show her face. She was a *soloist*. She flopped onto her bed, let her wet head sink into the pillow, closed her eyes, whispered, "I am a *soloist*," and smiled.

She'd always believed she had a good voice—but not really. It was one thing to believe something, and another to have proof that other people believed it. You could tell yourself over and over that you had a great voice, but if Ms.

Froiken never gave you a solo, you couldn't help wondering whether you were deluding yourself. Like maybe you couldn't truly hear how you sounded because your voice was entering your brain through your tonsils instead of your ears. Reva was always a little startled when she heard her own voice on a tape.

But now, the world—or at least Ms. Froiken—had finally acknowledged what Reva had always believed: she had a great voice. A magnificent voice. A soloist's voice.

A voice as good as Darryl J's.

Well, not that good. Nobody sang as well as he did. Besides, she was a girl, so she couldn't really compare her voice with his anyway.

But if she was good enough to sing a solo, she might be good enough to sing backup for Darryl J. She'd been fantasizing about that ever since Kim had brought it up last week, and now the fantasy was a few steps closer to reality. How cool would it be to sing backup for him? She could dress in something slinky and black and semi-sheer, with lots of silver jewelry, and she could do a simple rhythmic step and rattle a tambourine—or she could learn some chords on a guitar. The guitar couldn't be that hard, and she was a lot smarter than some of the kids she knew who played the instrument. Talented enough for a solo meant talented enough to learn a few chords, right? Darryl J could teach her.

The phone rang. She thought about ignoring it and letting her mother answer, except her mom was getting dinner ready and washing the champagne flutes—twice as many glasses as she would have had to wash if she hadn't impulsively invited that kid and his father upstairs for ginger ale. Reva hadn't minded including those people—at the moment, she didn't mind *anything*. The boy had been okay, less creepy than most boys his age. He didn't do anything gross or obnoxious, like pick his nose or go on and on about video games or other geek subjects. And his father seemed okay, too, although all his comments about the fireplace and the floors were kind of strange.

One thing Reva was learning about guys was that they became obsessed with weird stuff. Her dad was fanatical about his Scotch, for instance. It had to be a certain brand, a certain age, a certain color—yet the whole point of drinking Scotch was to get drunk, and once you achieved that goal, who cared about the brand, the age and the color?

So the umbrella man was fanatical about fireplaces. In the grand scheme of things, Reva considered that a better obsession than Scotch.

The call was probably from her father. She'd left a message on his machine at home, and he always called her back when she left messages. Pushing herself up, she grabbed the phone from her night table, lifted the receiver and hoped her father had gotten to the answering machine before Bony did. She'd rather not talk to Bony.

"Hello?"

"Um…Reva?" A boy's voice, deep but not man-deep yet. Familiar. She tried to place it, all the while wondering what boy would be calling her. Someone who needed help with homework, no doubt. She didn't hang out with the dating kids, so boys generally didn't phone her unless they wanted something, like the reading assignment or her answer on the third math problem.

"Yeah, who's this?" she asked, doing her best to sound bored.

"Luke Rodelle?"

"Oh." Luke Rodelle was pretty cute, and he'd score only a two or three on the creep scale, which went all the way to ten, except for Danny Vandrick, who was easily a twenty. Luke's hair was thick and kind of long, and he dressed mostly in baggy khakis and untucked polo shirts, and his

upper lip had a smudged appearance, as if he'd been suck-
ing on pencils. He ought to start shaving. "Hi."

"Yeah, so I was wondering—would you shut up?" he
said, not to Reva but to someone on his end of the line. At
least, Reva hoped he wasn't telling her to shut up. She'd
hardly even said anything.

She heard some laughter in the background and sighed.
So help her, if Luke had phoned her on a dare and was
going to ask her whether she smoked after sex or something,
she would hang up so fast he'd feel the slam of the phone
like a slap right through the wire. And then she'd tell everyone in school tomorrow that he was a jerk, and they'd take
her seriously because she was a *soloist.*

"Sorry," he said, sounding sincere. "I was wondering,
Ashleigh Goldstein mentioned this musician you know?
Darryl something?"

Reva could hardly claim she *knew* him. But he'd asked
her name the last time she'd seen him at the park, and then
he'd sung a song just for her. The next time she saw him, he
probably wouldn't even recognize her, but for now, she saw
no reason to correct Luke. "Yeah. Darryl J," she told him.

"See, I'm kind of searching for something new. Music-
wise, I mean. Hey, I heard Froiken gave you a solo."

Reva puffed up a little. She remembered what her mother
had said—that Ms. Froiken didn't *give* Reva the solo; Reva
had *earned* it. She wouldn't say that to Luke, though. It
would come across as bragging.

Through the phone she heard a high-pitched howl, some
guy in falsetto pretending to sing something operatic. That
unpuffed her pretty fast.

"Would you just—jeez," Luke said to the screecher, and
then, to Reva, "That's just Micah Schlutt. He's such an asshole."

Reva didn't know whether she was supposed to agree.

Luke hung out with Micah, after all. If they were friends, it wouldn't be very nice for her to say he was an asshole, even if she happened to think he was.

"Anyway, I'm on the committee for the holiday dance—I'm not sure how that happened, except Matt Staver put me up to it—but anyway, I think the whole deejay thing is getting old, you know? So I was wondering, where does this Darryl dude play? I'd like to check him out."

Reva bit her lip to keep from blurting, "At the Band Shell in Central Park." For one thing, as autumn grew colder, he might not be playing outdoors that much longer. For another, he was way too cool to perform at a school dance, for God's sake. For yet another, he was *hers*. She wanted him to have the biggest possible audience, but she also wasn't ready to hand him over to the rest of the world in the form of Luke Rodelle and his committee. "He plays in the park," she said vaguely, because she had to say something.

"Central Park? 'Cause, you know, there's sometimes some music action down in Washington Square Park."

Was Luke up on street musicians? Did he actually travel all the way to Greenwich Village in search of decent singers? Reva could just imagine asking her mother if she could spend the day in Greenwich Village. If her mom ever allowed it, which was highly unlikely, she'd make Reva go with friends and bring the cell phone, and call home every half hour just to say she was safe, even though her dad lived only a few blocks south of there. Her mother treated her like such a baby sometimes.

Luke rose considerably in her esteem because he was knowledgeable about Greenwich Village musicians. "Maybe Darryl J plays in the Village, too," she said. "I've only seen him in Central Park."

"So, he's good, huh?"

"Yeah, he's good."

"Okay." Luke had apparently run out of things to say, which made the gross-sounding background belch noises from Micah hard to miss. "Yeah, well, so anyway, I thought maybe you could show me where this guy plays."

"Sure," Reva said. Her voice was steady, but her heart started thumping like an out-of-control metronome. Was Luke asking her out? Or did he just want her to lead him and his committee to Darryl J's spot by the Band Shell, and then her job was done and she should disappear? Since she wasn't one of the dating kids, she wasn't real skilled at reading the nuances. How could a girl tell whether a guy was asking her out or just asking her a question?

"So, like, when would be a good time for you?" Luke asked.

If she said after school one day this week, it wouldn't be like a real date. It would just be an after-school activity, sort of. If she said Saturday, the whole thing would become more serious. What did she even think of Luke Rodelle? He seemed nice enough, but her only real contact with him was in math and history, where he didn't really say much although at least he didn't make stupid comments, and more generally from the fact that they'd both been attending Hudson forever and it wasn't such a big school that you didn't get to know all your classmates to a certain degree.

Did she like Luke enough to suggest Saturday? Or would she be better off playing it safe and saying Thursday? If this was only about finding a musician for the holiday dance and all he wanted was for her to point out Darryl J to him and then go away, she'd just about die if she'd devoted a Saturday to that. But if he actually intended to share Darryl J with her and they went on Thursday, then they could only spend like an hour together before she'd have to go home, because her mother would shit a brick if she stayed in the park past four-thirty.

She was keenly aware of the silence between them. She had to decide. "Saturday?" she suggested.

"Okay."

Omigod. He'd said okay. "What time?" she asked.

"One o'clock?"

"Okay." So they wouldn't have to eat anything while they were together, which was probably good.

"We could meet somewhere. The Band Shell's gonna be too crowded."

"How about the mosaic at Strawberry Fields?"

"Okay."

"Okay," she said. "Well. Bye."

"Bye," he repeated, then hung up.

After setting down her phone, she sprawled out on her bed and reran the conversation in her head. This wasn't a date, she told herself. He just planned to observe Darryl J for some stupid school dance.

Well, so what? She didn't want to be dating Luke—or anyone else, for that matter. Her heart belonged to Darryl J. And she'd be helping him by generating some new fans for him, which was a very loving thing to do. Let Luke hang out with a turd like Micah, who thought making belching noises was funny. Reva didn't like him that much.

She was a *soloist,* after all. That was way cooler than Luke Rodelle could ever hope to be.

Libby scrutinized the video box in her hand. Its computer-printed label gave the title of the video as *Scenes of a Childhood.* It purported to present a visual narration of the life of one Jeremy Tartaglia from his birth to his fifth birthday party.

"Tara, could you watch this video for me?" she asked her assistant.

"Is it X-rated?" Tara inquired.

Libby considered the scene of Jeremy Tartaglia's birth. "There might be some nudity in it," she said.

Laughing, Tara accepted the box from Libby and handed her three pink message slips. "Louise Streitmeister phoned three times. She said she wants to talk to you about the donation she intends to make to the Hudson School."

"She should discuss it with someone in the business department, or the fund-raising chairpeople," Libby said, accepting the pink squares of paper and frowning. "Why does she want to talk to me?"

"I assume her donation is contingent on the status of Aidan Streitmeister's application," Tara explained.

"Wonderful." Libby tossed down the message slips as if they were radioactive. "If the woman's handing out bribes, she might as well make a donation to me, not the school."

"Oh, yeah, like that would really work. You're so corrupt." Tara started toward the door. "Your interviews begin at ten-thirty today. I'm gonna go scare up a VCR to check out this flick." She glanced at the label. "It isn't Swedish, is it? There was some Swedish flick with a title like that. *Scenes of a Marriage,* I think. I had to watch it in my film class in college. It went on forever. Very long and boring."

"If that's long and boring, we won't accept the kid," Libby promised, then waved Tara out the door.

Alone, Libby stared at the pink message slips. The audacity of applicants—or, more accurately, their parents—astonished her. Did this Streitmeister woman really believe she could buy her son a place in next year's kindergarten class by making a huge donation to the school?

Maybe the idea wasn't all that far-fetched. Only a couple of generations ago, that was exactly how things worked at elite private schools like Hudson. Families offered endowments and their offspring attended the school. Applications were just a formality. A top-flight education could be bought and sold like a loaf of rye. A very, very expensive loaf of rye.

If only she *were* corrupt. If only parents like Louise Streitmeister made donations to her instead of the school…

No, she didn't need Streitmeister money. Harry would come through for her.

She hadn't heard from him since Sunday, but that was an auspicious sign. If he'd decided to deny her any assistance, he would have phoned to let her know. He loved to say no.

Still, it would be nice of him to phone and say yes.

As if on cue, her phone rang. She glanced at her watch— ten-fifteen. Harry wouldn't call her this early unless he had an emergency, and he never had emergencies. They were too messy.

Maybe it was Louise Streitmeister, calling to ask whom she should make the check out to. Libby chuckled and reached for the phone, knowing Tara was off searching for a VCR so she'd have to take her calls herself. "Libby Kimmelman," she said.

"Hi, this is Ned Donovan."

Ned. The other subject that was haunting her. Ned and his dimple and his baby blues, rhapsodizing about her parquet floors. Ned sheltering her under his umbrella. Ned asking personal questions about her marital status. Ned believing her fireplace was a treasure. Libby had experienced more than a few moments since yesterday afternoon when she wasn't sure which posed a greater challenge: putting together financing to buy her apartment, or Ned Donovan.

She wasn't sure *why* he was a challenge. He was only the parent of an applicant—and not the sort of parent who dangled bribes in front of her, unless the use of an umbrella on a rainy afternoon constituted a bribe.

Damn it, Ned Donovan didn't have to bribe her to make her feel corrupt. Just one sizzling look from him, one wicked smile and she'd found herself, for the first time in much too long, yearning to shut herself up somewhere with a man and beg him to corrupt her.

Which wasn't like her at all. She was the sort of woman people wanted to introduce to nice, responsible bachelors from the synagogue, not rough-hewn construction guys with Irish last names and gazes that could pierce a woman's defenses more easily than a syringe full of flu vaccine could pierce her upper arm. She and Tara had already concluded that Ned Donovan deserved a prime month in their fantasy Hudson Hunks calendar. Hell, he deserved twelve prime months. And a centerfold.

He was no doubt calling her to see how his son's application was progressing. Wasn't that ultimately why every parent of an applicant called her?

"Hi," she said, keeping her voice light and crisp. "Thanks again for sharing your umbrella yesterday. That was very kind of you." Cripes. She sounded like a Hallmark card.

"Thanks for the ginger ale. Excellent vintage." He laughed. "You're working, and so am I, so I won't take up a lot of time, but…"

She listened to the background noises through the wire— a muffled banging, the sound of a hammer pounding nails. "But?" she prompted.

"Well, your fireplace." He sighed. "I can't get it out of my mind."

Was this a joke? He was no longer laughing. For all she knew, he had some odd perversion when it came to fireplaces. Perhaps he slept with a smile on his face, dreaming about hearths and mantelpieces. Perhaps when he saw blazing logs resting on andirons he had to take a cold shower.

"I'm convinced you've got a marble mantel. The vertical molding might be marble, too. It wouldn't take much effort to strip off the paint and see what's under there."

How could he make the word *strip* sound so sexy when he was talking about her fireplace? Maybe *she* was the one who needed a cold shower, simply because he'd mentioned wanting to "see what's under there."

"I can't let you do that," she said abruptly. Thank God he couldn't see her panic. She sounded like a prude, valiantly protecting the virtue of her fireplace.

"Why not?"

"Two reasons. One, it's not my fireplace. Technically, it belongs to my landlord."

"You rent?"

"Temporarily. It's a long story." And none of his business, she reminded herself, although she'd love to share it with him. He seemed easy to talk to, and he had not just a professional knowledge but a kind of weird passion about apartments. And he wasn't Harry, so he wouldn't try to make her feel guilty or incompetent just because she couldn't afford to buy the place on her own.

"If you removed all that ugly paint from the fireplace, you'd probably enhance the value of the apartment. Why would your landlord object?"

"What do you mean, ugly paint?" The paint *was* ugly, but her faded old furniture and well-worn rugs didn't exactly shout *beautiful*. She was used to the paint. It had been there when she'd waddled into the apartment as a pregnant young bride, and it was still there today, which was more than she could say for her ex-husband.

"I'm sorry," Ned said, sounding as though he was choking on something. Laughter, she suspected. He probably considered her a Philistine because she didn't care about the paint. "What was the other reason you don't want me to salvage your fireplace?"

"I can't afford you." The blunt statement resonated inside her, settling into layers. Financially, she couldn't afford Ned Donovan's fixer upper fees. Ethically, she couldn't afford to develop a friendship with an applicant's father. Romantically…

For God's sake, he lusted after her fireplace. Not her. *Romantically* had nothing to do with it.

Except that he had asked her about her marital status. And when he'd bumped shoulders with her and gripped her arm to keep her from stumbling, she'd felt…

It didn't matter what she felt. She couldn't afford him.

"I wasn't planning to charge you," he said.

"You're going to renovate my fireplace free?"

"I was thinking more of a peek—just removing a bit of paint to see what was underneath. If it turned out I was right about the marble, then we'd see."

"We wouldn't see. I can't afford you."

"You won't even let me take a teeny tiny peek?" She could practically picture him sulking—and even with his mouth shaped in a pout, she could visualize his dimple.

"What would a teeny tiny peek entail?" she asked warily. She couldn't afford this, she really couldn't…but honestly, just one teeny tiny peek? How bad could that be?

"I'd chip a small piece of paint from the underside of the mantel shelf. Maybe another piece inside the hearth, someplace where it wouldn't be noticeable. Then, because you were so generous to let me chip the paint, I'd take you out for a drink."

Oy. If he wanted to take her out for a drink, he wanted more than her fireplace.

Closing her eyes, she contemplated the nice Jewish bachelors Vivienne hoped to set her up with. Opening her eyes, she noticed the dial of her watch, which informed her that her first interview was scheduled to start in five minutes. Ned had asked to look at her fireplace and have a drink with her. She needed to make up her mind, and the seconds were ticking away.

"Does this have anything to do with Eric?" she asked, because the ethical layer was at least as important as the financial layer. For all she knew, Ned wanted to buy her a drink so he could charm her into accepting his son into the school.

"Eric isn't old enough for the kind of drink I had in mind," Ned said. "Ginger ale he can handle, but I was thinking of something a little more grown-up."

Had he deliberately misunderstood her? Was finessing his son's application so far from his mind it wouldn't even occur to him to use the occasion of a drink with Libby to win her favor on Eric's behalf? He might not realize how eagerly other parents would ply her with liquor if they thought it would improve their offsprings' chances of joining the Hudson community. Ned was a country guy, after all, from the pristine wilderness of Vermont. He might have no idea how most parents played the prep-school applications game.

Three minutes until her first interview. She couldn't dither. "If the fireplace means that much to you—"

"Your fireplace means more than you can imagine," he said, so solemnly she knew he had to be joking.

"How is Friday? I could probably—"

"Friday is fine."

"Okay. Stop by Friday after dinner—seven-thirty. And you can chip off only a teeny tiny bit of paint."

"You'll be astonished by my restraint," he promised. "I'll see you at seven-thirty on Friday. Thanks, Libby." The line went dead.

She'd barely lowered her own phone into its cradle when it emitted a shrill ring, forcing her to lift it back to her ear. "Libby Kimmelman," she muttered, her mind lingering on the last call, mulling it over, trying to determine whether she'd been conned. *Teeny tiny?* What kind of man used words like that?

"Libby?" Tara's voice bubbled through the phone. "I watched a little of the Jeremy Tartaglia video. It looked like he was saying *mama* while he was still too young to sit up.

I think his parents doctored the film, dubbing in a voice. No baby can say *mama* at that age."

"And here I thought we expected all Hudson students to be verbally precocious. Reva could say *mama* in the womb. Don't tell me you weren't able to do that."

"If there wasn't a cell phone in the womb, I wasn't talking," Tara said. "Your first interview is here. Melanie Agapakis and enough relatives to stage a touring production of *My Big Fat Greek Wedding*. One of them brought stuffed grape leaves."

"It's a change from chocolate, at least. Bring Melanie to the interview room. I'll meet her there. I'd just as soon avoid the extended family."

"Coward," Tara teased.

Libby hung up and closed her eyes one last time. A drink with Ned Donovan. She didn't do things like that.

But she was going to do it Friday. After he mutilated her fireplace, which wasn't even hers—and might never be, if she couldn't get the funds together.

Somehow, thoughts of her teetering finances and her insecure housing situation were nowhere near as unsettling as the thought of spending an evening with Ned.

Eleven

"It's marble," Ned Donovan said.

He was half in and half out of Libby's fireplace, his long, denim-clad legs stretched across the hearth and into the room. Armed with a small chisel, a bottle of solvent, some rags and a penlight, he'd been fussing with the fireplace for a half hour. Libby would have thought it would take five minutes to gouge enough paint off to find out what was underneath, but Ned had promised to do the job carefully, indulging in his teeny tiny peek without spoiling the appearance of the mantel.

While he'd been digging around in her fireplace, she'd wandered in and out of the living room, wishing she weren't so conscious of his presence in her home. He had big feet—well, not *big,* but much bigger than any other feet in the apartment. She wasn't used to such massive, thick-soled shoes leaving tread marks on her rugs.

The second-biggest feet in the apartment right now were his son's. Ned had phoned her fifteen minutes before arriving with the news that the teenage girl from down the hall who had promised to stay with Eric that evening had just been diagnosed with strep, and Libby had blurted out that she had a teenage girl who could stay with Eric and wasn't suffering from any contagious diseases at the moment. After hanging up, she'd belatedly asked Reva if she would mind babysitting for Eric. Reva had acted exceedingly annoyed until Libby offered to pay her. Intense financial negotiations had ensued, but Libby had held firm at ten dollars. Eric, after all, was a self-sufficient kid. Reva wouldn't have to feed him or change his diaper. And Libby and Ned weren't going to be gone long. How long did it take to have a drink?

As soon as the Donovans arrived, Libby had directed Eric to the den, which was furnished with a TV and a computer. Eric had ignored the TV and asked if he could play a computer game. Recalling his enthusiastic descriptions of various software programs during his interview at Hudson, Libby had figured he knew what he was doing when it came to computers, and told him to make himself at home with her machine.

After getting Eric settled in, she'd prowled. Whenever she found herself watching Ned for more than a few minutes— not so much watching as ogling, even though she couldn't see his face; his body was definitely ogle-worthy—she abandoned the living room for the den to check up on Eric, or the dining room, where the table groaned beneath multiple stacks of applications. Reva had shut herself up inside her bedroom, where she was either gloating or sulking over the ten bucks Libby had promised her. Libby wasn't going to open that bedroom door until she had to.

"So, it's marble," she said to Ned's feet.

He slithered out from under the hearth's opening and

gazed up at her from the floor. "Dark green, with lots of veins. Want to have a look?"

Dark green? What would she do with a dark-green marble mantel?

The same as she did with a painted white mantel—display on it the cut-crystal vase she'd got from her cousin Sarah for her wedding, a framed baby photo of Reva and a few other tchotchkes, and dust it every six months if she remembered. She'd dusted it earlier that evening, of course, so Ned wouldn't think she was quite as lackadaisical a housekeeper as she actually was.

Dark green would actually look lovely, she thought. Bold and vivid. As if she could afford to pay Ned what stripping and refinishing the entire mantel would cost.

"Come here." He beckoned her to the hearth, and she cautiously dropped to her knees next to him. "Gotta get in a little closer," he said, casually arching his arm around her shoulders and guiding her head inside the fireplace. She tried not to lean back into him, even though she found maintaining her balance difficult without using his chest as a backrest. She admonished herself not to act as though lying this close to him was a sin. He probably flung his arm around the shoulders of all his marble-fireplace clients. She ought to be as nonchalant about it as he was.

He turned on his penlight, and its small circle of white guided her gaze up toward the underside of the mantel. "There. See?"

She saw dark green, with lots of veins. "Wow," she said, because she felt some comment was called for.

"Of course, this is what's under the shelf." He ran the light beam the length of the mantel. "The vertical trim appears darker—" he used the penlight to direct her attention to an area along the side edge of the fireplace, where a small patch of dark poked through the thick white paint "—but it might be more of the green marble. Hard to tell without stripping all the paint off and buffing it up. The top of the mantel feels like it's got a veneer of wood attached to it."

"Why?" she asked, feeling the heat of his body surrounding her. Did they really have to have this conversation stuffed inside her fireplace? He was much too close. His chin was a millimeter from her ear, and given the proximity of his hips to her tush, he could easily discern how thirty-five years of gravity and a pregnancy had redistributed the fat in her body.

"Beats me. Someone stupid enough to cover a marble mantel with paint is stupid enough to glue a slat of wood onto the marble, too. Maybe they thought it would hold the paint better." He shimmied out of the fireplace and she scrambled out, as well, eager for light and space and the chance to put some distance between Ned and her. She wasn't sure how old he was, but gravity hadn't done a damn thing to his body. He was so solid. And warm. And *male*.

She slid farther back on the floor and reminded herself that he was here as a carpenter, an expert, someone passionately devoted to fireplaces. He was Eric Donovan's father. His hips had no interest whatsoever in her tush.

He stood, leaned over and snagged her wrist to help her up. Even his hand was solid and warm and male, the palm smooth and hard with callus, the fingers thick and blunt. As soon as she was on her feet, she eased free and he smiled. "You want me to strip it?"

Strip what? The mantel, she reminded herself. "I told you, Ned, I don't own this apartment, and I can't—"

"Whoever owns this apartment would throw himself at your feet if you did him the favor of restoring the fireplace."

"I don't think the management company would throw themselves at my feet," she said, finding the image of those heartless, anonymous suits prostrating themselves before her rather amusing. "But it's more than that. I can't really—"

"I'd do it free," he said.

She gazed into his eyes. They glittered like jewels, and staring at them made her feel like a gold digger pressed up against the window of Harry Winston's, dazzled by a spectacular gem. But she couldn't afford the gem, or Ned Donovan, any more than she could afford to make changes in an apartment she couldn't afford without her ex-husband's financial assistance.

So Ned would renovate her fireplace free. And in exchange, she would…what? Let Eric enroll in the Hudson School? A renovated fireplace sure beat chocolate and flowers, to say nothing of loofahs.

"I can't let you do that," she said quietly, turning away so she wouldn't have to admire his eyes anymore, or the sexy dimple creasing his right cheek. "I can't accept gifts from the parents of Hudson applicants."

Ned laughed. "That wasn't why I was offering. Libby, your fireplace…" He paused, then changed course. "You know what? Let's go out, get a drink and talk. Okay? And just to make sure we're both clear about this, I'm paying for the drinks and it's not a bribe. It's a guy thing. The guy pays for the drinks."

Grinning, she turned back to him. "What century are you living in?"

"Early twentieth, just like that fireplace. Will you let me buy you a drink, or are we going to have an embarrassing argument in front of a bunch of witnesses at a café?"

"I'll let you buy me a drink," she relented.

"Good. Where's Eric? I want to tell him we're leaving."

Eric was still in the den, either building or blowing up virtual civilizations. Libby could never tell with computer simulation games, all of which seemed to feature numerous explosions no matter what their premise. He barely nodded when Ned said he and Libby would be gone for about an hour.

Libby tapped on Reva's bedroom door before inching it open. "Mr. Donovan and I are going out for a little while," she said. "Eric is playing on the computer."

Reva sat cross-legged on her bed, her math textbook open beside one knee and a spiral notebook open beside the other. "Yeah, okay."

"I've got the cell phone if you need us."

"Uh-huh. Mom, I've got to do my homework, okay?"

"Fine. Do your homework." Libby closed the door and shook her head. The minute she and Ned left the house, she suspected, Reva would slam her books shut, phone Kim and whine about how she couldn't IM her because some twerp she was babysitting for had taken over the computer. But she'd get ten dollars for her inconvenience, so Libby felt no sympathy for her.

She donned a wool blazer and Ned put on his denim jacket. Neither she nor Ned spoke as she locked the door and strolled with him down the hall to the elevator. The silence continued as they waited for it to arrive, and as they got in and rode downstairs. Whenever she sneaked a glimpse of him, she found him watching her, a tentative smile curving his mouth. Why did this feel as awkward as a first date?

Well, it was. Sort of.

Not really. No.

She didn't date the fathers of Hudson applicants. She didn't date gorgeous guys she barely knew. She didn't date, period.

Sure she did. Vivienne had set her up with a few guys over the years, all of them nice Jewish professionals, not the least bit like Ned Donovan. She'd dated one fellow for nearly a year. Marty Weinberg hadn't been one of Vivienne's finds. He'd been a sweet, slightly bald arts administrator whom Libby had met while rummaging in the cheese case at Bloom's. He'd been on a desperate quest for feta and one thing had led to another. Marty had never turned her world inside out or upside down, which had been fine with her. They'd been compatible, they'd enjoyed each other's company and the whole relationship had been…sweet and slightly bald. When Marty was offered a position at the Smithsonian, he'd asked her if she wanted to move to Washington with him and she'd said no, and that had been that.

But Marty had left her life three years ago, and she'd discovered, shortly after his departure, that she didn't really miss him that much. Reva had confessed she'd always considered him a weenie, and really, if her mother was going to go out with guys, couldn't she at least go out with cool ones?

Ned Donovan would qualify as a cool one, but Reva hadn't even commented on him. Which proved to Libby that this wasn't an actual date. If it was, Reva would have grilled Libby at length and then offered an unexpurgated critique of him.

They left the elevator and headed through the lobby and outside. The evening air was bracing, and it helped to clear Libby's mind. "The thing about the fireplace is—"

"Libby." He cut her off. "It's a magnificent fireplace." He motioned with his head toward the corner, and they started walking. "I don't get to work on that kind of restoration very often. Up in Vermont, I did lots of restoration work. I loved it. I miss it. It would be fun for me."

"Fun? To scrape paint off a marble mantel?"

"Yeah." At the corner, they turned down the side street in the direction of Broadway. West End Avenue was primarily residential, offering no bistros or cafés for two people to enjoy a drink. They'd have better luck finding a place on Broadway. "If you want to get permission from the building's owner first, fine. You don't have to clear it with them if you want to hang a picture, do you?"

"Hammering a nail into the wall is a little different from removing the paint from the fireplace." She sighed and shoved her hands into the pockets of her blazer. "Anyway, the situation is complicated. I'm trying to put together the funding to buy the apartment. If I start messing with it, who knows what the current owners will do? Jack up the price, maybe?"

"If you pay for the improvement—which you wouldn't actually have to do, since I said I'd work free—I don't see how the current owners would enter into it. Sure, the reno-vated fireplace would increase the unit's value, but they wouldn't assume the cost of that increase. So it's no skin off their noses."

"Well…" Having the fireplace restored to its original beauty would be nice. Having Ned Donovan working in her apartment over a stretch of days would be…dangerous. Probably quite nice, too. "I'll think about it."

They'd reached Broadway. A few shops remained open despite the late hour, but most of the activity buzzed around several eateries that occupied the block. One was a pizza place, one a Cuban-Chinese restaurant. One was a grungy neighborhood bar, one a chic place with enough twenty-somethings gathered around the open front door to make Libby feel like someone's grandma.

"Which place would you recommend?" he asked.

"I've never been to any of them," she admitted.

"Never? Hmm." He gestured toward the grungy bar. "Let's try that one. If it looks worse inside than outside, we'll leave."

It looked better inside, dark and cozy, with aged panel-ing and wooden booths along one wall. The television above the bar was tuned so low it was inaudible once Libby and Ned settled into a booth. A waitress came over while they were removing their jackets. Ned ordered a Pete's Wicked Ale, Libby a glass of merlot.

As soon as the waitress left, Ned leaned back in the booth and regarded Libby. "So, where do you go on dates?"

Thank God she didn't already have her wine. If he'd asked his question while she was taking a drink, she probably would have choked—or spit the wine all over him. "I beg your pardon?"

"When you go on dates," he asked, "where do you go? What are some of the better places in this neighborhood?"

"I have no idea," she said, hating herself for allowing him to fluster her. First the awkward silence in the elevator and now this. Reva probably had more poise around guys than Libby did.

The waitress arrived with Ned's ale, Libby's wine and a bowl of shelled peanuts dusty with salt. She left everything and disappeared.

"You don't date much?" Ned asked.

Why was he posing such personal questions? Did stripping the underside of her mantel give him the right?

The way he asked, though, gently and with a lilt of amusement underlining the words, calmed her down. This was his idea of getting-to-know-you, nothing more. "No," she said, deciding to go along with him for now. "I don't date much. How about you?"

He poured some ale from the bottle into the frosted mug the waitress had provided. "I've only been in New York City for a few months," he reminded her. "I haven't had time to meet anyone down here."

"But in Vermont—"

He let out a snort.

"Not much of a social scene in Vermont?" she asked. She liked being the one pitching the questions rather than getting beaned by them.

"I wouldn't exactly call it a scene," he said, "but yes, folks date in Vermont. I sure as hell tried."

She couldn't believe a man with his charisma would have any trouble dating, if that was what he wanted to do. "What happened?"

He took a drink of beer. "Eric and I were living in Wood-stock, Vermont—the same town as my in-laws. My wife had grown up there, and she and I moved there after we finished college and got married. It's a great town. I started a business renovating old houses and barns. We had Eric. Then one day, Deborah suffered a brain aneurysm and died."

"It must have been horrible."

"It wasn't a barrel of laughs." He sipped a little more beer, and Libby drank some wine. "After about a year, Eric and I decided it was time to start living again. So I invited a woman out to dinner. And call me crazy, but I asked my in-laws to babysit for Eric."

"What's crazy about that?" Libby asked.

"What was crazy about it was that my in-laws didn't think it was time for Eric and me to start living yet." Ned scooped up a handful of peanuts and tossed them one at a time into his mouth. "They were furious that I'd dare to go out with a woman who wasn't Deborah. They found out from Eric what restaurant I'd gone to, and the next thing I knew, my mother-in-law was standing at our table, telling my date all about what a wonderful wife Deborah was, how much we all missed her." He laughed, although Libby noticed a flicker of pain in his eyes. "Needless to say, my date and I lost our appetites. Afterward, I had a huge fight with my in-laws. They thought I was some kind of heartless bastard for wanting to meet women. They thought I should spend the rest of my life mourning Deborah. Don't get me wrong—I loved her very much. But she was dead."

Libby nodded to show she understood and sympathized with what he was saying. "It sounds as if your wife's parents weren't ready to start living yet."

"Not even close to ready," Ned confirmed. "I went out a few more times, and every time, one of them showed up—at the movie theater, at the restaurant, wherever. I took a lady up to Middlebury College to watch a hockey game, and my in-laws showed up at the arena. I went out a few times with one woman, a music teacher in town, and my mother-in-law intercepted her in the school parking lot to tell her I was still in mourning for my wife, that I was terribly wounded and didn't really know what I was doing. The next time I phoned her, she suggested it would be better if we didn't see each other for a while." He shook his head. "I realized that if I hoped for my life back, I'd have to leave Vermont."

"So you moved to New York?"

"Yeah. A friend of mine from college had a renovation business—Greater Manhattan Design Associates—and he made me an offer I couldn't refuse." Ned washed down a few more peanuts with a swig of beer. "Deborah's parents are good people. They just couldn't accept that Eric and I were handling her death differently than they were." He stretched in his seat and bumped her feet with his under the table. An apologetic smile brightened his face as he shifted his legs. "Actually, it was Eric who got us both back on track. He looked at me one day and said, 'I'm tired of being sad all the time. Is it okay to stop being sad?' And I realized I was tired of being sad, too. Deborah's parents obviously weren't tired of being sad. We decided we had to put some distance between them and us."

"New York is quite a distance from Woodstock, Vermont."

"It's not that far," he argued.

"I wasn't talking about miles."

He grinned. "Right. Eric and I have come a long way."

"And now you want to date."

His gaze met hers and his smile widened. "Now I want to be right where I am, having a drink with you."

Did that mean this was a date? He'd just told her more than any guy would tell a woman on a first date. They were two friends having a drink, that was all. If Libby allowed herself to think of this as a date, she'd start measuring each silence the way she had in the elevator, and paying too much attention to his dimple, which had disappeared when he'd talked about his wife and in-laws, but was once again punctuating the corner of his smile.

"So, that's my story. What's yours? You don't have a dead husband making you sad."

"No, I've got a live one making me crazy," she joked, then laughed. "Not really. We get along most of the time. It's one of those civil divorces."

"If you're going to get a divorce, that's probably the best kind to have." Ned shifted again, leaning forward this time. "So why don't you date much?"

Two friends having a drink together, she reminded herself. As long as this was nothing more, he could ask a question like that. "It's hard to find the time to meet anyone," she acknowledged. "My sister-in-law tries to set me up with guys."

"Your brother's wife?"

She laughed. "No, my ex-husband's sister. I won custody of his family in the divorce."

Ned digested that news with a philosophical shrug. "I hope that's okay with you."

"They're great," she said. "Yentas, one and all, but I don't mind. Vivienne—my sister-in-law—is always meeting single men in her synagogue. Now that she's married, I guess she figures they shouldn't go to waste, so she tries to foist them on me."

"And you turn them all down?"

"It never gets that far. I don't have the time or energy for the whole thing. If someone really clicked with me, then maybe…" She faltered, realizing that someone *had* clicked with her. He was sitting across the table from her right now. He wasn't a nice Jewish guy from the synagogue, and he had a son applying to Hudson, and *they were just friends having a drink.* She settled herself with a sip of wine and said, "If I weren't basically happy with my life the way it is, maybe I'd put more effort into changing it. At the moment, I'm trying to put my effort into keeping it the way it is."

"You like being single, huh?" Even if Ned was relatively new to New York, he'd probably met more than a few women desperate to get married. Libby might seem like an oddball for not sharing their desperation.

"Being single is fine. It's my apartment I'm trying to hold on to. If things remain civil enough between me and my ex-husband, I should be able to do that." She explained to him about the last remaining rentals in the building going co-op, and about her determination to buy her apartment so she wouldn't lose it. "One thing about New York—finding a great apartment that's also affordable is a hell of a lot harder than finding a husband. Or a wife."

"So, if I salvage your fireplace, I'd be doing it for you, not for this management company that owns the apartment now."

"If I can buy it. I'm hoping my ex-husband will help with the financing."

"That would be generous of him." Ned drained his mug of beer. "I'd rather rehab the fireplace for you than for some stranger in a suit. I'd do it anyway, for the fireplace's sake—"

"The fireplace's sake?" Libby burst into laughter. "Do you think the fireplace cares?"

Ned smiled, but he didn't laugh. "Yes. I do think it cares. It wants to break free of that paint and be all that it can be."

He was serious. Libby stopped laughing. He obviously

had a passion about his work. She admired that, even envied it a little. She loved her colleagues at the Hudson School, and the students—whom she was helping to be all that they could be by choosing them for admission to the school—but she couldn't imagine doing what she did free, just for the love of it. No one listened to a five-year-old who wasn't a blood relation sing an aria from *Madama Butterfly* for the love of it.

She finished her wine, and Ned asked if she'd like another. She checked her watch and shook her head. They'd been gone nearly an hour. "We should get back," she said. "I promised Reva we wouldn't be out too long."

Ned conceded with a shrug. He summoned the waitress and paid for their drinks.

The night had cooled considerably during the time they'd been indoors. It wasn't yet cold, but autumn carried a preview of winter in the breezes that lifted off the Hudson River and gusted down the side streets. Broadway was still hopping; the crowd in front of the chi-chi bistro appeared to have doubled in size, and the sidewalks teemed with people walking in brisk, committed steps. Central Park on a sunny afternoon was full of amblers, but Broadway on a Friday evening attracted mostly marchers.

Libby didn't feel like marching. Reva expected her home, and she'd get there soon enough. But talking to a man about grown-up matters was a rare pleasure, and Libby saw no reason not to prolong the pleasure as much as she could. If she let Ned work on her fireplace, the talking could continue. She wished she could afford to pay him so she wouldn't have to think of his labor as a bribe.

She also wished she could afford to buy the colorful boots on display in the window of the shoe boutique two doors down from the tavern. She paused to study them: cowboy style, with multicolored patches of leather. "I'd love to get those for Reva," she said, imagining her theatrical daughter waltzing around in such a flamboyant pair of boots while practicing her *Tommy* solo.

Ned gravitated toward the window with her, then ushered her into the recessed doorway so they could study the boots from a different angle. "You should get them for yourself," he said.

"Oh, please!" She laughed. They were not the sort of boots a mother should wear.

"They'd look great on you. Too bad the store is closed, or you could go in and try them on."

"I'm sure they're uncomfortable. The toes are so pointed." Reva never cared if shoes were uncomfortable, as long as they were cool. But Libby was a huge fan of pain-free feet.

"They probably feel better than they look," Ned said.

"You think so?" She twisted to see him and found him much closer than she'd expected. In the shadowed alcove of the store's entry, his face was barely an inch from hers.

"Lots of things feel better than they look," he said.

"Like what?" If he weren't so close, maybe her voice wouldn't have sounded like a rusty hinge.

He didn't answer. He only gazed at her in the shadowed alcove. He'd been closer to her inside her fireplace, but then they'd been discussing fireplaces. Now she had no idea what they were discussing. Something about boots, maybe, or about things feeling good.

God, he was close. All he had to do was tilt his head the slightest bit and his lips would be touching hers.

He tilted his head the slightest bit.

Okay, so they weren't just friends having a drink. That was her last lucid thought before Ned lifted his hands to frame her face, wove his fingers into her hair and turned the kiss from lips touching lips to something wonderfully, unexpectedly wild.

Had she ever been kissed like this before? She didn't think so, and while she knew it wasn't a wise idea—things would be a lot safer all around if she went back to the friends-having-a-drink premise of this outing—she wasn't about to bring this kiss to a halt until she'd given the experience its due. Surely they could revert to being friends in a minute. Or five. Or ten.

The only time she noticed the nerve endings in her lips was when they were chapped and split—until now. Now that flesh seemed unnervingly sensitive, picking up changes in pressure and heat and moisture like a high-tech weather station. When Ned angled his face, her entire mouth hastened to adjust. Being kissed at *this* angle instead of *that* made everything entirely new.

Then there was her tongue. Or, more accurately, there was Ned's tongue. Tongues were for tasting, right? For speaking and swallowing, vital functions like that. She hadn't realized tongues were also for dancing, for teasing, for stroking. She hadn't realized tongues were so downright phallic. But what Ned was doing with his tongue…

A shudder began at the back of her throat and rippled the length of her body. In all the years she'd lived in Manhattan, she'd never before felt like having sex with a man while standing in the entry alcove of a shoe boutique on Broadway. To be sure, they already *were* having some kind of sex. In case there was any question in her mind of that, he twined his fingers deeper into her hair and shifted his legs just enough to align her pelvic area with his.

His hips might have had no interest in her slightly spongy thirty-five-year-old tush when she and he had been tangled up inside her fireplace. But she had no question that his body was extremely interested in hers right now.

At some point within the next minute or so, she was going to have to breathe. She didn't particularly want to. In her mind, breathing seemed synonymous with ending the kiss. Both were good ideas. She just wanted to enjoy this bad idea for a few moments more.

Evidently, Ned needed to breathe even more than she did. He leaned back and sucked in a deep, ragged lungful of air. Then his gaze met hers and he smiled. "Well," he said.

Well what? *Well, we're in a hell of a lot of trouble here,* she thought. *Well, that was the most mind-boggling kiss I've ever participated in. Well, we've got two kids waiting for us back at my apartment, and one of them is trying to get into the school where I'm the director of admissions, and maybe you're betting there's some rule about a father's kissing skills contributing to a kid's chances for acceptance. Well, this might be your first kiss since you escaped your in-laws in black crepe, so you're probably just flexing the old muscles to see if they still work. Well, this kiss probably doesn't mean a damn thing.*

He apparently wasn't going to tell her *well what.* All he did was lower his hands from the sides of her head, leaving her cheeks chilled and her jaw suddenly aware of the absence of his thumbs. He caught one of her hands in his, interlaced their fingers and ushered her out of the alcove and onto the sidewalk, steering them near the buildings to avoid getting trampled by the high-speed traffic of their fellow pedestrians.

She'd already established that the last time she'd been kissed so magnificently had been never, so she tried to recall the last time she'd held hands with a man. When she was eight, she recalled holding her father's hand while they crossed a busy intersection together. She'd held hands with boys as a teenager. But with a man? Harry wasn't a hand holder.

Ned was both a hand holder and a kisser.

And this, she acknowledged as they turned off Broadway in the direction of her apartment, was a date.

Twelve

"Look," Vivienne said. "Someone's going to snatch up all those available men if you don't come to synagogue with me today."

Libby yawned, then filled a second mug of coffee without bothering to ask Vivienne if she wanted any. Dressed in dove-gray slacks and an orange tunic as bright as a traffic cone, her hair and makeup meticulously done, she appeared brisk and chipper, clearly not in need of caffeine. But Libby had never known her sister-in-law to turn down a cup of coffee.

Libby herself was desperately in need of caffeine. She'd hardly slept last night, and she felt foolish about her restlessness. A grown woman shouldn't be plagued by insomnia just because a gorgeous man had kissed her.

Okay, so Ned Donovan was more than a gorgeous man. He was a gorgeous, unattached, age-appropriate man. In New

York City, most gorgeous men in their thirties were either married, gay or chasing after babes barely out of high school. Libby hadn't met the synagogue fellows Vivienne seemed so determined to introduce her to, but she'd bet that if they were unattached, they were either not age-appropriate or not gorgeous.

Vivienne accepted the steaming mug from Libby with a grateful nod. Before she could ask for artificial sweetener, Libby pulled a few packets of Splenda from the cabinet and tossed them onto the table. Then she slumped into a chair and tried to stifle yet another yawn.

"I really shouldn't stay," Vivienne said as she emptied the sweetener into her cup. "I'd hate to miss the service." She took a sip, then gazed around the kitchen. "You didn't happen to get to Bloom's this week, did you?"

"I bought bagels, if that's what you're asking. If you want one, they're in the fridge," Libby said, gesturing toward the refrigerator. "Help yourself."

"That's all right. I'll eat at the kiddush. You shouldn't refrigerate bagels, Libby. It makes them dense." She took another delicate sip of her coffee, managing not to smear her coral-hued lipstick. "You sure you don't want to come to shul with me? One of the men, Harvey Golub, is in the fur business. You could do worse, Libby. Just think, he could have you in a nice little mink by New Year's Eve. Maybe you could get a discount on something for me, too. A fun fur, nothing fancy. Leonard is never going to buy me a fur."

"How do you know that?" Libby asked.

"He said, 'I'm never going to buy you a fur.'"

"I guess that's an indication."

"He's afraid someone'll throw fake blood on it. He said, 'I should spend all that money so someone can throw fake blood on you?'"

"He has a point."

"Yeah, right between his ears." Vivienne planted her mug on the table, shoved herself out of her chair and crossed to the refrigerator. "I'm thinking, just one bagel. I'll skip the schmear. I need to lose a few pounds."

Vivienne didn't need to lose any weight, but Libby lacked the energy to argue with her. "I've got low-fat cream cheese," she said.

"Low-fat? Well, okay, maybe just a little." She pulled the bag of bagels and a tub of cream cheese from the refrigerator, then helped herself to a plate and a knife. "So, you're not interested in meeting some nice Jewish men? What, you want to live the rest of your life like a nun?"

"Are those my only choices?" Libby asked. "Nice Jewish men or marriage to Christ?"

"What other choices do you want?"

Libby closed her eyes and her mind filled with an image of Ned. Tall, dimpled Ned with strong, callused hands and a mouth a more gifted woman could write poetry about. Libby had never been particularly poetic. At best, she could probably scrape together a haiku about him: *This man has a tongue/He knows how to use it/Ned Donovan is hot.*

"Libby Kimmelman," Vivienne clucked. "You're blushing."

Libby's eyes jerked open. "I am not!"

Vivienne slammed her plate down on the table and dropped into the empty chair. "Tell me *everything,*" she demanded in a firm voice.

"There's nothing to tell."

"She went out with a guy last night," Reva announced from the kitchen doorway. "Hi, Aunt Vivienne."

"Sleeping Beauty! Have I ever seen you up this early on a Saturday morning?" Vivienne asked, rising to give Reva a hug. Libby prayed for Vivienne to ask Reva about school, her friends, her solo in *Tommy*—anything to keep the discussion from focusing on what Libby had done last night.

The reprieve didn't last, however. Vivienne returned to her chair and glowered at Libby. "You went out with a guy? What guy?"

"We didn't go out," Libby said. "I mean, technically we did, in the sense that we left the apartment and went outside. He's going to fix the fireplace."

"What's wrong with the fireplace?"

Eager for something to distract Vivienne from this interrogation, Libby watched with hope as Reva entered the kitchen. She had on faded jeans that were tight on top and flared at the bottom, and a skimpy knit top that revealed a sliver of belly. Her hair was brushed to a high gloss. "Are you going someplace today, Reva?" she asked.

"I *told* you. I'm meeting some people at the park." Reva slid a bagel from the bag and bit into it without bothering to slice it or add cream cheese.

Ned Donovan might be hot, but he hadn't emptied her brainpan last night. "You never told me you were going to the park today."

"I did. You probably just weren't paying attention. We're meeting at the Imagine mosaic."

Libby didn't comment on Reva's accusation. Of course she'd been paying attention. She always paid attention to her daughter. If Reva had mentioned this Central Park outing, Libby would have remembered.

But she didn't see much value in arguing about it. If Reva *had* discussed the outing with her, she would have given her consent. "Will Kim be there?"

Reva shrugged. "She can't come. Her sister's playing in some stupid recital. I'm just, like, gonna hang with some other kids."

"What other kids?" Ashleigh with the black nail polish? Libby wondered.

Reva's shrug this time was accompanied by a look of transparent annoyance. "Some Hudson kids."

Libby considered pressing her, but saw only flaring tempers and a contest of wills at the end of that route. Hudson kids were generally good kids, she reminded herself—and Reva was a good kid. And the day was sunny and Reva knew Central Park. "What time are you meeting these Hudson kids?"

"Around noon. So Aunt Vivienne—" Reva turned the tables on Libby "—Mom went out with this guy and she made me babysit for his kid."

"You went out with a *father?*" Vivienne seemed to find this shocking, for some reason.

"His son is ten years old," Libby said. "And when we came back home," she added, slanting a glare in Reva's direction, "this poor, put-upon babysitter was busy playing computer games with him."

"He's pretty good at Space Colony. That's kind of like the Sims, only in outer space," Reva explained.

"I like the Sims," Vivienne remarked. "Maybe I'd like Space Colony, too."

"Yeah, it's a good game. I just watched him play awhile—until Mom and his dad got back."

"So, who is this man?" Vivienne directed her question to a space midway between Libby at the table and Reva, who had hoisted herself up to sit on the counter. Obviously, Vivienne assumed that if Libby didn't answer, Reva would.

"He's a fireplace guy," Reva obediently told her. "His kid applied to Hudson."

"What's his name?"

Reva was chewing. Libby had to field this question. "Ned Donovan."

"Ned Donovan?" Vivienne's voice rose to a coloratura pitch. "Irish?"

"I think he's American," Libby said dryly.

"Still, *Donovan*...that's not a Jewish name."

"No," Libby said. "He's not Jewish. He's from Vermont," she added, hoping that would forestall further questions.

"Vermont? They don't have Jews in Vermont, do they."

"In the big cities, maybe," Libby said.

"What big cities do they have in Vermont?"

Libby sent Reva an imploring gaze. Reva was clearly not inclined to help her mother. She only grinned before taking another hearty bite of her bagel.

"Burlington," Libby finally said, because Vivienne's frown was intensifying by the second. Were there any other cities in Vermont? Did Burlington even qualify as a city? Did Libby care?

"What does he look like?" Vivienne pressed. "Does he look Irish?"

"What does Irish look like?" Libby retorted. "Give me a break, Viv. He came over to check out the fireplace. Then we took a walk." She edited out the part about their having a drink in a bar, because Vivienne would probably consider that tawdry, and she edited out the part about the kiss, because that would freak out everybody, including her. "And then we came home, and he picked up his son and left."

"You took a walk? What kind of date is that?" Vivienne glanced at Reva. "He sounds cheap. Harvey Golub, you're talking mink coats. And this guy's idea of a date is to take a walk?"

"It wasn't a date," Libby said with finality. She might not be able to convince herself of that, but surely Vivienne should be easy enough to fool. The woman was eating Libby's bagels, after all. The least she could do was believe Libby. "Reva, did you tell Aunt Vivienne about your solo?"

Reva leaped off the counter, suddenly too excited to sit. She talked about the solo. She sang it. She described the auditions, did a hilarious impersonation of Muriel Froiken, sang her solo again, analyzed whether she should try to add a British accent to her pronunciation "because *Tommy* is set in England" and went on at such length that Ned Donovan, the cheap Vermont Irishman, was forgotten. By the time Reva wound down, Vivienne had to leave to get to synagogue if she hoped to catch any of the service.

Good work, Libby silently praised her daughter. Dating might not be so difficult if she could count on Reva to distract Vivienne. Not that Libby wanted to keep Ned a secret from them—not that she was dating him, anyway—but until she knew what the hell was going on in her life, she saw no reason to let anyone else meddle in it.

Reva really wished Kim had been able to join her, but she had that stupid recital to go to. "My sister's playing Schoenberg," she'd told Reva. "So, like, even if she plays everything perfectly it'll sound awful. But I've got to go, my parents said. Besides, you don't want me tagging along if you're going to be with Luke Rodelle."

"I don't think it's a date," Reva had explained. "He didn't ask me like it was a date."

"But he asked you for a Saturday. That means it's a date."

Reva doubted that. But even if it *was* a date, she would want Kim along for moral support. She had never gone on a genuine date before, but she'd heard around school that bringing your best friend along on a date was perfectly acceptable.

If only Kim's sister didn't have to play Schoenberg. Reva wasn't sure who Schoenberg was, but if Kim said his stuff sounded awful, it probably did.

Luke had said he'd meet her at the Imagine mosaic at one,

but Reva had told her mother noon so she'd have an excuse to leave early. She'd been too restless in the apartment, pacing her room until she stubbed her toe on her night table, then schmoozing with Aunt Vivienne, then wandering into the living room and trying to picture the fireplace green. "A dark green, with lots of veins," her mother had described it last night. Dark green with lots of veins sounded disgusting, like a monster in a cheesy horror flick. "If you'd like to see the marble, get the flashlight from the kitchen and crawl into the fireplace. You'll find a couple of spots where Ned scraped off the paint."

One thing Reva wasn't going to do was crawl into the fireplace. Even though she couldn't remember a fire ever blazing there, the whole idea of wedging herself into a place where stuff was supposed to burn grossed her out.

In order to avoid a fight with her mother, she wore her fleece jacket even though it was too warm, and she took the cell phone with her. The ten-dollar bill she'd earned doing nothing last night was stuffed into her purse, along with her sunglasses, lip gloss and a tube of mascara, which she'd apply to her lashes once she got far enough away from the house.

She had time to kill, so she headed to 72nd Street and window-shopped. Too many of the stores had been there forever, like even Grandma might have shopped there when she was Reva's age. Broadway had much cooler stores, but Broadway wasn't going to lead Reva to the park.

While she walked, she plotted in her mind how she ought to act with Luke. Friendly but not too friendly. Like she understood this wasn't a date, unless of course he took it in a major date direction, in which case she'd just go with the flow. Up to a point, of course. This was the first time she and Luke were actually together, and she wasn't going to do any of that stuff that Larissa LeMoyne and the other divas were rumored to do. Monica Ditmer had told Reva that the divas did it to guys with their mouths, which struck Reva as remarkably disgusting, plus maybe it could affect your voice. Like, imagine if you were about to sing your *Tommy* solo, but your voice wouldn't come out right because your throat was all clogged with boy gunk. *Gross.*

Reva didn't even know why she was thinking about it. This was not a date.

The showcase window of a shoe store that specialized in really ugly footwear—fat, rounded toes, thick brown leather, flat heels, the kinds of shoes her mother would probably love—was trimmed in shiny chrome, and Reva used the chrome as a mirror to put on her mascara. Just a light touch to darken the tips of her lashes. She didn't want to come across as Goth or anything. It wasn't like she was trying to impress Luke with her eyelashes, anyway. She just happened to look better with a little mascara on. And her lip gloss. She wore a shade that was the same color as her lips, only more so.

And if he wanted to fall in love with her, well, she wasn't going to stop him. Even though Reva didn't hang out with the dating kids, and she didn't go down on boys and she was actually kind of a total dork in some respects, Luke might just like her. Stranger things had been known to happen.

She checked her watch and quickened her pace. She didn't want to arrive at the Imagine mosaic ahead of Luke, but she didn't want him to wait too long, either. She always thought girls who deliberately made guys wait for them were bitchy.

She hit Central Park West at exactly one o'clock. Perfect timing, she thought, slowing her stride down a little. She didn't want him to think she'd raced to reach his side, either.

The crowd in Strawberry Fields was small, nothing like

the mobs that filled the plaza by the Band Shell to listen to Darryl J, but that made sense because there was nothing to do except stare at the Imagine mosaic and feel sad and maybe leave a candle or a dead flower or something. Reva had no difficulty spotting Luke, because he was tall and had long floppy black hair. She was glad she hadn't arrived too early.

Drawing nearer, she realized he wasn't alone. Katie and Matt Staver were with him, and—oh, shit—Micah Schlutt.

The Staver twins were okay. Reva had never heard them make belching noises or anything. But Micah? Yuck. And how had this turned from Reva taking Luke to hear Darryl J into a fricking group activity?

Disappointment settled like a cold, wet towel on her shoulders. She ducked behind a tree for a minute and took a deep breath. She'd *known* this wasn't a date. She'd known it all along. But maybe she'd hoped, just a little bit, that it would be a sort of date because she would be graduating from the lower school in a matter of months and she'd never gone with a boy and Luke was tall and quiet and kind of nice.

And he hung out with Micah Schlutt, she reminded herself.

Her eyes got a little misty, and she batted them quickly. Tears would not do, especially when she was wearing mascara. She didn't want to wind up with black *schmutz* all over her eyes.

Okay. She was going to be okay. This had never been about Luke, anyhow. It was about Darryl J, the guy she really loved. Today was about expanding Darryl J's audience, getting him on more people's radar, maybe scoring him a gig at the Hudson School, although he seemed way too cool to perform there. The moment Luke saw her and Darryl J together, he probably would figure out that he was way down on her list. Her heart belonged to Darryl J. And she'd get to see him today, and maybe he'd remember her name, even if she didn't put a dollar in his case. Which she couldn't, because she didn't have any singles. Just the ten-dollar bill her mother had given her last night.

Squaring her shoulders, she tossed her head to get her hair to lie smoothly, and stepped back onto the path that led to the mosaic. Luke spotted her first and waved. Then Katie jogged over to her. Reva liked Katie, even though she was too rich. She couldn't help it that her ancestors came over on the *Mayflower* or something. She and Matt spent summers on Nantucket, which seemed like such a cool thing, except it meant they never could hang out with their school friends during vacation. Katie once confessed to Reva that she wished she could stay home in the summer and just do New York things.

Matt Staver greeted her with a cheerful, "Hey, Reva." Micah didn't make any belching or farting noises. And Luke had an awfully nice smile, even though Reva hated him for having brought so many people with him.

"I can't wait to check out this musician," Katie babbled just as Luke said hi, so Reva almost didn't hear him. "Ashleigh Goldstein said he was really good."

"He is," Reva said, feeling superior because she was the only one in the group who knew just how good Darryl J was.

"We're all on the dance committee," Katie continued. "So we all have to hear him before we can even talk about hiring him. I'm not sure if the school will let us hire a singer. But they've got a budget for a deejay, so I don't see why we can't use that budget for a singer, instead. How much did they budget for the deejay?" she called to Matt as the group started down the asphalt sidewalk toward the Band Shell.

"A couple hundred bucks or something," Matt said. He and Micah flanked Luke, with Reva and Katie a few steps behind them. That wasn't right. Reva should be in front, since she was the one who knew Darryl J.

But she couldn't just elbow her way through the guys. Sooner or later they'd figure out that she should take the lead. In the meantime, she was just going to stay cool.

What a joke, the boys all together and the girls all together. And to think Reva had wasted a minute of brain time on the idea of going down on a boy. She would never do that. Never. Boys were so dumb, why would you let them put that part of them in your mouth?

"We just want to do something different," Katie continued. "Nine years we've all been in that school, most of us anyway. We started in kindergarten, and this is our last winter dance, and you know? It's like, let's do something different for once in our lives."

"Darryl J would be different," Reva confirmed.

"You ought to join the committee, Reva. You're such an expert about music. I hear Froiken finally gave you a solo." Katie wasn't in the chorus. "Like, hello? What was she waiting for? The next millennium?"

"There are lots of good singers in the chorus," Reva said modestly. "She gave other people solos."

"Everybody knows you've got a fabulous voice. It's about time, that's all I can say. Hey, guys, do you have any idea where we're going?" Katie called to the boys, who had stretched their lead.

They stopped and turned around. "The Band Shell, right?" Luke asked.

Reva wished she didn't have to answer. She was still pissed at him, even though she knew she shouldn't be. But she had to remain mature and above it all. "That's right," she said.

He smiled again. She decided she hated his smile.

The usual assortment of kite-flying dweebs and Frisbee

throwers covered the Sheep Meadow. In another week or
two, it would be too cold to hang out at the park. People
would bundle up and use the paths only to get from one
place to another. Reva wished Kim could be with her, enjoying what might turn out to be the last really nice park day
of the year.

As they approached the mall leading to the Band Shell,
she caught an aromatic whiff from a vendor's cart, hot pretzels and roasting chestnuts. She was too irked to have an appetite, and no one else was stopping to buy food. She
wondered if Luke had intended to treat her to something,
then stifled a sarcastic laugh. Of course he hadn't. He'd
brought the whole damn dance committee today. You didn't
buy a girl a snack while a committee was watching you.

Beyond the vendor, Reva spotted the guy who juggled
teddy bears. A few feet south of him was a guy in an Uncle
Sam outfit doing an acrobatic dance on in-line skates. South
of him was that dumb-ass mime, still trapped in his invisible box. Maybe it was sealed with invisible duct tape, Reva
thought with a smile. Maybe it was actually an invisible
prison cell. Maybe the mime was sentenced to invisible life.

Music drifted toward them from farther down the path,
but Reva didn't recognize it. She heard two women singing
in close harmony, accompanied by a guitar and a country
fiddle. They sounded good, but they weren't Darryl J.

Behind them loomed the Band Shell, the huge, arched
concrete stage. People stood around the singing women,
gnawing on hot salted pretzels and nodding in time to the
song. Reva edged past the crowd, then sprinted ahead of
Luke and the other guys, searching the plaza.

He wasn't there. Not in his usual spot. Not in any spot.
Darryl J wasn't there.

Shit. Luke was going to think she was a real loser now.
Maybe he'd think she had totally invented Darryl J—al-

though he'd heard about Darryl J from Ashleigh, so inventing Darryl J would have involved some ridiculous scheming and planning. And Reva had far more important things to do with her life than to pretend a nonexistent singer existed.

"Where is he?" Luke asked.

She surveyed the audience pit in front of the Band Shell, the grass and trees beyond, the path winding farther south. "I don't know," she said, her voice wavering. Shit, shit, shit. She couldn't cry. She wouldn't. Not here. She could fall apart when she got home, but right now she had to tough it out.

Luke patted her shoulder, making her flinch. "Maybe he's somewhere else."

"What do you mean?"

"Like, maybe he's playing down in Washington Square, or in a subway station or something. Does he only play in Central Park?"

"I don't know," she said, hearing that quiver in her voice again and hating it. "I've seen him here a bunch of times."

"Well, if he's not here, he's not," Katie said sensibly.

"Why don't we go look for him?" Luke suggested.

"Now?" Reva peered up at him. He'd stopped patting her shoulder, thank God—she wasn't a baby who needed to be comforted—but he was still close to her. Close enough to see her eyelashes. Close enough to see her tears if she let herself cry—which she absolutely wouldn't.

"Why not?" he said. "We could go down to the Village. Maybe he's there."

Her mother would shit a brick if Reva went to the Village. But if she didn't go, she'd be the biggest loser at Hudson, if not in the entire city. She was already under a cloud of suspicion for having dragged all these people to the Band Shell—not that she'd chosen to include the Staver twins and

Micah—and Darryl wasn't there. She could just imagine the scene at Hudson on Monday, when Luke and the others related to everyone in school how they'd schlepped all the way to Central Park to see this fabulous singer Reva was so high on and he wasn't even there, and then she refused to go to Greenwich Village with them because she was afraid her mommy would shit a brick. Or if she phoned her mother on the cell phone to ask permission—they could make a big deal about that. "Reva Kimmelman can't even take a subway downtown without asking her mother's permission."

She was nearly fourteen, for God's sake, and she was with a bunch of friends, including three boys, including one boy who was as tall as a man, and it was the middle of a sunny afternoon. She'd been to Greenwich Village with her father and it was no big deal. Lots of college kids, some stoners, musicians…regular New Yorkers, just like in Central Park. Traveling downtown was no big deal. And Reva was *not* going to be a loser.

"Okay," she said. "Let's go."

Thirteen

Eric wanted to spend Saturday afternoon at the Museum of Natural History. "Okay," Ned said, "but you've got to bring along a friend." It was already mid-October. The kid should have connected with a few classmates by now. If he didn't get into the Hudson School, he would have to survive in the public school system, and he wouldn't survive if he didn't have friends. Ned had made a new friend last night, and while Eric was way too young to be developing friendships like the one Ned was embarking on with Libby, he needed some pals he could call on a Saturday and say, "Hey, wanna go to the Museum of Natural History with me?"

Eric accepted his father's edict without protest. After five minutes on the phone, he announced that Gilbert would be joining them.

"Gilbert? Isn't he the boy who pushes everyone?"

"Yeah, but he doesn't push me," Eric said.

Gilbert arrived at their apartment twenty minutes later. A scrawny boy with short hair, coloring that implied that an assortment of races had swum in his gene pool and trousers featuring more pockets than any human being could ever possibly require, he didn't appear hefty enough to push anyone. He had a friendly smile, and when he called Eric "Monty," he did so good-naturedly. And he called Ned "Mr. Donovan," which Ned took to mean that someone had taught him manners.

Before they left for the museum, Eric showed Gilbert his bedroom. "Wow, look at that!" Gilbert's voice drifted out to where Ned waited in the living room. "You sleep up there?"

"Yeah. It's a loft bed."

"And you can hang out underneath it? That's so cool."

"My dad built it," Eric boasted, making Ned's chest puff up a little. "He's a fixer upper. He fixes things up."

"That is so cool," Gilbert repeated. "You could hide stuff under there that you didn't want your dad to know about."

Ned's grin waned, and he made a mental note to peek behind Eric's desk and bookcase, which were wedged under the loft bed, to see what he might be hiding. Eric was probably too young to be interested in hiding anything really dangerous, but Ned could imagine uneaten food, broken toys and important notes from his teacher vanishing into the darker recesses of his bedroom.

"Let's go, guys," he hollered toward the door, deciding to get their outing under way before Gilbert gave Eric any more good ideas.

The museum was crowded, as it always was on Saturdays. Ned didn't mind, even though the throngs meant he had to remain extra vigilant not to lose track of the boys. He maintained a particularly close watch on Gilbert to make sure the boy didn't shove any of the other gazillion kids shrieking and giggling and racing around the exhibits, but Gilbert kept his hands to himself, usually tucking them into various trouser pockets. He and Eric insisted on visiting the Hall of Fossils, which was jam-packed and echoing with strident voices yakking about the dinosaurs, and then moved on to the Hall of Ocean Life, which was much less crowded. Gilbert darted from showcase to showcase, shouting, "Hey, Monty, check this out!" and, "Hey, Monty, you ever see a shell this big? Man, you hold that shell up to your ear, you don't just hear the ocean. You hear the New York Philharmonic!"

"And it's playing that thing they always play on the Fourth of July, with the cannons and the church bells," Eric elaborated.

"Yeah, and all the fireworks, too. You could get fireworks out of a shell like that."

All right. Eric had a friend.

In the relative quiet of the Hall of Ocean Life, Ned felt safe resetting his attention on the boys at seventy-five percent, which left him twenty-five percent to devote to his own interests. *Interest,* singular.

Libby Kimmelman.

You could get fireworks out of a woman like that, he thought with a private smile. They'd lit a few sparklers last night. He wouldn't mind igniting a Roman candle or two with her.

A school administrator. Well-groomed, mature, not terribly self-involved. Nothing flashy about her, although she'd look damn good in those boots she'd contemplated buying for her daughter.

The hell with her daughter. Ned wanted to see Libby wearing those boots—and nothing else.

All right, so her life wasn't exactly simple. Any woman

past the age of thirty whose life was simple wasn't fully engaged in the world. You reach a certain age, and of course there'll be a little wear and tear, a couple of scars, a few chapters of history. That was what made a person interesting.

Libby interested him, even more than her fireplace did.

"Dad, we're starving," Eric announced, planting himself in front of the bench where Ned sat, right across from a display charting the evolution of algae. Gilbert nodded in vigorous agreement.

"How about some seafood?" Ned joked, waving at the display.

The boys wrinkled their noses. "We were thinking of ice cream," Eric explained.

Ned stashed his thoughts of Libby in a safe nook of his mind and led the boys to the Big Dipper Café in the food court, where he treated them both to Stellar Sundaes and bought himself a lemonade. While they shoveled sticky spoonfuls of ice cream and toppings into their mouths, they evaluated their classmates, their ratings accompanied by assorted snickers and guffaws. This one always sounded as if she had the hiccups when she talked. That one was always trying to borrow stuff. A certain young fellow named Peter had a habit of eating his own boogers, which, Eric pointed out, was better than if he ate someone else's boogers. This observation prompted so much laughter that the boys had to put down their spoons, rock in their chairs and bump knuckles a few times.

Ned sipped his lemonade, grateful that he hadn't bought any food for himself. If he'd been hungry, the conversation would have made him lose his appetite.

Libby had raised a daughter. Did little girls discuss boogers?

He wondered about Libby's divorce. What idiot would

leave a woman like her—and their daughter? Ned had had his share of arguments with Deborah, but even when he'd been angry enough to want to throw things—he usually resorted to throwing his socks against a wall, which allowed him to let off steam without damaging anything—he couldn't imagine ever leaving her. Not if leaving her would have meant leaving Eric.

Booger jokes notwithstanding, the boys polished off their sundaes without any difficulty. They announced they wanted to do the lizard hall—reptiles and amphibians—and Ned downed the last of his lemonade and chased them out of the food court.

Museums were tiring, he realized an hour and a half later, after he and the boys had stormed through the lizard exhibit, the primates exhibit and the North American Birds Hall. Ten-year-old boys fueled on ice cream and enthusiasm were tiring, too.

"How about it, guys?" he said. His watch informed him it was a quarter to five. The museum would remain open for another hour, but he was too weary to stick around and help the janitors lock up. "I think we got our money's worth."

The boys insisted on visiting the gift shop, where they oohed and aahed over a variety of toys and Ned repeatedly said no. By five they were willing to let him tear them away from the shop. Outside, twilight lay golden over the Upper West Side. In another couple of weeks, with the end of daylight savings time, the city would be dark by this hour.

Ned and Eric walked Gilbert home, the boys frequently nudging each other and pointing out objects worthy of ridicule—"Get a load of that stupid baby stroller!" "That dog is *ugly!*" "This is the grossest garbage pail I've ever seen!"—and laughing uproariously. Ned felt a light pain tapping at his forehead from inside his head, but he knew it was nothing a couple of aspirin couldn't handle. A couple of aspirin and a phone call to Libby.

He just wanted to say hi to her, maybe tell her about the afternoon, maybe discuss a time he could get started on her fireplace. He wanted to hear her voice, hear her laugh, water the seeds of their friendship so it would grow. He didn't want to rush into anything with her.

Like hell. He'd be real happy to rush into sex with her.

But he was a responsible adult, and waiting would only make the sex better when it happened, if it happened. Last night's kiss gave him hope that sex with Libby was a matter of when, not if.

Gilbert lived in a boxy modern building near Lincoln Center. He and Eric said goodbye by bumping knuckles again, and then he vanished into the building. "Did you have fun?" Ned asked as he and Eric headed west toward their own building.

"Yeah. Those stuffed eagles were cool. The ice cream was good, too," Eric said.

"He seems like a nice kid," Ned commented, angling his head back toward the building where they'd left Gilbert.

"He's okay." Eric shrugged. "I think I'd make more friends at the Hudson School."

So much for that plan, Ned thought wistfully. The kid still had his heart set on Hudson.

Which meant the woman Ned had kissed last night, the woman he would be phoning in just a few minutes, the woman who had occupied every bit of brain power he didn't have to devote to Eric and Gilbert today, the woman he wanted to see naked except for a pair of colorful boots, held his son's happiness in her hands.

He led Eric into their brownstone, and they climbed the two flights to their floor. Eric bounded up the stairs ahead of Ned, manifesting far more energy than anyone should possess after a long afternoon at a museum. He reached their door while Ned was still trudging up the last few steps, and Ned tossed him the keys. Eric caught them and unlocked the door. "What's for dinner?" he asked.

Ned groaned. Takeout was for dinner, he decided. One of the wonders of New York City was that so many restaurants delivered. Chinese, Italian, Indian, Thai, Greek, deli, sushi, pizza, kosher pizza—a simple phone call could bring to his door more cuisines than existed in the entire state of Vermont. "We'll figure out dinner in a few minutes," he said, following Eric inside and locking up behind them. "I want to make a phone call first."

"Okay." Eric charged down the hall to his bedroom. Ned paused for a minute, contemplating what treasures the kid might have stashed under his loft bed, then shook off the thought and strode to the kitchen. He picked up the phone and punched in Libby's number.

She answered on the first ring, her voice sharp. "Hello?"

"Hey," he said. "It's Ned."

"Oh." She sounded disappointed.

He cleared his throat to buy a minute. Why would a call from him disappoint her? She'd been there last night, just like him. She'd kissed him every damn bit as much as he'd kissed her.

"I really can't talk," she added. "This is a bad time."

It was fast becoming a bad time for him, too. Dreaming about this call had sustained him throughout the long, exhausting afternoon. Had he been crazy to think she might be pleased to hear from him? He'd sure thought talking to her would make him happy, but happy was the last thing he was feeling right now.

He sank against the counter and rubbed the back of his neck, where the pain from his forehead had migrated. "What's wrong?"

"It's Reva. She's in a bathroom in Greenwich Village. At least, that's where she was when she phoned. Now she's turned the cell phone off and I have no idea where she is."

"A bathroom?" Did the girl phone her mother when she had to pee? Or was she kidnapped? He'd seen more than one movie in which a kidnap victim had insisted on using the bathroom, and then she'd left a message—lipstick on the mirror, a scribble on a square of toilet paper—alerting the world to her plight. In the age of cell phones, he supposed a phone call would work even better. "Is she okay?"

"Who the hell knows? She's with friends. She didn't have permission to go downtown, and I don't know where they are now, and I swear she'll be grounded for life the minute she walks through the door." Libby issued a mumble that might have contained a few curses, then said, "She hasn't walked through the door yet."

"If a lifetime grounding is waiting for her, she may be putting that off as long as she can," Ned pointed out.

Libby clearly didn't appreciate his wry humor. "I've got to leave the line open. Maybe I should call her father. He lives downtown."

"What's he going to do? Search bathrooms for her?"

"What is wrong with you?" Libby roared. "My daughter is in the Village somewhere with her damn cell phone turned off! Don't you get it?"

Actually, Ned didn't. He and Eric had gone to Greenwich Village a couple of times and it didn't strike him as a particularly hazardous place. "I'm sure she's fine," he said helpfully.

"You have no way of guaranteeing that. I've got to go."

"Call me when she gets home," he requested, partly because he'd like proof that his claim about her being fine was true, and partly because once Reva was home Libby's mood would improve and he'd be able to have a more rewarding conversation with her.

"Goodbye," Libby said abruptly. Hearing the phone click dead, he lowered the receiver and cut loose with a few pungent words.

What the hell was her problem? Reva was fine. She was an eighth-grader and she was with a group of friends in Greenwich Village. She would come home, Libby would chew her out, they'd scream at each other, and eventually the smoke would clear, the dust would settle and all those other postbattle clichés would kick in.

So why was Libby taking out her rage on him? Because he was a convenient target for her anger? Because he'd dared to call in the middle of her crisis? Or because maybe she didn't want his friendship after all?

I am a bitch, Libby thought, staring out the living-room window as if she could will Reva to materialize on the sidewalk below. Ned Donovan was the most exciting thing to happen to her since Reva learned how to say *Mama,* and Libby had just blown him off.

Screw it. He deserved to be blown off. Making jokes about Reva's disappearance? Teasing that she should ask Harry to search the bathrooms of Greenwich Village for her daughter? The asshole!

Just wait until his golden boy hit adolescence. Just wait until earnest Eric got whomped by a barrage of hormones and went on a tear. Ned wouldn't be making light of the situation then. He'd know just how devastating it felt to realize that your child was out there in the world, doing foolish things, and you couldn't protect her.

Not that Libby would wish this kind of distress on Ned. She wouldn't wish it on anyone.

How could Reva behave so recklessly? How could she go traipsing off to Greenwich Village without asking permission? She wasn't even with Kim. Of course, if she had been, Kim would have talked her out of traveling down there against her mother's wishes. Kim was a well-behaved child.

Reva most definitely was not.

She'd phoned ten minutes ago—nearly an hour after Libby had started checking her watch and feeling the first flutters of anxiety in her gut. Reva knew her mother expected her home from Central Park before daylight started to fade, but Libby had tried not to worry as the minutes ticked by. But by five, daylight was fading and Reva hadn't come home.

Libby had dialed the cell phone, but Reva didn't have it turned on. This had led to a frantic parade of worst-case scenarios in Libby's imagination: one of Reva's pals had brought along an illegal substance, and the kids were all shit-faced somewhere, oblivious to the time. Or Reva had gotten separated from the group, and she was lost, and she was too proud to phone her mother and ask for help. Or Reva had been kidnapped, and the kidnappers had tossed her cell phone into a Dumpster, and they were holding her somewhere in New Jersey and subjecting her to God knew what horror. Or Reva had gotten hit by a car and was lying unconscious in an emergency room, and her idiot friends—the not-Kim group—had freaked out and abandoned her there. Or they'd gotten hit by cars, too, and all of them were lying unconscious in an emergency room.

When the phone had rung, Libby's panic had formed such a dense knot in her throat that she hadn't been sure she'd be able to speak. But she'd answered, and when she'd heard her daughter's cheerful voice saying, "Hi, Mom, it's me," she'd wanted to use language she generally reserved for maniacal cab drivers, hypocritical politicians and Harry during the early years of her divorce.

However, she'd remained composed, figuring she could

spew her rage once Reva was safely home. "It's late," she'd said. "Where are you?"

"I'm in this bathroom in the Village," Reva said. "We're having a really good time. I'll be home later."

"What do you mean, *later?* When?"

"I don't know. Whenever?"

"I want you home now," Libby had demanded.

"Yeah, well, nobody else is ready to leave yet. I'll see you later. Bye!" A click as the phone went dead, and Libby had heard nothing from her since.

Ned had sure chosen the wrong time to call.

She felt her hair turning gray. Her scalp itched; her roots ached. Her daughter, Reva, her sweet, beautiful, smart, talented child, had turned into a monster. A demon. A teenager—and an AWOL one, at that.

Where the hell was she? A bathroom in the Village? What bathroom? In a restaurant? In an NYU building? In some fleabag apartment where a stranger was plying her with illegal substances?

The phone rang again. Libby flinched, then sprinted across the living room, through the dining room and into the kitchen, where she grabbed the receiver before the second ring. "Hello?"

"Libby? It's Gilda."

Shit. Just what Libby needed: her ex-mother-in-law. "Gilda, I can't talk right now. I—"

"What's all this about you dating an Irish person?"

"Gilda, I—"

"Vivienne called me after synagogue today. She said you told her you're dating an Irish person."

"I'm not dating him." Even if last night had been a date, he probably never wanted to see her again, after her brusqueness on the phone. She didn't know if she wanted to see him again, either, if he could mock her in the midst of this disaster.

"Not that I want to interfere," Gilda said, although Libby understood that interfering was exactly what Gilda wanted to do, "but it's easier when everyone is of the same faith. I know you don't go to shul that often. Let's face it, neither do I. Once a month, I try. It's good to go at least once a month, just to keep your hand in. You should go once a month, Libby. Vivienne will take you."

"I'm sure she will." What if Reva was attempting to phone her again? What if she'd moved from a bathroom to a bus kiosk? What if her friends were all planning to drag her off to Brooklyn, and she needed directions from Libby on how to get home? "Gilda, I can't talk now. I'm expecting an important call."

"You should get Call Waiting. Vivienne has Call Waiting. She says it's worth its weight in gold."

How much did Call Waiting weigh? Libby shook her head to rid herself of that inane thought. "I'll phone you tomorrow, Gilda, okay?"

"Okay. I want to hear all about this Irish person. Is he Catholic?"

"I have no idea."

"It's important. You should find out before this thing goes too far."

"All right. I'll find out." Libby would have promised to vet his baptism records if such a promise would get Gilda to hang up. "I'll talk to you later," she said before pressing the off button to disconnect the call.

I am a bitch, she thought.

She was still holding the cordless handset when the phone rang again. It vibrated against her palm and she flinched, then jammed her thumb against the connect button. "Hello?" *Please, let it be Reva,* she prayed—although God probably wasn't listening because she didn't go to shul once a month to keep her hand in.

"Libby?" A familiar man's voice, but not Ned's. As if he'd ever want to talk to her again, after she'd treated him so rudely.

"Harry?" she guessed.

Correctly, as it turned out. He sounded pissed off when he said, "Reva is here."

Libby's scalp relaxed and her hair felt dark brown again. Who cared if Harry was pissed off? He spent a significant portion of his life pissed off. Libby, on the other hand, was ecstatic. "She's there? At your apartment?"

"She showed up with a group of kids, Libby. What the hell is she doing here?"

Testing the limits. Spreading her wings. Being an obnoxious brat. "Perhaps you ought to ask her," Libby suggested.

"Bonnie and I have plans for tonight. I'm supposed to see Reva tomorrow. I always see her on Sundays. But suddenly, she shows up with four kids and says, 'We were in the neighborhood, sort of.' How can someone be in a neighborhood sort of?"

"Ask her," Libby said. As her anxiety drained away, it created a vacuum inside her, and given nature's abhorrence of a vacuum, rage was rushing in to fill the empty space. She took slow, deep breaths to keep her anger from erupting. Right now, all that mattered was getting Reva home. "Do you know who the other kids are?" she asked, as if Harry kept up with Reva's social circle. If Reva had introduced him to her friends, though, he might remember a name or two.

"No idea. There's another girl and three boys."

"Three boys?" Libby felt her hair turning gray again.

"They seem like nice kids. Clean-cut. No pierced noses. Listen, Libby, I don't want these kids here. Bonnie has tickets to a concert at the Japan Society for tonight," Harry said. "We're supposed to hear some woman play bass koto and shakuhachi."

Now, there was something Libby could be grateful for—
that she was not going to spend the evening listening to
someone play bass koto and shakuhachi. "If you don't want
them there, send them home."

"Reva asked me to drive them home. I can't fit them all
in my car. I've got only five seat belts."

"Then put them in a cab."

"I'm not going to pay their cab fare," Harry retorted. "I
don't even know who these kids are. And they wouldn't all
fit into one cab, either. Do they have enough money to pay
for their own cabs?"

"I have no idea." Let Harry be a father, Libby thought
churlishly. She'd spent so much time fretting over Reva
today; now it was Harry's turn to fret. "I don't want them
taking the subway at this hour," she added.

"It's not that late. If I send them off now—"

"Can they take a bus? There are fewer nutcases on the
bus."

"They're all gathered around the flat-screen TV. Bonnie?" he said away from the phone. "Hide the remote." Back
into the phone, he said, "Why did you let Reva travel down
here by herself? She isn't even fourteen yet."

"I didn't let her. She told me she was going to Central
Park," Libby informed him.

"Maybe you need to keep her on a shorter leash."

Oh, great. Harry was going to turn this into a criticism
of Libby's parenting skills. As if she'd done anything wrong,
other than to trust her daughter. As if *he* ever did anything
of significance when it came to raising Reva. He'd walked
out on them, hadn't he? He'd fled from fatherhood. Sure,
he saw Reva on Sundays—and he could dazzle her friends
with his fancy-schmancy flat-screen TV—but who the hell
was he to tell Libby how short a leash she should keep Reva
on? As if Reva were a poodle.

If he thought her parenting skills were lacking, would he demand custody? And if he did that, would he decide not to help her buy her apartment, because she wouldn't need such a big apartment if Reva weren't living with her? Was her entire life about to crumble because her daughter had pulled this meshuggeneh stunt?

"I don't want you to miss your koto and shackalacka concert, Harry—"

"Shakuhachi," he corrected her. "I'm not exactly sure what that is. Bonnie would know."

"I'm sure she would. Why don't you usher the kids to the nearest bus stop and stay with them until they board a bus uptown. I'll take it from there."

"The bus is a schleppy way to get home. They can catch the IRT. The one, two, three and nine all stop down here. They won't even have to change trains."

He wanted to send Reva into the subway after dark, and he thought Libby needed to put their daughter on a shorter leash?

But there were five kids, three of them boys. And although it was dark, it wasn't that late yet. People would be heading out for dinner now, or uptown for bass koto concerts. The sane-to-crazy ratio of subway passengers wouldn't be that awful.

"All right," she snapped. "Just send them home."

She hung up the phone and groaned. She'd managed to be nasty to Harry, Gilda and Ned, all within fifteen minutes. Once Reva got home, Libby was sure she'd be nasty to her, too. She was a lousy mother, an impatient daughter-in-law, a shrewish ex-wife…and to Ned she was what? A former friend? A reject sweetheart?

A bitch.

As long as Reva got home safely, Libby swore to herself that she didn't care.

Fourteen

Reva had more important things on her mind than whether her mother was upset. Like, where was Darryl J?

Okay, so autumn was beginning to grow cold. Maybe he'd found a place to perform indoors so his fingers wouldn't freeze. Or maybe he'd left the city and headed south. Maybe he was right this minute standing on a street corner in Washington, D.C. because it was ten degrees warmer down there, and the president might be strolling down Pennsylvania Avenue, and he'd stop all the secret service guys and say, "Listen to that dude! Isn't he incredible?" And Darryl J would mention to the president that while it was warmer in D.C., he sure did miss Reva, his biggest fan in New York City.

Maybe Dee-Dee would hear him, too—except she rarely went into the city, even though Bethesda was about as close as you could get to Washington without being *in* Washington. Dee-Dee wouldn't like Darryl J's music much, anyway. She listened to Tony Bennett and that kind of thing.

Maybe Darryl J had gone even farther south. Maybe he was hanging out in the Florida Keys with that guy who sang about margaritas.

Or—it pained Reva to consider this possibility—maybe Darryl J had quit. Maybe he'd given up. Maybe he couldn't survive on the spare change folks tossed into his guitar case, and his parents said, "Come on home, Darryl J, go back to school, get a degree. Become an accountant."

God. Darryl J as an *accountant.* The mere idea nauseated her.

Wherever he was, Reva, Luke, the Stavers and Micah hadn't found him. They'd taken the IND downtown, disembarking at the Times Square station and again at 34th Street and wandering around the platforms to see if he might be playing there. The last station they'd checked was West 4th Street, and then they'd climbed back into the afternoon sunshine. Reva was kind of glad they didn't find him in a subway station, because the platforms were gloomy and smelled like petroleum. She wasn't sure why, since the trains were powered by electricity, but the atmosphere in subway stations seemed oily to her.

She'd actually had a pretty good time in the Village, even though Luke had hardly paid attention to her. Katie Staver and Reva had found plenty enough to talk about, so they'd ignored the guys and the guys had ignored them. Boys their own age were such dorks.

That was just one of the many reasons Reva liked Darryl J: he was way too mature to be a dork. He would never laugh through his nose so hard he wound up snorting like a pig the way Micah did. He would never shout, "Lance Armstrong! Lance Armstrong!" at a bike courier pedaling down the street the way Matt did. He would never go nuts over some weird hubcaps the way Luke did.

Reva supposed even guys in their twenties might go nuts over weird hubcaps, but only if they'd stopped maturing somewhere around their fourteenth birthdays.

"I think Luke likes you," Katie had confided to Reva at one point.

"Who cares?" Reva had said with a shrug. Not that she wasn't flattered—assuming Katie was right about Luke, which was highly doubtful, given how little he acknowledged Reva's existence—but he'd continued to talk about those stupid hubcaps three blocks after they'd passed them. Who needed that?

Well, she was never going to see Luke Rodelle again outside of school, because she was never going to see *anyone* again. The way her mother was acting, Reva would be lucky if she was allowed to walk around the block to buy a bottle of milk before she died. Everyone—even Bony—was shitting bricks just because Reva had gone to the Village. God, you'd think she'd killed someone or something.

Her mother kept walking in circles—through the living room to the den, out to the hall and into the entry and then into the living room again. Occasionally, she'd pace a minicircle without leaving the living room. Just watching her walking around and around made Reva dizzy.

Reva sat on the sofa with her feet tucked under her and her arms folded. She felt no obligation to look sorry or rueful. Even if she apologized, her mother wasn't going to forgive her, so why knock herself out pretending she regretted what she'd done?

"I can't believe you'd do something like this," her mother said for about the hundredth time since Reva had gotten home. She was saying it more softly now, at least. The first few times, she'd screamed it—well, as close to screaming as possible without disturbing the neighbors. Early in the discussion—which had really been more of a monologue because her mother had done all the talking—Reva could practically see fiery little exclamation points shooting out of her mouth. But her mom was finally calming down, pacing more slowly, speaking with commas instead of exclamation points.

"You act like the Village is on the other side of the world," Reva grumbled. "It's just a few subway stations away."

"The problem isn't the Village," her mother explained. "The problem is that you went there without telling me, without asking permission—"

"I'm supposed to stop everything, in front of everyone, and call you and ask for permission?"

"Yes."

"No one else had to call their mothers."

"Maybe because their mothers don't care where they are. *I* care."

Right. Her mother was just so wonderful because she expected Reva to check in with her every hour on the hour. Reva ought to nominate her for the Nobel Prize in Motherhood.

"I didn't know who you were with—"

"I *told* you! Katie Staver and her brother Matt, and Micah Schlutt and Luke Rodelle."

"Yes, you told me now. You didn't tell me when you left the house this morning. Is that mascara on your eyelashes?" Her mother leaned toward her and squinted.

"No," Reva lied. She was already screwed. One little fib wouldn't blacken her soul any further at this point. "Anyway, you can look up Luke and Micah and the Stavers at work on Monday. They're all Hudson students. They'd meet your seal of approval."

Her mother must have heard her sarcastic undertone. She pursed her lips and paced another circuit. "What were you doing in the Village, anyway?"

"Nothing."

Unlike the lie about the mascara, her mother wasn't going to swallow this one. She glowered at Reva. "You traveled all the way downtown to do *nothing?*"

Too many lies was not a good strategy. One or two Reva could pull off, but pile on a bunch and her mother might suspect everything she said, even the truthful stuff. She decided to try a little sincerity. "We were searching for this guy who sings and plays the guitar," she said, opening her eyes wide in the hope that she'd seem even more honest. At the moment, she *was* being honest.

"A musician?" That brought her mother to a dead halt.

"Yeah. He always sings in Central Park, so we went over there to hear him, but he was gone."

"What do you mean, gone?"

"Well, he wasn't in the park today. So we thought maybe he'd set up downtown. Sometimes musicians set up in Washington Square, so we decided to look for him there."

"I see." Her mother dropped onto one of the chairs and studied Reva. Reva sensed no exclamation points spewing from her, not even any serious heat. Either she'd exhausted herself by marching laps around the apartment or else the whole idea of Reva searching for a musician appealed to her. "What kind of music does he play?"

"Guitar, and he sings. He writes his own songs, too. He's real good."

"And you wanted to see him because…?"

"Luke and the Stavers are on the winter dance committee, and they thought instead of a deejay we should have a live musician. And they thought maybe a street musician would be fun. And affordable," Reva added.

"A street musician at a Hudson School dance?"

"Why not? Tracy Chapman started out as a street musician," Reva reminded her.

"I doubt Tracy Chapman performed at private-school functions." She wiggled her fingers a bit, a gesture not too far from wringing her hands. "Does this fellow play dance music?"

As if people went to dances to dance. But the mood in the living room had definitely improved; her mother hadn't yelled "I can't believe you did this!" in the past ten minutes. "We were going to ask him," Reva said. "And Katie wants me to be on the dance committee, too."

She'd hoped her mother would be impressed that people wanted her on their committees. But unfortunately, her mother stayed on topic. "So you went to the Village in search of this street musician."

"It was Luke's idea to go there. He goes down to the Village all the time to hear musicians." *His mother treats him like a grown-up,* she wanted to add, although he sure had seemed pretty immature when it came to those stupid hubcaps.

She braced herself for her mother's expected comment—something along the lines of how she didn't care where other kids were allowed to go and how if other kids were allowed to jump off the Empire State Building, did Reva think her mother should give her permission to jump off the Empire State Building, too? But her mother surprised her by asking, "So…what kind of music does this person play?"

"Good music. Kind of like Paul Simon when he's doing ethnic stuff, like 'Me and Julio' or that *Rhythm of the Saints* album." Demonstrating knowledge of and respect for her mother's musical tastes ought to earn her a few points. And she desperately needed some points.

Her mother rose, wandered in another uneven circle around the living room that ended in front of the fireplace, stared at it for a long minute and then turned back to Reva. "If this musician—what's his name?"

"Darryl J."

"Darryl J? Is Jay his last name?"

"No, it's just a letter. Like an initial or something."

"Darryl J," her mother said awkwardly, as if trying to wrap her tongue around some long, foreign-sounding word. "Well, if you couldn't find him, I don't suppose he's going to be able to play at your school dance."

"We aren't done looking for him yet," Reva said, then bit her lip and wondered if her mother would say something like, *You bet you're done looking for him, young lady. You're banned from leaving the apartment ever again, except for school.*

"What are you planning to do? Comb all five boroughs in search of him? Do you realize how impossible that would be?"

"We could still look a little more. He might be somewhere."

"Sure. And while you're at it, maybe you can find Jimmy Hoffa," her mother muttered. Reva didn't know who Jimmy Hoffa was, but she didn't care enough to ask. "None of this would be a big deal if you'd had the courtesy to phone me first. Why bother to take the cell phone if you're just going to turn the damn thing off?"

Reva had taken it because her mother had forced her to, but she didn't mention that. Nor did she mention the humiliation of having to call and check in with your mother in front of a group of friends. She doubted her mom would understand that being grounded for the rest of the century was preferable to acting like a baby in front of witnesses.

"Didn't it occur to you that I'd be frightened, not knowing where you were? Didn't it occur to you that I have a right to know where you're going, and with whom?"

That was exactly it, of course. Reva *didn't* think her mother had that right. But to say so would make about as much sense as attempting to stop a speeding cab by stepping out into the middle of the street and holding your hand up. Only a suicidal idiot would try such a thing.

"I'm trying to hold everything together," her mother continued, her voice shivery with tension. "I've got Hudson School applications out the wazoo, I've got interviews with applicants lined up all next week and I have to figure out a way to buy this apartment so we can continue to live here. The last thing I need is to be worrying about my daughter because she's traipsing around the city with her cell phone off."

You're also seeing some guy who wants to overhaul our fireplace, Reva added silently. That might have something to do with her mother's hysterical state. Whatever had happened with Mr. Donovan last night was unquestionably a big deal. The woman didn't date. Maybe the men she met were hung up on hubcaps, too. Maybe they never grew up. This new guy's fixation with the fireplace might be…what was the word? *Sublimation.* In English class, Mr. Mullin talked about how Laura in *The Glass Menagerie* sublimated her desire for a boyfriend by obsessing about her glass unicorn. Reva had considered that a stupid play because she thought guys were much more likely than girls to have desires they needed to sublimate. Most girls—even if they were crippled like Laura—would just as soon skip the crystal tchotchkes and go to a movie with their friends, preferably a movie starring someone really cute. Someone like Darryl J, for instance.

Did Mr. Donovan sublimate something by obsessing about fireplaces? Did he want to renovate her mother's fireplace because he really wanted to take her mother to bed? Gross.

"Are you hungry?" her mother asked.

She wasn't. They'd eaten pizza in the Village, and of

course Luke hadn't paid for her slice, which proved to Reva that he didn't really like her, regardless of what Katie thought. But things might go smoother with her mother if she agreed to eat something. "Sure," she said. Maybe once they were eating, the subject of Reva's afternoon in Greenwich Village would get forgotten. Her mother still hadn't told her what her punishment would be, probably because she hadn't yet decided on an appropriate sentence. But even without much appetite, Reva would rather eat than find out she was grounded until her fiftieth birthday.

"We'll have to eat in the kitchen," her mother remarked. "The dining-room table is covered with applications."

Like Reva was blind or something. She'd have to be not to notice the mess on the dining-room table. "The kitchen is fine," she said, hoping her mother would make something light—a salad or scrambled eggs. Reva would force herself to eat a bit, she'd be polite, and as soon as she was done she'd shut herself up in her room, phone Kim and discuss the situation.

Situations, plural. She needed to tell Kim about Luke, her mother's fireplace guy and, most important, the disappearance of Darryl J.

Macie Colwyn kept fluttering like a red cape in front of Ned. Not that he was a bull, but she certainly seemed to be inviting him to charge at her.

Ned was not in the mood. He was enraged at the world, most especially that part of the world occupied by Libby Kimmelman, who had not phoned him since their terse, snarly conversation Saturday evening. What had he done to deserve her wrath?

All right, so *wrath* might be an overstatement. She'd snipped and snapped at him, clarified that her daughter's well-being was more important than he was—a legitimate claim; he wouldn't quarrel with that—and implied that she would let him know once Reva was home, safe and sound.

Now it was Monday, and he still hadn't heard from her.

He assumed Reva had made it home. If she hadn't, the newspapers would have been full of stories about a missing young teenager from the Upper West Side. Even in New York City, Reva's disappearance would have made headlines.

So Reva had returned home and Libby hadn't called. Add it up and the sum didn't appeal to Ned.

Let her hate him. Let her cut him out of her life. He could survive that. But whatever she had a bug up her ass about, if she let it influence her decision on Eric's admission to the Hudson School, he would never forgive her.

"What I was thinking," Macie said, her hair featuring some new coppery highlights that clashed with the purple ones, "is pillars in the bathroom."

"The bathroom?" Ned nearly dropped the tape measure he'd been using to block in the locations for the major appliances in what would eventually be her kitchen. "You want columns in the bathroom?"

"Just the master bath," she clarified.

"Why?"

"It'll give the room a Roman-orgy feel. What do you think?"

One thing he thought was that a bathroom didn't strike him as a particularly promising location for an orgy. The master bath in this apartment would be spacious by Manhattan standards, but it certainly wouldn't be big enough to hold an orgy in. All those hard surfaces wouldn't be too comfortable, either.

"We've already talked about the tub design," Macie continued. "Marble, sunken, dramatic. If you framed the tub with two pillars—I envision the Corinthian kind, just like in the living room—it would be terribly sensuous."

Emphasis on *terrible,* Ned concluded grimly. He inched backward because Macie was standing too close to him, her pointy high-heel boots nearly touching his steel-toed work shoes and her perfume, something heavy and musky, clogging his nostrils. He didn't like standing so close to a client, especially while discussing terribly sensuous tubs.

"You'd lose valuable floor space," he argued.

"How valuable is floor space in a bathroom?"

He sighed. "Then there's the cost…."

"Money is no object," she told him. "You're a flexible man, Ned. You can be flexible about this."

Ned's flexibility had limits. Perhaps if Macie had hit him up with this orgy brainstorm when he'd been in better spirits—another outing with Libby on his agenda, maybe a date that would entail some time alone in a more private place than the alcove of a shoe store on Broadway—he'd say what the hell and order some Corinthian columns for Macie's master bath. But he wasn't in good spirits. "What does your husband think?" he asked.

"About the bathroom? He doesn't care, as long as it's got a toilet." Macie dismissed Ned's concern with a wave of her hand. Mitch had mentioned that Colwyn was significantly older than his punk-artist wife. The poor guy might have a coronary if he wandered into the master bath and found himself in the midst of a Roman orgy. Of course, more than columns were required to make an orgy, but an old man with a frisky wife and a sunken marble tub… Ned didn't want the man's death on his head.

"I don't think the columns would work in the bathroom," he said, because he wasn't in the mood to accommodate anyone right now, not even the client.

"In the bedroom, too," Macie said, as if he hadn't even spoken. "A couple of columns sort of framing the bed. That entire part of the loft could have a sybaritic feel."

Great. She wanted sybaritic. He wanted some socks to throw against a wall. "Macie, let me be frank with you," he said.

"I wish you would," she purred, shifting closer to him again. He eyed her boots with some concern. The toes were so pointed he wondered if they could puncture the leather covering his insteps.

"Sybaritic is the sort of thing you count on a decorator for. You can go with big pillows, animal skin prints, whatever. I'm focused on the structure. Where the rooms go, how they make sense, how they'll contribute to comfortable living. Anything else, you should work with an interior designer."

"But you do the pillars, don't you?" She peered up at him and batted her eyelashes. Given the unnatural smoothness and immobility of her forehead, he figured she must have undergone more than a few Botox injections between her eyebrows in the not too distant past. She was lucky she could still blink.

"They're columns," he emphasized, just to be contrary. Pillars, columns—what they really were was pretentious. "Right now, let us finish framing the rooms. We can deal with the cosmetics later."

"I thought it would be easier if you ordered the pillars—I mean columns—in bulk."

Oh, sure. Column manufacturers loved bulk orders.

Fortunately, he didn't have to respond, because the cell phone hooked onto his belt started chirping. It belonged to Mitch, or more accurately to the company. Mitch liked to be able to contact his crews, so he supplied the foreman of each crew with a cell phone. One of these days, Ned supposed he'd have to subscribe to his own personal cell-phone service. Sooner or later, Eric would deem himself old enough to roam the city with his friends, and Ned wouldn't want to go nuts worrying about him the way Libby worried about Reva.

"Excuse me," he said to Macie, grateful for the excuse to turn away from her. He unclipped the phone, flipped it open and pressed the button. "Ned Donovan here."

"Ned?" Mitch's secretary said. "You just got a call here at the office from a woman named Libby…Kibble, I think. She said she's at work and you could call her there."

Libby Kibble. Ned permitted himself a grin. "Did she say what it's about?"

"No, just that you can call her at work. Do you need the number?"

Ned wasn't in any rush to return her call, but he balanced his clipboard against one of the studs in a wall that wasn't yet finished and jotted down the number the secretary provided. After thanking her, he flipped the phone shut.

He stared at the number for a minute, then tucked the clipboard under his arm and yanked the tab on the tape measure. If he looked busy enough, maybe Macie would leave him alone. Let her go bug one of the other guys. They had the boom box tuned to a Latino station and they were happily chatting about an acquaintance who did a brisk business bootlegging cigarettes from Virginia, where the retail price of a pack was about two bucks less than in New York. Maybe they'd like to discuss whether someone wearing shoes as pointy as Macie's would be able to stub out a cigarette on the ground.

The Sub-Zero would go here, he thought, measuring the dimensions carefully and marking them on the floor. The dishwasher had to go right next to the sink to simplify the plumbing. Screw Libby Kibble. He'd phone her when he felt like it, and not a minute sooner.

Unless, of course, her call had something to do with Eric's application.

Shit.

He snapped the tape measure shut though he remained kneeling on the floor, staring at the dusty boards but seeing too many other things: boots—not Macie's but wild, colorful patchwork cowboy boots. Eyes, large and dark and framed with a few lovely, human lines. Hair that was silky and wavy and natural. A mouth…

Shit.

If the reason she'd called him was to discuss Eric, when there was so much else they should be talking about, so much else they should be aiming for, he'd hate her. And if the reason she'd called him was to discuss all those things they should be talking about, well, he'd hate her for having not called him sooner.

Either way, he wanted to throw socks.

He'd call her back later. Much later. Maybe.

Fifteen

By the time Libby phoned Ned's work number, she'd already spent two hours interviewing prospective Hudson kindergarteners. She'd listened to five-year-old Anna Weinblatt recite a garbled version of the Gettysburg Address, after which she'd admitted that she had no idea what Gettysburg was but its address was too long to fit on an envelope. Libby had also discussed the environment with five-year-old Anna Pelletier, who'd explained that global warming was something like what happened to Hot Pockets in the microwave. And she'd witnessed five-year-old Anna Rossini's rendition of a song from *Annie*—her favorite musical, because it almost had the same name as her. Anna Rossini had an unfortunate speech impediment, and the song had come out as "It's a hard-wuck wife," but Libby had somehow managed to keep a straight face throughout the entire performance.

She'd also interviewed five-year-old Justin Belkow, who

was oddly fixated on rye bread. "I like the kind with seeds in it," he'd told her. "Those seeds, you know what I mean?"

"Caraway seeds," she'd said helpfully.

"Yeah. They look like dirty fingernails."

Libby had decided she would never again eat seeded rye.

As she emerged from the playroom with Justin, Tara caught her eye. "Your husband phoned while you were doing the interview," she said.

"Harry?"

"Yeah. He's at his office and he wants you to call him ASAP."

I'd rather call him a-s-s, Libby retorted silently, annoyed that he would identify himself as her husband. She shut herself in her office and dialed his work number. Her gaze strayed to her desk calendar. Three more interviews with prospective students today, and one meeting with a mother. She'd inked a star next to the mother's name, which meant either the mother was a Hudson alumna or she'd promised a huge donation to the capital fund. Neither detail would guarantee her kid a place at the school, but if Libby had that kind of information about the parent ahead of time, it helped. Forewarned was forearmed.

Harry's secretary answered and Libby gave her name. She was put on hold.

Swell. She had a crammed schedule, she was still recovering from Reva's delinquent behavior on Saturday, she was still recovering from whatever had happened between her and Ned Donovan on Friday, and Harry put her on hold. The bastard.

"Libby." He broke the silence on the line.

"I'm very busy, so—"

"I just had an appointment cancel on me. I have two hours open this afternoon. Meet me at the bank and you can get your mortgage application started."

The calendar before her went blank. Or maybe it was her

mind that went blank. What exactly had Harry said? "My mortgage application?"

"For the apartment."

"Are you serious?"

"When am I not serious?"

She realized the answer was never. "Why? I mean, what made you decide—"

"I told you, a client canceled on me." He said nothing for a moment, then, "Reva needs stability in her life. After the *mishegas* she pulled this weekend, she needs parameters. She needs roots. We can't have her roving around the city not knowing where her home is."

"Okay." Libby wasn't sure a connection existed between their daughter's unplanned jaunt to Greenwich Village and her need to continue living in the same apartment, but she wasn't going to argue with Harry. "When do you want me to meet you at the bank?"

"I'll be there at two-thirty. Set it up." With that, he disconnected the call. Typical Harry: even when he was doing something nice, he had to be unpleasant about it.

The calendar came into focus again, with all her appointments written on the page. Libby buzzed Tara and asked her to rearrange the schedule. Tom Hedrick, the math specialist who was one of this year's faculty members on the admissions committee, could interview the children. The wealthy-alumna mother could be rescheduled. Libby was going to buy her apartment.

Oy. The thought of signing that mortgage and committing herself to a loan big enough to support a rural village in China for several years scared the hell out of her. Losing her home scared her even more. So she'd commit herself to a crushing debt for the next fifteen years. So what? That was better than moving to Jersey.

She phoned the bank, begged and pleaded, and won a

place on a mortgage officer's schedule for two-thirty. Hanging up, she glanced at her watch. A few minutes past one. She'd have to stop off at home to get her paperwork—the sales contract she'd been sent by the management company, with its nonnegotiable insider price, and all her documents attesting to her wealth, which was skimpy enough that the word *wealth* really didn't apply. If she left at one-thirty, she'd make it to the bank in time.

She looked at her watch again. She had to tell someone what she was about to do.

The first person she thought of was Ned.

She should have phoned him yesterday. Or Saturday evening, once Reva was safely home. He'd asked her to call him, but she'd been too upset with Reva on Saturday and too upset with herself on Sunday. What kind of mother was she? How could she have raised a daughter who would do such a thing? Reva's misbehavior was all Libby's fault because she was the custodial parent. Okay, maybe Harry deserved a tiny sliver of blame for having walked out on his wife and daughter, but Libby had obviously failed Reva far more profoundly.

Ned was a single parent, and his son was charming—bright, funny, poised and polite. Unlike Reva, who used to be all those things but had turned like a container of milk two weeks after its sell-by date. How could Libby telephone a perfect father like Ned and tell him what a loser she was?

Yet now, when she was about to become a proud but deeply indebted homeowner, the first person she wished to tell was Ned. Not Vivienne, not Gilda and Irwin, not even Reva, whose hopes Libby preferred not to raise until the mortgage application was approved and the sale went through, and who was still on Libby's shit list, anyway. She wanted to call Ned.

And say what? "I am unworthy, but I wanted to share my

happiness with you." No, because the mortgage application might fall through. "I am unworthy, but I wanted to share my *potential* happiness with you." "I am a lousy mother and a lousy friend, and I'm still not sure if Friday night was a date, but I wanted you to know that the fireplace can be renovated without the management company being dragged into the process."

That was it: she'd tell him he could work on her fireplace. With her insecurities foaming all over the surface of her ego, she didn't think she could discuss anything else with him. But he dreamed of giving her fireplace the chance to be all it could be, so she'd tell him he now had clearance to actualize her hearth.

His work number was filed with Eric's application. The woman who answered told her Ned was at a job site and would have to call her back, and she'd promised to inform him of Libby's call. Libby stared at her phone for a few minutes, hoping he would call back immediately, but it didn't ring. Sighing, she packed her briefcase, donned her blazer and headed for the apartment that she could once again think of as her home.

She stored her papers regarding the apartment in a drawer of her dresser. Her apartment folder contained letters from the management company, the sales offer, the sheets of scrap paper on which she'd calculated what she could afford each month in mortgage, taxes and common fees, the amount she could use as a down payment…God, those numbers seemed paltry, she thought as she thumbed through the folder to make sure no documents were missing. If Harry truly wished to increase the stability in Reva's life, maybe he could contribute more than a quarter of a million dollars toward the down payment. A third of a million dollars would make Reva more stable, wouldn't it?

The local bank where Libby had her savings and checking accounts offered competitive mortgage rates. She figured they would be more likely to approve her because she'd been banking there for fourteen years. Of course, in those fourteen years, the bank had undoubtedly familiarized itself with her finances, which might work against her.

But Harry would be there. They couldn't possibly say no to Harry. He was a corporate attorney with a very big income.

She spotted him standing inside the glass-enclosed ATM lobby as she approached the bank's Broadway entrance. If he'd been waiting a long time, he might be in a cranky mood. Well, screw it. He had left her on hold, after all. He could wait.

Weren't banks supposed to shout money? Libby's local branch bank shouted airline terminal, and when she joined Harry inside the entry she half expected to hear a disembodied voice reminding her not to leave her bags unattended. The floor was linoleum, the walls pale and unadorned, the chairs molded plastic, the lighting bright and bluish. As Harry surveyed the bank, his expression grew pinched. He was probably used to banks with plush carpeting, paneled walls and Winslow Homer prints in gilt frames. The banks where he did his business likely resembled Libby's office at Hudson. A venerable private school, a venerable financial institution—all that class required high-quality decor.

"Thank you," she said effusively as they left the ATM lobby for the main room. "I really appreciate this."

Harry nodded, and Libby noticed a slight softness underlining his chin. He was aging. In the not too distant future he'd have jowls, just like his father. The possibility made her smile.

"We've got to keep a closer eye on Reva," he said.

Libby's smile faded. By "we" she knew he meant *she* had to keep a closer eye on Reva. Fine. If he'd help her buy the apartment, she'd put Reva on a leash, or maybe get her one of those electronic ankle bracelets that could track her movements. Was there some sort of satellite-controlled global positioning system parents could hook their teenage children up to?

If there was, Harry would have to pay for it. Once Libby was done signing all the papers the bank would require of her, she wouldn't be able to afford a pen to write "Reva, call home" on a Post-it.

The mortgage officer was a thin man named Sharma, with an Indian accent and tawny cheeks covered in peach fuzz. The Hudson lower school matriculated students who looked older than him. Libby didn't like having to beg for money from someone at least ten years her junior, but she needed what he had.

Sharma seemed perplexed that a divorced couple was buying a single unit. "You are not going to live there together?"

"No," Harry and Libby said in unison, perhaps a bit too emphatically.

"You are going to buy this apartment together, but not live there together?"

"She's buying it," Harry said. "I'm just helping." Libby was both touched by his generosity in presenting her as the apartment's future owner, and irked by his insinuation that she couldn't buy it without his help. Which she couldn't, but still.

Now was not the time for pride. Stoically, she provided Sharma with all the numbers requested: her monthly gross income, her monthly net income, her savings, the current sum in her pension fund, photocopies of her last three income-tax returns, projections of future earnings, Harry's child-support payments, any possible inheritances on the horizon—gee, maybe her parents would do her a favor and die soon—and on and on.

She signed papers. Harry cosigned everything she signed. If she allowed herself, she would fret about what, besides her entire financial future, she was signing away. Her independence? Her autonomy? Her right to call herself a self-supporting single woman?

"Face it, Libby—you need someone to cosign," Harry muttered to her while Sharma was shuffling and sorting his countless multicolored forms. "If I don't cosign, they'll turn you down."

Once again, Libby was irritated by Harry's ability to give with one hand while taking with another. He was probably right that the bank would reject her application without his signature on it, so she really ought to be grateful. But she hated having to depend on him. She'd never shared his ambition about earning big bucks in a Wall Street firm, and now he was making her feel like a hypocrite for tapping into those big bucks of his.

Practicality trumped ego, however. She'd let him cosign, she'd accept his down payment—hell, she'd give him a key to the apartment if he'd enable her to purchase it.

Ninety-four minutes after they'd entered Sharma's office, Libby found herself standing outside in the fading sunlight with Harry. Sharma had said the application process would take roughly a month, and an appraiser would contact her for an appointment to visit the apartment, even though he acknowledged that the insider price was obviously below market value. "With Manhattan real estate," he'd said in his crisp accent, "you can never be too careful."

Of course you could be too careful, Libby believed. If she'd been too careful, she would have moved out of the city long ago, found herself some middle-management job at an office park on Long Island and raised her daughter in a safe suburban house on a third-acre lot, just like the safe suburban house she'd grown up in outside Washington. Her daughter would never have attended Mostly Mozart concerts or visited the Frick Museum. She would have watched the Macy's Thanksgiving Day parade on TV instead of in person, standing on a windswept corner amid a crowd of thousands and shrieking with joy when the gigantic Cat in the Hat balloon drifted down Broadway above her head. She would never have discovered some grungy street-corner singer named Darryl Something in Central Park.

Reva hadn't been too careful. She took after her mother that way, unfortunately.

"Where is Reva?" Harry asked, as if he'd tuned in to Libby's thoughts.

Libby checked her wristwatch again. "Home."

"By herself?" He scowled, his symmetrical brows dipping above his nose and his thin lips tightening. "She's home all by herself?"

Libby inhaled for strength. "I work," she reminded him. "If she has an after-school activity, she stays at Hudson and we go home together. If she doesn't, she goes home alone. I can't end my workday at three-thirty just because she ends her school day then."

"You should hire a babysitter for her."

"Oh, for God's sake," Libby snapped. "She's thirteen. Old enough to babysit herself." She'd babysat for Eric Donovan on Friday, hadn't she?

"How do you know she's home?" Harry pressed. "She could be gallivanting around the city every afternoon while you're still at your desk."

"And while you're at yours."

"I'm not the custodial parent," Harry said, his brow pleating with more creases as his frown intensified. "You are. I'm providing the home. You have to provide the controls."

Anger flared inside her. "You're not providing the home! All you're doing is giving me a little financial assistance.

And we both have to provide the controls. You're not going to turn me into the bad cop while you get to be the good cop."

"I don't have a problem controlling her," Harry argued. "I'm not the one she disappeared on."

Libby drew in another deep breath to keep from lashing out at Harry—or bursting into tears. The fact was, Reva had disappeared on *her*. She was the bad cop. The lousy mother.

When she'd sold her autonomy and self-sufficiency, she'd apparently also sold Harry the right to make her feel like shit. At least she'd gotten a high price.

"I'm going home," she lied, knowing she had to detour back to her office to touch base with Tara and collect some more applicant files to read that evening. She might be a bad cop and lousy mother, but she was a semidecent liar, because Harry didn't berate her further. With a quick nod, he stalked down the street and vanished into the subway kiosk at Broadway and 72nd, his impeccable suit fitting him better than Ken's Mattel apparel ever fit the doll.

The phone rang just as Ned ran the last dinner plate under the spout to rinse off the suds. Eric was old enough to do the dishes, but Ned couldn't yet bring himself to turn over that chore. Back in Vermont they'd had a dishwasher, and he felt guilty about moving Eric to a residence lacking that basic appliance, even if Eric had wanted the move as much as Ned had.

But asking Eric to do the dishes meant asking him to be just a bit older, a bit more responsible, a bit less Ned's little boy. The kid was already growing up too fast. Surely Ned could handle the dishes for another year.

At least Eric had helped clear the table before bolting to the computer to do some stuff, as he'd put it. Just as well; Ned wanted to be alone. He'd had difficulty staying cheerful while Eric had regaled him with news of his day at public school. Apparently, a classmate named Simon had unspooled an entire roll of cellophane tape in art class that day. Eric clearly considered both the mess and the ensuing hysteria on the part of the art teacher quite entertaining, and he'd described the entire incident in excruciating detail. "Then this girl Melissa got tape in her hair and she was screaming, and Ellen started to cry because she always cries, and Richard tried to wrap the tape around his neck and Ms. Engelhart threatened to call the police…."

Ned had had to pretend he cared. It wasn't Eric's fault that his father was tied in knots over Libby.

By the time he'd tamed his resentment enough to call her back that afternoon, she was out of the office, and her being unreachable had made his resentment return, more potent than before. If she'd wanted to talk to him, she should have stuck around to receive his call. Or she should have tried him again. In fact, she should have called him yesterday, or Saturday night.

He was a jerk for being angry that she'd stepped out of her office. He was a jerk for letting her get under his skin. He wanted to kiss her again. He wanted to sleep with her. He wanted to meet a dozen other smart, attractive women who could make him forget about her. He wanted not to care about her as much as he didn't care about Simon's excellent adventure with the roll of tape. He wanted Deborah to be alive so he wouldn't have to go through all this courtship shit.

The phone rang a second time while he dried his hands on a towel. He grabbed the receiver before it rang a third time. "Hello?"

"Ned? It's Libby."

He felt a muscle tick in his jaw. Did this call qualify as courtship shit, or had she finally remembered her promise to update him on her daughter's situation? Until he knew, he wasn't going to say anything.

"You can do my fireplace," she said.

Hell. He wanted to do *her.* "Your fireplace," he said.

"I applied for a mortgage today. If I get approved, the fireplace will officially belong to me. You can refinish it."

He tried unsuccessfully to summon some excitement. "Gee," he said. "That's…" He sighed. "Great."

"I tried calling you earlier today." Her voice wavered. "I don't know if you got my message…"

"I was working," he said, avoiding the question she hadn't quite asked.

"I'm just…" Her voice wavered again, and she paused. "I'm sorry, Ned. I'm feeling overwhelmed."

That covered a lot of territory. "Is Reva okay?"

"She's fine. I'm a wreck."

"And you think my fixing your fireplace will help?"

"No, but I want you to fix it anyway. You said my fireplace would want it."

"What do *you* want?" he asked.

Another, longer pause. "I want to have a perfect home and be a perfect mother with a perfect daughter, and I can't have that. So I'm thinking maybe I should settle for a perfect fireplace."

"I can't give you that," Ned said, realizing that Libby was serious. "I can give you an improved fireplace. But perfection is way beyond me."

"It is?" She sounded almost pleased.

"What do you want, Libby?" he asked again. The bitter edge was gone from his voice.

She said nothing for a minute, then admitted, "I don't know. I thought maybe I could start with a fireplace and see what happened."

He suspected she was no longer talking about her apartment, but damned if he could cut through the crap. Women loved talking around a subject. Maybe it was part of the courtship shit, but he just wasn't sure how to play that game.

Keep it simple, he advised himself. "All right," he said. "I'll fix your fireplace."

"Thank you," Libby said.

He heard something beyond *Thank you* in her tone, but again he was at a loss as to what it might be. When he saw her, he'd figure it out. Maybe. Or else he'd just kiss her again, the way he did the last time, and she could take it from there. She could slap his face or she could kiss him back. Last time she'd kissed him back.

"You're welcome," he said, choosing to act as if he knew what the hell they were talking about. "When should I get started?"

"Whenever you'd like. Some evening this week?"

"Wednesday," he said, to give himself a couple of days to think over what he was getting himself into.

"Wednesday would be good." Another tremulous silence.

"I'll be over around seven, seven-thirty," he told her.

"Fine."

One more silence and he'd have to throw socks. "So I'll see you Wednesday," he said.

She murmured a goodbye, freeing him to hang up the phone.

Christ. What was that all about?

Hopefully, it was about his winning a second chance to get close to her. Physically close, and emotionally close, too, if she wanted that. And if he wanted it, which he wasn't so sure about. Perhaps by Wednesday he'd have a clearer idea where he and Libby were heading.

Two short steps carried him out of his minuscule kitchen—God, he lusted for her kitchen as much as he lusted for her, and he was a man, not a chef. Maybe once he finished her fireplace she'd let him play with her kitchen. New cabinets, a tile floor, a polished oak sill for her window—she had a fucking window in her kitchen! Yeah, he could work some magic there. Then he could move on to her entry, refinish that parquet floor, hang some French doors in the entrance to the dining room….

If he couldn't make love to her, he'd make love to her apartment. That wouldn't be as satisfying, but it was better than nothing—and a hell of a lot better than Macie Colwyn's loft.

Eric was at the computer in the den, studying what appeared to be a Web page. "What's up?" Ned asked, relieved to be dealing with his son. No games necessary here, no courtship shit. Just two guys who more or less understood each other.

"It's a Web site I created," Eric told him. "Gilbert got me this software."

"What software?" A bootleg copy? Were Eric and Gilbert breaking copyright laws?

Eric shrugged. "I don't know. He just had this copy he gave to me. You can make your own Web sites. I was experimenting with it."

Ned propped himself on the back of Eric's chair and squinted at the screen. It showed a photo of a grouchy-looking white-haired woman in a green sweater, surrounded by soft-focus roses and pastel swirls that resembled diaphanous veils. Beneath the roses, in a florid golden script, ran the words *Eau de oatmeal—the scent that sticks to your ribs.* A bottle of perfume appeared at the bottom, with a pair of walking shoes next to it, the sort that older people wore when they power-walked around malls.

"What is this?" Ned asked, his head starting to thump with an incipient headache.

"It's a make-believe ad. A Web site for Mrs. Karpinsky's perfume."

"She doesn't wear perfume."

"If she did," Eric pointed out, "it would be this stuff. Check this out." He clicked the mouse and more florid script spread across the bottom of the screen: *Fragrance for your grandmother. For your breakfast. For you.* "It loads real easily," Eric said.

Okay. This was kid humor, the twenty-first-century equivalent of the comic strips he and his friends used to create about their teachers. Ned had designed a whole series about Mr. Nylund, the eighth-grade social studies teacher who'd always seemed intoxicated in class. In the comic strip, Ned had had Mr. Nylund tripping over his own feet and imagining strange winged beasts while garbled lectures on the Louisiana Purchase rose in cartoon bubbles from his mouth. Ned's buddy Joey had specialized in strips about Mr. Blunt, the sadistic gym teacher. They'd both had stay-at-home mothers, so they hadn't had the opportunity to write silly comic strips about babysitters.

"I hope you don't plan to load the Web site anywhere," Ned said. "I'm not paying for Web space for you."

"We've got free Web space through our ISP," Eric said.

"Yeah, well, Mrs. Karpinsky knows how to use a computer. If she stumbled upon this, she'd be insulted."

"She probably wouldn't even get it," Eric argued, but he shrugged again. "I can trash it when I'm done. I'm just experimenting."

"So you said." Ned straightened up. "Did you finish your homework?"

"Hours ago."

"I'm going to catch some TV and read the paper. I want that Web site gone before you shower."

"Yeah," Eric said, tuning Ned out with a click of the mouse.

Ned abandoned the den for the living room. He opened the cabinet doors that hid his TV, grabbed the remote and settled on the couch. He wasn't really interested in any shows; the World Series would start next week, but no playoff games were on tonight. It didn't matter. He wanted the noise, a babble of voices to serenade him while he read about turmoil in other parts of the world. They made his own turmoil seem petty.

He'd go to Libby's apartment on Wednesday. He'd do her fireplace and see what happened. If nothing worked out… Well, he had a lot of socks and some sturdy walls.

Sixteen

Life sucked sometimes, Reva thought as she unwrapped her Muenster-and-sliced-tomato sandwich. In fact, life sucked a lot of the time. Here she was, grounded for the rest of her life—and her Sunday afternoon with her father convinced her he was in total agreement with her mother regarding the punishment, so she couldn't even play her parents off against each other. Even worse, she had no idea where Darryl J was. And Luke Rodelle, who was an asshole anyway because he was obsessed with hubcaps and hadn't paid for her pizza, was schmoozing at the diva table when she'd entered the cafeteria a few minutes ago. She saw him leaning over Larissa LeMoyne, talking intimately to her, tossing his head every now and then to get his hair out of his eyes. Larissa was wearing a sheer white fitted blouse with a black tank top under it. All her friends were wearing the same thing. Seeing Luke surrounded by so many sheer white fitted blouses with black tank tops under them had curdled Reva's already sour mood.

After he was done talking to Larissa, Luke wound up sitting with Micah Schlutt at the other end of the dining room from where Reva settled. She shouldn't have told Katie Staver she'd serve on the dance committee, because now that she'd made the commitment she was stuck having to work with Luke. And Micah, the little turd.

Across the table from her, Kim pulled the cardboard lid off a disposable foil tub filled with tempura. Reva could see the big pieces were shrimp. The smaller pieces were probably vegetables, although who could tell with all that batter clinging to them? The shrimp held her attention, though. She'd kill for shrimp.

Not that she'd kill Kim, of course. Kim was her best friend, and now that Reva was majorly grounded, Kim could serve as her lifeline to the world. While Reva was imprisoned in her apartment, Kim could use her cell phone to call her and report in. "It's sunny out," she'd say. "I'm at a hot-pretzel stand, and I'm going to buy a pretzel and eat it in your honor, since you can't be here to eat it yourself."

God, if Kim did that, Reva might just have to kill her after all. Reva would rather have a hot pretzel than a Muenster-cheese sandwich. She'd rather have tempura than a hot pretzel. She'd rather have *anything* than the life she was living right now.

Well, she wouldn't rather have whatever weird vegetarian thing Ashleigh had packed into her insulated bag. Ashleigh dropped into the chair next to Kim's, her long gray skirt fluttering around her legs and her hair so black it looked as though she'd spilled ink on it. "Hey," she said much too cheerfully. "I hear Luke Rodelle likes you."

"Where'd you hear that?" Reva snapped.

"Mia Nussbaum told me. She was at my dad's office

yesterday getting a new retainer. This is her third replacement. She threw the last one down the compactor chute by mistake. The one before that got run over by a bus. Anyway…" Ashleigh busied herself peeling the silver foil off a spinach wrap with weedy green stuff spilling out of it. "My dad's office is on the first floor of our building, so I stopped in before going upstairs, and I saw Mia, and she told me Luke likes you."

"I don't think so," Reva muttered.

"Reva's in a bad mood," Kim warned Ashleigh.

"I am not," Reva argued, then sighed.

Ashleigh appeared genuinely sorry. "How come?"

"She's grounded," Kim said.

"For how long?"

"I don't know," Reva answered, softening. Having sympathetic friends eased her resentment. "Probably till I finish college, at least."

"What did you get grounded for?" Ashleigh asked, gathering the sprouts her sandwich was shedding and stuffing them back into the wrap.

"It's a long story," Reva said, even though it wasn't that long. She just didn't want to have to go through it. "I didn't check in with my mother every five minutes when I was searching for Darryl J this weekend."

"He's disappeared," Kim added.

Ashleigh frowned. "No, he hasn't. He's playing in the subway."

Reva could barely keep from leaping out of her chair. She was so excited to hear Darryl J was still in Manhattan that remaining seated seemed physically impossible. She jiggled both feet and bounced her knees to burn off the excess energy. "Where was he? Which station?"

"Seventy-second and Broadway," Ashleigh said.

"How'd you find him?"

"It was really bizarre." Ashleigh settled into her seat and grinned, obviously thrilled to have a really bizarre story to tell. "I was walking home through the park yesterday—" Ashleigh lived on the East Side "—and I detoured down to the Band Shell to see if he was there. He wasn't, but that mime was."

Oh, yuck. The mime. Reva scowled.

"So I figured, what the heck, and I asked him if he knew where Darryl J was."

"You asked a *mime?*" Kim gaped at her.

"Well, he's a human being. I figured, what the heck."

"What did he say?" Reva asked.

"He didn't say anything. He's a mime."

Reva decided Ashleigh was enjoying this story a little too much. Her impatience grew and she jiggled her feet harder.

"He was doing this whole routine, pretending to sew his fingers together," Ashleigh continued. "But there was hardly anyone watching him, so I interrupted him and asked if he knew where Darryl J was. He's, like, blinking. His face is so white. He has no skill when it comes to makeup."

Neither did Ashleigh, but Reva was too polite to mention that.

"So he points to where Darryl J used to stand, and mimed strumming a guitar. And I'm nodding and telling him, 'Yeah, yeah, that's the guy. Do you know where he is?' And the mime starts doing this thing like he's walking downstairs. He gets shorter and shorter, like he's about to disappear into the ground. It was really cool. And I'm thinking, Darryl J has gone to hell."

"Why would he go to hell?" Kim asked. "He seems like a nice guy. Plus he's so cute."

"Well," Ashleigh said, drawing the story out, "I asked the mime, 'What, you're saying he's underground?' And the mime shakes his head and sticks one hand in the air and

starts trembling and rocking. He looked exactly like someone riding a subway train. He was really good. If I'd had any
money on me, I would have given him some, just for that
subway routine. Well, I did have some money, but I need it
to buy my kid sister a new Minnie Mouse watch, because
she ruined hers because I told her it was waterproof and she
was dumb enough to believe me, so she wore it in the bath-
tub and this was somehow *my* fault."

"So Darryl J's in a subway?" Reva pressed. Damn. She
and Luke and the Stavers had guessed right on Saturday—
but they hadn't found him.

Ashleigh nodded. "So I asked the mime which line,
which station, and he falls to his knees and spreads his arms
out…" She put down her icky green sandwich and dropped
to her knees, arms extended like one of the Marx Brothers
at the end of *Duck Soup*. When Reva and her mother had
watched that movie on the VCR, her mother had explained
that the Marx Brothers were spoofing minstrel singers. Reva
wasn't exactly sure what a minstrel singer was.

"I didn't get what he was doing," Ashleigh continued.
"Not a clue." She stood up, dusted off her skirt and flopped
back into her chair. "So then he pretends he's holding a mi-
crophone, and he's mouthing some song—I don't know
what it was, but I tried to read his lips and I think he was
singing that schmaltzy song from *Cats*. You know which one
I mean?"

"'Memory,'" Kim guessed.

"That's it." Ashleigh nodded energetically. "All I'm
thinking is *Cats*. And then I got it. Broadway. So I said, 'Is
Darryl J on the Broadway IRT?' and the mime hugged me."

"Gross!" Reva and Kim shouted in unison.

"Yeah." Ashleigh laughed. "It was gross, but at that point
I was on a roll. So I asked if he was playing on the subway,
and the mime did the shaking, swaying thing again, then

tapped on this imaginary subway door and then stepped through it and did the imaginary guitar-strumming thing. So I guessed Darryl J was playing in a subway station, and the mime hugged me again. That made me feel better about not giving him any money. I mean, he was getting paid in hugs."

"Gross," Kim muttered again, although she seemed full of admiration for Ashleigh.

Reva admired Ashleigh, too. She couldn't believe she and Luke and the Stavers had wasted Saturday checking out the IND stations instead of the IRT. They'd been on the right track—but on the wrong tracks. Damn, damn, damn.

"So I asked which Broadway station," Ashleigh continued, "and he starts pawing the ground with his foot like one of those circus horses that can supposedly do arithmetic? After a while, I just guessed 72nd Street, and he did this stupid little dance."

"So Darryl J is playing in the subway station at Broadway and 72nd?" Damn! That was so close! Her own neighborhood! "Do you think he'd be there now?"

"Reva." Kim sounded sterner than Reva's own mother. "You're already in trouble. You're not going to cut school to find him."

"But after school—"

"You're grounded, remember?"

Leave it to Kim to be obedient. Reva didn't want to get in worse trouble than she was already in...but if Darryl J was in the 72nd Street station, that was just a few blocks away. Chorus wasn't rehearsing today, and the dance committee wasn't meeting, thank God. Reva's mother would be working late because she had all those applications to deal with. Reva could leave school, check out the station to see if Darryl J was there and be home before her mother ever found out.

"Okay, I'm grounded," she said with a shrug. Like what

more could her mother do to her if she found out Reva had taken a minor detour to the subway kiosk at 72nd on her way home from school? Add another year to her life sentence?

Her mother wouldn't have to find out. Kim wouldn't have to find out, if she couldn't stand the pressure of participating in Reva's brief jailbreak. All Reva meant to do was check on Darryl J, find out where he was going to be when, and then go home. No big deal.

He might not be there today, anyway. And shit, she'd have to buy a fare card just to see him, unless he was playing in the entry, outside the gates. She hoped he was, because the odds of her earning any more babysitting money watching the fireplace guy's kid play Sim games on the computer were pretty low, not only because she was grounded but because her mother hadn't said a word about the fireplace guy for days.

Darryl J was worth the fare, of course. And if Reva wasn't allowed to go out ever again, she wouldn't have much opportunity to spend her money on anything else. So she'd pay to find Darryl J.

He'd just better be there.

Eleven o'clock. Libby stared at her fireplace, a farewell visit with the thing. Tomorrow Ned would do whatever he was going to do to it—chip it and strip it, work a miracle, fix it up. She wanted to be excited, but she felt like *drek*.

Reva hadn't gone straight home from school today. Libby knew because she'd phoned home at 4:00 p.m. and Reva hadn't answered. Libby hadn't bothered to leave a message on the answering machine. What would she say? "Reva, you're breaking my heart!" But she'd asked about it over dinner—a meal she'd had to choke down, she was so upset—and Reva had said, with only the slightest hesitation, that she'd taken a nap when she'd gotten home from school. She must have slept right through the phone's ringing.

Reva was a teenager. The sensory nerves in her body were wired to vibrate wildly at the sound of a ringing telephone. No way could an eighth-grade girl sleep through that sound.

"You should have left a message, Mom," Reva had had the audacity to scold her. "I would have called you when I woke up."

Her daughter was lying to her. Libby had realized it then, when Reva had issued her phony defense at dinner, and she understood it now, in the silence of her dimly lit apartment in the minutes before she went to bed. Reva was slipping right through her fingers. Libby recalled her own mother's warnings when she'd been a teenager: "Someday you'll experience what I'm feeling right now. May God give you a daughter who causes you pain the way you're causing me pain."

Of course, Libby hadn't had to do much to cause her mother pain. She often achieved that tragic feat simply by dressing in what her mother considered unflattering clothing, or refusing to wear lipstick on a date. She hadn't misbehaved the way Reva did, sneaking around and lying about it. Then again, her mother probably thought that going on a date without lipstick was more shameful than what Reva had been doing.

Damn. Libby didn't even know what Reva was doing.

She was a terrible mother, that much was certain. Her own mother had been a stay-at-home mom—busy with her volunteer work when she wasn't whining about how this or that organization was refusing to pay her for her efforts. Libby recalled a few conversations with her mother during which she tried to explain the concept of volunteerism, which was that a person wasn't supposed to get paid, and those discussions had usually concluded with her mother moaning, "You should only have a teenage daughter someday who does to you what you're doing to me!"

But Libby hadn't sneaked around. And when she'd misrepresented her activities to her mother, her lies had been awfully benign: saying she'd been at Jenny's house when she'd actually been at Laurie's house, or saying she'd bought a piece of fruit to snack on when she and her friends had in fact gone to the Cone Zone for ice cream.

She'd been in the suburbs, for God's sake. How much trouble could a suburban teenage girl get into? Bethesda wasn't Manhattan.

She stared glumly at her fireplace and pondered the likelihood that her choices of late represented one huge mistake after another. The hugest of all had been signing all those papers at the bank in order to buy this apartment. Buying it meant that not only would she never be able to retire, but she'd have to be reincarnated so she could finish paying off the mortgage and Harry's loan in her next lifetime. She would never be able to come home at three o'clock to keep an eye on Reva, and Reva would run wild through the city, looking for some scummy street musician who was probably strung out on drugs. If he was any sort of decent musician, he'd be taking classes at Juilliard during the day and practicing his scales at home at night.

And Ned…another huge mistake. She couldn't even guess what was going on between them; she just knew that whatever it was, it was wrong, especially since his son hoped to get into the Hudson School.

She was a failure. She didn't deserve a revitalized fireplace, and she certainly didn't deserve getting one free. She couldn't afford to be indebted to Ned, given how indebted she was to Harry and the bank. Every flake of paint Ned removed from the mantel would represent one more bit of evidence that she was a disaster. And she couldn't kiss him ever again, because lousy mothers up to their eyeballs in debt weren't entitled to such pleasures.

If she tried to explain, he wouldn't understand. He didn't seem to possess the gene for guilt. Not only wasn't he Jewish, but he was from Vermont. Did they even know what guilt was in Vermont?

She could phone him and tell him not to come tomorrow. Right, at 11:00 p.m. He'd appreciate that.

Okay. She'd call him tomorrow, as soon as she got home from work—except that as soon as she got home from work she'd have to interrogate Reva. And if Reva lied to her again... She couldn't bear to consider that possibility.

She turned off the lamp, said goodbye to her fireplace with its layers of thick white paint and trudged to her bedroom, certain she wouldn't sleep.

She wound up not calling him. The one time she'd tried to phone him on the job, a few days ago, he'd never bothered to call her back. That was then, this was now, but she didn't want to open herself up to getting not called back again. The woman who'd taken her message last time would recognize her voice. She'd think, *This is the ditz who keeps calling Ned.*

Libby didn't call him after work, either. The admissions committee included two teachers and generally didn't meet until after their teaching hours, which meant they didn't convene until three-fifteen. The first ten minutes of their allotted time was consumed by filling their mugs with coffee and arguing whether three-fifteen was too late in the day to ingest caffeine. Once they'd finished stirring and sipping and bickering, they would review the applicant pool so far, the numbers of openings and the tenor of the kindergarten class they hoped to assemble for next year. That discussion generally continued until at least five o'clock. It didn't leave a spare second to phone Ned.

By the time she staggered into her apartment, her briefcase bulging and her left hand barely able to close around a thick stack of mail, much of it Christmas catalogs from companies that sold sterling-silver martini sets, ergonomic neck pillows, fleece blankets featuring patterns of mallard ducks and other such luxuries that Libby would never be able to buy because she'd already committed herself to crushing debt, it was nearly six. She was exhausted, yet her heart raced. Would Reva be home? Would she lie to Libby about how she'd spent her afternoon? Would Libby call her on it? Would Ned arrive ninety minutes from now to find the two of them dead on the floor with their hands wrapped tightly around each other's necks?

Reva waltzed out of her bedroom, looking far too cheerful for someone who'd been grounded. Libby faked a smile. "Hi, sweetie. What have you been up to?"

"Homework," Reva said. She looked far too cheerful for someone who'd been doing homework, too, but Libby couldn't give her the third degree. There had to be some trust, even if Libby didn't trust Reva at all these days.

In fact, Reva remained suspiciously bubbly and chipper as she helped Libby prepare dinner—without being asked. She talked about her solo, about how important singing was, about how she was convinced the world would be a more peaceful place if everyone sang at least once a day. "Like at the U.N.," she explained, "you'd get all those delegates singing 'I'm With You' at the top of their lungs, and by the end, they'd all love one another."

"'I'm With You'?" Libby asked as she slid a pan of chicken pieces under the broiler.

"It's a song by Avril Lavigne," Reva told her.

Levine, Libby thought. A nice Jewish girl, so how bad could the song be? Still, while she was in this not-trusting-Reva phase, she ought to listen to what Reva was listening to, just to be sure her music of choice didn't contain lyrics offering instructions on how to run away from home.

Over dinner, Reva chattered happily about the dance committee, about her stepmother's promise to buy her a new outfit to wear when she sang her solo, about Ashleigh Goldstein's conviction that organized sports were a metaphor for militarism and about the unit on electricity her science class had just begun. Libby wondered vaguely what ever happened to the unit on dead leaves. If Reva ever did a project with those leaves she collected, Libby hadn't heard about it.

They were washing dishes when the doorman buzzed them to announce Ned's arrival. So much for calling him and canceling tonight's visit. Let him fuss with her fireplace. Let him make his dream of it come true. She'd review applicant files, or maybe thumb through the glossy catalogs that had been crammed into her mailbox, and familiarize herself with all the gifts she couldn't afford.

Her doorbell rang as she propped the last dish in the drying rack. Reva, being unnervingly helpful, said, "I'll get it." Libby thanked her, relieved to have a moment to collect herself before she had to face Ned.

Collect herself? Ha. She had about as good a chance of collecting herself as a colander had of collecting water. She scooped up her poise, only to watch it dribble out of her through a million tiny holes in her ego.

"Hi, Reva." Ned's voice spun through the apartment. He had an absurdly sexy voice, Libby acknowledged with a sigh. The last time she'd seen him, she'd kissed him. Since then, her life had turned inside out and she'd botched everything, and she was losing her daughter, and she was broke.

"Mom?" Reva sang out. "Mr. Donovan and his son are here."

Ned had brought his son? Well, why not? He shouldn't have to pay for a babysitter when he wasn't even charging Libby for this job. She dried her hands on the dish towel, noticed her unpolished nails, wondered whether her hair was as shabby as her hands…and then screwed her courage and emerged from the kitchen.

He was more attractive than she remembered, even with his son standing right next to him in the foyer. Clad in jeans, work boots, his denim jacket and a lumpy wool scarf that appeared to have been hand-knitted by someone who wasn't very good at knitting, Ned carried a large canvas duffel. She tried to imagine the tools inside that bag, tried to imagine what those tools could do to her fireplace…and then lifted her gaze to his face and forgot the duffel.

Oh, God. All she could think of was his kiss.

"Hi," she said. "Hi." Two times, as if her brain had stopped functioning—which, in a way, it had. Maybe Ned would assume the second "Hi" was for Eric. "Take off your coats. Can I get you anything to eat?"

"We're here to work," Ned said with a hesitant smile. "Actually, *I'm* here to work." He dropped the duffel and gestured toward Eric's compact backpack, which the boy carried slung over one shoulder. "Eric brought some stuff to keep himself busy. I hope you don't mind."

"Not at all," she said, forcing herself to play her role as the proper hostess even as her brain clung stubbornly to her memory of kissing Ned. "If you'd like, Eric, you can watch TV or use the computer."

"I'd like to use the computer," Eric said politely. "I've got this new software I'm working on." Not bothering to remove his jacket, he carried his backpack into the den.

Reva approached Libby. "If you want me to keep an eye on him, ten dollars—"

"I'm not paying you to sit for him." Libby cut her off. "Ned and I aren't going out." *Because if we go out, we might kiss again, and that can't happen.*

Scowling, Reva pivoted on her heel and stomped down the hall.

"What software is Eric going to put on my computer?" Libby asked.

Ned shrugged, then removed his jacket and unwound the scarf from his neck. "Something illegal, I think."

From the corner of her eye, Libby noticed Reva pausing halfway down the hall. *Illegal* had apparently caught her interest.

"What kind of illegal software?" Libby asked. "Are the MP3 police going to break down the door and take me away?"

"He's been playing with a bootleg copy of some software you can use to create Web sites. He and his buddies have been making silly Web sites for whoever they don't like." Ned handed her the jacket, and she remembered she was supposed to hang it up. "Fortunately," he went on, "he doesn't have any Web space, so he can't post the Web sites publicly. If he did, we'd all be in trouble. And his after-school sitter would probably quit."

"He doesn't like her?"

"He doesn't like the way she smells," Ned answered.

Reva reversed direction and wandered into the den.

Fine, Libby thought. Let the kids make phony Web sites using bootlegged software. Let Ned stop staring at her with his seductive blue eyes and get to work on her fireplace. Let Libby hide in the dining room, surrounded by walls of file folders.

"Rough few days, huh," Ned said.

Damn. He was going to get personal. And she was going to do something embarrassing, like cry. "I'm okay," she said, sounding about as okay as a prisoner discussing the fit

of her blindfold in front of a firing squad. He continued to
stare at her, and she smiled and backed toward the dining
room. "I've got tons of work to do, so I'll just stay out of
your way. Give a holler if you need anything." Before he
could stop her, she escaped to the cluttered dining-room
table.

She sat in the chair nearest the window, which overlooked
an airshaft. Her ghostly reflection in the dark pane informed
her that yes, her hair was as poorly groomed as her hands. The
cardigan of the sweater set she'd worn all day was slightly
askew.

Turning her back to the window, she picked up the folder
closest to her, opened it and shuddered. It contained the application materials of Samantha McNally, the pint-size soprano who'd submitted the CD on which she'd tackled
Puccini and taken him down.

From the living room drifted an interesting assortment of
sounds: a zipper, the rustle of heavy cloth, a tapping. The
clank of tools, more tapping. "Libby, I'm going to open a
window," Ned called to her. "It's cold out, but when I'm
using a solvent, I need the ventilation."

"Go right ahead," Libby hollered back.

She hunched over Samantha's application, but the words
danced across the page, a blur of neat print. The famous aria
from *Madama Butterfly* resounded inside Libby's head, but
unfortunately, the rendition she heard was Samantha's, not
Maria Callas's. The shiver that spun down her back Libby
blamed on the window Ned had opened, not her tattered mood.

"Wow," she heard Ned say, followed as closely as an
echo by Reva murmuring, "Wow."

Libby folded Samantha's file shut, shoved away from the
table and marched to the living room, hugging her cardigan
more tightly around her as the chilly night air struck her.
She'd expected to see Reva watching Ned and exclaiming

over whatever he'd been wowing about, but Reva was still in the den. Her wow must have had something to do with Eric's software.

Libby had no idea what Ned's was about. He had draped a thick white drop cloth across the floor in front of the fireplace and inside it, and he knelt half in and half out of the opening. An assortment of ratty old towels, a square of steel wool and a tinted glass bottle lay within reach.

The man sure knew how to fill a pair of jeans, Libby thought. Considering what a lousy mother she was, she had no right to think such a thing, but she couldn't help herself. "Why did you say wow?" she asked.

Ned ducked his head out from under the fireplace arch and smiled up at her. "Come here," he said, extending his hand. "You've got to see this."

Once again, he was dragging her into the fireplace with him. Once again she was going to wind up pressed close against him. Maybe the fireplace represented hell. Maybe Ned was Satan. Except she didn't really believe in hell or the devil. As Gilda had once put it, "There's no such thing as heaven or hell. There's only *naches* and *tsores.*"

Joining Ned in the fireplace qualified as *tsores.* But he was waiting for her, and running away would be rude. To say nothing of ridiculous.

She eased herself onto the cloth, carefully smoothing her tailored wool slacks over her knees, and tilted her head to peer inside the fireplace. Ned had used the solvent to remove a large swath of paint from the inner trim. He aimed his flashlight at the cleaned area, and Libby saw the long expanse of green marble, silky smooth and rippling with veins.

The marble definitely merited a wow. She tried to utter one, but her voice caught in her throat.

Ned drew her against his chest. She would have resisted if she'd had any balance, but given her position, she tumbled right into his arms. "I'm not attacking you," he whispered. "Just tell me what the hell is going on."

They were inside a fireplace. Their offspring were in the next room, wowing over the computer. Ned's chest felt too warm in the cold room, too solid. His arm felt too possessive. And she was supposed to tell him what the hell was going on?

"I'm a terrible mother," she whispered back. "I've applied for a mortgage as big as the *Titanic*. I'm beholden to my ex-husband because he's contributing the down payment. I'm buried under applications to the Hudson School." *And all I want is to kiss you,* she almost added.

"You're not a terrible mother." His breath ruffled her hair with each syllable he spoke.

"I am. Reva is lying to me. She's rebelling. She's—"

"A teenager," he said. "They're supposed to do that."

"Eric doesn't do that. He's so well behaved."

"He isn't a teenager yet." Ned's hand moved gently on her upper arm, as if he could stroke her back to equanimity. "But you're right. He's well behaved. Remember that while you dig yourself out from under all those applications."

She was tempted to elbow him in the gut; positioned as they were, it wouldn't have been hard. But his caress *was* stroking her back to equanimity. She hadn't felt this good since…

Since the last time she was with Ned. Friday night. Before Reva turned off her cell phone and became a teenager.

"Reva's home," Ned pointed out. "She's safe. She's acting civilly toward a boy three years younger than her. I'd say her mother must have done a damn good job."

"You're trying to butter me up so I'll accept Eric into the Hudson School," she muttered.

"No. I'm doing the fireplace so you'll accept Eric into the Hudson School. Just kidding," he quickly added when she stiffened against him. "Check out this marble. Is that beautiful or what?"

It really was beautiful. Undeniably wow-worthy. "Is the outside going to look like that?" she asked.

"I hope so. The outside has more paint on it. We'll just have to see."

His arm was still arched around her, his chest still cushioning her spine. One of his knees nudged the outer surface of her thigh. His chin brushed the crown of her head. "I really should get back to work," she said faintly.

He tightened his hold on her. "I'll let you go in a minute." He turned off the flashlight, depriving her of her lovely patch of green marble. "When can I see you?"

"You're seeing me now," she reminded him.

"When can I see you outside a fireplace?"

"Ned…"

"Come on, Libby. We've got something here, something with potential. We should follow through on it." He shifted slightly, his knee bumping her thigh again, his belt buckle pressing into her tush. "And I don't think your being pissed at your daughter is a reason to avoid me. Correct me if I'm wrong."

He was so wrong she couldn't even imagine of where to begin. So she kept her mouth shut.

"When can we get together?" he asked again. "Like a date or something."

"A date." She felt dazed, as if someone had clubbed her with a two-by-four.

"Yeah. We go someplace together, talk, enjoy each other's company, maybe fool around a little afterward…. Maybe fool around a lot, depending on how things go. Or maybe not fool around at all, if that's what you want."

She wanted to fool around a lot. She wanted to feel so carefree and guiltless that going someplace with Ned and fooling around a lot would serve as her general life plan. "I don't know," was all she could manage.

"Check your calendar. I'm free Friday night and Saturday night." With that, he released her, then gave her a little push to evict her from the fireplace. She felt a rush of cold from the open window and the absence of Ned at her back.

She didn't have to check her calendar to know she was free both Friday night and Saturday night. She was free every night, much to Vivienne's chagrin.

Ned didn't seem to care that she was upset. He still wanted her.

"I'll check my calendar," she said to his rugged work boots. But he was whistling and doing things to her fireplace's interior, so she doubted he heard her.

Seventeen

"That is so cool!" Reva leaned toward the computer monitor while the kid clicked some keys. He was really fast, and obviously computer-savvy. But he wasn't like the usual nerdy little boys who obsessed over computers. He didn't wear eyeglasses, he didn't dress like a geek and he didn't get all excited and start spitting saliva when he talked about techno stuff. For a ten-year-old boy, Eric was okay.

The software he'd brought with him constructed Web pages. He showed her some of the pages he'd created. One featured his after-school babysitter, and it was hilarious. The sitter was obviously an old lady, and he had one page designed like an ad for a musty-smelling perfume and another page full of *Wise Sayings from Granny Carpet-Stinky.* "Her real name is Mrs. Karpinsky," Eric explained.

The sayings were really dumb, like: "Roughage is Mother Nature's Roto-Rooter" and "If God wanted us to watch TV, He would have wired the Garden of Eden for cable," and "Because I said so." A third page was labeled *Fashion Tips from Granny Carpet-Stinky,* and it included things like, "Hats are more attractive than frostbitten ears" and "Big sleeves make the arthritis in your fingers less noticeable." The way he wrote *arthritis* looked wrong—Reva was pretty sure there was no *u* in the word—but she thought the joke was pretty funny, and much more subtle than the jokes she heard from guys in school.

"You must really hate this babysitter," she said.

"I don't *hate* her. She smells kinda funny, but…" He shrugged. "I wish I didn't have a sitter at all. I wish I went to a school with a good after-school program, so I could just hang out there until my dad came and got me. Like at the Hudson School. They've got good after-school programs."

"I hope you get in," Reva said, meaning it. "I'd tell my mom to make sure you got in, but she's mad at me right now."

"Why?"

Reva answered with a shrug of her own. If she told Eric the truth—that her mother insisted on treating her like a three-year-old—Eric might tell his dad, and then his dad would tell her mom at some point when they were on a date or whatever. And then her mom would come down hard on her for complaining.

Reva couldn't ask Eric for a copy of his software, even though she desperately needed to build a Web site. If her mother found her in possession of bootlegged software, she'd shit a brick. Reva was in enough trouble without breaking copyright laws or whatever all the fuss about bootleg software was about.

"I'm wondering," she said, instead, shifting her chair closer to Eric's so she could view the monitor with less distortion, "if you could build a Web site for me."

"Sure. It's easy," he said. "You could build one yourself. I can burn you a copy of the CD—"

"No." She didn't want to turn him off by talking about the legalities of sharing software, so she said, "I'm such a doofus about computer stuff. If it's easy for you, then you can do it."

"Well…" He flipped through the old-lady pages he'd created. "It's pretty much wysiwyg—"

"Huh?" She really felt like a doofus now.

"Wysiwyg. What you see is what you get. Some Web site software, you've got to do things in code and then download them onto the page. This, you just block out what you want and type in the text, or click and drag the image." He gazed at her. "What kind of Web site do you want?"

She lowered her voice slightly, just in case her mother was eavesdropping. "It's for a musician," she explained.

Reva had found Darryl J after school on Monday, right where Ashleigh had told her he'd be, performing on the platform of the subway station at 72nd Street and Broadway. Naturally, her mother had checked up on her while she'd been in the subway, and Reva was pretty sure her mother hadn't bought her explanation about missing the call—that she'd slept through it. Yeah, right. Like anyone could sleep through all that ringing. But her mother hadn't accused her of lying, not in words. She'd accused her with her eyes, though, and days later her eyes still looked accusing. Her mother didn't trust her anymore.

So what? Who cared? She'd seen Darryl J. He'd seen her. Even better, he'd remembered her. She'd had to remind him of her name, but he knew who she was. "Right. Reva," he'd said, giving her a smile so big it made the underground station seem as bright as Central Park at noon.

But it wasn't Central Park. "What are you doing down here?" she'd asked. "Why aren't you playing in the park?"

"It's too cold out there. My fingers don't work when they're cold." He'd run his left hand up and down the neck

of his guitar, tapping his fingertips against the strings so
quickly they produced fluttery notes. "The acoustics are
fine down here, as long as no train is rumbling through.
Money's good, too. I had to audition to get this spot, 'cause
the money's so good. Everyone wants to play in the subway."

"Yeah, but…" But Reva had had to pay a fare just to go
downstairs to see him. Not that he wasn't worth every penny
she'd spent on the fare card. "I didn't know where you were.
You have fans, and if you change locations, people can't find
you."

"Fans?" He'd tossed back his head and laughed, and all
his little braids had vibrated as if they were laughing, too.

"Yeah. Like me. And my friends. And lots of others, I
bet." She'd been sort of amazed that she could talk to him
this way, as if they were buddies, so close she could give
him advice and he'd take it. "What you need to do is find a
way to alert your fans to where you are."

"You think?" He'd strummed his guitar, and the entire
station resounded, all the steel and concrete surfaces boun-
cing his chords through the air. "How do I do that?"

"Flyers? You could post them around the neighborhood."
She'd design them for him and attach them to every vertical surface in the city. She'd run rows of them on the construction walls lining sidewalks, and on bus shelters, and in
store windows. She could be his assistant, and he'd fall in
love with her because she did such a fabulous job of publi-
cizing him.

"They'd get torn down. Or ruined in the rain."

"Can you run an ad? Like, in *Gotham* magazine or the
New York Times or something."

He'd laughed again. His laughter was as musical as his
singing. "Reva, Reva, Reva," he'd crooned. Then he'd begun
a song, which, she realized after a moment, he'd made up on

the spot. "Reva…I could never leave her…I could not deceive her…."

Reva had thought she'd die, right there, on the downtown IRT platform. No one had ever sung a song to her like that. No one had ever made up a song, just about her—unless you counted her mother's silly lullabies when Reva had been a baby, when instead of singing "Hush, little baby," she'd sung, "Hush, little Reva."

But Darryl J wasn't her mother. He was the man she loved, the man she would someday sing with, and marry. "I'll figure something out," she'd promised him. "I'll make you famous."

Now, thanks to Eric Donovan, she'd figured something out.

"So, who's this singer?" Eric asked. "Does he do hip-hop? I like hip-hop."

Reva curled her lip. "Hip-hop sucks. You need to listen to good music. Like Darryl J's. That's his name—Darryl J."

Eric hit a few keys to clear the screen. Another few keys, and a grid appeared, different rectangles outlined in dotted lines. He typed *DARRYL JAY* in one of the boxes.

"No. It's just the letter—*J*. Without a period," Reva informed him. "I guess it's an initial or something, but I don't know what it stands for."

Eric accepted that with a faint "Humph." He deleted the *AY* and hit the enter key. "I can play with fonts and stuff, colors, whatever. You probably need some artwork, though, like a picture of this guy or something."

"I'll have to get that." Just seeing Darryl J's name on the monitor and imagining an entire Web site about him excited her.

"So, what else are you going to want on this?"

"His picture, of course—" because he was so cute and that would attract fans "—and a list of where and when he's performing. Like a concert schedule."

Nodding, Eric moved the cursor to another box and typed *Concert Schedule*. "You know, this isn't going to show up on the net or anything."

Reva's excitement transformed into uneasiness. "Why not?"

"You have to pay for Web space and register a domain name."

"I have Web space," Reva told him. "We get some space free with our ISP."

"Oh. That's good. You still need a domain name, though. DarrylJ.com or something."

"How do we get one of those?" Reva asked.

Eric glanced at her. Maybe he was reacting to her use of the word *we*. But she saw them as partners in her mission to make Darryl J successful. Eric was the tech and she was the creative. She was also the marketing and the management, and maybe someday she'd be the missus, too, although she couldn't imagine ever using that title, even if she got married. She'd always be Ms. Reva Kimmelman. She hoped Darryl J wouldn't mind.

"You have to go to a service, reserve the name and pay for it," Eric explained.

"Pay for it?" Shit. How was she going to do that? She didn't have a checking account or a credit card. She had some savings in her bank account, but she could only withdraw that in cash, and couldn't very well mail cash to whoever was in charge of the domain names.

Eric doodled on the computer for a while, saying nothing, letting her stew. She watched as he opened a second window, scrolled through a list of items and clicked on *guitar*. The picture of a folk guitar appeared in the window, and he click-dragged it onto the Web page.

"That's the wrong kind of guitar," Reva muttered. She felt the way she had years ago, when her father and Bony had taken her to the Hamptons and every time she'd built a sand castle it had collapsed. Her Darryl J Web site sand castle was collapsing now.

"Um," Eric suddenly said. "I might be able to use my dad's credit card, but you'd have to pay him back."

"Your dad would let you do that?" Mr. Donovan had to be the coolest father in the world. Reva hoped he'd keep seeing her mother. Maybe some of his coolness would rub off on her.

"I don't know if he'd let me. I did it before and he didn't kill me. It's just a possibility."

"If we could do that... Omigod, it would be perfect. As long as my mom didn't find out about it."

"Why? She doesn't want you to do this?"

"She doesn't want me to do *anything*," Reva complained.

"Is she..." Eric glanced at her again. His sweatshirt looked a little small on him, his wrists sticking out. She wondered if he would wind up as tall as his father once he was done growing. "Is your mom in love with my dad or something?" he asked.

"Of course not," Reva said. "I'm not even sure if she and your father are dating. She used to tell me stuff, but she doesn't anymore."

"It's not that I mind or anything," Eric said solemnly. "I would just want to know."

"So would I." Reva sighed. "Are your parents divorced, too?"

"No. My mom died," Eric told her. "That was back in Vermont. I think my dad wants a girlfriend."

Reva felt a pang of sorrow for Eric, but she did her best not to reveal her emotions. As much as she hated her mother right now, and her father, too—and she'd never been crazy about Bony—she was so lucky both her parents were alive. Death was awful. Especially the death of someone young.

Great-grandparents you expected to die, but not a kid's mother.

"Well," Reva said, "if your dad wants a girlfriend, he shouldn't have picked my mom. She never dates."

"Never?"

"She's had a few boyfriends," Reva conceded. "But no one serious. I wouldn't count on her falling in love with your father. She doesn't do that kind of thing."

"Okay." Eric deleted the picture of the guitar from the Web page, went back to the list and clicked on another item. A curving musical staff appeared, with a graceful treble clef at the left end and little notes dancing along the ribbon of lines. Eric click-dragged it to the Web page. Reva liked the guitar better, but she didn't want to criticize him. His mother was dead, after all.

"I'm going to get a photo of Darryl J," she said. "Maybe a couple. We could have one on the home page and one on a link that lists his performance schedule, and maybe another on a third page that has his biography. Does that sound good?"

"I guess." Eric didn't seem totally convinced. But then, he liked hip-hop. Reva would be wise not to depend too much on his aesthetic judgment.

She'd have to get photos of Darryl J. Kim had a digital camera. They could use it to shoot pictures of him, if he didn't already have some photos he wanted them to use. Reva also had to get his performance schedule. He'd have to update it regularly, which meant he'd have to stay in touch with her.

"So, you'll buy this domain name we need?" she asked, just to make sure.

He glanced at her, then turned his attention back to the screen. He still had a baby nose, small and soft. Reva had noticed that most guys didn't start getting their real noses until middle school. "Yeah, I'll take care of that—but you've got to pay me back."

"Of course." Reva hoped it wouldn't cost, like, hundreds of dollars. In less than two months she'd be getting more money—Hanukkah gelt from both sets of grandparents and from her father, too. He gave her presents, but he also always gave her some money. Bony would lecture her about how she should spend it on something of quality, not trash, but once the money was Reva's, she could do whatever she wanted with it. And this Web site wouldn't be trashy. Darryl J was a quality musician, and his Web site would reflect that.

"I need your phone number," Reva said, pulling a sheet of paper from the printer and a pen from the drawer in the computer desk. "My mom probably has it, but I don't want to have to ask her for it." Reva didn't want to ask her for anything. These days, whatever she asked her mother, the answer was no.

Eric wrote down his phone number and his e-mail address. Reva folded the paper four times and stuffed the thick rectangle into her hip pocket. "Thanks," she said. "This'll be cool. We can work on it while your dad and my mom do whatever they're doing." Eric seemed on the verge of asking her what she meant, and he was too young, really, for her to go into all the implications, so she added, "The whole fireplace thing. God knows why they're so excited about a stupid fireplace that we never use anyway."

"My dad's a fixer upper," Eric told her. "He'll make it beautiful."

"Well, okay, then."

"Eric?" Mr. Donovan called into the den. "It's getting late. School night."

"It's not that late," Eric said to Reva, but he dutifully closed the Web site window and pulled his CD out of the computer. "So, I guess I'll see you," he said kind of shyly.

Reva realized he probably didn't hang out with many older girls like her. He was, what, a fourth grader? Most eighth-grade girls wouldn't acknowledge his existence. She hoped he didn't think there was anything too special going on here. They were just kids of parents who were…well, making the fireplace beautiful. There was a cute euphemism, Reva thought cynically.

Still, if his father and her mother were going to beautify the fireplace, Reva might as well get along with Eric for as long as the beautification lasted. They could be friends, even if he was way younger than her. Especially now that they were partners in the creation of Darryl J's Web site, they could wind up being really good friends.

Not long after Ned and Eric left, Reva said good-night to Libby and disappeared into her bedroom. Libby knew her daughter hadn't gone to bed; she considered herself much too mature to retire for the night at nine-forty-five. She was just freezing Libby out.

Reva's icy detachment wasn't necessary. The open living-room window was freezing Libby quite effectively.

She slid the window shut. It stuck in its tracks, and she had to exert herself to get it completely closed. Once she owned the apartment, sticky windows were going to be her responsibility. But they would be *her* sticky windows, and this would be *her* fireplace, which she hoped would eventually look better than it did now, streaked with stripes of paint and semidiluted paint and marble more gray than green. Ned had only worked on one side of the hearth so far. He hadn't even started on the mantel shelf.

But it was *her* fireplace.

The hell with it. She flopped onto the sofa and grinned. The hell with the fireplace, the sticky window, her bitchy daughter and her loans.

Ned desired her.

She tried to remember the last time she'd felt so utterly desirable. The few relationships she'd had over the years had always been stable and sweet and…well, not exactly passionate. She'd been seeking safety, a man who wouldn't walk out on her and Reva the way Harry had, a man who considered a hardworking single mother in an unglamorous job perfectly acceptable.

And indeed, she'd felt acceptable. But not *desirable*.

What a fabulous word that was. She rolled it over her tongue, then experimented with the word *sexy*. No, she didn't quite feel sexy. Her tush was too spongy to qualify as sexy, and her hair was too ripply—not stylishly wavy but lumpy and unkempt, no matter how carefully she brushed and styled it. She dressed in unsexy clothes and spent most of her days asking five-year-olds what their favorite letter of the alphabet was, and she came home tired and cooked utilitarian meals and struggled with her daughter. There was nothing sexy in that description.

In spite of all that, Ned desired her. She reveled in the knowledge.

She would see him Saturday. Friday she'd be too frazzled, after a day at Hudson, to give her all to anything resembling a date. Saturday she'd be better rested. They'd make a plan, just the two of them, something more substantial than a drink at a neighborhood pub and a stolen kiss in the alcove of a shoe boutique. They'd talk about their favorite movies and books, and she'd ask him about his childhood, and they'd argue politics. Or maybe not. Maybe they'd just spend the whole evening gazing at each other, and she would read his desire for her in his eyes.

Not that she'd let him follow up on that desire. Not yet. She was still much too new at this.

But it felt good. After too many days filled with anger,

anxiety and guilt, Libby lounged on her old sofa, inhaled the cool air, which still carried the slightest scent of solvent, studied her splotchy, smeared fireplace and smiled. Tomorrow she'd get back to suffering from guilt again, but right now…

Right now, she was desirable, and it felt good.

Eighteen

Saturday morning found Libby entering Congregation Beth Shalom with Vivienne. Her life seemed so bewildering at the moment, she figured a dose of religion might help her regain her bearings.

The only problem was, she wasn't sure she wanted to regain them.

She'd agreed to attend services with Vivienne on a whim. Also, she didn't have any fresh bagels, and she figured that on her way home she could stop in at Bloom's and stock up. Before she'd left the apartment, she'd given Reva permission to invite Kim over, but insisted that they would have to stay in the apartment—a semigrounding.

Maybe by allowing Reva to socialize with her best friend when she was under house arrest, Libby was spoiling her. Maybe if Libby regained her bearings, she would feel bad about that. Maybe spending a couple of hours at Congregation Beth Shalom would clear her mind and teach her the importance of being a strict disciplinarian, especially when one was a single mother and one's daughter was plunging headlong into adolescence.

"So this thing with the Irish guy, it's serious?" Vivienne asked in a hushed voice as they wove through the crowds milling in the vestibule of the old limestone building. Vivienne had on a hot-pink sweater with a fringed collar. The color was blinding in contrast to the more sedate apparel of most members of the congregation. Beth Shalom was a conservative synagogue, and the majority of the people schmoozing their way toward the sanctuary were dressed soberly. No one except Vivienne dared to wear neon-pink. The color alone would keep Libby awake if the service made her drowsy.

Libby had worn a simple wool below-the-knee skirt and a demure sweater. Although her parents had had a love-hate relationship with organized religion, her mother had indoctrinated her to groom herself properly for temple. Libby might have defied her mother in all other fashion circumstances, but she'd understood the importance of dressing correctly for God.

"Because if it's not serious," Vivienne continued, still in a near whisper, "I could introduce you to Harvey Golub. And there's a very nice young man, maybe a little younger than you, but why not, you know? His parents have been in the congregation for years, and now he's attending services with them while he looks for a new job."

"He's living with his parents?" Libby asked. "How young is he?"

Vivienne poked her arm. "He has a PhD. How young can he be?"

Wonderful, Libby thought with a barely suppressed snort. An unemployed PhD living with his parents. Just what she wanted.

In fact, just what she wanted was Ned Donovan. He'd come to the apartment yesterday evening to continue working on her fireplace. He'd brought Eric along again, which was fine with Libby, since Reva seemed willing to treat Eric civilly, for some reason. The two of them had huddled at the computer, whispering and giggling and ignoring Ned as he scraped and scrubbed and filled the living room with the chemical scent of solvent and the nippy evening air.

Libby had tried to ignore Ned, too. She'd sat at her dining-room table, diligently reviewing the application of James Quimble, who, according to his mother, wanted to be a lion when he grew up. That alone was enough to place him on the "recommended for acceptance" pile.

But as hard as she tried to remain focused on the applications, she couldn't shut off her awareness of Ned. And it wasn't just because of the smell and the cold evening air wafting through the living room, across the entry and into the dining room. Nor was it because she could hear his tools making rasping and clanking noises, or because she could hear muffled thumps as he shifted position, as his huge boot-clad feet clomped around her floor.

He whistled. Like a dwarf in a Disney movie, he whistled while he worked, a pleasant, unrecognizable tune. Did he always whistle on the job, she wondered, or was his whistling a special expression of the joy he took in rehabilitating her fireplace? Or maybe the joy he took in being in her apartment, doing something for her? Or his joy at thinking she would have to let his son into the Hudson School because he was doing something for her?

Actually, she believed he was doing this for himself more than her. He was the one who was so psyched about her fireplace's potential.

"Hey, Libby—you've got to see this," he called to her at one point.

"I'm not crawling into the fireplace with you," she called back. She'd already done that twice, and both times had left her discombobulated.

He resumed whistling and chiseling and whatever else he was doing. Ten minutes later, he appeared in the dining-room doorway and announced, "I'm dying of thirst. Any chance I can get a glass of water?"

"Help yourself. The sink works," Libby said, trying to stifle her grin as she gestured toward the kitchen doorway. His hair was mussed—undoubtedly from crawling in the fireplace—and he'd rolled up the sleeves of his flannel shirt to his elbows. He had the sexiest forearms she'd ever seen. That she would even notice his forearms and think of them in terms of their sex appeal rattled her.

"I don't know where you keep your glasses," he pointed out.

With a great show of reluctance, she shoved away from the table and preceded him into the kitchen. Just as she reached up to open the cabinet door, he planted a hand on her shoulder, turned her to face him and covered her mouth with his. "This is what I'm dying of thirst for," he murmured between the first kiss and the second.

She ended the second kiss before it lasted as long as the first. "The kids—" she murmured.

"Are at the other end of the apartment." He completed the sentence before zeroing in for a third kiss.

She broke that one off, too, even though she would have had to think long and hard to come up with anything she'd rather do than stand in her kitchen kissing Ned. She'd never considered solvent as an aphrodisiac before. By the end of the third kiss, she'd never consider solvent as anything but an aphrodisiac.

She was going to see him tonight, just the two of them. On a date. Spending her morning in prayer seemed like a good idea.

She followed Vivienne into the sanctuary and chose a seat near the back, in case Vivienne's sweater failed to keep her awake during the service. The moment they settled on the upholstered bench, Vivienne gave her a sharp nudge. "That's him," she whispered.

"Who?" Libby asked, peering around.

"Ari."

"Harry?" What was Harry doing here? Couldn't he be religious downtown in his own neighborhood?

"Ari," Vivienne stressed. "The younger man."

Libby's gaze followed Vivienne's discreetly pointed finger to a thin young man in khakis and a white shirt, an ill-fitting yarmulke sitting askew atop his thick brown hair. He appeared absurdly young. Libby was already financially linked to Sharma, the boy-man mortgage officer at her bank. She certainly didn't intend to start a relationship with a boy-man possible lover, especially one who didn't know how to wear a yarmulke properly. Even Ned would look better in a yarmulke than Ari did.

He smiled shyly at Vivienne, who smiled back and fluttered her fingers in a wave. "He's really very sweet," she confided to Libby.

He lives with his parents, Libby wanted to retort. But who cared? She didn't need Vivienne to set her up with anyone.

"That's Harvey," Vivienne whispered, motioning with her chin to Libby's left. Libby glanced in that direction and saw a beefy man with dense black curls covering his head and creeping down into the collar of his shirt. He probably had a hairy back. He probably looked as though he was wearing a fur coat when he was naked. Libby shuddered…and then stopped shuddering when she thought about Ned's back. If it was hairy—and she simply couldn't believe it was—at least his hair would be fair, not black and wiry.

Not that she was going to see his back anytime soon. A few kisses were one thing, but removing clothes… No. She was a long way from that.

She turned back to Vivienne and found her smiling warmly at Harvey, who smiled back. "Where's Leonard?" Libby blurted.

Vivienne's smile waned. "He's having brunch with a friend."

"What friend? Why didn't they invite you to join them?"

"It's a guy he went to college with. I didn't care to join them. When they get together, all they talk about is Brandeis. It's boring."

In truth, Libby often found Leonard boring, even when he wasn't talking about Brandeis. Vivienne loved him, so he was fine with Libby. But she'd rather attend services than listen to him discuss his alma mater.

Still, she thought it odd that Vivienne had a glowing smile for Harvey Golub and baby-faced Ari, and her smile disappeared when Libby mentioned Leonard. If Vivienne mentioned Ned, Libby wouldn't be able to stop smiling. Maybe it was easier to smile when the man in your life was a boyfriend and not a husband.

Was Ned her boyfriend? Just contemplating the possibility caused the corners of Libby's mouth to twitch upward. *Boyfriend.* Such an adolescent term. Reva was the right age for boyfriends—well, no, she wasn't, but in a few years she would be. Libby, though… Wasn't a boyfriend someone you were supposed to meet at your locker? Wasn't a boyfriend someone who gave you his ring to wear on a chain around your neck? Wasn't thirty-five too old to have a boyfriend?

The cantor entered and started chanting in a sonorous voice. Vivienne straightened and affected a pious expression. Libby commanded herself to stop thinking about Ned and pay attention.

The cantor sang and the rabbi spoke. Libby had a vague idea of what the prayers meant, although what little she knew of Hebrew had pretty much evaporated in the days immediately following her bat mitzvah. Harry had been more religious than Libby, and she'd made an effort for him. She still remembered her first seder as his wife. Gilda had hosted it, and Libby had missed most of it because Reva had fussed and demanded to nurse the entire time, and popping a breast out of her blouse at the seder table to feed the baby wouldn't have been appropriate. She'd sat in Gilda and Irwin's bedroom, nursing Reva and burping her, rocking her and changing her diapers, while the aromas of wine and rich chicken soup with matzo balls and pot roast and a potato kugel wafted in from the dining room. By the time she and Harry had gotten home, she'd been ravenous. She'd put Reva into her crib and then stuffed a peanut-butter sandwich into her mouth. Harry had gone ballistic because she'd eaten bread.

Next to her, Vivienne leafed through the prayer book, running her index finger right to left along the Hebrew text the way people did when they wanted to pretend they understood what was being said. Occasionally, the rabbi would lapse into English. Libby tried hard to pay attention, but her mind drifted. What should she wear tonight? And what about her hair? Should she borrow Reva's straightening iron? Imagining Ned's reaction if her usually bushy hair suddenly fell sleek and limp past her shoulders made her smile.

She glanced at Vivienne's prayer book, then at her watch. She shouldn't have accompanied Vivienne to shul, except that Vivienne had been asking her for weeks. Did Leonard ever go with her? Or was he always having brunch with that old Brandeis gang of his? True, the last few times Vivienne had tried to drag her to synagogue, Libby had instead convinced her to stay at the apartment and eat bagels, their own minibrunch.

If she'd stayed home today, though, she would have wandered around the apartment in a frenzy, worrying about what to wear and all that other adolescent crap. Worrying about the adolescent crap and getting a dose of God at the same time was far more efficient.

Finally, the service ended. Vivienne insisted that they go downstairs to partake of the kiddush, which consisted of challah, wine that tasted like cough syrup, cheese that had been sliced so long ago it had dried to the consistency of roofing shingles, bowls of warm, limp grapes and coffee cake stale enough to serve as packing foam. Libby put her plastic cup of wine down after one sip and concentrated on the grapes.

Vivienne cornered Harvey Golub and dragged him over to meet Libby. She tried to signal Vivienne with a subtle shake of her head, but Vivienne on a mission was unstoppable. Harvey had a thick nose, thick fingers and black hair on his knuckles. Imagining those hands stripping the pelts off adorable little minks and foxes made her queasy. Or maybe what made her queasy was the bad wine.

No, what was making her queasy was the way Vivienne kept smiling at Harvey.

Libby swallowed one last lukewarm grape, told Harvey it was a pleasure meeting him, then clamped her hand over Vivienne's shoulder and steered her away from the table. Apparently, the basement room doubled as a preschool, because the half of the room not being used for the kiddush was cluttered with boxes of toys and art supplies and a tyke-size plastic kitchen, complete with a plastic stove, a plastic refrigerator and a colorful plastic sink filled with plastic toy dishes. Libby wondered if the kitchen was kosher.

"What are you doing?" she asked Vivienne through gritted teeth.

"What, what am I doing?" Vivienne sipped her wine and

looked gravely put upon. "I'm trying to set you up with a nice Jewish man."

"You're flirting with him."

"What? You're crazy! Completely *meshugge*."

"You keep smiling at him," Libby said. "And he keeps smiling at you."

"He's a mensch. We know each other. I'm trying to set him up with you."

"I'm not interested," Libby said firmly, then added, "and you're married."

"You want to go out with an Irish chimney sweep? Be my guest." With that, she spun away from Libby and stalked back across the room, nearly kicking a plastic toy vacuum cleaner en route.

Libby remained where she was for a moment. Was she crazy? Was she so besotted with Ned, or with the mere idea that she would be going on a date tonight, that she read flirtation into an innocent exchange of smiles? And why were all the toys housekeeping toys, anyway? Did the preschool encourage its male students to learn domestic skills, or did the boys all get to play tag while the girls hung out in the little plastic kitchen, cooking little plastic hamburgers in the little plastic skillets and then using the plastic vacuum cleaner to clean up the plastic crumbs afterward?

A cloud of misery descended upon her. She hadn't meant to pick a fight with Vivienne. Instead of sharing her giddy excitement with her ex-sister-in-law, she'd alienated her. If Vivienne wanted to smile at hairy Harvey, let her. Her idiot husband was off singing the Brandeis equivalent of "Boola Boola" with his buddies. Vivienne deserved to have a little fun, too.

Still, even after Libby apologized to Vivienne, forced down a slice of desiccated cheese to prove there were no hard feelings, and then left, telling Vivienne she had a lot to do that afternoon, she felt unsettled. The sky was a gentle blue, the sun tunneling light down to the sidewalk between the towering apartment buildings as she strolled toward West End Avenue. Reva would be in a good mood when Libby arrived home, because she'd allowed her to invite Kim over. And tonight Libby would see Ned. She ought to be dancing home, bursting into song in the middle of the sidewalk the way Reva had the day she'd gotten her solo. But Libby felt uneasy.

Nerves, she thought.

When she arrived home, Reva and Kim greeted her at the door. They must have heard her key in the lock, because they were standing in the entry, gazing at her so hopefully her panic increased. "What did you break?" she asked as she tossed the mail—mostly bills—onto the table and removed her coat.

"Nothing," they said simultaneously.

"We were just wondering…" Kim began.

"Please!" Reva added.

All right. They hadn't broken anything. Libby could scratch that worry off her list.

"The thing is," Reva said in a singsong voice, "Kim's got a piano at her house."

"And my mother said it was okay with her."

"What's okay?" Libby asked.

"Me sleeping over at Kim's house," Reva said.

Libby took a deep breath. The air carried a trace of chemical smell. It didn't smell like an aphrodisiac when Ned wasn't around. It smelled like turpentine.

Trying not to think about the smell, she analyzed Reva's situation. The girl was supposed to be grounded. She *had* been grounded for a week. Kim was her best friend, and she had a piano. "A piano?"

"So we can practice *Tommy,*" Kim explained. "Reva needs the practice."

Reva needed the practice the way Harry needed an ego.

"And my mother said it was okay with her. We already checked," Kim continued, beaming her sweet, innocent smile. Libby had always considered Kim a good influence on Reva, smart and kind and obedient. But the girl was cunning, she acknowledged. Her innocent smile hinted at a fair amount of finagling.

"Let me call your mother," Libby said. The instant the words were out of her mouth, she realized they contained her decision. If Reva were truly grounded, Libby wouldn't be phoning Kim's mother. She'd be saying no.

Her brain was kaput. The overloaded wiring had short-circuited. A morning with Vivienne and God was enough to erase Libby's memory of punishments meted out.

She strode into the kitchen, grabbed the cordless phone and punched in the memory button for Kim's number. Marise Noguchi answered, and within minutes she was chattering away about what a lovely girl Reva was, and how exciting it was that she would be singing a solo and Kim would be accompanying the chorus on the piano, and Reva's sleeping over tonight would in fact work out to the Noguchis' benefit, because Kim's older sister was having friends over, and Kim always got whiny when her older sister was entertaining, but if it was all right with Libby, Reva could keep her occupied so she wouldn't whine tonight.

"Sure," Libby said. "Fine." She could have suggested that Kim stay over at her place, instead, but since she was going to be out for at least part of the night—at *most* part of the night—she'd feel better knowing Reva and Kim were someplace that parents would be present.

She disconnected the call, turned and found the girls crammed into the doorway, staring at her with wide eyes. "Okay," she said, and was assaulted by shrieks of ecstasy. "But you'll go directly to Kim's place and you'll stay there," she warned.

"I promise I'll phone you every ten minutes," Reva said, bursting into the kitchen and flinging her arms around Libby. The last time she'd had arms around her in the kitchen they'd been Ned's arms. And she shouldn't be thinking about that while her daughter was hugging her.

"Don't phone me every ten minutes," she said. "Just leave the cell phone on so I can reach you."

"I promise. I promise I'll leave it on until the battery dies."

"And then recharge it."

"You can always call the apartment," Kim sensibly pointed out. "You won't need to call Reva on the cell, because we won't be going out."

What a good girl. So much better behaved than that crowd who'd led Reva astray last weekend. "I guess I could do that," she said, wondering if she actually would.

Thank God for healthy babysitters, Ned thought as he left the apartment. Lindsay from the other end of the hall was over her strep throat and happy to empty Ned's bank account by staying with Eric for a few hours. Eric had grumbled that he was too old to need a babysitter, but at least Lindsay didn't smell of oatmeal, so he kept his complaints to a minimum.

Ned headed down the stairs at a sprightly pace. He'd had mixed feelings about moving into a walk-up, but walking down was a breeze. Eric liked to grip the railings and hurl himself down the last three steps of each flight, as if he were maneuvering some sort of indoor ski jump with lots of ninety-degree moguls. And given the difference in price between a walk-up and an elevator building, well, Ned could use the exercise.

He'd cleaned the apartment that afternoon. He'd dusted while Eric vacuumed—the kid liked noisy equipment with wheels. Ned had also put a bottle of white wine in the fridge and left a bottle of red handy on the sliver of counter space between the stove and the sink. He'd even fluffed the cushions on the sofa.

Hell, what was he thinking? As promising as things seemed between him and Libby at the moment, exactly one week ago he'd been ready to write her off—or, more accurately, he'd been sure she'd written him off. He knew her, but he didn't *know* her. Tonight he'd take her out for dinner and they'd talk…and if the talk went well and she wanted to return to his place, he had wine ready. And fluffed sofa cushions. And maybe by the end of the evening he'd know her a little better. His expectations went no further than that.

The doorman at her building stopped him, asked who he was and then phoned her apartment. "You can go up," the man muttered, giving him a begrudging stare. Ned couldn't imagine why he'd aroused the guy's suspicions. He'd put on khakis and a gray shirt with a pattern woven into the threads that the salesclerk at the Gap had told him was really cool, and on top of that his dark gray wool blazer. He'd shaved, showered, shampooed, and shined his loafers. If he didn't pass muster with the doorman, then the guy's standards were too high.

Riding upstairs, Ned gave himself a final pep talk. If Libby turned out to be last week's bitchy incarnation, he'd get through the meal and call it quits. If she turned out to be the smart, funny incarnation he'd seen when he'd first met her, and the past few nights when he'd worked on her fireplace, he'd be a very happy man.

At her door he paused. He felt unarmed. No tools, no solvent, no drop cloth. Just himself. Tonight he wouldn't be the guy who restored Libby's fireplace, or the dad with the kid who wanted to go to Hudson. He would just be…

Chill, he ordered himself, then rang the bell.

Libby swung open the door, and he was glad to just be himself, a man taking a woman to dinner. She looked incredible.

Actually, she looked like Libby, only more so. Her hair was wild with waves but soft and lustrous, and she'd done something to make her eyes appear darker, emphasizing just how large they were. She wore black slacks that gave her legs a long, slender shape, and a matching black jacket over a white shirt that was more lace than fabric. Not to tear her jacket off and see what she looked like covered in nothing but tantalizing lace took all his willpower.

"Hey," he said, hoping he didn't sound as horny as he suddenly felt.

She smiled shyly. "Is this okay?" she asked, gesturing toward her outfit. "I didn't know where we were going, so…"

"It's fine," he said, his voice catching slightly. God, did she have any idea how seductive he found her? Wasn't there some sort of law that said mothers in their thirties weren't supposed to be this sexy?

"Good." She seemed a little nervous, her smile too bright. "Will I need a coat? How cold is it?"

"Kind of warm," he told her, not bothering to add that he'd gotten a lot warmer in the past thirty seconds.

"Okay." She stepped out into the hall, locked the door and slipped her key into a small black purse.

They waited for the elevator in silence. Still not a word as they got into the car, with its tasteful paneling and brass. If he didn't speak soon, the heat and tension would overcome him and he'd do something stupid. "It's not like we don't know each other," he said.

She shot him a quizzical look.

"I mean, we've gone out before, we've spent time together, we've kissed each other. This is just, well, dinner."

Her smile lost its artificial brilliance. "Of course," she

said, sounding relieved that he'd given them both permission to stop being nervous.

"How's Reva?" he asked, realizing he hadn't seen her lurking behind her mother. Maybe she'd been hunched over the computer, working on her Web site. Last Wednesday, Ned had asked Eric about what had him and Reva so occupied when Ned was stripping the paint off the fireplace, and Eric in turn had asked if he could pay for a domain name with Ned's credit card. "I think it's a surprise for her mother," Eric had explained, "so she can't get the money from her. She'll pay us back, but she doesn't have a credit card. You do. I'll set everything up. You just have to let me use your account."

Ned couldn't stand in the way of a surprise for Libby, so he'd let Eric charge the domain name on his card. Yesterday, when he and Eric had been back at the Kimmelmans' apartment, Reva had given Eric the money and he'd reimbursed Ned. Ned hoped the Web site would be spectacular, perhaps a grand apology to Libby for having gone to Greenwich Village without permission last weekend.

"She isn't home," Libby said.

"Oh? She's been sprung?"

"She's spending the night at her friend Kim's house. I gave her permission."

Then no one was home at Libby's apartment. Ned could have gone inside. He could have torn off her jacket. They could have had wild sex in every room. They could have made love with their heads inside the fireplace.

His internal thermostat rose another ten degrees.

And then dropped back into the polar zone when he acknowledged that Libby hadn't invited him in. A few brief words and she'd been out in the hall with him, locking the door. She hadn't wanted to be alone with him in her apartment.

So she didn't want to have wild sex in every room with him tonight. Okay. He wasn't a maniac; he could accept that. They'd be civilized, have dinner, maybe kiss a little, and spend the night alone and bummed out.

He'd made a reservation at a romantic bistro in the neighborhood, a place with soft music and candles on the tables and no crowd of twenty-two-year-olds in spandex lined up outside the door. Libby seemed pleased by his choice. "I've always wanted to try this place," she said as they took their seats.

They ordered—some sort of chicken thing for her, a slab of steak for him, a glass of chardonnay for her and an ale for him. He thought of the white wine chilling back at his apartment, and then thought of her apartment with its lack of children, and then he thought of her rushing him away from her door rather than inviting him in, and he stopped thinking about what would happen once they were done eating.

"So," Libby said, her eyes the color of dark chocolate. "Tell me the story of your life."

"In twenty-five words or less?" She smiled. He swallowed a bracing sip of his ale and tried not to let her eyes and her rippling hair and her smile distract him. "I grew up in Altoona, in central Pennsylvania," he told her. "My dad's a cop, my mother runs the house and one of my brothers teaches math and coaches lacrosse at a high school a few towns away. My other brother is an optician. He lives in San Francisco. Have I used up my twenty-five words yet?"

"No," she told him. "I'm counting. Keep going."

He laughed. His childhood had been stable and loving. He'd been a Boy Scout for a few years but quit when Little League took over his life. He'd devoured superhero comic books, collected stones that resembled arrowheads but probably weren't, and walked the family dog when he got home from school. He'd helped his father with household repairs and developed some excellent carpentry skills. He'd lost his virginity at seventeen—a birthday present from Jenny O'Neill, his steady girlfriend through high school. It had been without question the best birthday present he'd ever received.

He decided not to share that last detail with Libby. "I decided to become an architect," he told her, "and I got a scholarship to the University of Pennsylvania."

"You're an Ivy Leaguer?" She seemed surprised.

He supposed most Ivy Leaguers didn't hammer nails for a living. He wondered whether his Ivy League degree would improve Eric's changes of getting into Hudson, but decided not to bring up the subject. He didn't want Libby's job or his son to be a part of this evening. "In case you haven't noticed, I'm a genius," he said with a smile.

"Penn has one of the top architecture programs in the country, doesn't it?"

"The undergraduate program was pretty comprehensive. I contemplated going on for a graduate degree, but…"

"But?" she prodded.

He couldn't avoid every subject—and he shouldn't. This was getting-to-know-you stuff. "I met Deborah, and we decided to get married, and we moved to Vermont."

"Because her family was there?"

"She loved the place, and once I saw it I loved it, too. It's beautiful up there. So…" He shrugged. What more could he say? That he'd been so crazy about Deborah he would have moved to Neptune if that was where she'd wished to live? That even as an undergrad, he'd always felt a little out of place in Penn's architecture program, a working-class kid who enjoyed the physical aspects of design and construction more than the intellectual aspects?

Their salads arrived, but Libby clearly had more important things than food on her mind. "Tell me about your wife," she requested.

Shit. If she was going to put him on the couch, she'd damn well better lie down on that couch with him—and remove her jacket before she went horizontal. "What would you like to know?" he asked, hoping he didn't sound testy. He supposed this fell into the getting-to-know-you category, too, and he didn't want her to think he resented her inquisitiveness or felt threatened by it. "She was an English major. She loved Emily Dickinson. She was a mediocre cook, she was tone deaf and she was incredibly sweet and generous. She was blond like Eric." Certainly that ought to be enough. But he preempted Libby before she could tell him it wasn't, and said, "Now tell me about your husband."

"Oy." She rolled her eyes, then dug into her salad. "Harry is not incredibly sweet and generous. Well, he has his generous moments," she amended. "But sweet he's not."

Ned listened while she told him, without hesitation or hedging, about meeting Harry at Columbia—"just like you and your wife, except that in your case it was obviously a good match"—and found herself pregnant in the spring of her senior year. She told him they got married and, thanks to Harry's law-school connections, they moved into the apartment she was now in the process of buying. Libby got a job as an assistant in the admissions department at Hudson, Reva was born, Harry finished law school and announced that he wanted a divorce. "I really can't blame him," she said, then shook her head and laughed. "Sure I can. He's a schmuck. He wanted a high-power job that paid tons of money. Dirty diapers didn't figure into his plans."

"His loss," Ned said simply. He'd done his share of diaper duty when Eric was a baby, and he hadn't minded. He would have gladly changed diapers for more kids, but Deborah had had a miscarriage, and that had sent her into a depression for a while, and she refused to attempt pregnancy. Ned had accepted her decision.

He was only thirty-seven, though. Still young enough for another kid. So was Libby.

Whoa. Where had that thought come from?

"So, what do you think of the president?" he asked, deciding it was time to change the subject.

Libby caught his eye and smiled. She must have agreed with him that enough had been said about their marriages, because she said, "I think most politicians are putzes. What do you think?"

He wasn't sure what a *putz* was, but he cheerfully concurred. "Definitely," he said. "*Putzes,* one and all."

Nineteen

Libby agreed to go back to his apartment, just for a few minutes. He wanted to show it to her, and she figured Eric's presence would keep them out of trouble.

Not that she feared trouble was imminent. She could just as easily bring Ned to her apartment and stay out of trouble. They didn't need their children to chaperone them. If she told Ned she didn't want to sleep with him, he would respect that decision.

The problem was, she *did* want to sleep with him. She'd considered him a hunk from the first moment he'd stepped into her office—the star of the Hunks of Hudson calendar she and Tara had fantasized about—and the more she got to know him, the more aware of his irresistible hunkiness she became. But sex was a big deal. It meant a lot to her. If it meant a lot to him, making love would imply a commitment she wasn't sure they were ready for. And if it didn't mean a lot to him, then he was an asshole and she shouldn't be sleeping with him.

It was only ten-thirty, though, and her options weren't limited to sleeping with him or saying good-night. So she walked with him back to his building on West 71st Street. He unlocked the glass front door and led her through the vestibule to the stairs, and they climbed. She was a little out of breath by the time she reached his floor. She ought to join a gym to get in shape. Maybe after she'd paid off her mortgage and her debt to Harry—she should only live so long—she'd be able to afford that.

Ned led her to one of the four doors in the hall and opened it. The quiet babble of a television reached their ears as they entered, and then the sound ended and a wiry girl with a pierced eyebrow entered the neat, square living room. "Hi, Mr. Donovan," she said, although her gaze fixed on Libby with blatant curiosity.

"Any problems?" he asked as he dug his wallet out of his hip pocket.

"Nope. Eric went to bed about ten. I hope you don't mind that I let him stay up that late."

"That's okay," Ned said. "It's a weekend." He handed her a few bills. "Did he watch any TV?"

"He mostly just did computer stuff," she said, cramming the money into a fabric purse and sliding its strap over her shoulder. "I can get home myself."

"No, I'll walk you." He turned to Libby. "It's just down the hall. I'll be right back."

She waited for them to leave, then surveyed the living room. The furniture seemed lived-in, the surfaces clean of dust. A faded Persian rug covered the hardwood floor, and a pile of magazines—*Newsweek, Computer World* and *Gotham*—stood in a neat stack on one side table. On a shelf a framed school photo of a stiff, freshly barbered Eric was displayed, and also a photo of a younger Eric, maybe five or six, with his parents. Ned also looked younger in the photo, the laugh lines framing his eyes a little less defined, his hair marginally shorter. The woman in the photo was blond and delicate, with a tiny nose, blue eyes and cheek-bones to die for. She was the exact opposite of Libby, at least in appearance. Probably in personality, too. Libby had a lot going for her, but she'd never really thought of herself as sweet. And her cheekbones left something to be desired.

She wondered if Ned still mourned for his wife. He had clearly loved the woman, but he didn't act like someone in the agonizing grip of grief. He seemed so blessedly normal, grounded, content. Why the hell was he wasting his time on a divorced single mother about to hurl herself into a bottom-less pit of debt?

He lusted after her fireplace, she recalled with a wry smile. And then there was his son's dream of attending Hudson.

She firmly shoved that thought from her mind. She was having too much fun on this date, enjoying Ned's company too much, to spoil the evening by worrying about what he might hope to get out of her.

He returned, whistling the way he'd whistled the other night while working on her fireplace. "Shh," she cautioned him. "You'll wake Eric."

"Eric could sleep through a nuclear explosion," Ned as-sured her. "Would you like a glass of wine? I've got white and red."

She'd already had wine with dinner, as well as decaffe-inated coffee and a flourless chocolate cake that Ned had forced her to order and she'd forced him to eat half of. She supposed another glass of wine wouldn't kill her. "Okay. Thanks."

He led her to a kitchen so tiny she understood why he

found her kitchen impressive. While she hovered in the doorway, since there really wasn't space for both of them in the minuscule room, he removed a bottle from the refrigerator, uncorked it and filled two goblets. "I didn't know you liked wine," she said as he handed her one of the glasses.

"It's not beer, but it'll do in a pinch." He tapped his glass to hers. "To Libby with the beautiful brown eyes."

For some reason, his toast struck her as remarkably romantic. She must have regressed to her giddy I'm-on-a-date mentality.

"So, this is the kitchen," he said, waving with a gesture far too grand for the room's puny dimensions. "And this—" he backed her out of the doorway "—is the living room. I added that wall." He escorted her to a wall of bookshelves. "I decided we needed a separate den."

The renovation was so natural and well proportioned she would have assumed it was part of the original design. The den was nearly as small as his kitchen, barely big enough to contain the computer desk and the love seat he'd somehow squeezed into it.

"My masterpiece is Eric's room," he continued, leading her back through the living room to a small back hall.

"I don't want you to wake him up."

"He can sleep through a nuclear explosion," Ned repeated as he nudged the door open. She peered into the gloomy room. Once her eyes adjusted, she saw an elevated bed that nearly doubled the available space. Tucked beneath the bed was a dresser, a desk and a bookcase, creating a clubhouse-like nook. A ladder at one end rose to the mattress, and she was able to make out a lumpy silhouette beneath the rumpled blanket. Heavy breathing just shy of a snore rose from the lump.

"It's wonderful," she whispered. "He must love it."

"Yeah. He thinks he can hide things from me under the

bed." Ned touched her arm, guiding her out of the room. He closed Eric's door. "Bathroom," he said, pointing to another door. "Linen closet." And then the final door. "My room."

Those two last words seemed to fill the snug space. *His room.* Was she supposed to say she wanted to see it? Had he built a loft bed for himself, too? If he had, Libby could dismiss any possibility of the evening ending on an X-rated note. No way was she going to climb a ladder for sex.

So why else would he want her to see his bedroom? Did he have a wall of bookcases he wished to show her? An interesting window treatment? A restored fireplace?

Damn it, she knew why he wanted her to see his bedroom. She just didn't know what to do about it.

In the sudden silence, he bowed his head and touched his lips to hers. *Oh, God,* she thought, *I'm on a date with a hunk, and his bedroom is on the other side of that door.*

And his son's bedroom was on the other side of a door, too. "Ned, I don't think... I mean, Eric—"

"Can sleep through a nuclear explosion," he reminded her, sliding his free hand along the edge of her chin and into her hair. He kissed her again, a light, teasing kiss. *Sweet,* she thought. Ned was sweet. His kisses were sweet. The promise in them was so sweet they ought to be banned from weight-loss diets.

She already assumed Ned was destined to be a weight-gaining experience for her. He'd bullied her into ordering that slice of sinfully rich cake, hadn't he? She'd been relieved that he'd eaten part of it—but now she tasted traces of chocolate on his lips, along with coffee and wine.

If only Reva weren't at Kim's, Libby would feel obliged to say good-night and go home so her daughter wouldn't worry about where she was. Not that it was so late, and not that Reva would spend a full second worrying about Libby. Libby was the family worrier, Reva the worried-about. Yet

Libby hadn't remembered to call Reva all evening. She'd been having too good a time with Ned.

She was a terrible mother. Her daughter's first time out of the apartment after last week's debacle, and Libby hadn't even spared her a moment's worry.

It was a bit late to start fretting about Reva now. It was also impossible. Ned was kissing the corner of her mouth, the rise of her cheek, her temple, his lips as light as a gentle rain on her face, and that rain washed away all thoughts of Reva.

He steered his lips back to hers and sighed happily when she opened for him. She kissed him eagerly, kissed him wantonly, kissed him the way she imagined women without daughters to fret over might kiss irresistible hunks.

Her fingers went numb around the wineglass she was gripping. If she dropped it, they'd wind up mopping spilled wine and broken crystal from the floor rather than kissing each other. Which might be a good idea—but kissing Ned seemed like a better one. She grazed the slightly rough surface of his chin, the edge of his jaw and then his mouth again. When his lips met hers, they were aggressive, his tongue sliding hard against hers. He dropped his hand from her hair to her waist and pulled her against him. She felt his erection and clutched her glass so tightly she came close to snapping the stem with her fingers.

"Ned," she murmured when his mouth released her.

"Yeah." His voice was hoarse, a little breathless.

"Ned, it's just…"

"Don't say it's Eric," he warned her. "He can sleep—"

"Through a nuclear explosion. You've told me. But…you *are* a daddy. I'm a mommy."

"How do you think we got that way?" he asked, his eyes bright with amusement. Gradually his smile faded. "This isn't about the kids, Libby. It's about you and me."

"I know." *You and me.* What an amazing phrase.

He touched his lips to hers. "I want you, Libby. I want to make love to you."

"I noticed," she said, then smiled nervously. "It's been…awhile for me. Since the last time I…well…"

"Me, too," he said, then grinned. "It's kind of like riding a bike—once you've learned it, you don't forget."

She laughed. She imagined making love with Ned was not going to be anything like riding a bike—except maybe for winding up with tired thigh muscles.

"Libby…" He kissed her forehead. "I'm crazy about you. Nothing that happens tonight is going to change that. If you say no, I'll still be crazy about you. But I really…" He brushed his lips against her brow again. "I really hope you'll say yes."

"Yes," she said, because she couldn't come up with any other response that made sense.

He opened the door to his bedroom. It was smaller than hers but bigger than Eric's, just barely wide enough for a queen-size bed flanked by twin oak night tables. A tall oak bureau stood against one wall, and another faded Persian rug covered the floor. A narrow chair was wedged into one corner. The curtains were drawn. A framed photo of Eric dressed in a colorful ski parka and knitted cap and holding a pair of skis against a backdrop of a snowy slope stood on the bureau, and an abstract art photo of a skyscraper under construction—steel girders rising into the sky like a jungle gym on steroids—hung above the bed.

In all its modesty, it was a lovely room. It reminded her of Ned—straightforward, honest, nothing frilly or phony about it.

He took her wineglass and set it beside his on one of the night tables. Then he gathered her into his arms. "Take this jacket off," he said. "I've been dying to see what's underneath."

Feeling a little shy, she removed the jacket. He sucked in

a breath. The top she had on was a long-sleeved T-shirt made of a white lace fabric that wasn't really sheer, although she'd never have the nerve to wear it without a jacket or sweater. "Nothing shows," she said as he stepped back to scrutinize her.

"It doesn't matter," he said. "That shirt is my favorite thing in your wardrobe."

"You haven't seen everything in my wardrobe."

"I don't have to. The shirt wins first prize." He pulled off his own jacket and tossed it onto the chair, then eased her jacket from her hands and laid it neatly on top of his. The sight of their two jackets draped together like that, one lying on top of the other with the sleeves tangled, struck her as erotic.

He moved his hand down the front of his shirt, undoing the buttons. *Stay focused,* her mind ordered. *Forget about the jackets getting intimate on the chair. This is about you getting intimate with Ned.* And it was about Ned's chest, which became exposed as his shirt fell open. She saw golden skin, rippling muscle, a small patch of honey-colored hair. Heat surged through her body and gathered in her womb, making her feel woozy. She sank onto the bed.

Ned accepted that as an invitation to kneel before her and remove her shoes. He slid his hands up her legs to her waist, popped open the button, eased down the zipper and stripped her slacks down her legs and off.

Okay, she thought as her heart thudded. *Stay calm. It's just like riding a bicycle.*

In less than a minute, they were naked. She acknowledged that Ned naked was one of the wonders of the world. He didn't resemble a buff model, some callow, cute pinup boy advertising Calvin Klein underwear on a poster in a bus stop shelter. He had a real body, a man's body, taut and healthy but lived in. Hairy legs but no hair on his back or on his knuckles, thank God. Broad, bony shoulders. An abdomen that a desk jockey would have to do a hundred sit-ups a day to accomplish, but that Ned probably obtained naturally, through physical labor.

Her abdomen was soft. It had endured a pregnancy and many years of her jockeying a desk. But Ned didn't seem to object to her lack of buffness. He kissed and licked and touched her with a healthy, uncritical enthusiasm that would have amused her if she could squeeze amusement into her mood. She had no room in her soul for amusement, though. Only arousal, deep and fierce, threatening to burn right through her.

He caressed her breasts. He caressed her arms. He kissed her collarbone and the tips of her fingers. Most men she knew would have started with her breasts and stayed there, leaving them only when it was time to move down to her crotch. Not that she was an expert, but the few men she'd been with hadn't considered her fingertips a particularly important part of her anatomy.

Ned did. The way he touched them, they became prime erogenous zones.

Libby touched him back. His fingertips were blunt, his palms smooth. His chest was firm muscle overlying the thick bones of his rib cage. Free of his work boots, his feet weren't as big as she'd expected. His hair was surprisingly silky.

She couldn't imagine he was as aroused as she was—it simply didn't seem possible—but his body was definitely ready for action.

Kissing her deeply, he slid one hand between her legs. Her body lurched at his touch. One brief stroke of his fingers and she came, so quickly she blushed with embarrassment. Ned's hand stilled and he lifted his head to gaze down at her.

She averted her eyes. "I'm sorry," she mumbled.

A roaring laugh escaped him. "You're *sorry?*"

"Well...that was so fast, and...I just..."

"You're *sorry.*" He fluttered his fingers against her, nearly making her come again. "Libby, love, by the time we're done, you're going to be sorry you were ever born."

His laughter was contagious, and she relaxed. She understood she could do anything with Ned—even come too soon—and not feel embarrassed.

He kissed her once more, then rolled away and reached into the drawer of his night table. "So we won't be *sorry,*" he whispered as he unwrapped the condom he'd pulled from the drawer. And then he entered her, took her, filled her so completely she couldn't imagine ever being sorry about anything ever again. His name fell from her lips as he moved inside her, long, deep thrusts that made her cling to his back and wrap her legs around his hips. She mouthed his name again as he pumped harder, as his hands fisted against the pillow on either side of her face, as he groaned softly and arched his back and grazed her lips with a kiss.

Her climax pulsed through her, and for a moment she felt as if she'd never had sex before. She'd had what she thought was sex, good sex even. But it hadn't been like this. Nothing in her life had ever been like this.

He shuddered in her arms, his breath escaping him in a broken sigh, then sank heavily against her, his cheek pressed to hers as she cupped her hands around his head and raveled her fingers in his hair. Was he as astonished as she was? As utterly blown away?

After a minute, he recovered enough to raise his head. He gave her a sly smile, then crooned the old Connie Francis song: "'Who's sorry now? Who's sorry now?'"

Laughing, she shoved him away. "Don't make fun of me when I'm—" *Falling in love with you,* she almost said.

He stopped singing, but he didn't stop smiling, and Libby

admitted that his smile was one of the main reasons she was falling in love with him, quite possibly as important a reason as what they'd shared just moments ago. "Don't go away," he murmured as he lifted himself off her. "I'll be right back."

He strolled out of the bedroom, totally uninhibited in his nudity. She wondered what he'd do if he ran into Eric in the hall, then remembered how many times he'd assured her his son was a sound sleeper. She heard the rush of water running in the bathroom, then the flush of the toilet, and then Ned returned, still smiling, still gloriously, gorgeously bare-assed.

He lifted one of the pillows, propped it vertically against the headboard and sat back against it, stretching out his legs, looping one arm around Libby's shoulders and handing her her wineglass. She leaned into him, even though that heightened the risk that she'd spill wine all over him. If she did, she supposed she could lick it off....

She drew in a cleansing breath. She couldn't lick wine off him because she had to go home, and if she licked wine off him they'd undoubtedly wind up making love again, and if they did that she might not ever be able to leave him at all. Could a person get hooked from only two exposures to an addictive experience?

"I'm not spending the night," she said.

He twisted to look at her. "What makes you think I'd want you to?" he asked, then broke into a laugh. "Of course you'll spend the night."

"I can't." She was absolutely certain about this. Spending the night with him would turn her into a Ned junkie.

He moved his hand up and down her arm, and reflexively, she snuggled closer to him. "You can if you want to," he said, emphasizing the words to imply that he'd be insulted if she didn't want to.

She wanted to, desperately. "I couldn't face Eric in the

morning," she said. "What would he think if he saw me here?"

"He'd think you spent the night," Ned said. He sipped some wine, then gave her a squeeze.

She supposed he could afford to be casual about the situation. He faced Eric every morning. She didn't, and she was sure confronting the ten-year-old son of the man who'd spent the night making love to her would be at best awkward and at worst traumatic. "Maybe I'm not sophisticated enough," she said, "but I'm not ready for your son to be aware of my sex life."

"Okay." He drained his glass and set it on the night table. "I can't walk you home now because I'd have to get Lindsay to come and sit with him while I was out, and it's too late to be bringing her back here."

"You don't have to take me home. I can get a cab."

"Oh, right. We get tons of cab traffic on this block at this hour." He shook his head. "You'd have to walk down to West End Avenue to get a cab, and by then you're halfway home. And you can't walk home alone."

"Why not?"

"I won't let you." He smiled. "It's late. It's dark."

"I know." The logistics loomed before her like a thunderhead. "So what are we dealing with? I'm a prisoner here until the next time your babysitter is available?"

"That's not a bad idea," he said, striking a thoughtful pose. "Imprisoned in my home, naked and willing."

"Who says I'm willing?" she asked indignantly, then allowed herself a chuckle when he laughed. "I could walk home once it got light out. When does the sun come up?"

"Around six? Six-thirty? Eric never wakes up that early on weekends."

"Are you sure?"

"I'll set the alarm for five-thirty and we'll see how light it is outside."

"Okay." She *was* a prisoner, forced to remain for hours and hours in Ned's bed, forced to sleep with his arms wrapped around her. By morning, she'd be totally addicted, hopelessly inebriated on the potent substance that was Ned. But really, what other choice was there?

He eased her nearly empty wineglass out of her hands and drew her into his lap. "Life stinks sometimes, huh. You're stuck with me."

"I'm feeling terribly sorry for myself," she told him.

"'You've had your way…'" he sang. "'Now you must pay…'" He planted a lusty kiss on her mouth.

"'I'm glad that you're sorry now,'" she finished, then made her peace with the inevitable and kissed him back.

Twenty

Reva's mother telephoned her at Kim's house around 8:00 a.m., which sucked because Reva and Kim were still sleeping. People weren't designed to wake up at eight-thirty on Sunday mornings, especially not after a sleepover.

Reva hadn't expected her mother to call at all. She'd phoned home twice last night, checking in like the good little girl her mother expected her to be, and both times she'd gotten the answering machine. That her mother wasn't around to answer the phone at eleven o'clock—well, all right, she was still out with Mr. Fireplace. But after midnight?

"I got home late," was all her mother said about that. If her mom had gotten home so late, though, how come she was up and making phone calls at eight o'clock?

Whatever. She'd probably been doing the nasty with Eric's daddy. A totally gross thought, but they were grown-ups. Ned Donovan wasn't so bad for an old guy. He'd fronted Reva the money to pay for Darryl J's domain name, so he was okay. If he wanted to get it on with her mother, that was their business, and the less Reva thought about it, the happier she'd be.

None of that excused her mother for calling her so early, though.

"I'm trying to work out the logistics," her mother said over the phone. "You have to see your father this afternoon. You should probably get home by ten so you'll be ready when he comes to pick you up."

Reva rolled her eyes. She sat on a futon mattress on Kim's floor. Kim had been asleep in her bed, but the ringing of Reva's cell phone had awakened her. She lay on her side facing Reva, listening to her half of the conversation and making goofy faces.

"You know what, Mom?" Reva said. "It's silly for Dad to drive all the way uptown to pick me up. I can get downtown myself." It was time for her mother to admit that she wasn't a baby. She was certainly old enough to take the subway down to SoHo.

"Your father loves driving his car," her mother reminded her.

"Yeah, but by the time Kim and I straighten up her room and eat breakfast—her parents are going to make a big brunch and they invited me to stay for it…."

Kim giggled. If her parents made a big brunch, it would probably be sushi and rice noodles, not ham and eggs or waffles and fruit.

"So what I was thinking is," Reva continued, "I should stay for brunch and then take the subway down to Dad's place. I know the route."

"You know the route because you went down to Greenwich Village without my permission last weekend," her mother reminded her.

So what? Reva was asking for permission this time, wasn't she? "I won't get lost," she promised. "I'll call Dad and tell him I'm taking the subway downtown. And I'll call you from Dad's place as soon as I get there." Jeez. Maybe she ought to keep her mother posted on how often she went to the bathroom every day, too.

Her mother didn't speak for a while. Finally, she said, "You have to phone me the minute you get there."

"The minute. I promise." Reva sent Kim a thumbs-up. She contemplated asking her mother whether she'd had fun last night, but her mother might think she was prying, or she might be embarrassed because of the specifics of the good time she might have had. "I'd better go," Reva said instead. "Kim and I want to help Mrs. Noguchi fix brunch."

"Be careful, Reva," her mother said. "Not with Mrs. Noguchi—I mean, of course, be careful in the kitchen, too. But on the subway, sweetie. Don't talk to strangers."

She rolled her eyes again. "I know."

"You're better off standing than sitting next to someone who looks suspicious."

"Okay."

"Or smells bad. You don't want to sit next to someone who's dirty."

"I won't, Mom. I promise."

"And remember to thank Mrs. Noguchi for having you over."

"I will." She struggled not to sound exasperated. If she came across as angry or resentful, her mother might change her mind about letting her take the IRT to SoHo.

"All right. I guess I'll see you this evening, then. And don't take the subway home. Make sure your father drives you."

"Okay. I will. I promise." She'd promise anything just to get off the phone before her mother rethought the plan. "I love you, Mom. Goodbye." She hit the disconnect button, cringed to think she might have been rude, then decided the "I love you" made up for her abruptness.

"She said yes?" Kim asked, sitting up. Even after a whole night's sleep—well, a half night's; she and Reva had stayed up watching *Nick at Nite* until about one-thirty—her hair looked perfect, sleek and straight. Reva's hair was undoubtedly a mess, and she'd have to do major work on it before she left Kim's place.

"She said yes," she confirmed as she tucked the cell phone into her backpack. "I can't believe I was on her shit list one week ago for doing what she's letting me do today."

"What do you think changed?"

Mr. Donovan, Reva thought, but she wasn't sure she ought to tell Kim about her mother's boyfriend. The whole thing was too new, and it could fall apart any minute. And then her mother might be heartbroken, and in her heartbroken state she might decide that Reva could no longer use the subway. Reva had a window of opportunity today, and she'd take full advantage of it. And she wouldn't jinx things by discussing her mother's love life with anyone.

"I guess she finally figured out I'm not a little kid anymore." Reva would have loved to flop down on the futon and go back to sleep, but she was too wired. Now that she had permission to use the subway, she wanted to get moving.

Instead of the brunch she'd lied to her mother about, she and Kim breakfasted on navel oranges, rice cakes with honey spread over them and tea with skim milk in it, which Reva felt very cool drinking, even though it tasted disgusting. Then they returned to Kim's room to ready Reva for her mission.

She'd packed her outfit for today—tight jeans, a ribbed turtleneck and sneakers—in the hope that her mother would let her ride down to her father's place on the subway. Thank

God she'd also brought her straightening iron with her, because her hair looked lumpy and mussed and in need of some heavy-duty work. She thought about putting on mascara, but with Kim's parents lounging around the living room, passing sections of the Sunday *Times* back and forth, Reva thought it would be best to add the mascara after she'd left the building.

She departed at about ten-thirty, after thanking Kim's parents like the polite guest she was. Around the corner from Kim's apartment, she stopped to apply her mascara, using a window as a mirror. She also dabbed some tinted lip gloss on her mouth. By the time she saw her mother it would be gone. Her father would never notice, and Bony would probably congratulate her for protecting her lips from the elements. Reva didn't think you could get sunburned lips, but the gloss had an SPF number so she figured she could say she was wearing it for health reasons.

At the 72nd Street station, she raced through the turnstile and flew down the stairs. Her timing was perfect. Darryl J must have arrived just minutes before her. He was still setting up, not yet playing.

A bunch of other people stood on the downtown platform, but Darryl J zeroed in on her. His eyes were so warm, the color of fudge. They made Reva's mouth water. "Hey, Reva," he greeted her, pausing as he uncoiled the electrical cord for his amp.

She loved that he knew her—her name, her face, her existence. He treated her like a genuine friend. She'd met him on the platform only once last week, that Monday when she'd found out he was here, because she hadn't wanted to press her luck with her mother. But Ashleigh had come to see him on Tuesday and had given him Reva's e-mail address. He'd e-mailed some photos of himself for the Web site, and a rudimentary schedule of when he'd be playing where—mostly in this particular station, although he'd mentioned in an e-mail that he was hoping to play in Grand Central Station sometime in the near future.

"Have you checked out the Web site yet?" she asked.

He grinned. "It's sweet, Reva. Is it gonna make me rich and famous?"

"I hope so." She tried not to gawk at him as he resumed his search for an electrical outlet. He had on baggy jeans, a textured sweater and red cloth high-top sneakers that were retro and very cool. She wished she could help him. Imagine holding his guitar… Or she could assemble his mike stand and test the mike by singing her *Tommy* solo, and he'd be so blown away by her fabulous voice that he'd ask her to perform with him.

The distant echo of a train in the tunnel brought her back to reality. "The site needs some more stuff, though," she said. "We could use some kind of biography of you. It doesn't have to be personal. It doesn't even have to be true. But fans like to know something about a person's life."

"My life is boring," Darryl J said with a snort.

"Yeah, right." How could someone so talented be boring?

"I share an apartment in Brooklyn. I sleep on a couch. I serve overpriced drinks at a bar three nights a week. If I don't turn this sidewalk stuff into a profitable venture by the end of the year, I've gotta go home and go to college."

"College isn't such a bad thing," Reva said, although the prospect of Darryl J going home—she assumed home wasn't that apartment in Brooklyn where he slept on a couch—made her heart twist. And then there was the possibility that he'd wind up majoring in something totally awful in college, like accounting. "Where's home?" she asked, praying it was someplace not too far away. Northern Jersey wouldn't be so bad, or Long Island or even Rockland County. As long as he was within commuting distance of the city.

"St. Louis," he said, and her heart twisted again. "Got into Mizzou and deferred for a year to see if I could make the music thing work. That's the deal I agreed to with my parents. One year. You make this Web site work for me, Reva, and I will worship you forever."

Reva nearly staggered under the onslaught of information. Mizzou—that must be some school near St. Louis. He would be a first-year student if he wasn't doing the music thing, which meant he really was eighteen or nineteen—not too old for her at all. And he would worship her forever if the Web site made him a success. *He would worship her forever.* Omigod.

"Well," she said, struggling to remain poised. "You could invent a biography if you want. You could make it something more dramatic. I could help you. You know, like maybe—" he handed her a coil of cable, and she felt like his roadie, which made her smile "—you could say you were a brilliant scholar, but the call of music was too strong to be denied. How does that sound?"

"Better than reality," he said with a laugh.

"And another thing…" She held the cable while he assembled his mike stand. "You should have a sound clip."

"Huh?"

"A sound clip on the Web site. So people can click on it and hear how good you are."

He stopped what he was doing and stared at her. The train she'd heard rumbling down the tunnel finally rattled into the station, making conversation impossible. It squealed to a halt, and the other people waiting on the platform boarded. A few people got off and glanced curiously at Reva and Darryl J. He adjusted the mike stand's height while he waited for the train to depart.

Once it did, he said, "How am I gonna get a sound clip? It's not like I've cut a CD or something."

"You could record it into a digital recorder, and then we could load it onto the Web site."

"Where am I gonna get a digital recorder?"

Reva thought hard. "I could ask around school. Maybe someone has one I can borrow."

"You're gonna borrow a fancy piece of tech equipment, and then you're gonna lend it to me? You must have some generous friends."

"I do," Reva said, although she doubted any of her friends were generous enough to let Reva lend their digital recorders to a total stranger. She mulled over her options. "If I could get someone to let me borrow a recorder, maybe you could come to my house and record a song there. How would that be?"

Darryl J scrutinized her. God, his eyes were so rich. And he'd said he would worship her forever. Until this exact moment, Reva hadn't understood what love was all about. Now she knew. It altered the way the world appeared, the way it sounded. Everything seemed more vivid: the steel girders, the mysterious puddles on the tracks, the unyielding concrete surface of the platform, the musty scent of the air. Love fine-tuned her senses. The 72nd Street subway platform would be sacred ground to her forevermore.

"Where do you live?" he asked, and this time when her heart squeezed inside her chest, it didn't hurt at all. It felt wonderful.

"When can I see you?" Ned asked. The question had been running circuits through his head ever since he'd kissed Libby goodbye Sunday morning at dawn. She'd crept out of the apartment like a thief, and why not? She'd stolen a piece of his heart.

But at least Eric hadn't staggered out of his bedroom and seen her. That surely would have been the end of the world. The end of Libby's world, anyway.

Ned would have spent Sunday with her, doing clean, wholesome family things—or even dirty rehab-the-fireplace things—but he'd promised Eric a visit to the Central Park Zoo before the weather turned too cold. Eric's buddy Gilbert had tagged along. He hadn't shoved anyone, and the boys had had a terrific time alternately shouting encouragement at the animals and acting as if they were too mature for zoos.

Ned had phoned Libby in the evening, and unlike his call after the last time he'd taken Eric and Gilbert on an outing, this time Libby had been happy to hear from him. But their conversation had been cut short by Reva's arrival home from her weekly visit with her father. Libby hadn't seen her daughter for more than twenty-four hours, so he'd generously told her to go talk to Reva, and had ended the call.

Now it was Monday, and he was standing in the middle of Macie Colwyn's loft, and Macie was suffering throes of rapture because her columns had arrived. Ned hadn't wanted them delivered just yet, but apparently, Macie had gone behind his back and conferred with Mitch, and Mitch reminded Ned of the importance of keeping customers satisfied. "There's another way you could satisfy Macie," Mitch had observed, "but since you won't do that, you may as well get her some columns."

The huge, unpainted cylinders lay in the middle of the framed-in living room, forcing the crew to detour around them. Macie minced back and forth, pacing the length of each column. Occasionally, she bent over and stroked one. Watching her, Ned realized she would have been disappointed with him. Even when he was fully revved and raring to go, he was a hell of a lot smaller than those columns.

What with the assorted construction noises, the thumping of salsa from the boom box and Macie's intermittent sighs of ecstasy as she fondled her columns, Ned knew he couldn't have a calm, civilized conversation with Libby right now. She probably didn't have time for a lengthy chat, either, swamped as she was with Hudson School applications. But he needed to hear her voice, so he whipped out the cell phone, crossed to the corner of the loft farthest from where the boom box was sitting and the guys were taping the drywall, and punched in her office number.

"When would you like to see me?" she asked.

"How about right now?" he suggested. "You could mosey on down and watch me spackle drywall. It's a thrill you don't want to miss."

She laughed. "How about if you and Eric come over for dinner sometime this week? Pick a day, as long as it's not today."

"Why not today?"

"If I'm going to make dinner, I've got to plan it out." She paused. "I should warn you, I'm not the world's greatest cook."

"Reva looks healthy enough. And Eric will eat anything." Ned smiled, picturing the four of them seated around her dining-room table—and then lost his smile at his vision of that table hidden beneath mountains of application papers. Maybe they'd have a picnic on the living-room floor, instead. "We'd love to come for dinner, Libby, but what I had in mind was more in the nature of just you and me, you know. Taking a bike ride, something along those lines."

She laughed again. "Now?"

He felt a pleasant twinge in his groin at the fantasy that they could toss aside their jobs and spend the morning naked and sweaty in each other's arms. "Now would be great, but I don't think we can manage it."

"When, then?" She sounded thoughtful. "This isn't going to be easy, Ned. I can't ship Reva off to her friend's house for a sleepover every weekend. And then there's Eric…."

"We could set the kids up at the computer and then hide

in your kitchen. If we close the door and we're very, very quiet…"

Her laughter this time sounded sad. "Reva and Eric really complicate things. I don't know how to do this."

He wondered how she'd done it with previous boyfriends. Maybe those men hadn't had children, and she'd gone to their places but returned to her own bed to sleep. Or maybe she hadn't had sex with them at all. Ned wasn't a jealous kind of guy, but he wouldn't mind terribly if she hadn't had a bunch of red-hot lovers before him.

"Do you get time off for lunch?" he asked.

Silence greeted him, and then, "Do you?"

"I could grab an hour. I'd have to spend a lot of that time in transit, though. This job is down in the Meatpacking District."

Another moment of silence passed before she asked, "What would happen if you grabbed an hour and fifteen minutes?"

"I'd return to work out of breath but smiling. Where should we meet?"

They decided to meet at her apartment at twelve-thirty. At noon, when everyone was breaking for lunch, he told the guys he had to run a few errands and might be awhile. They were pros; he didn't have to micromanage them as they finished taping the nail holes and seams in the drywall. They nodded and made a few sarcastic remarks about getting a gold star for each errand he completed, and he politely laughed and said he'd see them later.

Then he bolted.

He'd never been so impatient for a subway to arrive, and so impatient for it to deliver him to his stop. Emerging at 72nd Street, he saw a guy strumming a guitar and singing at the station. The singer actually had some talent, and Ned would have stopped for a minute to listen and toss a dollar into his guitar case if he wasn't pressed for time.

He sprinted up the stairs two at a time, practically knocked three people over in his dash for the door and flew the few blocks to Libby's building. He spotted her approaching from the corner. She was walking, not running. Did that mean she was less eager for this than he was?

No, it meant she was wearing high heels. He admired her elegant legs as he caught his breath, and smiled when he noticed her accelerating her pace once she saw him. She smiled back, and the sheer force of her joy at being with him was enough to knock the breath right out of him again.

"This is crazy," she whispered as he gathered her in a quick hug, then slung his arm around her and hustled her into her building.

Yeah, it was crazy. Unlike Saturday night, he hadn't showered or shaved. He was dressed in his work clothes, and while he'd taken a minute to wash his hands and face before he'd left Macie's loft, his jeans were layered in dust and his shirt had a smear of plaster on the sleeve. In contrast, Libby was impeccably groomed, just as he would expect of someone who'd spent her morning evaluating the offspring of millionaires at a posh private school. Her skirt was neatly tailored, her blouse smooth and silky, a colorful scarf tied around her neck. Her legs—he allowed himself another admiring glance—were sheathed in stockings.

Real stockings? With a garter belt? Hell, he was lucky she'd agreed to meet him for a quickie. He shouldn't push his luck.

The doorman gave them a suspicious look as they sped past him and ducked into the elevator. The instant the door slid shut, Ned had his arms around her and his mouth locked with hers. They both groaned—with relief, with excitement, with everything. Heat flooded him, stoked not just by Libby herself, by her fluffy hair and her soft skin and her dazzling eyes, but by the situation. This was almost illicit. It was hurried. It was like his first time, with Jenny O'Neill. They'd done it in the den of the Sekowskis' house, where she'd been babysitting. She'd sneaked him in after the kids were asleep, whispered, "Happy birthday," and handed him a condom. They'd made love and he'd been out the back door within twenty minutes, and while it had hardly been the most satisfying sexual encounter in his life, he'd had nothing to compare it to at that point, and he'd believed it was fantastic.

He had plenty to compare today with, and he knew just from kissing Libby in the grand paneled elevator of her building that it would be fantastic.

And it was. On the rug, on the floor in front of her half-finished fireplace. Walking all the way to her bedroom would have taken too long, so they'd done it right there, Ned chivalrously bearing the brunt of the floor's hardness by lying under her—as if having Libby on top of him, with her skirt bunched up around her waist and her blouse open, her bra hanging slack below her breasts and her body tight and hot and wet around him, was such a noble sacrifice. Thank God he'd had a condom with him. He'd figured after Saturday night that he ought to be ready at all times with Libby, because they probably wouldn't be able to predict when the opportunity for sex would present itself.

As soon as he felt her climax, he let go. No time to hold back, to play her for a second orgasm, to prolong the moment and show her what a restrained, skilled lover he was. Not when he had to be back at the Colwyn loft before too many minutes had elapsed. She sank limply onto him and he stroked her back, smoothing the wrinkles in her blouse and the tangles in her hair.

"Hey," he murmured when a minute passed without her moving.

"That was quick," she said, then propped herself up and grinned at him. "I'm not complaining."

"Good." He grinned back. "I hate to fornicate and run, but it's one of those days."

"We'll have to do this again," she said.

"Just say the word and I'll come running. Literally." As soon as she rolled off him he got busy hauling his jeans back up—they'd spent the past few minutes tethering his ankles—and buttoning his shirt. He'd have to return to work, but he'd be back. Whenever Libby said the word, he'd be back, and he'd be sure to have a condom with him.

Twenty-One

"What do you mean, he's coming over? *Who's* coming over? And whoever he is, he can't come over." All right, so Libby was babbling. She was allowed to babble. Tonight she would be hosting her dinner party with Ned and Eric, and she was stressed out. She'd prepared Hawaiian chicken, a recipe she'd gotten from Gilda years ago and recalled loving, but she hadn't made it in ages and the memory could play tricks on a person. Maybe Gilda's Hawaiian chicken wasn't as tasty as Libby remembered it. Maybe Eric hated pineapples. Maybe she'd blown the recipe by doing all the prep work last night. Maybe leaving the chicken breasts marinating in the fridge for a full day before sliding them into the oven would cause them to be too chewy or sweet.

Adding to her panic was her suspicion that it would take several hours and a forklift to clear all the application papers off the dining-room table. She didn't have several hours. It was quarter to five, and Ned and Eric were due at six.

And now, halfway home from the Hudson School, Reva had announced that some musician would be dropping by. "I told you," she asserted. "I told you Darryl J was going to come over and record a sound clip for the Web site."

"When did you tell me this?" Libby demanded. She sped up a little, practically jogging the last block before their building.

Reva jogged along beside her. "Last night."

She must have mentioned it while Libby had been measuring the barbecue sauce, or browning the breasts, or draining the liquid from the canned pineapple chunks. Libby had undoubtedly nodded and said, "Fine, fine," without realizing what she'd agreed to.

Apparently, she'd agreed to let her daughter invite a stranger—a street musician, no less—into their home to make a recording. "Why tonight?" she asked. "Mr. Donovan and his son are joining us for dinner."

"Eric'll want to hear him. He helped design the Web site. Although he's got sucky taste in music. He likes hip-hop."

Libby ignored Reva's critique of Eric's musical preferences. "What Web site?" she asked as they entered the building. Reva kept pace with her as she detoured to the mail room to pick up the day's bills, gift catalogs and credit-card solicitations.

"I told you. I made a Web site for Darryl J. Actually, Eric made it with my guidance. We have to put a sound clip on it so people will realize how talented he is."

Darryl J. Wasn't that the singer Reva had been searching for when she'd turned off the cell phone and journeyed down to Greenwich Village a week and a half ago? Libby hadn't completely lost her mind—she definitely remembered Reva telling her about the street musician.

But she didn't remember anything about a Web site, let alone giving permission for this Darryl person to come to her apartment.

Maybe she should be glad Ned would be there. Not that she needed a big, strong man to protect her and Reva from the stranger Reva planned to welcome into their home, but…

"When is Darryl going to arrive?" Libby asked as they rode the elevator upstairs. She'd never been impressed with the elevator until she'd started viewing it through Ned's eyes. His passion for old architecture hadn't quite rubbed off on her, but thanks to him, she'd developed an appreciation for it. The building's maintenance fund—which she would be paying into as soon as Sharma approved her mortgage application—must include a budget for polishing the elevator's honey-hued paneling and brass trim. The lustrous walls made her feel as if she were standing in a very, very small gentlemen's club, one of those elite retreats where men smoked cigars and sipped brandy and closed billion-dollar deals.

Libby wouldn't mind a billion-dollar deal. A brandy would be nice, too. The cigar she could do without.

"I'm not sure exactly what time he'll arrive," Reva answered.

"You couldn't do this another night?"

"No, because for one thing, Katie Staver loaned me her digital recorder today, and I can't just hang on to it forever. And besides, Darryl J works some nights, but he was free tonight."

"Where does he work?"

"I don't know. He serves drinks somewhere."

"He works at a bar? How old is he?" Oy vey, Libby thought. Her daughter had been traipsing through the city in search of some guy who worked in a bar.

"Well, he's only eighteen or nineteen. 'Cause he just got

into college, which means he's smart, right? But he's taking a year off to try to make it as a musician. I think you can serve drinks if you're eighteen. You just can't drink them."

Why her daughter would be up on the intricacies of labor law was beyond Libby, unless it was because she wanted to keep abreast of Darryl J's employment situation. "What are you going to do if he arrives just when we're sitting down to dinner?" she asked.

"I guess I'll ask him if he's hungry."

Libby suppressed a curse and tried to recall how many chicken breasts she'd marinated. She probably had enough for one extra mouth. "What's he like?" she asked.

"He's very nice," Reva said, her eyes glowing like hundred-watt bulbs. *Wonderful,* Libby thought. *Reva's in love.* She was in love with an eighteen- or nineteen-year-old boy who worked in a bar. Not good.

Libby would have liked to collapse on the living-room couch and experience a complete meltdown, but she had no time. As soon as she and Reva swept into the apartment, she mentally enumerated everything she had to do. "I could use your help clearing off the dining-room table," she announced, "but first I've got to get the chicken into the oven and start the rice."

Reva gave her an alarmed look. "You're making rice?"

"You like rice."

"But it always boils over, and then you get all upset."

"I won't get upset if it boils over tonight," Libby promised, a vow she was likely to break. At least that wasn't as great a sin as not having enough food for guests.

Mollified, Reva shed her jacket and carried her backpack to her bedroom. Within a minute, she was in the dining room, scrutinizing the mess on the table. "What do you want me to do with all this?" she asked.

Toss it down the compactor chute, Libby silently replied.

She peeled the foil off the Pyrex dish with the chicken in it and slid it into the oven. "It's in piles," she called from the kitchen. "Keep it in the same piles and move it to my bed." Ned wouldn't be seeing her bed tonight.

"What about the multimedia stuff?"

Libby straightened, closed the oven door and turned. Reva stood in the kitchen doorway, holding up Samantha McNally's greatest-hits CD and Jeremy Tartaglia's video-tape. *Compactor chute,* she thought, but said, "Leave them on my dresser."

She measured the rice and water into a pot and set it on the stove. Then she assembled the salad fixings. Did she have bread? She should have bought a loaf. Guys ate bread at meals. But what kind of bread went with Hawaiian chicken? Luau loaf? Poi sourdough?

The doorbell rang. They couldn't be here already, could they? And why hadn't the doorman announced their arrival?

Libby dropped the cucumber she was rinsing, shook the water off her hands and hurried from the kitchen in time to see Reva racing for the door. What a pair they were, both of them eager for the arrival of their sweethearts. Only Reva's sweetheart was a much-too-old street singer who served drinks in a bar.

Reva swung open the door. "What are you guys doing here?"

"It was my idea." Reva's friend Ashleigh, pasty faced and draped in a long, swirling black velvet skirt, barreled into the entry, followed by the more modestly attired Kim. "We want to hear Darryl J make his sound clip. I talked Kim into coming because she's so musical. You should have some-one musical to judge if the recording is good."

"I hope you don't mind," Kim said. "Ashleigh called me at home and said you desperately needed me here. Hi, Ms. Kimmelman," she added, acknowledging Libby, who stood in the dining room, dripping water from her hands onto the floor.

"No problem," Reva said rather presumptuously. What did she mean, *no problem?* Libby was hosting a goddamn dinner party. She was the one with problems.

She heard a hiss coming from the kitchen. Shit. The rice had boiled over.

Abandoning the girls, she dashed back to the kitchen to rescue the rice. Were Ashleigh and Kim expecting to stay for dinner? She'd prepared eight chicken breasts; if no one wanted seconds, she'd be okay. Libby wasn't planning to eat seconds, anyway. Thanks to the revival of her sex life, she had a vested interest in keeping her tush from getting any bigger than it already was.

Wiping the sizzling, milky rice water from the stove, she practiced breathing deeply. Why should she be rattled about having Ned and Eric over for dinner? Ned clearly approved of her tush, and every other part of her. He'd had sex with her on the floor of the living room. Surely she didn't have to impress him with her elegant hostess skills, of which she had none. And Eric was just a kid, and a male kid at that. Boys didn't care if the stove was a little messy or the cucumbers sliced unevenly. She only hoped he wouldn't mind the lack of bread.

She was cautiously placing the pot back on the burner when the doorbell rang. She moved the pot to a cold burner before leaving the kitchen.

Once again, Reva beat her to the door, this time with her giggling posse in tow. She swung open the door and smiled. "Hi," she said, although it sounded more like a sigh.

Darryl J was here. Libby braced herself to meet the man. She already hated him because he had the power to break her daughter's heart. Reva had no business getting a crush on a man so much older than she was, at such a different point in his life from the one she was in hers, but crushes were irrational and often uncontrollable. Libby saw this situation ending in disaster.

Kim and Ashleigh had fallen back a step, as if to give the visitor more room. He entered the apartment, a compact fellow—Ned had him in both height and weight, thank God—with skin the color of mocha and braided black hair and a huge guitar case. He wore jeans, but they weren't torn or stained. In fact, he was dressed more neatly than Ned had been on Monday, when he'd raced from his work site to her apartment for their lunch-break tryst.

"Hey, Reva," Darryl J said, then nodded at Ashleigh and Kim and then turned to meet Libby. "Hey."

Hey? This was how the man who would break her daughter's heart greeted her? "How do you do?" she said stiffly.

"Mom, this is Darryl J. Darryl J, this is my mom, Libby Kimmelman."

If he called her Libby, she'd throw his guitar down the compactor chute.

He won a few points by extending his hand and saying, "Thanks for letting us borrow your place to do this recording, Mrs. Kimmelman."

She shook his hand and decided not to tell him it was "Ms." rather than "Mrs." She was already feeling marginally better about the situation. He might even make his recording and leave before Ned and Eric arrived. And when he left, he could take Kim and Ashleigh with him. "I'll be in the kitchen," she said.

"Try not to make any noise, okay, Mom?" Reva called over her shoulder as she led Kim, Ashleigh, Darryl J and his guitar into the den.

Right. Libby would keep the rice from boiling over and not make any noise. At least Reva had gotten most of the clutter off the dining-room table. Things could be worse.

She wiped off the outer surface of the rice pot, which was streaked with white from the water that had boiled over, and set it back on a burner adjusted to Low. Trusting the pot—undoubtedly a foolish thing to do, but she couldn't spend the next half hour hovering over the stove, awaiting another eruption—she returned to the dining room to clear the last few folders from the table.

As she carried them to her bedroom, she passed the den. Darryl J was tuning his guitar while the three girls crowded around him like guardian angels, or maybe Muses. If he objected to their nearness, he didn't say so.

Libby objected to their nearness. She'd prefer that her daughter put a few more inches between herself and the eighteen-year-old bar waiter.

She was in the bedroom, adding her folders to the piles neatly arrayed across her bed, when Darryl began to strum. Not bad, she thought, remaining where she was so she could listen. The girls chattered for a minute—"We'll just record it to see if you're close enough," Reva said. "I think it's called a sound check"—and then he started to sing along with his strumming.

Not bad at all.

The doorbell chimed, interrupting his song. The girls keened at this dreadful interruption. *It was only a sound check,* Libby wanted to remind them as she strode down the hall, passing the den on her way to the front door.

Ned and Eric stood on the threshold, Ned carrying a bottle of white wine and Eric a large bouquet of flowers. Libby's eyes filled with tears, even though she knew the flowers were from Ned and not his son. "Thank you!" she gushed as she waved them inside. "Come on in. This bouquet is gorgeous! I've got to find a vase."

They stepped inside, Ned sending her a private smile, which, she supposed, would be the limit of their intimacy tonight. To her relief, he didn't try to kiss her in front of Eric. She wasn't ready for the kids to see her and Ned in PG mode, let alone NR-17.

At the sound of a guitar chord, Eric tilted his head in the direction of the den. "Is that Darryl J?" he asked.

"Yes. He's recording a sound clip," she reported, as if she actually understood what this whole enterprise was about.

"Wow. Can I go watch?" He thrust the flowers into Libby's hands and raced to the den, yanking off his jacket as he went.

Alone at last. Ned stole a quick kiss that made Libby sigh. "A sound clip, huh."

"It's for a Web site your son and my daughter are making. When did they do all this?"

"When we were otherwise distracted," Ned said, grinning slyly and stealing another, slightly less rushed kiss. Libby sank into it for a moment, then nudged him away. The kids were so wrapped up in their Darryl J project she and Ned probably could have torn off their clothes and gone at it in the entry without their noticing, but she still felt funny kissing him when Eric and Reva were just a few rooms from them.

He set the wine bottle on the mail table and removed his jacket. "Who exactly is Darryl J?" he asked.

"Some stray my daughter picked up."

"Hey, could you guys keep it down?" Reva scolded. "We're recording in here!"

Libby rolled her eyes. "We're not allowed to make any noise," she warned.

"Well, that lets out some activities," he muttered, wiggling his eyebrows lecherously.

Libby didn't think they were that noisy—but then, in the heat of passion, she was hardly aware of whether she was breathing, let alone moaning or screaming or… She felt her cheeks grow warm and busied herself hanging up Ned's jacket. "I'm figuring we'll wait with dinner until they're finished," she whispered. "Is that all right with you?"

He shrugged. "I can work on the fireplace while they're doing their thing."

In khakis, a dark plaid shirt and loafers instead of his clumpy work boots, he wasn't dressed for fireplace work. But he'd gotten most of the messy part done already. The paint was completely off and he'd removed the wooden board someone had glued to the mantel shelf. A residue of glue remained. Perhaps that was what he intended to work on. Libby had told him to leave his tools, solvents and drop cloth at her place instead of schlepping them back and forth, so everything he needed was already here.

"You can't make any noise, though," she reminded him. "The impresarios will throw a fit if you do."

"Well, I sure wouldn't want them to throw a fit. I can work quietly."

"I'll be in the kitchen," she said, giving his arm a pat and carrying the flowers and wine with her. She hoped the rice hadn't boiled over again. She also hoped she could remember where she might have a vase. The last time she'd had flowers on display in the apartment might have been after her wedding, when she had insisted on bringing home one of the centerpieces. She'd held the artfully arranged bouquet on her lap during the cab ride home after the dinner, and the floral fragrance had made her queasy. But then, everything had made her queasy during her pregnancy.

She hadn't needed a vase for those flowers, because they'd been wedged into green packing foam in a plastic bowl. What she'd needed then was a table to put the flowers on. The dining-room table hadn't become a part of her life until she was eight months along, her belly so huge she could barely push in her chair.

Entering the kitchen, she heard the lid of the rice pot rattling, but the water wasn't boiling over. She checked the chicken again—nothing burning there—and rummaged through her cabinets for a vase. Unable to find one, she grabbed a jar of pickles from the refrigerator door, discarded the pickles, rinsed out the vinegar and spices and stuck the flowers in. Not exactly elegant, but it would do.

Darryl J's music reached her faintly. Words spilled out of his mouth so fast she couldn't decipher them, although they had an infectious rhythm and she found her feet moving to the syncopated beat. God help her if those lyrics were some sort of catchy rhyme about shooting up or shooting guns or enjoying unprotected sex with whores. Libby hoped she'd raised her daughter to have good taste when it came to music. But Reva was thirteen, so all bets were off.

Libby carried the pickle jar into the dining room, then decided the table's surface was too scratched to go naked. She pulled a tablecloth from the sideboard and shook it out, trying to remember when she'd last used it. It had a pale pink stain on one end. Wine? Cranberry sauce? For the life of her, she couldn't remember the occasion. She vaguely recalled that the tablecloth had been a wedding gift from some distant relative. She wouldn't be surprised if the last time she'd used it had been when she was still married to Harry.

The stain wasn't too bad. She'd cover it with the salad bowl—if she ever finished making the salad.

She was once again attempting to slice a cucumber when the intercom buzzed. Three groups of visitors had arrived at her doorstep without being announced; apparently, the doorman had suddenly decided to do his job. She would have to yell at him for his failure to stop Darryl J, Reva's friends and the Donovans. Once she owned her apartment, maybe she'd get a seat on the co-op board and yell at the doormen on a regular basis.

She dried her hands on a sheet of paper towel before lifting the intercom receiver. "Yes?"

"A woman named Vivienne is here to see you," the doorman reported lethargically.

"Send her up," Libby said, wondering why Vivienne would be visiting. Libby peeked into the oven and counted the chicken breasts in the roasting pan, as if a few more might have miraculously materialized.

Maybe Vivienne wouldn't stay for dinner. And Libby would send Kim and Ashleigh home. Darryl J, too. He might be a fine singer, but he was eighteen years old. He could find his own food.

Libby closed the oven and finished hacking the cucumber into slices before the doorbell rang. The chime prompted howls of outrage from the technicians in the recording studio.

After tossing the knife onto the counter, she darted through the dining room to the entry. She saw Ned approaching the entry from the living room, a rag in one hand and a jug-shaped can in the other. "I wasn't sure—" he began, but was cut off by more howls.

"Could you *please* be quiet?" Reva scolded.

"No, Reva, we can't," Libby retorted. "Aunt Vivienne's here. Once I let her in, we'll shut up."

She opened the door and Vivienne stormed inside, dragging a small wheeled suitcase behind her. Her hair was wind tossed and she wore a dramatic lime-green coat over drab brown slacks. "Hi," she said, slamming the door behind her, causing the safety chain to clang against the jamb. The moans from the den were so dramatic a person would be forgiven for thinking the kids were sitting shivah for a dead loved one in there.

"We're not allowed to talk," Libby warned, her gaze sliding to Vivienne's suitcase. Questions crowded her mind—the sort of questions she didn't think she'd like the answer to.

"What do you mean, we can't talk?" Vivienne asked, then turned to stare at Ned. "Who are you?"

"Ned Donovan," Libby whispered. "Ned, this is my sister-in-law, Vivienne Schwartz."

Ned passed the rag from his right hand to his left, extended his right hand, then thought better of offering it to Vivienne. "Solvent," he explained.

"Is this your Irish guy?" Vivienne asked Libby, her expression an odd combination of skepticism and awe.

"Mom! Puh-leez!" Reva whined from the den.

"All right, all right," Libby shouted back, then took Vivienne's arm and steered her through the dining room. Vivienne dragged her suitcase behind her; the little wheels squeaked ominously against the hardwood floor. "Reva is recording something," she explained to Vivienne once they reached the kitchen. "We're not allowed to make noise. What's in the suitcase?" Maybe it was full of books Vivienne wanted to donate to the Hudson School. Maybe Vivienne had bought new luggage and wanted to give her old suitcase to Reva.

"Leonard and I had a fight," Vivienne announced, the answer Libby had been dreading. "Can I stay here?"

"Of course," Libby assured her, then spread her arms. Vivienne accepted her hug, rested her head briefly against Libby's shoulder, then apparently decided not to fall apart. She stepped back and shrugged bravely. "Just a little fight. Not a big one."

"Big enough that you came here with a suitcase."

"To teach him a lesson," Vivienne muttered.

What lesson? Libby wondered. The lesson that if you act like a jerk, your wife will go away and leave you to eat pizza while watching professional wrestling on TV, pee without closing the bathroom door and take over the whole bed? Some lesson.

What bed would Vivienne take over? As it was, Libby wasn't sure where she herself would sleep, now that her own bed was heaped high with application materials.

The practicalities would work themselves out later. For now, her sister-in-law was in the midst of a marital crisis.

She didn't look critical. Her eyes were dry, her lips were curved in a slight pout and her blouse—visible as she unbuttoned her coat—was a riot of color that hurt Libby's eyes. "What happened?" she asked. "Can you talk about it? Should I send Ned to your place to beat Leonard up?"

"Would he do that?" Vivienne asked hopefully. She glanced out of the kitchen, but Ned must have returned to the fireplace. He wasn't visible from where she and Libby stood. "No, I don't believe in violence. He's cute," she added, tilting her head toward the living room. "What's with the solvent?"

"He's stripping my fireplace mantel," Libby said, studying Vivienne, gauging her. She'd just packed a bag and walked out on her husband. Why didn't she seem traumatized? "It must have been a terrible fight. You're here instead of at home, making up with Leonard."

"It was a ridiculous argument about his ridiculous Brandeis buddies and their ridiculous brunches. And their ridiculous get-togethers for a drink after work, and their ridiculous Sundays when they watch football on the tube and eat *chazzerai*. I've had it with his ridiculousness."

"Are you going to leave him?"

"I already did." Vivienne gazed at her suitcase, then lifted her eyes back to Libby. "Divorce him, you mean? I didn't bring enough stuff with me to divorce him."

"Okay." The lid on the pot of rice had stopped rattling, and Libby turned the burner off. She didn't want to know if the rice had overcooked. Who cared about rice when Vivienne had just realized that her husband was ridiculous? "Ned and his son came over for dinner, but we've got plenty."

"As if I have an appetite." Vivienne attempted a pathetic sigh, then said, "It smells good. What did you make?"

"Hawaiian chicken. Your mother's recipe."

"Well, maybe I'll have a little."

The doorbell rang again, without benefit of the doorman's warning. Libby flinched, and when Vivienne caught her eye, she saw her own panic reflected in Vivienne's expression. Could Leonard have followed her here? Not that Libby feared him, not that she thought he had enough chutzpah to stalk his wife, but still… That doorman was going to be severely reprimanded once Libby owned her apartment.

This time, the resounding chime didn't provoke shrieks and curses from the den. Libby walked through the dining room, Vivienne trailing her and the suitcase trailing Vivienne, as if she couldn't bear to part with it. Ned remained by the fireplace, wiping a corner of the shelf so hard she wouldn't be surprised to find a dent in the green marble once he was done. His hair was scruffy, his sleeves rolled up, and she paused for a moment, thinking of how lucky she was to have him in her life, rather than someone like, say, Leonard, or…

Harry. She stared at her ex-husband through the peephole in the door. Despite the hole's fish-eye lens, he looked like a Ken doll. A Ken doll made out of Silly Putty.

She opened the door and glowered at her ex-husband. Perhaps the doorman had recognized him, since he came to the building so often, dropping Reva off after her weekly visits. The doorman still should have announced Harry, though. Harry was not welcome right now. Harry was rarely welcome.

He had on an elegant suit and carried a fancy leather briefcase that Libby assumed was one of those brands that advertised in the biannual "Fashions of the Times" section of the *New York Times*. His tie was an iridescent silk that shimmered blue and silver. Even though the time was—she checked her watch—six-thirty, which meant the chicken had been in the oven long enough to have developed a texture not unlike that of Harry's briefcase—not a hint of beard shadowed his jaw. When he was married to her, she was positive he used to sprout stubble. Had Bonnie figured out a way to suppress his facial hair?

Harry ignored Libby and gaped at Vivienne. "Viv! What are you doing here?"

"None of your business," Vivienne retorted, sounding like the bratty kid sister Harry had always considered her.

"I had to meet with a client in the neighborhood," he said to Libby, entering the apartment without awaiting a greeting from her. "So I thought I'd drop by. We have some things to discuss. Is that a suitcase, Viv?"

"None of your business."

He narrowed his eyes, then widened them at the sight of Ned, who once again approached the entry with his rag and bottle of solvent. The sharp chemical smell overpowered Harry's fancy cologne.

Libby sighed. This was one of those awkward moments people wrote to advice columnists about: *Dear Ms. Know-it-all: What is the proper etiquette for introducing one's former husband to one's current boyfriend?*

Just do it, she answered herself. "Harry, this is my friend Ned Donovan. Ned, my ex-husband, Harry Kimmelman."

"How's it going?" Ned said pleasantly, extending his hand. Obviously, he'd wanted to protect Vivienne from exposure to the solvent, but Harry's delicate skin he didn't care about.

Clearly nonplussed, Harry shook his hand, then squinted at his palm. "What is it?" he asked, pointing at the bottle.

"That doesn't concern you," Libby said, just to be contrary. "We're having a dinner party, Harry, so—"

"She made Mom's Hawaiian chicken," Vivienne told him, a nyah-nyah undertone to her voice.

"A dinner party?"

"Dad?" Reva bounded in from the den, slightly flushed and beaming. "Oh, Dad, this is so cool! You've got to come and hear this! Eric put this sound clip on the Web site, and…"

Before she could continue, the rest of the recording engineers spilled out of the den, followed by Darryl J, carrying his guitar. "It came out so good, man!" he crowed. "You've gotta hear this. Eric, you the man!" He slapped Eric's hand. Eric seemed to take the praise in stride, though he was grinning.

"Well, I want to hear it," Ned said enthusiastically. "Come on, let's go hear the sound clip."

Libby could tell from Harry's scowl that he didn't want to hear the sound clip. He eyed Darryl J with blatant distrust, Eric with condescension and Libby with overt suspicion. "What the hell is going on?" he muttered.

"You have no right to turn into a grouch," Vivienne chided. "Nobody asked you to come here."

Nobody had asked Vivienne to come here, either. But how could Libby object when the poor woman was having marital difficulties? Besides, Vivienne had been announced by the doorman. Harry hadn't.

"Dad," Reva said, grabbing her father's hand and dragging him down the hall. "Listen to the sound clip."

Harry appeared deeply annoyed as he trudged along with Reva. The den was barely big enough for them all to fit in, but they managed to clear a path for Eric to reach the computer desk. He sat down, clicked the mouse, and the room resonated with a flourish of guitar chords and then Darryl J's voice, crooning, "'You can't leave her, you've got the fever, she's in your blood, you're delirious. In a way it's almost hilarious. And you're hooked, brother. She's your drug, brother. You got it bad, brother. She's your dru-u-ug.'"

Wonderful, Libby thought. A song about drugs. Well, not really—a song about love, using drugs as a metaphor. Perhaps he could have chosen a different song for his Web site, one that likened love to, say, spring flowers or sharks. But then, the first time she'd made love with Ned, she'd feared—rightly, it turned out—that she'd become addicted.

If looking as though one was about to shove his fist through a wall was a sign of approval, Harry approved of the song. Libby could practically feel waves of anger and indignation rolling off him. He turned to her. "We have to talk," he growled.

Ignoring him, she smiled at Darryl J and then at Eric. "The sound clip is great."

"It is, isn't it?" Reva said, sighing passionately. "Dad, isn't it great?"

"It's great," he snarled. "Your mother and I need to talk. Excuse us, please." He acted as if he were the host, in charge of the evening, and Libby realized some of the waves of anger and indignation she felt were rolling off her.

She held her ground. "We'll talk in a few minutes," she called after him as he stomped out of the den.

"Oh, my God!" he shouted from the entry. "What the hell did you do to the fireplace?"

"Libby didn't do that," Ned said, ignoring the quick shake Libby gave her head. She didn't want Ned to intervene. Whatever Harry had a bug up his butt about, Ned was not responsible for debugging him. Neither was Libby, but she'd been married to him and she had a certain familiarity with his bugs, as well as his butt.

Ned sauntered through the entry to the living room, Libby right behind him. He joined Harry, who stood stiffly, studying the fireplace and seething visibly. "See," Ned said amiably, "this is a beautiful marble fireplace, but someone slathered tons of paint onto it. I hope it wasn't you."

"Of course it wasn't me. Do you think I'd waste my time painting a fireplace?"

Ned shot Libby a smile, as if to assure her he wasn't insulted. *He'd* been wasting his time *un*painting the fireplace—except, of course, it hadn't been a waste of time. Libby loved the way it looked.

Reva sidled up behind her father. "Darryl J is packing up now," she informed Libby, "and then I guess Ash and Kim are gonna leave, too. So how do you like the fireplace, Dad?"

"I'm in shock."

"Eric says his dad is a fixer upper. He sure fixed up our fireplace." She smiled at Ned. Obviously, after the hour she'd spent with Darryl J, she had smiles for everyone.

"Who the hell is Eric?"

"Stop saying *hell*," Libby told Harry reproachfully.

"Eric's my son," Ned said.

Harry's gaze shuttled between Ned and Libby. His stubble-free cheeks lost a little color. "We need to talk, Libby." He reached for her elbow, but he must have sensed that she'd inflict pain to a sensitive part of his anatomy if he touched her. He let his hand drop. "Where can we go to get away from all these people?"

Acknowledging that Harry had promised to lend her a huge sum of money, she relented. "No one's in the bedroom. Reva, honey, say goodbye to your friends for me." With that, she stalked down the hall to her room.

Harry followed her in, slammed the door and suffered yet another visible spasm of horror at the sight of her files spread across her bed. "Libby, what the *hell* is going on?"

She wondered if he'd deliberately emphasized the word *hell* to piss her off. "What do you mean, what the hell is going on? I'm hosting a dinner party. If you'd called before dropping by, I would have told you that tonight isn't a good time for you to visit."

"A dinner party? You're hosting a zoo! That man—that fixer person—he's, what? A boyfriend?"

Vivienne would have answered "None of your business." But Libby shared Reva with Harry. That made his current wife her business, and, she supposed, her current boyfriend his business. "Yes," she said.

"He's a laborer! He smells like turpentine!"

"Not all the time," she said.

"He comes in here, into my daughter's home, and does that to my fireplace?"

Libby caught herself before erupting. "First of all, Harry, it's not your fireplace. Second of all, he made the fireplace look much better. Third of all, he loves that fireplace more than you ever did." So did she, especially after she and Ned had christened it with their midday fun and games a few days ago.

"And my sister—what the hell is she doing here?"

"She got mad at Leonard."

"So she left? Why didn't she stay home and make him leave?"

"I don't know," Libby said coolly. "I assumed it was a family trait. You let me stay and you left."

"I wasn't mad at you," he muttered, his dark eyes flashing. "I'm mad at you now, though. You've opened your house to all these people. You're parading your boyfriend in front of Reva and letting him mangle the fireplace. And that man—that musician. Who the hell is he?"

"He's a friend of Reva's."

"A friend? He's old enough to be—"

"Her older brother," Libby said.

"In case you didn't notice, he's the wrong race to be her brother."

"Do you have a problem with his race?" She could list plenty of reasons not to be happy with Reva's friendship with Darryl J—his age, of course, and his occupation, and his songs about drugs. As far as she was concerned, his race was a nonissue.

Obviously, Harry was bothered by it. "I always thought you were sensible, Libby. What, are you having a midlife crisis?"

"I'm not old enough for that," she retorted.

"I can't believe this. I feel like I've fallen down a rabbit hole. A strange black man hanging out with my daughter, some little boy using the computer I bought Reva, a handyman sleeping with my wife and—"

"Your *ex*-wife," Libby interrupted. "And you have no right to discuss my sex life. You have no right even to think about it."

"You're the mother of my child," Harry roared, "and you're acting completely irresponsible."

"And you're acting like a complete schmuck."

"That's it." He shook his head and waved his hands in a show of profound indignation. "I came here to make arrangements for transferring funds into your account so you can buy this damn apartment. And I'm looking around and wondering why the hell I should hand over all that money so you can host a circus here. Give me one good reason I should pay you for turning my daughter's home into chaos." He eyed the mess on her bed and winced.

"Here's one good reason. You promised," she said, fear clawing at her innards. He wouldn't renege, would he? He wouldn't back out now, when Sharma was well into the process of arranging her mortgage. He wouldn't dare.

Apparently, he would. "I'm going home, Libby. And let me warn you—" he jabbed his finger into the air barely an inch from her nose "—if you don't rein Reva in, there will be consequences."

Before she could respond—before she could slap his face, which was the first, and probably the best, response she could come up with—he pulled the door open so forcefully he nearly tore it from its hinges, and strode down the hall. She heard him open the front door, then slam it hard enough to leave the building shuddering in his wake.

She remained where she was, trembling with rage and dread. "Hey, Mom?" Reva hollered from the kitchen. "The rice burned!"

Libby couldn't move. She could scarcely think.

She was homeless once again.

Twenty-Two

Ned checked the address once more. The guys on the crew had told him Spring Street was a block before Broome Street, so if he hit Broome he'd know he had gone too far. Greater Manhattan Design Associates had renovated a loft in SoHo last year, before Ned had joined the firm, so they all were familiar with the neighborhood.

Ned was getting familiar with Manhattan's neighborhoods, too. He suspected that by winter he would feel like a true New Yorker. The city didn't take long to suck a person in and transform him. Already he was walking faster, talking faster, getting by on less sleep—and not even noticing the white noise of city traffic when he did finally crawl into bed.

He wanted to crawl into bed right now—with Libby. Instead, he was marching downtown to do something that would probably make her feel a whole lot better than sex.

Purple shadows stretched across the narrow downtown streets as the sun slid past New Jersey to the west. Ned paused at a corner when the light turned red—one sure sign that he wasn't yet a true New Yorker. Most of the other pedestrians hurrying home after work would never let a mere red light stop them. They charged across the street, glaring fiercely at any car that dared to honk at them. Ned had foolishly hesitated at the curb, and the cars surged into the intersection, denying him the opportunity to jaywalk.

He hoped Harry Kimmelman had hurried home. Ned would hate to have begged Mrs. Karpinsky to stay with Eric an extra hour—and begged Eric not to whine about staying with Mrs. Karpinsky an extra hour—and walked all the way from the Meatpacking District to Kimmelman's place on Thompson Street, only to find the SOB not home. Ned could have phoned ahead, except that if he had, Harry might have told him not to come. And damn it, he was going to set the bastard straight. Face-to-face, mano a mano.

Every time he thought back to last night, he suffered a surge of fury. He'd spent most of the day staring at one of Macie Colwyn's grandiose pillars or her heating vents or the pickled-maple kitchen cabinets, which had been delivered that morning, and finding himself pondering not the job at hand but the tension that had tightened Libby's mouth throughout yesterday evening. He remembered the flashes of panic in her expressive eyes, the way she'd choked on small talk and picked at her food and let her whacko sister-in-law dominate the dinner conversation. While Libby had silently stewed, Vivienne had held forth on her belief that men watched televised sports to avoid thinking about sex— a laughable theory, given that men thought about sex all the time, even during the Superbowl—and her complaints about the quality of wine served after services at her temple, and her concerns about whether her parents had enough money socked away to retire comfortably in ten years, "Because I won't be able to give them much. And Harry's such a *putz,* who knows what he'll do?"

Ned had heard the rise and fall of Harry's voice in Libby's bedroom yesterday, just before the guy had taken off. Harry and Libby had exchanged words heated enough to transform the entire apartment into a tropical paradise. But Libby clearly hadn't wished to discuss the argument in front of the kids and her sister-in-law. She'd put on a show after Harry's departure, smiling gamely, setting the table, scraping the charred rice out of the pot and calling everyone into the dining room for dinner. She'd eaten little, but downed three glasses of wine, one more glass than Vivienne had consumed. And Vivienne had walked out on her husband. According to the wine-o-meter, whatever Harry had done to Libby in the bedroom was worse than a marital rupture.

Vivienne had insisted on hanging around in the kitchen after dinner, helping Libby clean up after the meal. Ned had wanted to be Libby's helper—he'd hoped that doing the dishes together would give them a chance to talk—but in Vivienne's presence, Libby hadn't said much. She'd only nodded whenever Vivienne cast aspersions on her brother. "That squash club he belongs to? It's all goyim. Forgive me, Ned," she'd added, although he'd had no idea what *goyim* meant. "He's such a snob, Libby. Did I ever tell you about the time we went on a vacation in the Catskills, and he spent the whole week kvetching because there was no place to go scuba diving?" She must have noticed Ned's confusion, because she'd explained to him, "Jews don't scuba."

"Sure they do," Libby had argued, but Vivienne had sounded so authoritative, Ned had taken her word for it.

"I can't believe he barged in here like that!" Vivienne had ranted. "No invitation, no warning, just 'Hello! Drop dead! Goodbye!'"

"Let's not talk about it," Libby had said, considerately not mentioning that Vivienne had also barged in with no invitation or warning. At least she'd seemed unlikely to tell anyone other than her brother to drop dead. "Where do you want to sleep tonight?" Libby had continued, deftly changing the subject. "You can have the living-room couch, but it's lumpy. Or you could share my bed. It's big enough."

Ned had suffered a stab of jealousy. He would have liked to share Libby's bed, but the odds of his getting his wish last night had been zero to none.

Eric had appeared at the door. "Reva and I changed the Web site a little. Wanna see?"

Ned had grabbed the opening. "Reva's Aunt Vivienne will check it out," he'd said. "Ms. Kimmelman and I have to talk." He'd punctuated this statement by giving Vivienne a pointed look.

She'd shrugged and spread her arms. "You want me to check out the Web site? I'll check out the Web site." Then she'd followed Eric through the dining room and out of sight.

Ned had closed the kitchen door, pried the dishcloth out of Libby's hand, turned her away from the sink and wrapped his arms around her. "Are you all right?"

"Of course," Libby had said, then made a little sound that was a cross between a laugh and a sob. "Harry decided not to help me buy this apartment, that's all."

"Why?" he'd asked in a level voice, even though anger had bubbled up inside him like some dangerous chemical reaction. He'd figured he would have to stay calm in case Libby exploded. They couldn't both explode.

She hadn't exploded. She'd made another hybrid laugh-sob sound, then eased out of his arms. "God only knows. He thinks I'm a bad mother."

"Why?" Judging by the result—Reva—Ned would

grade Libby pretty high on the parent scale. Higher than him, for sure.

"Because Reva's friendly with a black musician? I don't know. Then again, Reva may have nothing to do with it. Maybe he's just pissed that you took the paint off the fireplace."

Ned reviewed the situation as he turned the corner onto Spring Street. He was going to pay a call on the *putz* and tell him that, fireplace or no, he'd made a promise to Libby and he'd better not break it. The apartment on West End Avenue was her home, hers and Reva's. If the fact that Ned had rehabilitated the fireplace—or, more likely, the fact that Ned had slept with Libby and hoped to sleep with her again in the near future—was enough to make Harry deny Libby her home, then he deserved to have his balls torn off, fricasseed and served with some of Libby's burned rice on the side.

From Spring Street, Ned headed onto Thompson and found the building. Libby hadn't supplied him with the address; he hadn't informed her of his plan to pay a call on Harry, because he'd been sure she would tell him not to. Ned respected her, and he believed in letting a woman fight her own battles. But this was about her fireplace, damn it. This was about Harry punishing her for including Ned in her life, and that made it *his* battle.

In any case, learning Harry's address had been simple enough. A person could find just about anything on the Internet.

Although the building was fairly large, only twelve names appeared on the intercom buttons. Two apartments per floor, Ned calculated. They must be huge apartments. Not surprising—Harry was rich, after all. A hotshot corporate attorney, Libby had told him.

Ned pressed the button next to Kimmelman. After a minute, a woman's voice crackled through the speaker. "Yes?"

"My name is Ned Donovan." He leaned toward the speaker and projected his voice. Shouting into intercoms in empty vestibules was one of those native-New-Yorker activities he hadn't yet grown used to. "I'd like to see Harry Kimmelman."

"Ned who?" the woman asked.

"Donovan. I'm a friend of Libby's." After a few seconds of silence, he added, "It's important."

The inner door buzzed as the lock was released. He opened it, went inside and summoned the elevator. Unlike Libby's elevator, this one had no paneling, no brass, no charm. The walls were gray, for God's sake. Elevators were inherently gray. Giving them gray walls was redundant.

He emerged on the top floor and pressed the doorbell for Harry's apartment. The woman who opened the door was thin and painfully chic, her streaked blond hair cut in an angular style, her eyes impeccably made up and her nose a bit too small for her face. She wore a brown slacks outfit in some fabric he'd never seen before, shiny but with little nubs texturing it, and the open neckline displayed her collarbones and her scrawny neck. She needed at least ten more pounds on her, and a normal hairstyle. Ned couldn't believe Harry would have left a real woman like Libby for a plastic one like this.

Then again, looks weren't everything. This woman might have the perfect personality for Harry.

"Hi," he said, attempting a smile he hoped was neither too friendly nor too scary. "I'm Ned Donovan. Can I talk to Harry for a minute?"

The woman eyed him up and down. Having come here straight from work, he wasn't at his most presentable. He hadn't performed too much messy labor today—mostly overseeing the work of the electrician and plumber as they piped and wired the kitchen—but a laborer couldn't leave a construction site without some crud on him. And Ned's clothes—stained denim jeans and an old U of P sweatshirt under his denim jacket—would seem shabby even if they were clean.

She twisted to call over her shoulder, "Harry? That man is here." She made the word *man* sound like a curse.

"I'm coming." Harry's voice echoed from the nether reaches of the apartment. He strode down the entry hall and joined the woman at the door. His suit was perfectly tailored to his lanky frame, and his face had about as much character as low-fat yogurt. Maybe some women considered all that bland symmetry attractive. At one time, Libby must have. That realization unnerved Ned a little.

"Hi," Ned said, reviving his neither-here-nor-there smile.

"So we meet again," Harry responded.

"We need to talk about last night," Ned said, wondering if they were going to have their talk across the threshold, him out in the elevator alcove and Harry safely inside the apartment. With only one other neighbor on the floor, Harry might not worry about anyone eavesdropping on their conversation.

Harry sized him up, then waved him inside. "Please, come in," he said.

Great. We're going to be civilized, Ned thought as he entered the apartment.

It was everything Libby's apartment wasn't: austere, tidy and chilly. Accompanying Harry down the hall, the walls of which were decorated with framed photographs of dead trees in silhouette, Ned passed a state-of-the-art kitchen much like the one he was building for Macie Colwyn. The hall ended in a spacious great room, in which everything— walls, windows, furniture—had been designed with a straightedge and protractor. The couches, chairs, bookcases, tables and area rugs were all rectangular. Ice cubes had more curves—and more warmth.

"Can I get you a drink?" Harry asked, loosening his tie as he crossed to a rectangular bar built into one wall.

Very civilized. If they shared a drink, Ned supposed no blood would be shed. He wondered if Harry's bar glasses were rectangular, too. "I don't suppose you've got a beer?" he asked.

Harry gave him a withering stare.

Okay. Ned would be civilized. "I'll have whatever you're having," he said.

Harry turned from him, plunked some ice into two high-ball glasses and filled them with Scotch. Carrying the glasses across the room, he gestured toward two of the boxy leather chairs. Ned lowered himself into one. It was as uncomfortable as it looked.

Harry handed Ned his drink and then sat facing him, cradling his glass without sipping from it. It was his prop. Ned needed a prop, too—and a glass of Harry's high-priced Scotch wouldn't do. A hammer would have worked. He should have brought one with him.

Lacking a hammer, Ned opted for directness. "The fireplace had to be stripped, so I stripped it. This doesn't mean you shouldn't help Libby buy her apartment."

Harry blinked. Evidently, he hadn't expected him to be as blunt as, well, a hammer. "What I do with Libby is none of your concern."

"Actually, it is my concern," Ned said. "She thinks you're backing out on her because of the rehab work I've been doing. The rehab work is *good* for her apartment. It increases the value of the place. By having me do this work, Libby's demonstrating how much the apartment means to her."

"If she can afford to have that rehab work done, then let her pay for the apartment herself," Harry snapped. "My daughter's home was a zoo last night. My *meshuggeneh* sister was hiding out from her husband there, and you were tearing apart the living room, and some street *schnorrer* was using the electronic equipment I bought for Reva. Why should I pour money into that kind of *tsores*?"

"That street *schnorrer* is a talented musician," Ned argued, wondering what a *schnorrer* was. "Maybe you ought to consider investing some money in him. He's going places."

"One place he shouldn't be going is Libby's apartment." Harry finally took a sip of his Scotch.

Ned took a sip, too. He wasn't much of a Scotch drinker, but this was definitely the good stuff. "If Libby loses the apartment, where is she supposed to go?" he asked. "Vermont?" The notion almost made him laugh. Libby would hate Vermont. The peace, the forests and the big blue sky would drive her crazy.

"Would it kill her to move to Queens?" Harry retorted. "There are lots of nice apartments in Queens. She could find a place as big as where she's living now for half the money."

Queens was another New York neighborhood Ned wasn't familiar with. He suspected that to Libby, it was as remote as Vermont. "Queens would put you farther away from Reva," he pointed out.

"I have a car. I could drive to Queens." Harry drank some more Scotch.

So did Ned. If he could afford this quality of booze, he might turn into a Scotch drinker. "You weren't the bozo who painted the fireplace, right?" he asked.

Harry's eyes hardened. "Why on earth would you even ask such a question?"

"Somebody painted it," Ned said. "Someone globbed multiple coats of white enamel over a beautiful marble structure. If it wasn't you, I don't see why you'd be so ticked about someone—namely me—removing that enamel."

"Who are you, anyway?" Harry shook his head. "Libby's opening her house to all sorts of strangers—"

"Libby and I are friends."

"She never mentioned you to me."

"Does she mention all her other friends to you?"

Harry mulled that over, swallowed some Scotch and sighed. "Let's not beat around the bush," he said, and Ned braced himself for the possibility that Harry would start wielding his own metaphorical hammer. "Libby can barely afford the damn apartment. She certainly can't afford paying people to renovate the place. I have some idea what handymen cost in this city, and let me tell you, it's made me wonder whether I made the right choice when I went to law school."

Yeah, sure. Handymen made more than corporate lawyers.

"I know Libby can't afford you," Harry continued, "so I put two and two together. You do something for her, and she does something for you. And I don't like it."

So that was Harry's swing of the hammer—and as far as Ned was concerned, Harry had seriously toed the nail. "You think she's sleeping with me in payment for my work on the fireplace," he said, not sure whether to laugh or to punch Harry's lights out.

"Women have done more for less," Harry said, as if he were some kind of expert. "And with my daughter living under Libby's roof, I—"

"Whoa." Ned held up his hand to stop him. "I'm not sure which I love more, Libby or her fireplace. Probably Libby— but I fell in love with the fireplace first. One thing has nothing to do with another."

"I'm supposed to believe that?"

"Not only are you supposed to believe it, but you're supposed to let Libby hang on to that fireplace once I'm done with it."

Harry mulled this over, then decided he needed more Scotch. He crossed to the bar and brought back the bottle so he could add a little to Ned's glass. Ned didn't object.

"My real concern is Reva, of course," Harry said.

"Of course," Ned echoed.

"Bonnie and I are married. You and Libby are not."

"And all Reva ever sees of me is when I've got my head stuck up the chimney, trying to bring that fireplace back to life. What, do you think that if you force Libby to move to Queens she's never going to date? She's a smart, beautiful woman. If she lived in Queens, I'd travel to Queens to see her. Kicking her out of her apartment isn't going to turn her into a nun."

"She's Jewish," Harry muttered. "Nunhood is out of the question."

Given what she'd told Ned about her sex life—or lack thereof—he didn't believe nunhood was out of the question at all. "What she is is a terrific lady," he said. "And you and she have a terrific daughter. And you're a good man. So let her and her daughter stay in their apartment. Help them out on the finances. Save the fireplace."

Harry drank. He stared at his glass. He stared at Ned. He drank again. But he didn't argue.

By the time they were on their third round, Ned had told him about Deborah, about his moving to New York and joining Greater Manhattan Design Associates, and about his love of old architecture—which was why he was so taken with Libby's prewar building. Harry had admitted that Libby was a fine woman, just not the woman for him— which Ned had no trouble believing, if the chic, skeletal woman who occasionally wandered into the room and made comments about a reception at a gallery in Westbeth was his type. Whenever she appeared, Harry would dutifully glance at his watch, tell her he was noting the time and remind her it never paid to arrive at these events early. Then he'd launch into another story about how often Libby had vomited during her pregnancy, or how bad her taste in home decor was. Ned would concede that she hadn't done much with her apartment—but then, she lacked the money. Harry and his wife apparently had plenty of money, and their home decor put him in mind of a bad science-fiction movie.

He kept his eye on the time, too. He'd given Mrs. Karpinsky the number of Mitch's cell phone, which remained clipped to his belt, and she hadn't phoned to ask him where he was and when he'd be home, so he let Harry run on. Somewhere between his second and third drink, Harry agreed once again to help Libby with the financing for her apartment. Somewhere well into his third, he mentioned that his law firm had done work for a local music promoter. "Your opinion is this street kid with the Buckwheat braids is good?" he asked. "I wouldn't know. I listen to bass koto and shakuhachi music. Japanese stuff. Don't ask. It's Bonnie's idea."

When Harry's wife reentered the room to harangue him about the reception, Ned was feeling no pain. "I really ought to get home," he said. "My son will be worried I fell down a manhole or something."

"And I've got to go look at ugly modern art." Harry stood, walked him to the door and shook his hand. "Don't be a stranger," he said, clapping a hand on Ned's shoulder as he sent him off.

Ned struggled to clear his head as the gray elevator carried him down to the ground floor. He'd accomplished his mission, and even gotten Harry interested in setting Reva's musician up with his partner's client in the music business. That his tongue felt slightly numb was irrelevant. Right now, he was thinking that if Harry was a *putz,* a *putz* wasn't such a bad thing to be.

Twenty-Three

Luke Rodelle had settled in with the divas two tables over from where Reva sat with Kim and Ashleigh. Announcing that she was no longer a vegetarian, Ashleigh had purchased a hot lunch, some kind of mystery meat with gummy brown gravy slathered over it. It smelled greasy. Or maybe the greasy smell came from Kim's teriyaki beef.

Despite her hunger, the aromas were getting to Reva. Only by holding her tuna-salad sandwich close to her face could she block the greasy smell from her nose.

She should be in a good mood. Her dad had acted like a dickhead on Thursday, and he'd put her mother in a majorly foul state, but Friday night Mr. Donovan had phoned her mother and cheered her right up. Aunt Vivienne had left Saturday morning after Leonard called to say he'd meet her at synagogue. She'd lectured him about how he wasn't supposed to use the telephone on Shabbat, but all in all she'd seemed in high spirits when she'd left, dragging her suitcase behind her.

Mr. Donovan and Eric had spent Saturday afternoon with Reva and her mother. They'd walked over to Riverside Park and hung out, which had been pretty boring. Maybe Eric and his dad got excited about viewing trees because they were from Vermont. But if Reva was going to hang out in a park, she'd much rather hang out in Central Park, which was full of people and musicians.

After staring at the trees and tossing bread crumbs to the pigeons for an eternity, Mr. Donovan had taken them all out for dinner at a local Italian place. Afterward, they'd gone back to the apartment, where her mother and Mr. Donovan had vanished into her mother's bedroom to watch TV on the small set. Reva would have suspected them of doing something private in there, but they'd left the door open and the TV on, and when Reva had peeked through the doorway she'd seen the two of them fully dressed, sitting side by side on the bed, with pillows propped up against the headboard, Mr. Donovan holding a bottle of beer and Reva's mother a glass of wine. They'd been laughing over some show about UFOs on the Discovery Channel.

Whatever was going on between them existed even when they were wearing their clothes. For what that was worth.

Mr. Donovan was a nice guy. Eric was okay, too. Both of them had been indispensable in setting up Darryl J's Web site. Reva should be happy her mother was dating someone who wasn't a dork or an asshole.

And she was, really. Her melancholy had nothing to do with her mother, or with Mr. Donovan, or with Eric, who even though he was okay was only ten years old. It had to do with herself. And with Darryl J.

She'd expected something more. Something magic. When the sound clip had been added to Darryl J's Web site, and everyone had been so excited, and Darryl J had expressed his gratitude... Reva had expected *something*. She wasn't sure what, but something more than, "Thanks. This is real cool. I appreciate it."

Okay, so Darryl J wasn't about to declare his love for her, especially in her mother's apartment with her father going ballistic and her aunt Vivienne acting flaky and Ashleigh and Kim and the Donovans all there to witness the moment. But Darryl J had her e-mail address, and he could have sent her a message. He wouldn't have to use the word *love,* but he should have communicated *something*. Like: "We make a good team, don't we?" or "This was so much fun we ought to work on some more projects together," or "I could use a backup singer—can you carry a tune?"

After everything Reva had done for him, the least he owed her was...*something*. Something more than silence.

Her stomach felt queasy, like just before her period. The aromas from Ashleigh's and Kim's lunches didn't help. Reva bit into her sandwich and chewed, willing the wet, salty flavor of fish and mayonnaise to soothe her digestive system.

"It looks like I'm going to trick-or-treat this year," Ashleigh said.

God knew, with her weird Goth outfits and her black nail polish, she hardly needed a costume. Reva didn't say that, though. Just because she was in a foul mood didn't mean she should be bitchy to her friends.

"Eighth graders don't trick-or-treat," Kim argued.

"They do if they're spoofing. My folks told me I have to take my sister around the building. If I'm going trick-or-treating with her, I may as well get myself up a little, you know? And collect lots of candy."

Maybe if Reva ate more candy, she'd grow a bigger bosom. Ashleigh had to be somewhere between a B and a

C cup. If trick-or-treating could produce that kind of result, Reva might do it. Then she remembered that bosom size was genetic, and Ashleigh's mother had such big boobs she'd had them surgically reduced. Ashleigh had inherited her figure. Candy had nothing to do with it.

Katie Staver approached, carrying an insulated lunch bag and smiling. "Hey, Reva," she said, flopping into the chair next to her. She flashed her even white teeth at Kim and Ashleigh. "Hey, Ash. Hey, Kim. Mind if I join you?"

She'd already joined them, but Reva nodded to inform her she was welcome, and shifted her chair to make more room for Katie at the table. "Thanks again for letting us borrow your recorder last week," she said.

"I checked the Web site. It's great." Katie meticulously unwrapped her sandwich and took a delicate bite. "Any chance we can get Darryl J to play at the dance?"

"I don't know." Since Reva hadn't heard from him since Thursday, she had no idea what Darryl J would or wouldn't do.

Katie seemed unconcerned. "Well, if we have to go with a deejay, we can hire the guy last year's eighth-grade class used. I heard he was pretty good." She leaned toward Reva and murmured, "Matt told me Luke likes you."

Reva scowled so hard the bridge of her nose ached. "He's over there with Larissa LeMoyne. That's who he likes." She waved her sandwich toward the diva table. A glob of tuna slipped out from between the slices of rye bread and landed on her napkin. Great. At least it hadn't landed on her jeans, she thought grimly.

"He can't stand Larissa," Katie told her. "He's probably just explaining the algebra homework to her. She's so dense. How did she get into honors math?"

"I can guess," Ashleigh said, winking slyly.

Reva could imagine Larissa using her body to get things,

but she doubted honors math would be her goal. In any case, Luke appeared to be having a mighty fine a time explaining the homework to her. They were probably talking about hubcaps. Larissa was probably telling him how much she admired his taste in auto accessories—and then, the instant he left the table, she'd giggle with the other divas and come up with insulting names for him behind his back.

Which would serve him right for spending time at that table. Anyone who flirted with the divas got what he deserved.

"The thing is," Katie said with great authority, "Micah Schlutt heard Luke say he liked you, and you know Micah. He couldn't keep it to himself."

"Oh, God." Reva's stomach clenched. "Who did he tell?"

"Just Matt, I think. And Matt told me. And I'm telling you. You could do worse, Reva."

She could do better, too. She could hook up with a brilliantly talented musician who could be a superstar if only someone paid attention. Someone besides Reva. Someone with power.

Except Darryl J hadn't been in touch with her for four whole days now. And Luke had apparently said he liked her, loud enough for Micah Schlutt to overhear. Assuming Micah wasn't lying, which was also a possibility.

For some reason, Reva's stomach settled. Maybe she'd gotten used to the fumes emanating from Kim's and Ashleigh's meals. Maybe she was getting used to the idea that Darryl J wasn't going to thank her by falling in love with her. She flicked a discreet glance toward the diva table and saw Luke writing something on a page of Larissa's notebook, and decided he actually could be going over the math homework.

Maybe he did like Reva. Stranger things had been known to happen.

* * *

Tara bounced into the office just as Libby lowered the phone to its cradle. A picture of blond effervescence, Tara wore a dress so short Libby initially thought it was just a big shirt. Around Tara's left wrist was a noisy charm bracelet that jingled whenever she moved her hand. "Just one more week," she said cheerfully as she placed three more files onto one of the piles circling Libby's desk. The stacks of folders rose along the perimeter, leaving her blotter clear at the center. It reminded Libby of the ice-skating rink at the heart of Rockefeller Center, a flat ground-level oasis surrounded by towers.

She leaned back in her chair and smiled up at Tara. Thinking about the impending application deadline bolstered her. After October 31st, no more applications would be accepted. The Hudson School had been deluged—submissions were up by fifteen percent over last year—but soon the flood would end and Libby could begin to mop up.

"So…that was Ned Donovan on the phone," Tara said.

Libby's smile expanded. Ned had called her from his work site to find out if she'd spoken to Harry on Sunday when he'd dropped Reva off after her weekly visit. Just as Ned had predicted, Harry had told her he would fund her down payment after all. He'd also mentioned that he considered his sister a nutcase. "She never should have married Leonard," Harry had said, as if he were some sort of expert on marriage. "The guy is immature, and he dresses like a schlub—his pants are too long and baggy, and his shirt's always untucked. I think the fireplace looked better when it was painted white, by the way."

Harry didn't give a rat's ass about the fireplace. What he'd given a rat's ass about was the man renovating the fireplace. Libby knew it, and apparently, so did Ned. Harry had been shocked to discover Libby had her own life—which included his sister and his daughter's friends and, yes, a smart, funny, drop-dead gorgeous man with a talent for taking drab old objects—for instance, a fireplace or a woman—and rejuvenating them.

Harry had no right to be threatened by the fact that his ex-wife was seeing someone. He had Bonnie, and Ned wasn't the first man Libby had dated since the divorce. He was, however, the first man who'd rejuvenated her fireplace.

"So, what's going on with you and the Hudson Hunk?" Tara asked. Because she answered Libby's phone and screened her calls, Tara was aware of just how often Ned was in touch with Libby during work hours.

"We're friends," Libby said discreetly.

"Yeah, right." Tara shook her head and giggled. "Like any woman could be *friends* with a guy like that."

"He's very friendly," Libby insisted.

"I'll bet he is." Tara tapped her fingernails against the top folder on one of the piles. "So what are you going to do about his kid?"

Adopt him, Libby almost said, although that was a bit premature. Sure, she and Ned were friends—crazy-about-each-other friends. Well, she was crazy about him. And honestly, would he have schlepped all the way to SoHo to twist Harry's arm if he wasn't crazy about her?

But crazy-about-each-other was a long way from marriage, from stepchildren, from adoption. Libby had a much more immediate concern when it came to Eric Donovan, and she suspected that was what Tara was asking her about. She'd already given the matter some thought, and she understood what she had to do. "I'll recuse myself."

Tara winced. "You interviewed the kid. How can you not participate in his evaluation?"

"I'll report honestly on the interview," Libby said. "He's

a great kid, and I'll make sure the committee knows that. If they think he should have another interview with someone more objective, they can set it up."

"You want him in," Tara guessed.

"Of course I do. And not because his father and I are…*friends*. Because he's smart and funny and he isn't like all the preprogrammed robot kids who apply here. He hasn't spent the first ten years of his life plotting his ascension to Harvard. He's a computer whiz and he can actually have a conversation with Reva, which requires a high degree of sophistication, to say nothing of patience. He's a great kid," she repeated, aware of how completely biased she sounded. That was why she maintained fierce scruples about the admissions process. Anyone with a personal connection to an applicant had to remove herself from the acceptance decision.

I'm going to be objective. Her mantra hummed through her brain. She had no objectivity about Eric, so she had to sit out his application process.

He'd probably get in without her influence, anyway. He was definitely a great kid.

Bonnie invited Reva to spend the night with her and Harry downtown that weekend. "I promised I'd buy her a new outfit for her solo," Bonnie told Libby when she'd called to make arrangements. "It's about time she started dressing with a little style."

In other words, Libby was a failure when it came to the sartorial education of her daughter. She couldn't argue. She'd taught Reva to shop by first searching for the Sale signs, then checking the price tag, and only after the first two steps had been taken assessing whether the article of clothing flattered her. "Style" was generally synonymous with "expensive," and Harry's child-support payments extended only so far. Libby supposed she could feed Reva a diet of potatoes and powdered milk and spend on apparel the money she saved on groceries. But if Reva subsisted on potatoes and powdered milk, she probably wouldn't look good in any of those high-priced, high-fashion items Libby would be able to afford.

So she fed Reva a healthy, well-balanced diet and taught her to buy clothing at discounted prices. Jeans were jeans, after all. Libby couldn't see spending fifty extra dollars for the brand patch on the hip pocket.

Bonnie had plans, though. "I'm going to take her around to some of the trendy boutiques down here," she said. "Let her go wild. She isn't a child anymore. What size is she now? Eight? Ten?"

"I think she's a four," Libby said, resentment sifting into her tone. She couldn't care less what size Reva wore, but she'd be damned if she'd let Bonnie convince Reva she was bigger than she ought to be.

"A four? Well, we should be able to work with that," Bonnie said.

"Remember, this outfit is for a school concert. It can't be risqué. No exposed navel."

"Now, Libby, if anyone understands appropriate fashions, I do."

Libby supposed Bonnie did. She edited a slick fashion magazine; that required a certain expertise. And if she wound up buying Reva a fashion that didn't pass the "appropriate" test, Libby would simply have Reva wear one of her old subdued outfits for the concert.

Ned was thrilled to hear that Reva would be sleeping down in SoHo Saturday night. He pretended he was delighted about Reva's shopping spree, but Libby knew the real reason her news made him happy. It made her happy for the same reason.

After lunch on Saturday, she swallowed hard and sent Reva off on the IRT. When Reva phoned her from Harry's house to report that she'd arrived safely, Libby headed for Ned's apartment. She huffed and puffed up the stairs and found him and Eric waiting in the hall outside their apartment. "We need your help," Ned announced. "We're carving a pumpkin."

They spent the afternoon creating an elaborate jack-o-lantern. Libby taught Ned and Eric how to roast the pumpkin seeds. She would have thought that in rustic Vermont, folks would know how to do this. Weren't they all back-to-nature types up there? Earth mothers and gardeners who canned their own produce? Apparently, Ned and Eric had never realized pumpkin seeds were edible. Libby suddenly felt like a cordon bleu chef because she could spread the pulpy seeds on a cookie sheet and stick them in the oven until they turned crunchy.

She, Ned and Eric also spent some time assembling Eric's costume. Originally, he'd thought he wanted to trick-or-treat as a bum, but as he explained it, he'd realized there were lots of homeless people in Manhattan and they might not think a "bum" was such a funny costume. His friend Gilbert would be trick-or-treating as Spiderman, but Eric didn't want to wear stockings, which eliminated most superheroes. Libby suggested a pirate, a cowboy and a fireman, but Eric seemed to think those ideas were juvenile. Finally, he decided he would be a handyman. Ned rigged a tool belt for him and promised to bring home a hard hat from work on Monday. With blue jeans, his hiking boots and a couple of dirt smudges on his face—"Fixer uppers get dirty on the job," Ned insisted—Eric would have an excellent costume.

They sent out for pizza for dinner. Reva loved pizza, and Libby suffered a pang of regret that her daughter would not be enjoying this treat with Harry and Bonnie tonight. They would probably take her to some exclusive restaurant where she'd have to order something with truffles or au poivre, and Bonnie would glower at her throughout the meal to make sure she didn't eat too much. But an extravagant and appropriately fashionable ensemble would be her reward for putting up with Bonnie.

After dinner, Ned, Eric and Libby played a cockamamie card game that Libby never quite caught on to. Then Eric went off to read—he'd just discovered *A Wrinkle in Time*—and Libby and Ned played gin, which Libby knew inside out. She took great pleasure in trouncing him.

Neither of them could concentrate fully on the cards, however. They were both thinking about the time, waiting for Eric to go to bed and drift into his nuclear-explosion-defying slumber.

Less than a minute after Eric fell asleep, Ned and Libby were shut inside Ned's bedroom, naked, going at it with the enthusiasm of lovers who had been celibate for years rather than not quite a full week. Libby didn't care what Ned said; this was nothing like riding a bike. If it was, she would quit her position at the Hudson School and find a job as a bicycle courier, just so she could feel this spectacular every day.

But of course, the only way she could feel this spectacular was if Ned was her bicycle, lean and strong, fitting so perfectly between her legs and carrying her to a gloriously carnal destination. He joined her there, groaning and pressing deep inside her, then nuzzled her cheek. "We're good at this, you know?" he mumbled.

"Yes," she agreed. A single-syllable word was pretty much all she could manage.

He rose slightly, propping himself on his arms. "You're not sorry, are you?"

She focused on his face above hers, his sly smile and his

mussed hair, and gave him a shove, although he was too big and heavy for her to push off her. Not that she truly desired to have him off her. "Don't you dare sing that song," she warned.

"Come on. I've got a great voice."

"Well, if you've got to sing something, choose another song. How about 'It Ain't The Meat, It's The Motion'?"

"How about 'I'm On Fire'?"

"Or you could do a few bars of 'Whole Lotta Love.'"

"Mmm." He moved his hips, stirring inside her. "'Gonna give you every inch.' Now, that's a song I can relate to."

She laughed, but when he moved his hips again her laughter faded. Even spent and half-soft, he could make her come. She gasped and let out a quiet sigh. Were other men so amazing in bed? If so, why hadn't she ever felt like this before?

He bowed to kiss her, slowly, softly, like Sleeping Beauty's prince awakening her from her trance. She opened her eyes again and saw Ned, only Ned. And she realized, with an odd mixture of joy and dismay, that she was insanely in love with him.

He eased off her, then wrapped his arms around her and pulled her against him. "Don't run away this time."

"I didn't run away last time," she said.

"No, you walked away—at six in the morning."

"Because Eric—"

"The hell with Eric." He laughed. "I don't mean that. Eric can handle seeing you over his pancakes in the morning."

"Maybe he can. I'm not sure I can handle him."

"You ought to get used to handling him." Ned twirled his fingers through her hair. Such a simple, casual motion, yet it very nearly made her come again. "We can't keep sneaking around like a couple of kids, Libby. We're grown-ups. We're allowed to have sex."

"I know, but—"

"And kids are smart. They can figure out what's going on. Wouldn't you rather be honest about it?"

"Kids in the abstract is one thing," she rationalized. "Eric and Reva aren't in the abstract. They're our children."

He stroked through her hair to her nape and traced gentle circles against her skin. "Is it such an awkward thing that you have breakfast with Reva and then you see her at the Hudson School?"

"Reva is my daughter," Libby argued. "It's completely different."

"Would it be awful if you had pancakes with Eric and then ran into him at school?"

"I don't eat pancakes," Libby muttered. "They're fattening. And while I can't say your scenario would be awful, it would be...uncomfortable."

"For you. Not for Eric."

"How do you know? Some kids would die of embarrassment if they realized their parents were having sex."

"Eric's not like that."

Libby wished she could believe Ned. Eric was his son, after all. Perhaps he was right and Eric wouldn't think twice about the Hudson director of admissions sleeping with his father.

"Okay," Ned said, relenting. "If you don't want to deal with this yet, we won't. But sooner or later we will. Because I think we've got something special, Libby. I'd like Eric to get used to your presence in his life. And once Eric starts attending Hudson, you'll be seeing him there."

A tickle of cold ran down Libby's spine, not from Ned's teasing caresses but from his words: *once Eric starts attending Hudson...* He sounded as if this was a given, as if not a single question existed, but that Eric would be accepted into the Hudson School.

Libby was the director of admissions, and much as she hoped he'd get in, even she couldn't predict whether he would.

She eased back from Ned and sat up. "Ned," she said. "I'd like to believe Eric will be attending Hudson next year, but he hasn't been accepted."

He blinked, his smile fading, his eyes quizzical. *"Yet,"* Ned said. "He hasn't been accepted *yet.*"

"If I had anything to do with it, Ned, he'd be in. No doubt about it."

Ned sat straighter, too. A line dented the bridge of his nose. *"If* you had anything to do with it? You run the show over there. You're in charge of who gets in."

"Yes, but I've recused myself from Eric's application."

"What?" The word burst out of him with the force of a nuclear explosion. She glanced at the door, half expecting Eric to stagger in, rubbing his eyes and whining about having been awakened.

"I won't participate in Eric's application decision. I can't, Ned. The process has to be objective, and I'm not objective about him. If I pushed for him, when we've got a personal relationship…it wouldn't be fair."

"Wait a minute." Ned appeared outraged. "You're telling me that you could get Eric in and you're not going to?"

"I'm going to step aside and let the rest of the admissions committee decide."

"Libby. Attending Hudson is Eric's dream. He's never asked for anything, but he asked for this. He deserves it. He *should* go there."

"I agree—"

"But you won't lift a finger to help him."

"I can't, Ned." His anger unnerved her. Surely if he looked at the situation logically and dispassionately, he'd understand her dilemma. She was a professional. She had to be objective. It was her job. "What if everyone on the committee had personal connections with some of the applicants? Getting into Hudson would be about nothing more than who you knew."

"Isn't that the way the world works?" Ned raised his eyes to the ceiling, as if it might contain instructions for how to regain control of his temper. Apparently, it didn't, because when he leveled his gaze back to Libby his face was etched with anger. "For once in his life, my kid asked for something. For once in my life, I knew someone. And you won't do a damn thing for him."

"I can't."

"Shit." He spun away from her, swung off the bed and stormed out of the room. She heard him in the bathroom, banging things, slamming things. Several minutes passed and she began to wonder whether he planned to remain in the bathroom until she was gone.

She began to wonder other things, too. *For once in my life, I knew someone.* Was that why she was in Ned's bed now? Was that why he'd made such sweet love to her? Was that why he'd fixed her fireplace and persuaded Harry to honor his promise of financial assistance? Was this all Ned's way of "knowing someone," someone who could get his son into a highly selective private school?

Some people gave her flowers and candy to ease their children's entry into the Hudson School. Some people gave her gift baskets and loofahs. Ned had given her a rehabbed fireplace, restored funding for her apartment and mind-blowing sex.

And she'd given him her heart.

Her heart wasn't what he wanted, though. What he wanted was a guaranteed slot for his son in next year's fifth-grade class at the Hudson School.

That was something Libby couldn't give him. As she

gathered her clothes from the floor where they'd fallen when Ned had torn them off in a frenzy, she fought back the tears that pressed against her eyelids, and tried to assure herself that she wasn't stupid. Godiva chocolates and pandering she was used to. Bouquets and bath oil she could cope with. Being bribed with love was way beyond her experience, though. Just because she'd fallen for Ned's con didn't mean she was a fool.

But she felt pretty damn foolish as she stalked down the hallway of his apartment, through the living room and out the door without a glimpse of him, without even a goodbye.

The sound of the front door slamming shut jolted Ned into action. He yanked open the bathroom door, raced down the hall, checked his bedroom to discover it empty and Libby's clothing gone, then continued to the living room. His hand was on the doorknob before he remembered that he was buck naked. He couldn't very well chase after her in his birthday suit.

Why the hell had she bolted on him? He'd been gone only a few minutes, figuring they'd both be better off if he got his anger under control before they continued the conversation. His justifiable anger. How could she abandon Eric to the whims of some anonymous school committee? How could she toss Ned's son away like that?

His anger surged and he wrestled it back down. He had to go after Libby, bring her back here and work this thing out. But he couldn't very well go after her with smoke pouring from his ears and rabid foam spilling from his mouth— and his butt exposed for all of Manhattan to see.

He couldn't very well go after her at all, he realized back in his bedroom as he tugged on his jeans. By now, she would already be halfway home—either in a cab or walking up West End Avenue. He glanced at his clock radio: 10:35. Not too dangerously late for her to be walking home alone, but he sure as hell hoped she'd found a cab. And anyway, before he could pursue Libby, he'd first have to see if Lindsay from down the hall could come over and stay with Eric. Sure, Eric was asleep, and he'd probably never even know that Ned had stepped out for a few minutes—but this was New York City, and Ned would never leave Eric, not even for the time it took to find Libby and return with her.

He lifted his shirt from the floor and slid his arms through the sleeves. It seemed inconceivable that just a half hour ago she'd been unbuttoning this shirt, pushing back the fabric, running her hands over his torso and pressing a kiss to his chest. His groin twinged at the memory.

"Fuck," he said. The anger was back, full-bore. He couldn't believe she'd run out on him—especially when she was in the wrong. She should have been waiting to greet his return from the bathroom with an apology and a vow to secure a place for Eric at the Hudson School.

He sprawled out on the bed and smelled her on his pillows. Then he jumped off the mattress as if it were on fire, grabbed the phone, dialed her number and leaned against the wall while he listened to it ring unanswered at her end. At least Reva wasn't home, so Ned wasn't disturbing her.

When her answering machine clicked on, he hung up and left his bedroom for the kitchen, where the cordless phone had a redial button. He dialed Libby's number again, let it ring four times, disconnected the call, waited a minute and hit Redial. Four rings, disconnect, count to ten and redial again.

On his fifth attempt she picked up. "Hello?" She sounded leery. She must have guessed who'd be calling her at this hour.

His anger rose again, swelling like an approaching storm cloud. That image reminded him of the time he and Libby had walked home from Hudson in the rain, sharing his umbrella. She'd already had him by then. One brush of her shoulder, one shared smile and he'd wanted her.

And now she was there when she ought to be here, in his bed, with him. He prayed for the cloud to keep its distance, because if it started flinging daggers of lightning, he wasn't going to accomplish much with this call. "Libby." He swallowed to smooth out his voice. "Come back."

"I don't think so." She sounded a little uneven, a little uncertain.

"Libby, I don't understand why you left."

"Well, you shut yourself up in the bathroom and didn't come out. I assumed you were throwing a tantrum."

"A tantrum?" Thunder rolled off the cloud. He took a deep breath and clung to what little control he had. "I was upset, so I went somewhere to cool off. That was no reason for you to disappear on me."

"It was one reason. There were others."

Patience, he ordered himself, even as he felt the first splatters of rain on his soul. "What other reasons?"

"Do I have to spell it out? You want your son to get into the Hudson School. Lots of parents want their children to get into the Hudson School, and they ply me with goodies. They try to bribe me to admit their kids. They send me gifts." She paused, then said, "You renovated my fireplace."

"You think I renovated your fireplace so you'd get Eric into Hudson?" A cold gale blew the cloud back, hinting at a different kind of storm. Now Ned wasn't just angry that she'd walked out on him. He was furious at what she was implying.

"It's not just the fireplace." She paused again, then continued. "You went and patched things up for me with Harry, and…and other things."

Other things. Like making love to her. Apparently, as the

song said, she *was* sorry now. Rage buffeted him with hurricane-force winds. This was one ugly, destructive storm.

"Libby," he said, forcing his voice out around the knot of bitterness clogging his throat. "Where I come from, if someone you care about has a problem and you're in a position to fix it, you fix it. Your fireplace had a problem, and I could fix it, so I did. You had a problem with your ex, and I knew I could fix it, so I did. This is what people do for the people they—" He couldn't say *love,* not now, not when he was drowning in a deluge of fury. "Care about," he murmured. "My son has a problem with public school, and you're in a position to fix it."

"I'm sure that's what all the parents who send me gifts and flattering notes think, too. They're in a position to send me chocolates, so they do. And I'm in a position to get their kids into Hudson, so in exchange for the chocolates that's what I should do."

"You think this whole thing was quid pro quo? You think…what? I seduced you to get my kid into Hudson?"

"Right now, that's how it feels."

Ned didn't know enough curse words to cover how it felt to *him,* but he mouthed a few of them. They didn't bring catharsis, though. They only made him feel as if he should suck on a bar of soap.

"So now what?" he said into the phone, once he was sure the words emerging from him wouldn't leave blisters on Libby's ear. "Are you going to tell your department that Eric Donovan shouldn't be admitted to the Hudson School because his father tried to bribe you by rehabbing your fireplace and giving you multiple orgasms?"

There was a really long pause this time. Maybe he'd blistered her ear after all. Finally, she spoke. "I told you, Ned, I'm going to recuse myself from Eric's application. That means I won't ease him in and I won't ease him out. The rest of the committee will decide."

"Fine," he growled. "Let the committee decide. You want to break my kid's heart, go right ahead." Break my heart, too, he almost added, but the storm was inundating him. He shivered in it. Deafening thunderclaps echoed inside his skull. He couldn't talk anymore.

He hit the off button on the handset and put the phone on the stand. Then he staggered down the hall. He stopped at Eric's bedroom, opened the door and saw the lumpy, motionless silhouette at the center of the loft bed. A whispery snore filled the room and he closed the door.

Oh, God. He was the world's worst father. Not because of anything he'd done but because he couldn't fulfill Eric's wish. Eric wasn't like most kids. He didn't pester Ned for expensive toys, video games, overpriced sneakers. He didn't march through life acting as if the world owed him something, even though it did. Eric had lost his mother and yet he refused to use that tragedy as an excuse. He simply accepted it and got on with things.

All he'd ever asked of Ned was the right to be happy— and a place at the Hudson School.

Ned had done his best to deliver on the first item, but the second—not only was it beyond him, but he might have ruined the kid's chances forever. He couldn't believe Libby was so vindictive she'd punish Eric for the sins of his father, whatever they were. But who the hell knew?

That stupid song drifted through his head: *Who's sorry now?* Easy question. Lousy answer. Ned returned to his bedroom, pulled a rolled-up pair of socks from a bureau drawer and slammed them into the wall.

Twenty-Four

*H*ey, Riva, whassup? The Web site is working its magic, thank your little buddy Eric for me. So this dude who says he knows your father got in touch with me, he's in the music business and he wants to book me into some small clubs and see what happens. When I got his e-mail, hey, maybe you heard me screaming all the way from Brooklyn. And then we met and made arrangements. Once I have the dates I'll be performing, I'll send you the info and you can get Eric to put them on the Web site. I am so incredibly grateful, Riva. Your dad turned out to be not such a bad dude after all, hey?

Reva reread Darryl J's e-mail and scowled. Three weeks had passed since he'd recorded his sound clip, and finally, he was bothering to communicate with her, and he couldn't even spell her name right. The turd.

All right, so he'd misspelled her name. She bet Eric

would be even more pissed off to know Darryl J had called him her "little buddy." Still, that her father had somehow put Darryl J in touch with someone who could book Darryl J into clubs was pretty awesome. Weird, but she was learning not to analyze things too much.

She thought about responding to Darryl J's e-mail, then decided he could wait. Instead, she instant-messengered Eric. She hadn't seen him in nearly as long as she hadn't seen Darryl J. And the strangest thing—which she also wasn't going to analyze—was that she kind of missed him more than she missed Darryl J.

At least they e-mailed each other. Something had gone rotten between their parents, and they were in the dark what it was. Reva had knocked herself out trying to analyze that, and she'd drawn a blank. So had Eric. Things had seemed so great between her mother and Mr. Donovan, and now all she had to show for it was a mother in a perpetual state of misery and a green marble fireplace.

Webman, she typed—that was Eric's nickname, because he thought he was some kind of genius at creating Web sites— *heard from Darryl J and he's gonna be famous, thanks to us.*

A few seconds later, Eric wrote back: *Riviera*—that was her nickname; it sounded a little like Reva—*good for Darryl J. We should charge him for Web hosting. We'll get rich.*

Reva laughed, then typed: *You can charge him. I'll get rich singing my own songs.*

Eric responded: *You're doing your solo tonight, right?*
Yup.
Nervus?

Reva considered her answer before typing: *Not really.*
I got this idea, he wrote.

Reva stared at the screen and waited for more words to

appear. He kept her in suspense for a while before writing:
Promise you won't think I'm nuts?

Never, Webman.

Again he made her wait. Ten seconds was a really long time when you were IM-ing. *I was thinking my dad and I could come to your concert.*

Reva couldn't help analyzing this idea. On the one hand, if her mother saw Mr. Donovan again, maybe she'd realize that whatever had broken them up wasn't so important, and they'd get back together, which would make everybody happy, including Reva and Eric. On the other hand, if Reva wasn't nervous now, having Mr. Donovan in the audience might make her nervous. Eric she didn't care about. Of course her mother would be there, and her father and Bony, and Bony would be yakking to everybody about how she'd picked out Reva's outfit, they'd found it in this little boutique on Mercer where only people who were seriously cool shopped, and didn't it flatter Reva and slenderize her? But Mr. Donovan… If he was there, her mother might become a wreck, and if she did, Reva would, too.

But on the first hand, if her mother and Mr. Donovan saw each other and realized they should get back together, no one would become a wreck, and Reva would sing like an angel.

You think I'm nuts, Eric wrote.

No. I think you're smart. Could be risky, though.

He probably won't want to go, anyway.

Probably not. For some reason, that thought saddened Reva. She liked Mr. Donovan. He'd been there the day she'd won the solo. He'd drunk a ginger-ale toast to her. He'd helped her buy Darryl J's domain name. If things weren't so screwed up between him and her mother, she'd want him at the concert.

It was just an idea, Eric wrote.

You're sweet, Reva wrote back. She hoped he wouldn't

take that the wrong way. *Gotta go drink lemon juice and warm up my vocal cords.* Ms. Froiken said lemon juice cleaned out the throat and singers should sip some before a concert.

Good luck. You're gonna sing beautifly, Eric assured her.

Reva's eyes suddenly filled and her throat felt so thick with tears she might need a gallon of lemon juice to clean it out. She wished badly that Eric and his dad could come to the concert. She wished things were right with her mother. Knowing everything was screwed up would spoil the evening, her great moment in the spotlight, her long-awaited solo. Even if she sang her heart out, she couldn't fix whatever was wrong, because she didn't have a clue what was wrong.

Catch you later, she typed, then shut off the computer. She sat in the silent den, struggling to collect herself. From the kitchen came the sounds of her mother putting together dinner. Reva had to be at Hudson by six-thirty, so her mom had gotten home early, even though she was right in the middle of admissions madness, and had brought with her two chicken Caesar salads from Bloom's. Reva couldn't possibly eat anything heavier than a salad tonight.

She shuffled into the kitchen in her socks, trying not to glance at the magnificent marble fireplace on her way. Her mother gave her a smile so big and beaming Reva assumed it was fake. "Getting nervous?" she asked.

"Why does everyone think I'm supposed to be nervous?" Reva snapped, then bit her lip and prayed for her mother not to ask who "everyone" was. Reva didn't want to tell her she was IM-ing with Eric. She covered with a convenient lie. "Kim asked me three times today if I was nervous. She's got to play the piano through the whole thing. If anyone should be nervous, it's her."

Her mother nodded and pried the plastic lids off the containers of take-out salad. "Maybe *she's* nervous, so she's projecting onto you."

"Yeah. I guess." Reva wasn't sure what her mother meant by that, but she let it go. "Are *you* nervous?"

Her mother shaped another supersize smile. "Why should I be nervous?"

"Well, maybe you were projecting onto me or something." Reva picked at her salad. The romaine was crisp despite the oily dressing. Bloom's takeout was always good. Too bad she didn't have an appetite. She forced herself to eat anyway, so she wouldn't faint from hunger in the middle of the concert. "So, are you doing the acceptances?"

"At Hudson, you mean?" Her mother carried two glasses of ice water to the table and dropped onto the other chair. The table was so small their plates practically touched. "Yes, it's acceptance time. Also rejection time."

Reva wondered if Eric was going to be accepted or rejected. The day she'd met him wasn't only the day she'd gotten the *Tommy* solo, it was the day he'd had his interview. They'd talked about Hudson a few times since then. He thought it was like Emerald City or Walt Disney World or something, this big, happy place where everyone was smart and no one ever acted mean. Of course, it wasn't like that at all. But it was better than most of the city's public schools, and Eric would probably love the place. He'd take over the computer lab and turn it into his own private playground.

Whatever reason her mother was pissed off at Eric's father, Reva hoped her mother wouldn't take it out on Eric by denying him admission to the school. The decisions were made by a committee, but her mother was the head of the committee. Did that give her veto power? Reva wasn't sure how the process worked.

She struggled for a discreet way to ask her about Eric's

status. "Are you doing the kindergarten applications or the older kids' applications?"

"We always start with the older kids' applications," her mother said.

She appeared fatigued to Reva, with gray shadows circling her eyes and her hair frizzier than usual. Her mouth looked tense and tight, even as she opened it to stick a forkful of chicken and greens in. She chewed slowly, as if her jaw hurt.

For the past couple of weeks, Reva had been annoyed with her mother for being such a crab and spreading bad cheer throughout the apartment. But today, when she should be thinking only of herself and her imminent glory at the concert, she suffered a pang of sympathy for her. The woman hadn't been sleeping. She was working too hard. Whatever had gone wrong in her life might be her own fault, but pain was pain and Reva's mother was deep in it.

"I hope things get better," Reva said, then shoveled in enough of her salad to sustain her through the concert, and stood. She swung open the refrigerator, located the little plastic lemon-shaped bottle on a shelf in the door and squirted some juice into her mouth. Her tongue curled reflexively and she grimaced as the bitter liquid slid down her throat. "Ms. Froiken said that's good for the voice," she explained. "I'm going to go get dressed. I'll eat the rest of this after the concert."

Before her mother could stop her, she hurried out of the kitchen, trying to fend off another wave of tears. She hated being so sad, tonight of all nights. Even more, she hated that her mother was so sad. Life would be simpler if she could ignore her mom's sadness, but she just wasn't selfish enough. So she carried her sorrow along with her own.

Thank God she at least had a really neat outfit to wear tonight. If she'd had to wear the same old outfit she'd worn to last spring's concert... Now, *that* would be sad.

* * *

"You want to go to the concert tonight?"

Fork in midair, spaghetti slowly unwinding from the tines, Ned gaped at Eric. "At the Hudson School? How did you even know the concert was tonight?"

"It's on their Web site," Eric told him. Marinara sauce stained his mouth like lipstick. "And Reva's doing her solo. Remember Reva?"

Did he remember Reva? Jesus. It took all his willpower not to fling his plate of pasta against a wall and howl. Of course he remembered Reva. He remembered her big, dark eyes, so like her mother's, and her sassy smile and her stick-straight hair—and the way she'd waltzed down West End Avenue in the rain, singing her solo at the top of her lungs. He remembered Reva's vanishing into the bowels of Greenwich Village and making Libby insane with worry. He remembered her shouting at everybody to shut up so her musician friend could record a song for his Web site.

He remembered sitting with her in the waiting area outside Libby's office the afternoon Libby interviewed Eric, when she was so excited she couldn't sit still.

"We drank a toast to her," Eric reminded him. "On account of her getting the solo. The concert is tonight. I think we should go."

Ned stared at his son as if he were a recent arrival from a distant planet. Same blond hair, same flinty eyes and stubborn jaw—although the jaw seemed just a little thicker lately, and the eyebrows a little darker. Eric had grown in the past few weeks, too. His head reached Ned's shoulder now.

And he wanted to go to a fucking concert at the Hudson School.

Ned lowered his fork to his plate and focused on twirling spaghetti onto it. "Look," he said, figuring that after three weeks without a word from Libby, without even a hint that she was aware of how she'd misjudged him, let alone been sorry for it, he had to come clean to Eric. "You shouldn't get attached in any way to the Hudson School. The odds of your getting in there aren't good."

"I don't want to go there to be a student," Eric argued. "I want to go there to hear Reva sing her solo."

"Yes, but you've got your heart set on attending there next year. And it's not going to happen."

Eric's eyes narrowed. "Did you hear from them? They rejected me?"

Ned shook his head. "We won't hear officially until the beginning of January."

"But you know something?"

"No." All he knew was what his gut told him: that he'd fallen in love with Libby and she'd viewed his love the way she viewed the bath sponges some other applicant's parent had sent her. All he knew was that he'd assumed she would extend a hand to his son and he'd assumed wrong. All he knew was that a woman who would walk out on him the way Libby had wasn't someone he could count on. "I'm just saying the odds aren't good."

"Well, yeah." Eric relaxed in his chair and devoured another forkful of spaghetti. "I'd still like to hear Reva sing her solo. Wouldn't you?"

As a matter of fact, Ned would. He leaned back in his chair and slugged down some iced tea, wishing it were beer. "The truth is, Reva's mother and I aren't on good terms."

"Duh."

"Okay, so that's not exactly a news flash. I just—I'm afraid seeing her at the concert would make us both uncomfortable."

"Well, I sure wouldn't want you to be uncomfortable," Eric said with the sarcastic swagger of a full-fledged adolescent.

Ned squinted at his son. He hadn't started growing a mustache. He hadn't sprouted pit hair. When had he acquired the attitude?

"I thought you liked her," Eric added in a gentler tone.

"I did."

"So what happened? She decided we're not rich enough or something?"

"No, of course not. Do you think I'd like someone who had those values?"

"So, what happened?" Eric ate another baseball-size coil of spaghetti. This conversation might have stolen Ned's appetite, but it hadn't had any impact on Eric's.

"That's none of your business," Ned said, cringing at how prissy he sounded.

"I guess that means you did something really bad to her, huh." The sarcastic attitude had returned.

"I didn't do a damn thing to her," Ned retorted. He shouldn't have to defend himself to his son. He shouldn't have to defend himself to anyone.

"She just dumped you for no reason?"

"She dumped me because she thought I was bribing her to get you into Hudson." Ned let out a tired breath. He probably shouldn't have told Eric, but the kid had goaded him. If he was old enough to act like an adolescent, then maybe he was old enough to hear the truth.

Eric laughed. "*Bribing* her? What were you bribing her with?"

Sex. No, Eric was not old enough to hear that truth. "The fireplace," Ned said.

"She thought you were fixing her fireplace in exchange for getting me into Hudson?"

"Something like that, yeah." Ned tried for indignation, but the words emerged sounding forlorn.

"Why would she think that?"

"Because other parents try to bribe her all the time. They send her gifts and letters and chocolate."

"Hey, for chocolate, I'd probably let a few kids into Hudson," Eric said. Ned glanced sharply at him and realized from his grin that he was joking. "Well, if that's what people do, and there you were, fixing her fireplace free while I'm trying to get into the Hudson School... Maybe you can't really blame her for thinking you were bribing her."

"Of course I can blame her," Ned snapped. This time Eric was the one to stare at him. He shrank beneath his son's critical gaze. Damn, but he'd like a beer. Maybe five beers. Maybe a whole keg, followed by a few glasses of that fine Scotch Libby's ex-husband had given him.

Ned stuffed some spaghetti into his mouth. Eric, incredibly, had stopped eating and simply regarded him across the table.

"What?" Ned asked. "You believe I can't blame her?"

"Okay, there's this kid in my class, Simon, right?"

Ned nodded, encouraging Eric to continue.

"So last month he wound up getting sent to the principal's office three times for being rude to Ms. Engelhart. So yesterday we're in the art room, and Ms. Engelhart hadn't come in yet, and Kyle Molino writes a bad word on the blackboard."

"What bad word?"

"Just a bad word, okay?"

"What bad word?" Ned demanded.

"Okay, *bitch*. So the teacher comes in and sees the word there, and she immediately assumes Simon did it. He didn't, but I mean, can you blame her? He's mouthed off to her so many times."

Ned considered this example of injustice. "Are you saying the art teacher was right to accuse Simon?"

"No. What I'm saying is, you can't blame her."

God. Eric had gone past adolescence to full maturity. How else to explain such wisdom? No ten-year-old should be so smart.

Ned set down his iced tea and stopped wishing it were beer. He shoved his plate away and checked his watch. "What time does the concert begin?" he asked.

Reva was spectacular. Libby would have believed that even if she weren't Reva's mother, but—God, she was amazing. The outfit Bonnie had bought her, a black satin pant suit that resembled a tuxedo as conceived by Picasso, with asymmetrical lines and buttons along one side and a deep-cut front that exposed the lacy edge of the white camisole Reva wore underneath the jacket, was so sleek and elegant that she looked like a high-fashion model in it—a short model, although her dress sandals added two inches to her height. The chic ensemble made her stand taller, too. She held her shoulders back and her chin up, and when she stepped forward and belted out "See me, feel me, touch me, heal me" in her crystalline voice, Harry, who was sitting next to Libby, with Bonnie on his other side and a big bouquet of roses for Reva resting in his lap, socked Libby in the arm and mouthed, *Wow!*

Wow. That about summed it up.

For the first time in weeks, Libby forgot herself. She forgot her anger about misjudging Ned and her grief about no longer having him in her life. She forgot the stress and exhaustion of her job, which had kicked into high gear as she and her committee plowed through the thousands of applications the school had received. Each application had to be read by the full committee. Then they had to discuss each applicant. Whoever interviewed the child had to report on the interview. They had to weigh the child's strengths and weaknesses, evaluate what the child would bring to Hudson and consider what Hudson could give to the child. More times than not, they had to make decisions they knew would disappoint families.

But tonight, as her daughter stood at the center of the stage in the lower school auditorium and sang her heart out, all Libby could do was kvell.

The choral arrangement of *Tommy* was the final performance on the program. Libby had already sat stoically through the orchestra's mauling of excerpts from Handel's *Water Music* and the school band's *Sousa Suite,* played at a tempo suitable for a funeral procession. Muriel Froiken had done a superb job with the chorus, though—and of course Reva had done the most superb job of all.

Tears of joy and pride blurred Libby's vision as Reva took her bow to enthusiastic applause. People continued clapping even after the lights came up. Libby dug a tissue from her purse and dabbed her eyes.

Bonnie leaned across Harry's lap. "That was really something," she said. Her hollow cheeks were rouged and her lips were slicked with a maroon lipstick. "How about her outfit? Gorgeous, huh?"

Gilda reached across Libby's seat back to hug her. She and Irwin, Vivienne and Leonard had all come to the concert, as well, and if Libby was a touch teary, Gilda was bawling. "Oy, my *bubbela* is such a princess! When did she become so talented?"

"She was always talented," Harry huffed.

Gilda glared at her son and resumed sobbing on Libby's shoulder, while Irwin fingered his tweed cap and beamed, his eyes suspiciously damp. Vivienne leaned toward Libby and whispered, "She's a mensch, your daughter. Can a girl be a mensch?" Next to her, Leonard looked mildly bored. But at least he'd attended the concert with her. Their relationship seemed to be improving.

With a final blubber, Gilda released Libby, and she turned to view the stage. The chorus had filed off. They'd be congregating in the hall outside the auditorium, where audience members could meet up with them. "Let's go find her," Libby said, edging along the row of seats to the aisle.

They trouped en masse out of the theater, working their way through the sluggish, chattering crowds to reach the hall. Squealing young voices ricocheted off the walls as sopranos and altos embraced one another and the few boys—who were mostly altos but were called tenors for their egos—scuffled manfully. All the singers wore black and white, but none was dressed as stylishly as Reva, whom Libby spotted near the end of the corridor, talking to a lanky boy with floppy black hair.

"I know that kid," Harry muttered. "He was with Reva the day she showed up with all her friends at my apartment."

Libby tried not to stare, but she couldn't help herself. The way the two of them talked—the boy's arm propped against the wall, his posture casually slouching and his head bent to Reva, who tilted hers up and smiled and—Libby wasn't sure, but it looked as if she'd applied mascara to her eyelashes, which she batted at him… Oy vey. Reva was flirting with that boy. The boy she'd been with the afternoon she'd vanished and Libby had aged ten years.

"Come on," Libby said, grabbing Harry's elbow. "Give her the flowers." They marched down the hall, passing dozens of giggling, babbling students and doting parents and one solemn young band member toting a tuba that was nearly twice his size.

Reva turned as they approached, and smiled. "Hi! How was I?"

"You were fabulous." Ignoring the boy, Libby swooped down on Reva and gave her a crushing hug. "Unbelievable.

I am so proud of you! Your father brought you some flowers," she said, releasing Reva so she could accept a hug from Harry.

"Oh, cool! Thanks, Dad! These are beautiful!" She dipped her head to sniff the roses, and her eyes glowed. Definitely some mascara on her lashes, Libby noted—but she supposed that on such a night, mascara wasn't out of line. "Mom, Dad, this is Luke Rodelle. He's a friend of mine. Luke, this is my mom and dad. They aren't married to each other," she added.

Luke straightened up and dutifully shook Libby's hand, then Harry's. 'We've met," Harry said, his voice carrying a slight threat.

"Right. Yeah." Luke smiled sheepishly. "Well, um, Reva, if you've got to be with your folks…"

"Why don't you just say a quick hello to the family," Libby suggested. "Grandma and Grandpa are here, and Aunt Viv and Leonard and Bonnie. Then you can talk with Luke some more."

Harry seemed less than pleased by the prospect of Reva spending more time with Luke, but he nodded to the boy and ushered Reva over to her waiting relatives, all of whom— with the exception of Leonard—had to hug her, as well. Bonnie appraised Reva's outfit—"All that hugging, it's going to get wrinkled"—and hugged her more carefully than Gilda and Irwin had.

"Let me say goodbye to Luke," Reva said once she'd been thoroughly hugged. She tugged her mother's wrist, and Libby took a few steps away from the Kimmelman mob. "Mom," she whispered, "he asked me to go to the dance with him. Is it okay if I say yes?"

"Do you like him?" Libby whispered back, allowing herself a glimpse of the young swain waiting at the end of the hall.

"Well, I mean, he's a guy. But yeah, I guess."

"Then if you want to say yes, by all means, say yes."

"Okay." Reva appeared luminous, more beautiful than the flowers in her bouquet. She took a step toward Luke, then turned back. "If you see Eric here, say hi for me, okay?"

Eric? Eric Donovan? Why would he be here? Libby couldn't ask Reva, because she was already hurrying back to Luke.

Libby spun around—and discovered Eric and his father chatting with Harry. Her stomach lurched upward, forcing her heart against her ribs. Emotional heartburn spread through her chest.

Ned looked...weary. Wary. And more handsome than she'd remembered. He wore jeans and a battered leather jacket. His hair was in need of a trim and his smile was rimmed with sadness as he talked to Harry. She moved toward them and he noticed her. His smile faded altogether.

"We wanted to hear Reva's solo," Eric announced, clearly far more chipper than his father. "She was great!"

"She's just down the hall if you want to say hello," Libby told him. She didn't think Reva would mind if Eric interrupted her tête-à-tête with Luke.

Lifting her eyes, she found Ned still gazing at her, still unbearably handsome, still not smiling. "Can we talk?" he asked.

Not with her ex-husband and all her ex-in-laws hovering around. "Excuse us, please," she said in a low, taut voice as she moved away from her curious relatives. Ned followed her down the hall and around the corner to a less-crowded corridor. The walls were festooned with artwork reflecting Hudson's revisionist view of history: "Christopher Columbus Was Not The First European To Visit The New World," proclaimed a banner above several drawings of Columbus's three ships. Another drawing was entitled "Leif Erickson

Day" and depicted a Viking ship that appeared oddly similar to the Columbus ships.

"Libby," Ned said. He stood so close to her she could feel his breath against her face. The slightest movement and she'd be in his arms. The slightest shift and her mouth would meet his.

But he'd used her. Like so many other eager parents, he'd plied her with gifts—the gifts of his time, his skill, his lovemaking…. She felt her cheeks warming with a blush at that thought.

"I love your fireplace," he said.

"My fireplace." She inched back so she could see him better.

He seemed perfectly serious. "I know you thought I renovated your fireplace to get Eric into Hudson. That's the irony. I didn't do it for you. I did it for me."

"For you?"

"The project I'm working on now—the woman's demanding Greek columns in her bathroom. She's a head case, but she's paying the firm a lot of money so we're going to give her as many damn Greek columns as she wants. When I saw your fireplace, I thought, now this is something I'd like to work on. This is old. It's real."

"You wanted to make it all that it could be," she recalled.

"Yeah. It was very nice of you to let me, but I was doing it for my own satisfaction. Not to earn points with you." He peered down at her, his eyes bright and earnest. "I hope you can believe that, because it's the truth."

She remembered his enthusiasm for the project, the satisfaction he took in the work. She remembered his calling her repeatedly to join him inside the fireplace, to admire his efforts. She remembered the nooner they'd indulged in on the floor in front of that lovely green marble mantel.

"You misjudged me," he continued, his voice low and

hypnotic. "And I blamed you for that, but I shouldn't have. Everyone in the world—or at least every parent in the city—is trying to earn points with you. How could you assume anything different about me? Especially when you knew how much I wanted Eric to get into Hudson."

"He's in," she let slip, then pressed her fingers to her mouth. "I shouldn't have said that."

"He's in?"

"We reviewed his application two days ago. I discussed his interview and my impressions of him, and I told them that when I interviewed him, you and I were just—well, we weren't anything. I told them that we'd later become involved and that therefore I couldn't vote on his application. But the interview report had been objective, and I urged them to use it in evaluating him. Then I left the room."

Ned lifted his hands to her shoulders and caressed them. "That must have been hard for you."

"Leaving the room wasn't so hard," she admitted. "Not being able to vote on Eric was hard."

"And telling a roomful of colleagues that you were involved with a prospective student's father?"

The hardest thing about that had been acknowledging that she and Ned were no longer involved. She'd lost the chance to help Eric get into Hudson, and she'd lost the man who'd lost her the chance.

"Are we involved?" he asked.

"Given the past few weeks, I would guess no."

"Can we change that?"

She heard a plea in his voice, an undertone of desperation. Was he as wretched as she was about their lack of involvement?

"You said Eric is in. That means I could be nice to you now, and you wouldn't suspect me of ulterior motives."

"You're not supposed to know about Eric. The letters don't go out until January 2. I should never—"

"I won't tell him. I won't tell a soul. Can I be nice to you now?"

She allowed herself a tiny smile. "That depends on your definition of nice."

He kissed her softly, gently. "As a matter of fact, I was thinking your parquet floors would really benefit from refinishing. When was the last time you had them refinished? They're pretty scuffed."

"You do have ulterior motives," she complained, her smile expanding. "You love me for my apartment."

"Ah, you figured me out." He kissed her again. "When I'm done with your floors, I want to tackle your kitchen. New cabinets, new countertops—it's a terrific kitchen by Manhattan standards, but I could make it better."

"Could you, now?"

"And then there's your bedroom. I'd really like to get to work on your bedroom."

She couldn't imagine any renovations her bedroom needed. "And do what?"

He smiled slyly. "Take me to your bedroom and I'll show you," he promised before kissing her again.

Actually, she thought as they stood kissing in the back hallway, with juvenile paintings of the ships of ancient explorers hanging all around them, her bedroom could use some improvement. An expanded closet, so there would be space for Ned's clothes. Some slight rearrangement of the furniture so his dresser could fit in. And a few extra pillows on the bed, just in case things got interesting.

Perhaps they could discuss it when he was done kissing her. But she hoped he wouldn't be done for a long time.

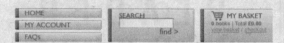

To save the lives of the GOOD would you make a pact with EVIL?

For years Agent O'Dell has been hunting Father Keller – the monster whose acts of brutality continue to haunt her.

Now, as she investigates a killing spree where the victims are all Catholic priests, Keller sinisterly returns to offer his help…in exchange for his own protection.

Is siding with the devil himself a risk too far? Or a necessary evil?

17th March 2006

MIRA